THE YARN OF
OLD HARBOUR TOWN

NAUTICAL FICTION
PUBLISHED BY MCBOOKS PRESS

THE YARN OF OLD HARBOUR TOWN

by

W. Clark Russell

CLASSICS OF NAUTICAL FICTION SERIES

McBOOKS PRESS
ITHACA, NEW YORK

Book and cover design by Paperwork.

Cover painting is *The Harbour at North Shields* by Joseph Crawhall (1861–1913), courtesy of Fine Art Photographic Library Ltd.

Library of Congress Cataloging-in-Publication Data

Russell, William Clark, 1844-1911.
 The Yarn of Old Habour Town / by W. Clark Russell.
  p.   cm. — (Classics of nautical fiction series)
  ISBN 0-935526-65-X (alk. paper)
  I. Title. II. Series.
PR5282.Y37   1999
823'.8—dc21

                                                99-046438
                                                CIP

The Yarn of Old Harbour Town was first published in London by T. Fisher Unwin in 1905. This text is based on the first American edition, published in Philadelphia by George W. Jacobs & Co. in 1906. A few corrections were made for consistency and clarity, but most of the original spelling and punctuation remains intact.

Distributed to the book trade by
Login Trade, 1436 West Randolph, Chicago, IL 60607
800-626-4330.

Additional copies of this book may be ordered from any bookstore or directly from McBooks Press, 120 West State Street, Ithaca, NY 14850. Please include $3.00 postage and handling with mail orders. New York State residents must add 8% sales tax. All McBooks Press publications can also be ordered by calling toll-free 1-888-BOOKS11 (1-888-266-5711). Please call to request a free catalog.

Visit the McBooks Press website at http://www.McBooks.com.

Printed in the United States of America

          9 8 7 6 5 4 3 2 1

"Have you ne'er heard the yarn of Old Harbour Town?

She was sweeter than Hinda or Haidèe;

When the hatches were flush with goods, victuals and lush,

The Captain made sail with the lady."

Old Rhymes, 1835.

CHAPTER I

LUCY ACTON

OLD HARBOUR HOUSE stood about a mile from the Harbour. It confronted the town which lay about one mile and a half off, right across a wide, romantic, heavily-wooded ravine. The banks of this gap sloped softly and pleasantly into a plain of meadows and two or three farms whose dyes of roof and cattle enriched the verdure; and down there ran a river singing in measures of music as it flowed into the Harbour and mingled its bright water with the brine of the deep beyond.

Above, on the placid slope of down close against Old Harbour Town, hung a straggler building or two, lonely in importance, or consequential in some trifling pomp of land; at the point of cliff on Old Harbour House side, a low, pursy lighthouse wheezed at night a yellow gleam that was a home-greeting or God-speed to some five score fishermen who dredged in these and further waters; and on the brow confronting the lighthouse a venerable windmill revolved its vans against the sky.

It has been said that Old Harbour House stood. The house takes its place as a beauty of the past. On Christmas Eve 1832, fire reduced it to a few blackened walls. All through the long night the flames made a wild, grand show; sea and land were illuminated for leagues and leagues. Out of the ashes of the beautiful building sprang that commonplace phœnix, the local poet, who celebrated the one tradition of Old Harbour Town in a copy of rhymes, of which the first verse should be found imprinted on the title-page of this book.

The house, or at least the front of it, was built after a design by Inigo Jones. The pediment was perforated by a circular window glazed with a casement whose frame resembled the spokes of a ship's wheel. A variety of antique symbolism resembling the hideous sculptures which sometimes close the chapters in books of the seventeenth century, under-ran the eaves. The tall, narrow windows gleamed blackly amidst the skeletons of the winter, or the coloured embroidery of the summer creepers. The hall door was noble and hospitable in expanse. A carriage drive swept from it on either hand the oval lawn to a handsome gate whose supports were crowned by the arms of the Actons on the one hand and the arms of a family into which one of the Actons had married on the other hand.

One bright morning in April in that memorable year 1805, Captain Charles Acton, R.N. (retired), stood on his lawn in front of the house watching a gardener who was at work at a flower-bed. He was a slightly-built but tall, very gentleman-like man, one of the last in a crowd to be picked out as a seafarer. He was pale, his nose aquiline, lips thin, and the expression of the mouth firm. He was dressed in a frill shirt, loose cravat of white cambric, red-striped waistcoat, long green coat with a high collar and small cuffs, tight breeches to the ankle buttoned to the middle of the thigh, and top-boots; a rather low-crowned, broad-brimmed hat sat somewhat cocked on his head. His hair was long, without powder, and tied a little way down the back in a sort of tail.

He was suddenly hailed from the gate by a loud, hearty voice.

"What cheer! How are ye, Captain, how are ye this fine morning? Have you heard the news?"

The gate was thrust open and there entered Rear-Admiral Sir William Lawrence, a round-faced, bullet-headed seaman of the old type. He was dressed in a bottle-green coat, metal buttons, red waistcoat, knee breeches and stockings, shoes and large buckles; and being totally bald he wore a wig, perched at the back of which was a little round hat.

Sir William again asked Captain Acton if he had heard the news.

"French landed?" enquired Captain Acton, as they strolled away from the flower-bed and paced the grass, in which the daisies were springing, in a quarterdeck walk, the Admiral taking about one and a half rolling steps to Captain Acton's one.

"Yes, the French have landed, but not just in the way they like.

One of our frigates—I haven't got to hear her name—chased a French privateersman ashore five miles up the coast yesterday afternoon; after taking out of her ten thousand pounds in gold, which the beggars had sneaked from a British West Indiaman off Dungeness two or three nights before, they set her on fire. I had a mind this morning to ride over and view the wreck or what remains of her."

"Lucy told me at breakfast this morning that on going to bed last night she noticed a faint tinge in the air as of the rising moon away to the eastward. 'Twas the burning wreck, I presume?"

"No doubt. She'd light up a wide area."

"I expect the frigate that chased her will be one of the Western squadron," said Captain Acton. "How finely those ships are doing their work! Since they've been sweeping these waters scarce a French picaroon dare put his nose out; when before, the seas swarmed like a tropic calm with bristling fins of sharks."

"You have to thank Pellew for the idea of those squadrons," said Sir William. "What a gallant fellow he is! Whenever I hear his name I recall the story told of him when he was a midshipman. He was aboard the *Blonde*. You remember Pownoll?"

Captain Acton nodded.

"General Burgoyne arrived alongside to ship for America. The yards were manned. The General climbed aboard, and looking aloft spied a youngster standing on his head on the main topsail yardarm. 'It's only young Pellew, one of my midshipmen,' says Captain Pownoll. 'But suppose he falls, sir?' said the General. 'Why, sir,' answers Pownoll, 'if he falls he'll sink under the ship's bottom and come up t'other side.'"

"Yes. Very characteristic. I rank Pellew after Nelson."

"Why, no, sir."

"Who, then?"

"I consider Cochrane possesses all the potentialities of Nelson. Then gallant old Jervis"—the Admiral interrupted himself and gazed with an arch leer at his companion.

"As you know, I have had the honour," said Captain Acton with slight sarcasm, "to serve under my Lord St Vincent when he was Sir John Jervis, I may claim to know him."

"Oh yes, thoroughly—very thoroughly."

"I admit the gallantry of his action with the Pegase. It was as brilliant as a hundred other actions between single ships, not one of
which nevertheless brought the victor an earldom. What made Jervis
a Lord? Was it his own, or the genius of Nelson? That manoeuvre of
the Commodore on the 14th won the battle. We took four ships
from the enemy, and two of them were captured by Nelson. But I
dislike St Vincent for opinions which he is at no pains to disguise.
He objects to the education of the poor."

"So do I, sir," said Sir William.

"We'll not argue the point. St Vincent objects to inoculation for
small-pox because he says that that disease is intended by God to
keep the population down."

Sir William laughed.

"He objects to service clubs. He said to a friend of mine, 'Take
my advice and have nothing to do with them; they are one of the
signs of the times of which I highly disapprove; these assemblies of
Army and Navy may in time become dangerous to the Government.'
When he was Commander-in-Chief he strongly discouraged matrimony. He hated to have married officers in his fleet, for he said they
were the first to run into port, and the last to come out of it. I do
not wonder that they declined to drink his health at Bath."

"I never heard of that," said Sir William.

"It was in 1802; a Naval dinner was given at Bath—St Vincent was
First Lord, I need not tell you—his health was proposed and refused
to be drunk by many of the company. The party broke up in confusion; some toasted him in a bumper and left the room; others
turned down their glasses and sat still. And you would rank this old
gentleman next after Nelson?"

"Talking of Nelson," said Sir William, "have you heard the yarn that
is told of Tom Cooke, the actor? He came on in the part of old
Barnwell, and when stabbed forgot the words, and would have died
speechless. His murderer whispered with agitation, 'For heaven's
sake, say something—anything,' on which Tom, throwing up his little three-cornered hat, shouted in his thick lisp, 'Nelson for ever!'
and died amidst louder applause than was ever provoked by the
finest strokes of Garrick or Siddons."

The story was to Captain Acton's taste, and he laughed with enjoyment.

"I should like," said the Admiral, "to have met Nelson. In all my going a-fishing I never fell in his way."

"Well," said Captain Acton, "I may say of Nelson as Pope said of Dryden: *Virgilium tantum vidi.* I was on the Hard when two Naval officers came ashore. I was thinking of other matters, and scarcely observed them until they were abreast or a little past me. Then my glance going to one I instantly perceived he was Nelson. His companion, I believe, was Troubridge. In the glimpse I got of Nelson's face I was struck by its paleness and careworn appearance. He looked at least fifteen years older than his age. They passed rapidly out of sight. I cannot express the emotions which that one-armed little figure excited in me—St Valentine's Day, the Nile, Copenhagen!"

"And how much more?" cried the Admiral, with a flush in his cheek, and with that expression of triumph and pride which lighted up the eyes of men in those days when they pronounced the magic name of Nelson. "I should like, I should much like to meet him, to see him, to grasp his hand, for a minute only before my windlass is manned for the next world."

"Who knows what lies before us?" said Captain Acton.

"Little enough before me, sir," exclaimed Sir William. "Sailors dream of a cottage ashore, but when they come to it—I like my little perch: 'tis not Old Harbour House," says he, casting his eye over the building, "but I could wish the sea were within range of its windows. I was down in the Harbour yesterday admiring the lines of your *Minorca.* She lay upright on the mud, awash to her garboard strake about, and I liked her lines in the run, and believed I could see a hint to our shipwrights in the cleanness and beauty of her entry."

"She is a pretty example of the French form," said Captain Acton. "I think I told you she was built at Bordeaux, from which port some elegant structures are sent afloat. But the French cannot approach the Americans as shipbuilders. Take that schooner of mine, the *Aurora*—by the way, she is due here shortly. I wish she may not have been taken by the enemy."

"I admire your venture," said the Admiral. "I believe if I could muster two or three thousand pounds I should be disposed to purchase a prize or two from the French, Spanish, or Yankees and follow your lead. Good interest on money is hard to get. Your ships do well for you, sir."

"I am quite satisfied," exclaimed Captain Acton complacently; "but, as you know, I was mainly actuated by the desire to promote the trade of this decaying place. The inheritance of this property," said he, sending his gaze over the wide grounds agreeably wooded afar by orchards whose boughs in a season's yield supplied cider enough to keep a parish merry through several generations, "brought with it urgent obligations. I could not view Old Harbour going to pieces without a resolution to do something that might serve to keep it together."

"You will add to your ships?" said Sir William.

"I think not. The prospect must brighten before I increase my fleet. The war risks are stupendous. I never see one of my vessels quit her berth, but that I say to myself, 'When I next hear of you, you'll be at Cadiz or Dunkirk, or at the bottom of the sea.'"

Sir William Lawrence halted in the quarterdeck walk the two were taking upon that bright green oval lawn, and looked at the ocean which ran in a white line, pale and faint as ice at the horizon, betwixt the two points of the ravine crowned on the right by the lighthouse and on the left by a windmill; but the waters of the Channel broadened down from their pearl-like margin into a delicate blue, which changed into dark green and brown as the sea shoaled into the land. The Admiral seemed to find something to delight him in the prospect, and Captain Acton standing at his side viewed a scene, very familiar indeed to him, with pleasure, which increased with the attention he gave it.

Indeed no piece of English landscape could have looked fairer on this fine April morning than Old Harbour Town and its Harbour, and little forefinger of pier; the windmill and the lighthouse resembled carvings, so delicately were their outlines traced against the silver blueness of the spring sky. In the Harbour against the wharves were visible the mounting masts and yards of several craft with sails hanging loose to dry, and the water of the Harbour was dotted with a few squab shapes of smacks and the figure of a moored brig-of-war.

The picture was tender and mellow with colour: the springing lights of the early growths of the young year, the venerable face of the cliff as it swept from the slope of down where the windmill was to the beach, the slow motion of violet shadows over green distances; and the impression of placid provincial life was heightened by the calm in the air which was scarcely vexed by the remote silver ringing of a chapel bell in High Street, Old Harbour Town.

"I often wish I was at sea again!" exclaimed Sir William, as the two started afresh on their quarterdeck walk. "What a noble, open, hearty, soul-stirring life it is! What good fellows one meets, what brave ships, what splendid crews! It is my hourly regret that my son should be out of it. Though I am his father, I say that this young man had in him—nay, he has in him—all the makings of a fine, dashing, even a great officer. But that devil drink—not that the vice is immoderate with him: but he takes too much; and when the fiend is in him, all that is weak in his nature appears, and he falls; drink—but not so as to justify the word drunkard—drink and gaming—these undid him. He was a favourite with all he sailed with, and yet, through his own accursed folly, he is forced to quit the Navy under circumstances which would bring the moisture into my eyes if half a century of hard weather had not dried all the dampness out of them."

Captain Acton looked at his companion in silence, but with an expression of gentle concern.

"He must go to the dogs," continued the Admiral, "if he lingers on in this neighbourhood. He can get nothing to do here, and idleness brings with it the temptation of drink. I hear of him at 'The Swan.' There he meets Lieutenant Tupman, and they grow merry together, God wot! over recollections. I wish he had Tupman's berth: a cabbage garden and a cottage and a pig-sty, and a gun-brig that is never ready. I wonder the Admiralty keep up this farce of gun-brigs stationed on the coast to guard against what they are never prepared for."

"I have heard Mr Lawrence highly spoken of. When I was last in London I met Pettigrew of the *Circe*, and he was telling me of a cutting-out affair in which your son was engaged in the West Indies—Antigua, I think. Nothing could have been more gallant than his conduct."

"He could have done well," sighed the old Admiral. "A few evenings ago I was waited upon by Mr Greyquill, a sleek and dingy little man whom I do not love the sight of. Such a visit must be an intrusion. I was sitting in the open window smoking my pipe, when he pushed the gate and sneaked up the path in his land-stealing way, but before he could fetch the door I hailed him: 'Hallo, Mr Greyquill,' says I, 'pray, what business brings you on this visit?' But in my heart I knew devilish well what he called about. He steps on to the grass over against my window, and with a low congee says, 'I am sorry, Sir William, to intrude upon you, sir, but I can obtain no satisfaction from your son, and at the same time I have no desire to go to extremities.' 'You'll not help your case by threatening me, Mr Greyquill,' said I. 'But look how the case stands, sir,' he cries, 'your son has had three hundred pounds from me.' 'No, sir,' I said. 'Well, sir, he owes me three hundred pounds.' 'For how much advanced?' said I. 'For two hundred in good cash,' he answered. I looked the old rogue full in the eye, and said, 'You should be a rich man, sir.' 'I want my money, Sir William,' says he. 'I trusted your son as an officer and a gentleman, and as the son of an officer and a gentleman—' 'Hold, sir,' I shouted, losing my temper. 'What right had you to trust me as an officer and a gentleman when you never gave me your confidence? Did you drop a hint to me that you were advancing money to my son? Do you suppose if I had known the truth, that I would have suffered you to accept my credit as a stake in these ignoble transactions?' 'Well, Sir William, I want my money,' said the old rascal, and must get it, though I hope not to be driven into extremities. Is Mr Lawrence in?' 'No, sir,' says I. 'Good afternoon!' and I got up and left the window."

"This man Greyquill has managed to clap the thumb-screw of debt upon the hands of a pretty good few in our district," said Captain Acton. "But what's the use of locking up a man who owes you money? Leave him at large and you stand to be repaid; but flinging a man into a debtor's gaol, not because he won't pay, but because he can't pay, seems to me folly as monstrous as locking up a man because being unable to obtain work his wife and children come upon the parish. Look at the cost you put the country to on this account! There is the expense of the maintenance of the man in gaol, and there is the expense of the maintenance of the wife and children on the parish. Now, by leaving the man at large you give him the chance of obtaining a day's work."

"I hope old Greyquill will not go to extremes," exclaimed the Admiral, with a flush in his face. "It is dishonour enough to be in his debt, but to be imprisoned! There is no good in his looking to me for repayment."

"I don't think he'll trouble your son in that way. He may be a Shylock, but he is not one of those money scriveners who demand your money or your flesh. At least, I should say not. I only know the man to nod to. Of what use would a pound of your son's flesh be to him? I believe, sir, that Mr Lawrence is not so immoderate in his love of the glass but that he might be entrusted with the care of a ship?"

"No, sir; 'tis gambling not drinking that is his weakness. But he has drunk and still drinks more than he should. Yet I have little doubt if he could find himself in a situation of trust, knowing now the hardships and difficulties of life, and the almost insuperable obstacles to a man's advancement when by his own folly he has ruined his professional career, that he would keep a stern watch over his appetite for drink. He has considerable powers of mind, an uncommon degree of spirit and resolution when he chooses to exert those qualities; and I say, with the assurance of his profound sensibility to his present melancholy condition, that he might be safely trusted to discharge any duties he may have the good luck to be called upon to execute."

"I think I told you, Sir William," said Captain Acton, after a short interval passed in reflection, "that the *Minorca* is in want of a captain."

"Yes, I remember. The master died in the homeward passage, and the ship was brought to port by the mate, to whom I suppose you intend to give the command."

"Well, he is a respectable though a very illiterate man, and I had half made up my mind to offer him the berth. But I am affected by your trouble. I should be glad to be of service to your son. Whilst we have talked I have been thinking, and if he is prepared to accept the position I am quite willing that he should take the *Minorca* out and home from the West Indies this voyage on the terms I am in the habit of giving—twelve pounds a month and a commission on the earnings of the voyage."

The Admiral stopped short and looked at his companion with a face that was warm, and with eyes that were dim with an emotion of gratitude that was almost the conqueror of his manhood. He extended his arm in silence, and the two officers clasped hands.

"Acton, you are good—this is indeed kind of you," said the Admiral after a moment or two of silence. "It would be a great weight lifted from my spirits to know that my son is shoved clear of the mischief of the idleness of this place, and that he is once more honourably employed. For, sir," said the old gentleman in a hearty, almost rapturous way, "to be in charge of such a ship as the *Minorca* is to hold a command as honourable, if not as exalted, as any afloat. I do thank you, sir. He will be most deeply obliged to you."

The two gentlemen released hands and continued their walk.

"Of course," said Captain Acton, "he is well up in navigation?"

"You will find him fully qualified in that, and in all else. A smarter seaman never trod shipboard."

"I like the idea," said Captain Acton, "of a naval officer being in charge of my vessel. The men of the Merchant Service are a very rough lot. Many of the masters and mates can scarcely read or write. They grope their way about by dead reckoning. They so little understand the treatment of men that their crews consider themselves as good as they, particularly when they bring the sailors aft, and hob-and-nob with the rum cask lifted through the hatch and broached in the cabin, till half the company lie motionless in drink, and the rest are fighting and running about mad. Two things the Navy teaches us: discipline and the art of it."

At this point the couple turned in their walk and confronted the house, at the hall door of which, in the act of descending the broad flight of steps, was a young lady putting on a glove, attended by a little terrier, who at sight of the gentlemen bounded along the grass and barked with fury up at the Admiral's face.

This young lady was Lucy, the only child of Captain Acton, one of the most charming, indeed one of the most beautiful girls of her time. The scene of garden and flower-beds quaintly shaped, and the backing of the noble, mellow, gleaming building with its pediment and symbolic carvings, was enchantingly in keeping with the figure and appearance of the girl, who by the magic of her looks and attire instantly transformed it into a picture charged with the colours of youth and health and a sweet and delicate spirit of life. Her apparel was prettily of the time: a straw hat, the brim projecting a little over the forehead and seated somewhat on one side, a plain light blue gown and long yellow silk gloves. The gown was without waist and bound under the bosom by a girdle. Her hair this day was dressed in tresses which hung around the face—not curls, but tender shadings of hair, as though the effect had been contrived by the fingers of the wind; but some curls reposed on her neck. Her eyes were unusually large, of a dark brown and full of liquid light. The eyelids were somewhat heavy, and looked the heavier because of their rich furniture of eyelash. The eyelashes indeed suggested at first sight that she doctored her eyes, as do actresses and others; but a brief inspection satisfied the beholder that all was Nature transparent, artless, and lovely. A conspicuous charm in Lucy Acton was her colour: her cheeks always wore a natural bloom or glow; this, as in the case of her eyes, might have been suspected as the effect of art, but she blushed so readily, even sometimes on any effort of speech, the damask of her blood so wrought in her cheek on any impulse of mood or humour, that it was quickly seen the mantling glow was a charm of Nature's own gift. No girl could have been more natural, and few more beautiful than Lucy Acton. Had she lived half a century earlier she would have been one of the toasts of the nation.

She was twenty-three years of age, and it will be readily supposed had been sought in marriage by more than one ardent swain. But she had kept her heart whole: nothing in breeches and stockings and long cut-away coat and salutations adopted from the most approved Parisian styles had touched the passions of Lucy Acton. She was like Emma as painted by Miss Austen: she loved her home, she adored her father, she was perfectly well satisfied with her present state of being, she could not conceive anything in a man that was worth marrying for, and being well, she meant to leave well alone.

Where did she get those wonderful eyes? From her mother, who in her day had been a celebrated Irish actress; Kitty O'Hara, famed in such parts as *Sir Harry Wildair,* the *Fair Penitent,* and *Ophelia.* Captain Acton, when lieutenant and stationed at Kingston, had seen Mrs Kitty O'Hara as "Ophelia" at the Dublin Theatre, and before she had been on the stage five minutes he lost his heart to her. The beautiful and accomplished actress was living with her mother, a noble-looking old gentlewoman who claimed to possess the blood of Irish kings. Acton made love and offered marriage, and was accepted. He had little more than his pay to live upon; nevertheless he refused to allow his wife to return to the stage. He was a sailor, and must by reason of his vocation be often long absent from home, and he declined to subject his beautiful young wife to the temptations of the stage. He might also have been influenced by the case of Sheridan after his marriage with Miss Linley, and sometimes quoted Dr Samuel Johnson's comment on Sheridan's decision: "He resolved wisely and nobly to be sure. He is a brave man. Would not a gentleman be disgraced by having his wife singing publicly for hire? No, sir, there can be no doubt here."

"Down, ma'am! cease your clatter!" cried Captain Acton to the terrier, whilst the Admiral saluted the young lady with a bow as full of homage as he would have conceded to royalty. "Where are you bound to?"

"I am going to Old Harbour Town to do a little shopping," answered Lucy, smiling at the Admiral and showing her milk-white teeth, the whiter for the red of her lips and the bloom on her cheeks. Can I do anything for you, papa?"

"No, my dear."

"Can I be of service to you, Sir William?" said the girl, picking up her dog to silence it.

"You do me service enough by suffering me to see you, madam," replied the gallant old sailor. "Brighter lights and fresher colours seem to attend you. Your grounds, sir, have grown gayer since your charming daughter made her appearance."

"I know nobody who turns his compliments so prettily as you, Sir William," exclaimed Lucy. "Do you know, sir," said she, addressing her father, "that Bates (the butler) just now told me there was a fire at sea last night."

"No, on the shore, Miss," said the Admiral. "A French corsair was chased ashore about five miles up and burnt."

"I saw the light from my bedroom window," said Lucy. "Who chased the Frenchman? Lieutenant Tupman?"

"He! More likely he was chasing one of his pigs, if indeed he was not in bed, sound under the influence of flip. As those brigs are not useful, and as they are not ornamental, why is the nation put to the cost of maintaining them? Had my son received Tupman's berth— oh, ma'am, I must tell you of a noble, generous deed of kindness your excellent, large-hearted father has been good enough to do me and Mr Lawrence. He has promised him the command of the *Minorca*."

Lucy looked at her father with an expression of surprise that vanished from her fine dramatic eyes in an instant.

"I am very pleased to hear it," she said. "I am sure Mr Lawrence will be glad to get away from Old Harbour Town. He has visited many parts of the globe, and to be limited to two streets, and such streets as High Street and Lower Street with their little shops and tame and commonplace interests, must be such a trial to a man of spirit, as every day can but make more and more a punishment."

"It gives me great pleasure to serve my old friend," said Captain Acton. "Mr Lawrence is an officer with a career full of gallant things; I have no doubt he is a capable navigator. Will you ask him to call upon me this evening?"

"At what hour?"

"Eight o'clock will suit me very well."

"He shall wait upon you at the stroke, sir."

"Good-bye, Sir William," said Lucy, and in silence the two gentlemen watched her walk to the gate and pass out.

CHAPTER II

WALTER LAWRENCE

LUCY ACTON made her way towards Old Harbour Town by a lane that struck down off the road used by the coaches and post-chaises. This lane was broad and in places steep and rugged, with long spaces heavily flanked with tall and spacious trees. Elsewhere the low hedge revealed the sloping meadow or ploughed field whose margin where it sank low was defined against the blue water of the ocean.

It was April, and some birds were in song; the sun shone brightly, and the breeze blowing from the sea sang pleasantly amongst the trees whose boughs were studded with little buds. The lane conducted Lucy to the valley where the river was, and here she stepped upon an old bridge. When half-way across she stopped to look in the direction of Old Harbour. The river flowed prettily under this bridge and melted its brilliance in the waters of the Harbour, where, when the tide was at lowest ebb, it always had a bed for its discharge into the brine beyond.

Lucy had often viewed this scene: her pause now was dictated by a trifling feeling of curiosity. Against the wharves on the left-hand side and over against the stump-ended projection of pier was moored her father's ship the *Minorca,* of which she had just now been assured Sir William Lawrence's son was to be offered the command. This vessel lay with two or three others, a brig or two and a schooner, at the wharves, and with her own and the drying sails of the others, the tall spars, the yards across, the complicated lines of the rigging, provided a bold and even ample figure of shipping to the eye. But in addition to these there lay in the harbour a number of fishing craft, and this side the extremity of the wharves within musket shot of where Lucy stood was moored the *Saucy* brig-of-war of about one hundred and eighty tons armed with thirty-two pounder carronades. She was one of a number of the like sort of brig which were to be found in that year (1805) on the coasts of

Sussex, Suffolk, and Norfolk. These brigs were usually hauled into creeks or laid up in snug corners where the Lieutenant, as Sir William had pointed out, had his cabbage garden and pig-sty. They were designed as a provision against the invasion of the French, and were quite worthless, as they were never ready, and always so anchored or so secured as to demand as much time in getting under weigh as would take a French army of invasion to march from Dover to Ashford.

This cool indifference on the part of the lieutenants in command of the brigs is rendered the more surprising by contrast with the sincere terrors which the prospect of invasion raised in the country. The alarm indeed was very seriously justified, for in that year the French Emperor had at his disposal at the Texel, Ostend, Dunkirk, Calais, Boulogne and Havre, a total of one hundred and eighty thousand men, with a fleet of twenty-one sail of the line, besides frigates and transports at Brest, a squadron at Rochefort, and a powerful fleet at Toulon, and at this time Spain had joined her forces with those of France against us. Nevertheless the lieutenants in charge of the gun-brigs stationed on the coasts took life with that unconcern which is one of the blessings of peace; they cultivated their cabbage gardens, they attended to their pig-stys, and they smoked their pipes and drank strong beer at taverns with sounding names such as "The Coach and Horses," or "The Maid and the Harp"; and one of the worst offenders was Lieutenant Tupman of the brig *Saucy*, which lay within gun-shot of where Lucy stood.

The thought of Mr Lawrence having received from her father the offer of the command of yonder little ship was put out of Lucy's mind by the image of placid sunlighted scenery she contemplated, taking full possession of her. Familiar as the picture was, her beautiful eyes, moving slowly, dwelt in their brooding way upon the objects she directed them at, and her native loveliness seemed to gain by the impulse which visited it, and she and the sweet and restful scene of cliff and distant blue water and quiet haven into which the fabrics that floated shook their lights and the delicate tracery of their gear, were blent, and it was as though she was the spirit of the place,

Close to lay the gun-brig reflecting her white band broken by ports in the calm surface. She looked to be ready for sea; all her yards were across, the white sails furled with that exquisite finish which expresses the pat of the man-o'-warsman's hand; but there was nobody visible aboard of her. Beyond, the eye went to the short length of timber pier, and on this side of it to some smacks which now floated at little buoys or at their own anchors, though at ebb of tide Old Harbour was mainly mud with the river's bed in the middle and vessels lying high, black and gaunt in several postures, whilst out in the south the ripple of the sea in smooth weather streamed to and fro with long lashings of black weed, and the air was salt and nimble with the smell of marine growths.

The wharves were old platforms black with tar or pitch, and at the back of them were three warehouses for the accommodation of such merchandise as this Old Harbour received or sent afloat. Perched midway on the slope that was terminated by the brow of the cliff where the windmill this morning was peacefully revolving its vans, was Old Harbour Town, a romantic grouping of little grey houses full of sparkling lozenge windows backed by a church spire, the whole looking in the distance like a toy that could be put into a box and set out according to taste upon a table by a child.

Lucy heard a church bell strike: she started from a fit of abstraction, and, turning to move on, confronted an old man who was crossing the bridge. The face of this old man was pale and wrinkled; his hair was long and quite white. His nose streamed down his face in a thin, curling outline; his mouth when his lips were compressed might be expressed by a simple stroke of a pencil. His eyes were deep-seated and extraordinarily luminous and swift in their motions, and his eyebrows, which were as white as his hair, were so thick and overhanging that they might have passed for a couple of white mice sleeping on his brow. His apparel had that dim and faded look which in fiction is associated with miserliness. His high and dingy white cravat and the tall build of his coat at the back of his head, so sloped his shoulders that they looked to make a line with his arms. He wore a faded red waistcoat which sank very low, and under it dangled a bunch of seals. His knee-breeches left painfully visible the pipe-stem shanks clothed in grey hose and terminating in large shoes, burdened with steel buckles.

He removed his little round hat and bowed low to Lucy.

"Good morning, Mr Greyquill," said the young lady, bestowing upon him one of those sweet and gracious smiles with which she favoured nearly all, thus rendering herself as much beloved for her cordial charm of manner as she was admired by the women and adored by the men for her singular beauty of face and graces of person.

He bade her good-morning with profound respect. Her dog barked in his face, and she silenced it by lifting it under her arm.

"I hope your cold is better, Mr Greyquill," said she, making to proceed in her walk.

"Much better—indeed, quite gone, I am greatly obliged to you, ma'am," he answered. "I find nursing of little account. Gruel and footbaths and a tallow candle for the nose do not help me so much as fresh air. Fresh air seems to dry the cold up."

She agreed with him with a smile, and with a pleasant salutation of the head, walked on.

The old man looked after her, and whispered to himself in admiration of her kindness and person. A wooden-legged sailor just then came up some steps from the river side on to that end of the bridge which the moneylender was approaching, and when Greyquill was close to, the tar, assuming a posture of abject despondency, pulled off his hat, and extending it begged for alms.

"I have bled for my country, your honour," said the man.

"But you don't say you were paid to do so," answered Greyquill.

"Ay, but I wasn't paid to lose my leg," called out the man.

Greyquill, who saw little to fear in the pursuit of a man with a wooden leg, turned his head upon his shoulder and cried back: "There are too many of us."

"That ain't my fault!" bawled the man at the receding figure.

"Yes, it is," cried Greyquill. "For people like you who can't get on ought to get out."

The laugh with which the malicious old fellow accompanied this sally caused the sailor to gaze eagerly round the ground as though for a stone to heave at him.

Meanwhile, Lucy crossing the bridge pursued the road to Old Harbour Town. She walked up an incline as gradual and pleasant as the lane which had brought her to the river. The hedges on either side stood thick, and the road was sentinelled by trees which when robed in their foliage transformed a long space of it into a beautiful avenue. The way took her straight to Lower Street, at the corner of which stood "The Swan" Tavern, a posting-house with a signboard that swang rustily through the long dark night, but behind its little lower windows a glimpse of old-world comfort could be caught: a sanded floor, a dark-polished table ringed with impressions of immemorial mugs of ale set down upon it, a little grate high perched in a setting of china, an old Dutch clock, and a black-board for the score.

This house contained a room which caused it to be the haunt of the seafaring men of the place. It was in the second story, and was lighted by a large bow-window with a seat running round it from which a fine view of Old Harbour was to be obtained and the spacious sea beyond. Here on a table in the middle of the room were to be found telescopes, newspapers, not older perhaps than a week, little sheaves of matchwood for lighting pipes at the fire in winter or at a floating oil-mesh in summer. This room always contained one or more seafaring men, and of a night, if there was a tolerable presence of shipping in the Harbour, it was sometimes full, on which occasions it was so heavily loaded with tobacco fumes that one was at some pains to see one's friend through the fog. Here were battles fought over again, and future victories planned and won. Here you heard the argument running high on the usefulness of certain sails in certain weather, on the best course to adopt when taken by the lee, on the wisest thing to do when chased by an enemy's cruiser. Here were told stories of admirals and captains whose names are shining stars in our national story; yarns of Hawke and Howe and Duncan, Rodney, and others. For this room was frequented by several very old men who lived in Old Harbour Town and had served the King; and one of them, like Tom Tough, had been coxswain to Boscawen.

Of this man, a toothless salt whose face was like an old potato, dark with the weather of vanished days and covered with warts, an affecting story was told: it was evening, and the room was full of seafaring men, and this man, whose name was John Halliburton, sat at the table with a long clay pipe trembling in one hand and a glass of hot rum and water in reach of the other. Several songs had been sung by members of the company, and someone, by way of a joke, asked old John to oblige. To the amazement of everybody the old man put down his pipe, took off his hat, out of which he drew a large red handkerchief with which he polished his face, and then, fixing his lustreless eyes upon the man who had asked him to sing, broke into a song in a strange, quivering, fitful note, as though you should hear a drunken sailor singing in a vault. The assembly was hushed into deep stillness. It was certainly a most unparalleled circumstance for old John to sing. In the middle of the second verse, some old nautical ballad popular fifty years before, he stopped, put his handkerchief into his hat, and his hat upon his head, and resumed his pipe, gazing vacantly at the man who had asked him to sing.

"Pray, go on," said the man. "We are all delighted, Mr Halliburton. Have you forgot the words? There's some here, no doubt, as are able to remind ye."

"Oh yes," said a voice.

"Are ye speaking to me?" said old John.

"Certainly," was the answer.

"What d'ye want?"

"We want you to finish the song you was just now singing and broke off in."

"*Me* singing!" exclaimed old John.

"Why, yes, of course."

"Me singing!" quavered old John, with a voice of amazement. "Why, I ha'nt sung this twenty year past."

It was easily seen that the poor old man was deeply in earnest and was to be speedily distressed. It was an affecting exhibition of mental decay, and rough as the company were, they had the good taste to change the subject.

Lower Street was not the street in which Lucy shopped. It consisted mainly of little houses with green doors and bright brass knockers, and lozenged windows which opened and shut in the French style, so that a small piece of the window could be opened at will. These houses were the dwelling-places of pilots, sailors, and fishermen belonging to the district. In the middle of the street was a Nonconformist Chapel with a burial ground spreading out in front of it till its outer confines were half-way upon the footpath; a wonderfully tended resting-place: its billows of grass marked in most cases the silent beds of seafarers; the decoration of flower or memorial was largely nautical: the anchor, the Liliputian bows of a ship as a headpiece, and here and there the headpiece was a gun. Tombstones whose inscriptions endless discharges of wet and the fretting action of the wind had rendered almost illegible, leaned as though for support in their weariness against the walls of the adjacent houses; so that a few bricks or stones might separate a row of dead men from a little parlour full of cheerful company where the fire crackled briskly, where the oil flame shook in ripples of yellow radiance upon the walls and the ceiling, where the atmosphere was good with the perfume of rum punch, and where a manly voice in an interval of silence might be heard singing a nautical ballad to the accompaniment of a fiddle.

Lucy walked on to High Street, into which she turned, and from nearly every person that she passed, she received a respectful salute or a ducking curtsy; and for all she had a kindly word and a smile as lovely as a fine May day, and sometimes she would stop and speak to a child, on which occasions she generally took a penny from her pocket.

This High Street was pleasantly furnished with shops: the butcher's, the owner of which shouted in talk to his customers as he dexterously chopped on his block; the baker's, with its little bow-window choice with buns and cakes, and pretty shapes of bread; here too was the post-office, which was like a pedlar's tray for variety of contents.

After Lucy had done her shopping—and the few articles were to be delivered punctually that afternoon—she walked along High Street, so as to return by the road she had come by. When her steps had brought her abreast of "The Swan," she saw two men standing in conversation in the doorway of that old hostelry. They both bowed low to her, but it might have been noticed that after she had saluted them in return, the fine natural glow of her cheeks slightly deepened and her step appreciably quickened. If her object was to escape these men she must either run, which would not have been seemly, or submit to being overtaken if pursued, which happened in the case of one of them, and within a few minutes a gentleman was walking at her side.

"Good morning, Miss Acton! I am going over to my father's. Are you returning to Old Harbour House? If so, I hope you will allow me to do myself the pleasure of accompanying you as far."

"No, sir," she answered. "I am not returning to Old Harbour House—not immediately. I am going to the Harbour—I am going for a little walk."

"How I am always being disappointed!" he exclaimed, and she might by the note in his voice, by a smile which did not show perfect self-control, and by a heated colour of complexion, have by this time suspected that this gentleman and his companion, who was Lieutenant Tupman, had not looked in at "The Swan" Inn only to find out what o'clock it was.

He was Mr Walter Lawrence, a son of Admiral Lawrence, and down to a recent period a lieutenant in the Royal Navy. He was something over thirty years of age, but drink, dissipation, the hard life of the sea and some fever which had got into his blood and proved intermittent, had worked in his face like time, and he might have passed for any age between thirty-five and forty-five. Nevertheless he was an extremely handsome man, of the classic Greek type in lineament, but improved, at least to the British eye, by the Saxon colouring of hair, skin, and eyes. His teeth were extra-ordinarily white and good for a sailor who had lived on gun-room fare in times when the ship's biscuit was flint, and the peas which rolled about in the discoloured hot water called soup, fit only for loading a blunderbuss with to shoot men dead. His eyes told their tale of drink, but they were large and fine and spirited; his light brown hair, according to the fashion of the age, was combed down his back and lay in a rope-shaped tail there. He wore a wide-brimmed round hat, and his attire, a little the worse for wear, consisted of a blue coat, white waistcoat, sage-green kerseymere breeches, and, needless to say, the cravat was high and full. He stood about six feet, his figure was extremely well proportioned, and in addition to these merits his carriage had the easy elegance which the flow of the billow and the heave of the deck infuse into all human figures not radically vile and deformed. His voice was soft, winning, and somewhat plaintive, and no man, whether on or off the stage, not even Incledon, sang a song with more exquisite feeling and sweeter sincerity of passion.

His companionship, however, in spite of his beauty, for more reasons than one, must prove, then, as it had proved on other occasions, extremely embarrassing to Miss Acton. Shortly after he had obtained his promotion he arrived home on a visit to his father, and meeting her, fell in love and offered her marriage. But Lucy had much good sense, which is not often allied with so much beauty as she possessed. Her heart admitted his fascination, and she had heard things of him that did him honour; moreover, he was a member of a profession which she adored. But it had come to her knowledge, by avenues difficult to determine, that he was a gambler and drank without moderation, and that his theory of life and morals was such as deserved severe condemnation as it would surely end in provoking heavy punishment.

She declined his offer, yet with a maiden's secret fretfulness over the perception that her judgment compelled her into a step against the wishes and sighs of her heart.

He went to sea again and did not return for two years, and when he arrived he came broken, to the grief and shame of his father. He had been court-martialled and dismissed his ship. His offence was singular and characteristic: he was in a foreign port, and at night-fall he walked to the quay to return to his ship. He was intoxicated, and on being challenged by a sentry, tumbled the fellow into the water and immediately sprang after him and saved his life. Some in the face of his gallant career thought the sentence too severe: others regarded it as lenient. His own view of it he betokened by conceiving a bitter hatred against the Service and by resigning his commission.

He returned to England, and went to his father ostensibly to seek a berth ashore, but for many months past he had been hanging about Old Harbour Town, an idler and a tippler, and handsome as he was, and brilliant as had been his short naval story, he was not

the man to commend himself to Lucy Acton as a husband whatever
may have been her secret feelings in regard to his person and some
points of his character.

"How," he exclaimed, "I am always being disappointed! If you turn
off at the bridge I shall not be allowed more than ten minutes' talk
with you."

"I shall turn off at the bridge," she answered. "It is not long since
that I was with your father. I left him in conversation with Captain
Acton at Old Harbour House. I believe I heard your name mentioned
as I passed away from them."

"What would they have to say about me?" he exclaimed, with a
rather unmeaning smile. "I can believe that Sir William grows weary
of my presence, and that he sometimes wishes me at the bottom of
the sea. 'Tis a pity that he did so ill in prize money. He was born
to no fortune, and married a moneyless lady, and here is my father,
an Admiral in the British Navy, obliged to dwell in a cottage fit only
to make a dwelling-house for a poet, whose calling is, I believe, the
poorest paid of any. I am much troubled," he continued in a maudlin
way, "to think that I should continue to be a burthen upon the old
gentleman. But I assure you on my honour, madam, if I am not independent of him this moment 'tis not because I have not been as
diligent as Old Nick himself in looking about me. But go where I
will and ask where I will, the door is shut, the place is full, the
answer is nay. What a sweet little dog is that! How happy to be for
ever frisking about you and often lifted and caressed!"

Here he sighed so loudly that she could not fail to hear him, and
looked at her a little while with a somewhat tipsy steadfastness.

"There should be plenty to be done," said she. "There is the Army."

"The Army!" he cried. "Could you put a greater indignity upon a
sailor than to compel him to shoulder a handspike and march up
and down as though he were a soldier?"

She fell a-laughing at his sottish indignation, but quickly recollected herself. He burst into a loud guffaw when he saw that he had
amused her, and said: "I was just now with Tupman. I wish I had his
berth." Here he looked behind him to see if the lieutenant was following, but as a matter of fact Tupman had re-entered "The Swan."

"He is stationed here to guard us against being invaded by the

French, which he provides for so carefully by lying a-bed until ten in the morning, then sulking over his breakfast of ale, new bread, and tobacco, then doing some work in his bit of garden—he is a great lover of vegetables—then lurching up to Old Harbour Town, where of an afternoon he may commonly be found sitting over a pot reading the newspaper and yarning with any man that will take a chair over against him, that I protest when I met him at 'The Swan' not an hour gone by he had not heard that a French privateersman had been chased ashore by one of our frigates last evening, and burnt after ten thousand pounds had been taken out of her."

"I think if the French intend to invade us, they will not be stopped by Mr Tupman and his brig."

"He thinks highly of his brig, though: says to me a day or two ago, 'I wish an enemy's cruiser would look in. She will not know that the *Saucy* is lying here. I believe I could make my carronades talk to her, and it would please me to see the pier and the shore dark with figures whilst I was towing my capture into Old Harbour.' I doubt if he would rise out of bed to give an order to chase even if a suspicious sail hove in sight. Here we are coming to the bridge, and you are going for a walk to the pier. Will you pluck me a daisy before you go? See, there are several amongst the grass just there. I have nothing to remember you by. I will wrap it in silver paper, and it shall be the only sacred thing I possess."

"Oh no, sir, you can do without a daisy from me," she answered, though her cheeks were warm with one of those sudden blushes which seemed to glow as though to prove that her lovely bloom was entirely due to nature and not to art, as the suspicious eye might fancy or the cynical eye desire.

"You will deny me even a daisy?" he cried, with a sudden passion in his manner which alarmed her, as he was not sober. He sprang to the side of the road, and picking a daisy returned to her, pulled off his hat, and said earnestly—indeed in a voice of emotion and sincerity that put a fine and appealing meaning into the expression of his eyes which by the power of the impulse then governing him were superior to the drink in his head: "Let me entreat you, madam, to put this little flower to your sweet lips, and return it to me. It is but a trifle I ask: you are too good and generous to refuse me."

She took the flower, put it to her lips, and handed it to him. His passion for her was very visible as he received the flower with his eyes fixed upon her face. He gave her a low bow, and then put on his hat, and going to the hedge pulled a leaf in which he wrapped the daisy, and carefully placed both in his waistcoat pocket.

"To prove my sincerity, madam," said he, "I could wish that the possession of this little flower might depend upon the result of a conflict between yonder brig with your humble obedient servant in command of her, and the biggest corvette the Frenchman has afloat."

"Why, sir, do not you think that a great deal of nonsense is talked by young men and old men to young women? But I believe your father will be glad to see you. I may have a reason to suppose he is waiting for you to return. Here we part, Mr Lawrence, and I wish you a good morning," and, sinking her figure in a curtsy fashionable in those days, she crossed the road and went down the little flight of wooden steps that led to the path by the river's bank and so to Old Harbour.

She had not intended to take this walk. At Old Harbour House dinner was served at two o'clock, and if she was not punctual Aunt Caroline would grow alarmed, and probably send the coachman on horseback in search of her. But it was only just noon, and there was time enough for her to arrive home at the dinner-hour, and also to make this little diversion to escape Mr Lawrence, who, she suspected, would have forced his company upon her even in this further walk had not she excited his curiosity by saying that his father was waiting to see him. He was not too far gone in liquor to understand that something of significance to him lay in her reference to Sir William, and when presently she was upon the river-side footpath and took a cautious peep over her shoulder, she observed him through the trees mounting the lane and walking somewhat fast.

"It is a very great pity," she thought to herself, "that so handsome a young man, and one so spirited and daring as he has proved, should abandon himself to his vicious tastes. The longer he remains here the more sottish he will become, and the lower will his manhood sink till he will be at no pains to relieve his father from the obligation of supporting or helping him, and the gallant creature who, if he took the right path, would march easily to fame and dignity and affluence, must end as a drunken, trembling, degraded wretch, the object of pity or scorn, and who has pity for such people?" The beautiful girl sighed.

She had no intention of crossing the river by the ferry to gain the pier. When Mr Lawrence had advanced well ahead, she intended to resume the road he was taking and go home. Her mind, however, was occupied by him, and yonder, lying at the wharves, was the *Minorca,* of which she understood he was to receive the command. She walked towards the vessel; she supplied an object for the little excursion, and the walk would give Mr Lawrence time enough to put the necessary distance between them. The river widened rapidly when it passed under the bridge. The smooth water at the mouth of it reflected the chequered band of the *Saucy* brig-of-war. Two or three smacks were hoisting their coloured canvas and sailing out to sea. On either hand the banks of the ravine sloped, well dressed in shrubs and wood, and here and there stood a little house. Some small boats lay in black specks away out between the two Heads fishing. Business was not very brisk in the Harbour just then, and the wharves were quiet. They were three; each of well-pitched timber long enough to supply berths stem and stern to two or three small vessels apiece. They were backed by a row of warehouses, some of which were Captain Acton's, and in these were stowed the rum, sugar, and tobacco which his two ships brought from the West Indies.

CHAPTER III

THE OFFER

THE SMALL amount of work in the shape of discharging and receiving cargo which was being done on the wharves of Old Harbour, had come to a pause when the labourers' dinner-hour struck, and but three or four figures were visible upon the tar-black platforms along which the little ships were moored. Of these one was a brig and the other a schooner, and one was the *Minorca,* a handsome coppered barque of five hundred tons built by the French, and, as we have heard, taken from that people.

The sails of these vessels had been furled, and the bright April breeze blowing from the sea sang in their clean rigging. A couple of planks communicated between the *Minorca*'s gangway and the wharf, and at the wharf-end of these planks stood a man of a sea-faring aspect, apparently belonging to the barque.

As Lucy advanced holding her dog lest the creature should skip in a fit of excitement into the water, the man viewed her as though on catching her eye, or receiving the encouragement of a look of recognition, he was prepared to salute her. Perhaps she did not heed him, but on drawing close to the vessel, she looked at him, and thanks to that gracious gift which by creating opportunities for tact, helps more to render the individual beloved or popular than perhaps any other quality, she immediately recollected the man, and not only the man, but his name, as Mr John Eagle, mate of the *Minorca,* who, when the vessel was last in harbour and she had gone on board of her with her father, had been introduced to her by Captain Acton.

He was a man of rough appearance whose hand had been in the tar-bucket for most of his life—a hard, reserved man, shy, so ignorant that he read with difficulty, and wrote his name as painfully as a hand tortured with gout inscribes with the pen.

"How do you do, Mr Eagle?" exclaimed Lucy.

He stiffened himself, and saluted her by a flourish of his hand to his brow, and answered: "Just about middling, thank you, Miss."

"I am sorry you are not better than middling," she said.

"It's the rheumatics. It's got into my feet and my shoulders. It's a pain as no spirits can stand up against."

"Are you doing anything to ease your suffering?"

"I drinks a drop of rum when it comes on very bad. I've given up rubbing. I've been rubbed till I've scarce got any skin left."

"I'll speak to Miss Acton. I am sure she will have something that is good for rheumatism, and if she has I will send it you."

"I thank you, Miss," said he, with an incredulous smile. "Was you going on board?"

"No. What a big ship she looks compared with the other two! It is difficult to think of her alone in the middle of the sea. I can only imagine her lying at a wharf with protecting hills on each side. Does she sail fast?"

"Give her a good breeze and she can find her legs, but she ain't to be compared with the *Aurora*."

"She will be arriving shortly, I think."

"Doo any day, Miss, unless she's been nabbed, but the vessel that's going to take the *Aurora* 'ull want more than wings."

"When does the *Minorca* sail?"

"Early next month, I believe, ma'am."

Her eyes reposed thoughtfully upon the hull of the ship, mounting presently in a stealing way to the heights, and her colour seemed to deepen slightly to the impulse of a romantic mood or fancy.

"If there was nothing to fear from the enemy's ships," she said, "and if the sea was always calm and the breeze gentle and mild, I believe I might wish to make a voyage in the *Minorca* to the West Indies."

"You'd be taken all care of, ma'am."

"But the sleeping berths are very little, and I am certain that the motion of the ship—" She shook her head and smiled, and then saying, "Good morning, Mr Eagle. If my aunt has a remedy for the rheumatism I will send it you," she returned the way she had come, mounted the steps, gained the bridge, and proceeded home.

Meanwhile, Mr Lawrence had gone about three-quarters of a mile and was now approaching his father's home. The Admiral's cottage was in a lane off the main road. It was such an umbrageous retreat as Cowper, had he been in earnest, would have hastened to when he sighed for some boundless contiguity of shade. It stood in a little land protected by hedges and walls full of orchards. The Admiral lived in the heart of groves of cherry, plum, apple, pear, and other fruitful trees which presently, in this month of April, would make the scene round about as beautiful as driven snow shone upon by the sun, with almond-white flowers.

The Admiral missed the sea; he was near it, nay, in heavy weather within sound of it, but not a glimpse of the blue deep could be caught through the windows. He had retired on a pension and on trifling private means which rendered this retreat the fittest he could have chosen for the convenience of his purse and for the simple tastes of his life. Here he lived with an old servant and a young girl, and now with his son; but he was always hoping that this last obligation would not be continuous, though the prospect of getting anything to do in such an obscure corner of the earth as Old Harbour Town was as remote as the possibility of Mr Lawrence ever becoming Prime Minister of England. Yet a secret hope, an indeterminable dream, one of those imaginations which make blessed the possessors of the sanguine temperament, buoyed the Admiral. Who could tell? Something might happen! Walter might fall in with a man who should prove a friend, even in that very haunt, "The Swan," which seemed obnoxious to his interests. Thus the old fellow would reason without logic, or even knowing what he was talking to himself about.

His mind was full of his son as he sat this day at his dinner, which was put every afternoon punctually at half-past one upon the table whether Mr Lawrence was at home or whether he was not. The window at which the Admiral was wont of a pleasant evening to sit with his pipe was open; the room was small, with a low ceiling, but one should say a very dream of comfort to a nautical man. Its walls were embellished with pictures of seafights, of frigates engaging forts, of encounters between line-of-battle ships. A handsome telescope, a gift for some deed of valour, lay in brackets over the small, richly-carved sideboard.

The Admiral sat at table before a meal that betokened total neglect on his part of all thought of digestion. The dinner in short, so far as it had been served, consisted of a round of boiled beef, carrots and turnips, and a dish of potatoes smoking in their jackets, a stout loaf of black crust, a dish of fine yellow butter, and at Sir William's elbow was a silver mug with a thick glass bottom, just filled foaming to the brim from a cask of the very best ale at that time brewed in England, and in those days a glass of fine ale was a more delicious draught, more thirst-quenching, more appealing to all the secret feelings of the interior than the finest liquor that has been drunk since, call it what you will.

Just as the Admiral was cutting a second helping for himself from the round of beef, which being English was choicely tasted, he heard his son's footsteps in the passage outside, and after a short interval, during which Mr Lawrence fitted himself for the dinner table, that gentleman walked in. He was almost immediately followed by the old housekeeper with hot plates. She was very fond of Mr Lawrence. She would listen for his footsteps. He was still "Master Walter" with her, and would remain so. She had once, on hearing of his money troubles, offered to lend him from her slender savings. But whatever may have been his character he was a sailor in this: he would not take money from a woman.

The Admiral viewed his son critically. The walk home, followed by a sousing of the face in cold water, had helped to attenuate the lingering fumes in the young man's brains, and on the whole his mind was about as steady as could be expected in one who was always more or less under the influence of drink.

"Have you dined?" asked Sir William.

"No, sir."

This question will not appear strange when it is understood that Mr Lawrence occasionally took a seat at an ordinary at "The Swan," served half an hour after noon.

The Admiral cut a plate of meat, and the pair fell to their dinner, the housekeeper reappearing to place such another silver tankard foaming full as graced Sir William's elbow, at the side of Mr Lawrence.

"I met Miss Acton as I was coming home," said Mr Lawrence, "and she said she had left you and her father talking about me."

"Captain Acton and I were talking about you this morning," said the Admiral. "I was lamenting your inability to procure a berth of any sort, and told him that I could see no hope for you whilst you continued to hang about Old Harbour Town, and to lounge in and out of 'The Swan.'"

"You'll admit, sir, that my failure to obtain employment has not been due to neglect in searching for it."

"But what is to be hoped for in a place like this? Here are no industries; there is nothing doing, you cannot turn smacksman or start as a pilot."

"I am extremely anxious to relieve you of the burden of maintaining me, and my fixed intention, if I can procure nothing to do between this and next month, is to work my passage out before the mast to the United States. If it should come to the backwoods, I am ready. I confess this life grows insupportable, and the more bur-thensome to me because it is a tax upon you, sir."

The Admiral buried half his face in his tankard, and after wiping the froth from his lips and looking earnestly at the round of beef as though he deliberated within himself whether he should take another slice, he said: "I am happy to say that I have good news for you. An opportunity has been offered which will do away with the need of your shipping before the mast and seeking your fortune in America. The *Minorca,* as you doubtless know, is in want of a cap-tain. I was speaking about you to Captain Acton this morning, and regretting, as I must continue to regret whilst I have the capacity of a sigh—I do not say a tear—left in me, that you should relinquish the Service in which, had you behaved with prudence, you were eminently calculated to make a shining figure."

The gallant old officer paused and looked at his son, and any one could have easily seen that he was equally moved by pain and pride. Indeed the man who sat opposite to him was one who by manly beauty of face, worn as it was by weather and excess, by vigorous bearing of shapely person, and by a story which, brief as it was, was as full of the stars of gallant deeds as a short scope of wake is alive with the brilliant pulses of the sea-glow, was one, let it be repeated, whom many a father's heart would rejoice in, and approve of, bit-terly as it must deplore those lamentable, if fashionable, weaknesses, gambling and a love of what Dibdin calls the "flowing can."

Mr Lawrence had closed his knife and fork and swallowed half his tankard of ale, when the Admiral halted in his speech. He regarded his father with eager earnestness. But the Admiral was not to be interrupted in his further disclosure. Having ascertained that his son wished for no more beef, he went to the fire-place and pulled a bell-rope, and it was not until the housekeeper had removed the joint and vegetables and replaced them by a dish of Norfolk dumplings with white sauce sweetened and brandied—a homely dish of which Sir William was uncommonly fond—that the old gen-tleman proceeded.

"I may now tell you," said he, "that Captain Acton this morning, on my expressing my regret that you could not obtain employment, most handsomely and liberally made you the offer of the command of a ship, the *Minorca*."

Mr Lawrence's face lighted up, but the expression was curious; it was composite; it seemed to be lacking in the elementary quality of exultation or rejoicing which naturally would have been sought for or expected.

"He is very kind," said he. "I should like the berth."

"He proposes that you should take the vessel out to the West Indies and bring her home. He pays twelve pounds a month, and gives a commission on the earnings of the ship. What do you say?"

"Why, sir, of course I accept without hesitation, and feel most deeply obliged."

"It is a step," continued the Admiral, "that may lead to other and even better things. But first and foremost it finds you in employment, and will put some money into your pocket, and relieve the pressure which not only you but I am made to feel. I do not choose that Mr Greyquill should visit me. Yet he calls to enquire after you."

"He is a very impertinent old man, and why he should call here to see me when he knows that every day I am within a stone's throw of his office, I cannot tell. He'll get his head broke if he troubles you, sir."

"Captain Acton wishes to see you at eight o'clock this evening. You'll be there?"

"Oh, depend upon it. This is a great offer. He is extremely obliging."

"And I must hope," said the Admiral, "since this opportunity has been brought about by me, that you will do me the justice to take care to present yourself in such a state as shall not excite his resentment, or, which is worse, result in the cancellation of his offer."

The old gentleman spoke with sternness, and held his eyes fastened upon his son, who cried: "Oh sir, I am not such a fool as to run any risks with this stroke of fortune."

"You will present yourself at eight," said the Admiral a little more softly, "and I have no doubt whatever that you will receive the offer which will be properly executed tomorrow. I believe that the *Minorca* sails early next month. You will have time to obtain the few clothes you may require. The dress of the Merchant sailor is inexpensive. Indeed, a man in the Merchant Service dresses as he pleases. It is a warm voyage, and you'll find a few white clothes useful. I do not suppose you'll be expected to know anything about stowage and the like. But you will pick up what you want as you go. Captain Acton spoke of the mate as a respectable, though illiterate man. He doubtless understands his part, and little more will be expected from you than the navigation of the ship to her port, a careful attention to your owner's interests, and a strict execution of such commands as you may receive with regard to obtaining a freight and matters of that sort, of which I confess I am ignorant."

Sir William now rose from the table and went to an armchair at the open window, upon the seat or ledge of which stood a jar of tobacco, some clay pipes, and a little machine for firing a match dipped in brimstone, a very ingenious contrivance as old as the days of the second Charles: namely, a little pistol-shaped fire-maker whose trigger struck a full and brilliant spark from the flint and kindled the tinder. He filled his pipe and lighted it, and sat in conversation with his son, in whom the particular humour or mood would have been extremely hard to settle by the most sagacious of critical observers. He was speedy in answering his father, and his language did not show much abstraction of mind; but even the Admiral noticed that there was an undercurrent of thought in his son which was pursuing a very different course from the stream as it appeared on the surface.

Sir William, however, was a man not in the habit of taking long or deep views. His son was thinking of his good luck, of his meeting that evening with Captain Acton, of the opportunities for advancement which now lay before him, and these reflections would naturally colour his manner and make him appear somewhat strange to those who knew him best.

Captain Acton received Mr Lawrence in his library, a small but very elegant room. It was lighted by wax candles on the table and wax candles on the chimney-piece. Its walls were covered with valuable books in finely carved cases. Captain Acton was reading when Mr Lawrence was announced. He immediately put down his book and rose. It would have been easy to see that he was struck by and pleased with the fine figure and handsome face of Mr Lawrence as he strode through the doorway, bowing with dignity and grace as he advanced. Of course the Captain was perfectly well acquainted with Mr Lawrence; he had been to his house to dinner on more than one occasion with Sir William; they had met at the Admiral's house and out-of-doors.

Yet Captain Acton appeared to find in Mr Lawrence this evening a quality of bearing, a character of masculine beauty which had not certainly before impressed him to anything like the same degree. He had carefully dressed himself; his manner betokened complete self-possession; his handsome eyes shone clear and steady, and his face exhibited a mind whose command over itself was complete. The worn look partly due to dissipation, partly due to the hard life of the sea which was often injuriously visible by daylight, was now concealed in the soft veil of light shed by the wax candles. They shook hands, and seated themselves.

"Your father has doubtless acquainted you with my object in asking you to call upon me this evening."

"He has, sir."

"Are you willing to accept the command of the *Minorca?* "

"I am indeed, and have no words in which to convey my thanks to you for your kindness."

"Oh, say no more, sir, about that. I am pleased with the idea of a Naval officer being in charge of my ship."

And here Captain Acton again viewed the face and form of the young man with a pleasure and satisfaction the other could scarcely miss, though it was delicately tempered by Acton's natural gravity and his well-bred air. And now for a short time the conversation wholly referred to the business part of the compact. Captain Acton named the terms, stated the nature of the voyage and his expectations, spoke of the cargo and the consignees, and of his agent at Kingston. Mr Lawrence listened with intelligence, and the questions which he put were all to the point.

"The rig of the vessel," said Captain Acton, "is unusual. She is called a barque. The idea of fore and aft canvas only upon the mizzen-mast is French. I am told that rig is very handy in stays. Do you know the ship, sir? "

"I was never on board of her, but I know her very well. I admire her figure, though I do not think she is so finely moulded as your schooner, the *Aurora.*"

"Oh, certainly not, and as a consequence the *Aurora* sails two feet to the *Minorca*'s one. That schooner is almost due. She is commonly very punctual. She earns more money than the *Minorca.* No doubt all will have been well with her until she enters the Chops. But the Western squadrons have done great work. They have swept the French corsairs off the narrow waters and huddled the lily-livered rogues into their own ports. The *Minorca* is lightly armed: four eighteen-pounder carronades, for her business is to run and not to chase. You'll have to keep a bright look-out, sir. Your business must be to give your heels to everything that stirs your suspicion."

"I assure you, sir," said Mr Lawrence, with a smile which added a freshness to his beauty by that light, "that I have no idea of taking command of your ship with a view to a French prison."

After some further conversation to this effect, during which it was manifest that Captain Acton was very well satisfied with the generous resolution he had formed that morning to offer the command of the *Minorca* to Sir William's son, he left his chair and conducted Mr Lawrence to the drawing-room.

Wax candles burning purely and softly in sconces and candelabra illuminated an interior of singular elegance and rich in luxury. Lucy started from the piano, the sounds of which had been audible outside before the gentleman opened the door. Her beauty, her costume were in exquisite keeping with the objects which filled that room, the repository of the tasteful and sumptuous selections of several generations of Actons. Lucy's garb was the picturesque attire of that age: the neck and a portion of the bosom were exposed; a handsome medallion brooch decorated the bust; the arms were bare to above the elbows; the girdle gave her gown a waist just under the bosom. In that light all that was tender and lovely in her gained in softness, sweetness, and delicacy. Her rich bloom had the divine tenderness of the flush of sunset when in the east the velvet deeps are enriched with the diamond-throb of the first of the stars.

Not far from the large old-fashioned hearth beside a little table on which stood a workbasket, sat in a tall-backed arm-chair fit for a queen to be crowned in, a figure that must have carried the memory of a middle-aged or old man of that time well back into the past century. She was Miss Acton, Lucy's Aunt Caroline, sister of Captain Acton, a lady of about seventy years of age, who trembled with benevolence and imaginary alarms, who was always doing somebody good, and was now at work upon some baby clothing for an infant that had been born a week or two before.

She belonged to a race whose extinction Francis Grose lamented. She was what was termed an antiquated gentlewoman whose dress was a survival of the fashion of two if not three earlier generations: consisting of a stiffstarched cap and hood, a little hoop and a rich silk damask gown with large flowers. She acted as housekeeper to her brother, and the keys of the cupboards jingled at her side. She was choice in her stores, which included cordial waters, cherry and raspberry brandy, Daffy's Elixir, pots of currant jelly and raspberry jam, and her stock also comprised salves, electuaries, and purges for the poor. When she walked she leaned, perhaps a little affectedly, on an ivory-handled crutch stick, and a fat pug dog rolled in her wake. This pug now snored alongside of her, and the little terrier slept with its paws upon the pug's stomach.

Mr Lawrence was extremely easy. There was nothing of the embarrassment in the presence of ladies which is often visible even in well-bred men who have fallen from their estate, and pass their days in liquor and in looking in and out of such haunts as "The Swan." Indeed, his well-governed behaviour had something of a pre-determined air as of a man who acts a part and with all the resolution of his soul means to carry it through, though he may be obstructed by physical pain or by mental distress.

After a few airy nothings of salutation and the like had been exchanged and all were seated, Captain Acton said: "Lucy, I am now to introduce Mr Lawrence to you in a new character; he is the captain of the *Minorca.*"

"What is that you say?" cried Aunt Caroline, starting in her chair and peering over her gold-rimmed glasses at Mr Lawrence.

"I have given Mr Lawrence the command of my ship, sister," said Captain Acton.

"The news does not surprise me," said Lucy. "I think I told you this morning, sir, that Sir William wished to see you. Do you like the idea of commanding the *Minorca?*"

"Very much indeed, madam. My inclination leans wholly towards the Merchant Service. I would rather command the *Minorca* than a line-of-battle ship."

He smiled faintly, as though he guessed she would not believe this, and she could not miss the expression of bitterness in his smile which, as she was well acquainted with the story of his career, she perfectly understood. In truth she felt a little grieved for him. It was pitiful to think of so handsome and gallant a young fellow descending from the lofty platform of the King's Service to take charge of a poor little Merchant vessel whose one officer, a mate, was as ignorant and common a fellow as any that could be found in the 'tween decks of a man-of-war, remote from the society of the ward and gun rooms, though on board the *Minorca* Mr Eagle would be Mr Lawrence's associate.

"Are you not afraid to take the command of a ship, sir?" enquired Miss Acton, who continued to peer at Mr Lawrence over her glasses.

"Afraid, madam!"

"Afraid, sister!" echoed Captain Acton. "Your question reminds me of a story of Lord Howe: a lieutenant having reported the ship on fire returned, and said that his lordship need not feel afraid as the fire was out. 'Afraid!' exclaimed Howe, 'How does a man feel when he is afraid? I need not ask how he looks!'"

"It is such a very serious undertaking," said Miss Acton. "I cannot imagine a more responsible position than that of captain of a ship. If she sinks or is consumed by fire or strikes upon the rocks and the people perish, the captain, whether he survives or not, is answerable. If he dies with the people he goes before God, who judges him. It is dreadful. If I commanded a ship and lost lives, I could never sleep. I should not know what to do for seeing the spirits of the dead. I should feel that they all looked to me to return them their lives, and how terrible it must be to feel helpless when you are pleaded to by spirits who wring their hands and wail."

Mr Lawrence viewed the old lady with silent astonishment.

"If all thought like you, aunt," said Lucy, "we should get no captains at all for our ships, and how delighted the French would be to learn that our men-of-war could not leave port because captains were not to be got."

She received a smile full of perception of her point from Mr Lawrence.

"Well, I did not think of it in that way," said Miss Acton, who was active again with her needle and talking at her work. "Of course we must have captains for our men-of-war. I hope there is no fresh news of invasion."

"Nothing more since the privateersman was run in," said Captain Acton.

"Oh, aunt, whilst I think of it," cried Lucy, "poor Mr Eagle, the mate of the *Minorca,* is suffering badly from rheumatism in his ankles. He can hardly stand. I told him that I would ask you to send him something to ease him."

"I am sure I do not know what is good for rheumatism," said Miss Acton, with the petulance that attends a sudden anxiety of benevolence. "It is a most troublesome disease. You may rub and rub, and you only make it fly to another place, and often rubbing takes the skin off. I will send him some sulphur to put in his stockings, and I will see what else there is to be done for the poor man." And here, looking over her glasses again at Mr Lawrence, she said: "Pray, can you tell me how Mrs Bigg is, sir?"

"Mrs Bigg, ma'am! I never heard of her."

"She lives at Uphill Cottage, and lay in of a very fine baby a fortnight yesterday, and has done very poorly since. You cannot tell me how she does?"

"I cannot, madam."

At this moment the door was opened and the butler entered with a large sparkling silver tray of refreshments—wines and spirits, and cakes of several kinds. But Mr Lawrence would take nothing. He had done very well, he said. He had supped handsomely with his father off a round of cold boiled beef. The hospitality of the tray was not pressed upon him; Miss Lucy took some wine and water, and a small draught of cordial waters was placed beside Miss Acton.

"Your father was telling me a few days ago," said Captain Acton, "of a narrow escape of yours, sir."

"I have met with several. To which did he refer?"

"To that of the punt in which you attempted to sail from Plymouth to Falmouth."

Mr Lawrence smiled. When his smile was dictated by some honest or candid emotion, free from irritation or contempt, or any of the passions which make merriment forced and alarming, the expression gave a particular pleasure to the beholder. It was full of heart, and seemed to lighten his beauty of much of its burden of wear and tear.

"What was the story, sir?" asked Lucy.

"A story of foolhardiness, madam, largely due to my difficulty in foreseeing issues."

The remark appeared to impress Captain Acton, who fastened his eyes upon the speaker.

"I had made up my mind to go from Plymouth to Falmouth in a small punt. She was fourteen feet long. When I had got some distance away, my hat was blown overboard. I secured the tiller a-lee, threw off my clothes, and jumped after my hat. As I was returning with the hat the sail filled, the boat got way on her and sailed some distance before she came up in the wind. I had almost reached her when she filled again. This happened three or four times. At length I managed by a frantic struggle to catch a hold of the rudder, but I was so exhausted that it was long before I had strength to get into the boat."

This tale induced Captain Acton to indulge in the recital of a hairbreadth escape of his own, but a flow of exciting anecdotes was arrested by Miss Acton declaring that she was not strong enough to bear to hear such horrid, moving stories, particularly just a little before bed-time.

Lucy was somewhat puzzled by Mr Lawrence. His behaviour was cool, gentleman-like, distant, cautious, entirely sober, and for the most part he expressed himself with a high degree of intelligence. She could not but remember that in the morning when, to be sure, he might be said to have been "flown with wine and insolence," he had, with a passion which assuredly borrowed nothing of heat from liquor, plucked a daisy and bade her put it to her sweet lips and return it to him, and he had then concealed the little flower in his pocket as the only sacred treasure he possessed. This evening his bearing was on the whole as formal and collected as though she was but an acquaintance in whose company he could sit without being overcome by her charms. The passion of the morning was genuine and sincere, drink or no drink; the behaviour this evening was calculated and extraordinary. Perhaps in the delicate candlelight she might not catch every expression of eye, every movement of mouth, every shade of change in the expression of the whole face, so that she would justly imagine she had missed through defective illumination the impassioned look, the swift pencilling by rapture of the lineaments which her maiden's intuition gave her eloquently and convincingly to know must be the secret homage of his heart, let him mask his handsome and worn face as he would.

"I wish, madam," said he, "that you would return to the piano at which we interrupted you.

"Papa will not thank me for making a noise."

"Oh, my dear, don't say that. I am quite sure that if you will play, Mr Lawrence will afterwards sing, and I shall be charmed to hear you, sir, for I recollect your sweet and powerful voice both here and at your father's."

"There is little that I would not do to oblige you, sir," answered Mr Lawrence, and going to the piano he stood beside it, as though waiting for Lucy to seat herself at the instrument.

"Lucy, my dear," exclaimed Miss Acton, "play 'Now, Goody, Please to Moderate,' or 'My Lodging Is on the Cold Ground,' or 'Sally in Our Alley.' I do not care which. They are all very beautiful, and I know no song, brother, that carries me back like 'Sally in our Alley.' Do you remember how finely our father used to sing it? He was at Dr Burney's one night, sir," said she, talking to Mr Lawrence, "when a famous Italian singer of that day—who was it now—she was as yellow as a guinea, and her hoops were so large there were many doors she could not pass through—who was it now? But no matter; after my father had sung she stepped over to him, and curtsying as though she would sit before him, she said: 'I have often heard this song sung and thought nothing of it. But now, sir, I shall ever regard it as the loveliest composition in English music.'"

"Ay, father had a very fine voice, to be sure," said Captain Acton, "and so has Mr Lawrence."

Lucy had now taken her seat at the piano, and as the airs her aunt desired were well known to her, she played them from ear, whilst Miss Acton in her stiff-backed chair, kept time, with much facial demonstration of enjoyment, with her starched cap and hood.

"Will you now sing us a song, Mr Lawrence?" exclaimed Captain Acton.

"With the greatest pleasure. What should it be?" As Miss Acton loved "Sally in our Alley," he would be happy to sing it.

Lucy touched the keys.

CHAPTER IV

THE "AURORA"

NEXT MORNING after Captain Acton had read prayers, he stepped on to the lawn to take the air for half an hour before breakfast, and was immediately followed by Lucy, who had hardly reached his side when Miss Acton appeared on the hall steps and carefully descended the broad flight, leaning on her crutch cane and followed by her pug.

It was a charming spring morning, warm as June and brilliant as a diamond. The sea was white with the light of the sun, and the radiance of the water clarified the sky into a tender azure, along which floated a number of little mother-of-pearl clouds brushed by a breeze which kept sea and land in motion with a feathering of ripples and the dance of shadows.

"I cannot think of anything but sulphur for poor Mr Eagle's feet," said Miss Acton, as she approached father and daughter. "I will give you a packet for him after breakfast. Is not this a morning to lift up one's heart in rejoicing? How fair is this prospect! How tender and promising this scene of garden! How quiet the old town looks upon the hill! The heart swells in gratitude to God on such a morning as this."

"Very true, sister," said Captain Acton, "and I hope we are all grateful; I am sure I am. I was very well pleased with our friend Mr Lawrence last night. I witnessed nothing in him that I could have wished not to see. I do not know that I ever met a more gentleman-like man. He holds himself very well. He has a fine figure, and I like his type of good looks; it is manly. The face is a little weather-worn perhaps."

"'Tis a pity he cannot command his appetites," said Miss Acton. "How would my heart bleed if he were my son! Poor, dear Sir William! with what Christian fortitude has he resigned himself to the wretchedness of seeing his son out of the Navy, and squandering his precious time in drinking with Lieutenant Tupman."

"He can control himself," said Captain Acton. "Did you observe, Lucy, that he refused all refreshments last night? Now, a man who is radically and incurably a sot cannot view a decanter of anything to drink, and the stronger the worse, without thirsting for it. And did ever such a man say no to an invitation to drink with the liquor standing up in a bottle in front of him?"

"I am sure he is a man of resolution," said Lucy. "I never look at him without seeming to see why it is he should be so gallant and desperate a fighter at sea. He has a cast of face that is very uncommon, full of power of thought, and the shape of his head is like that Greek bust in the library. How is it that a man with his spirit is unable to deny himself what he knows must speedily bring him to ruin?"

"It is not only drink," said Miss Acton. "They tell me he is accustomed to bet very heavily."

"He will mend. He shall have a chance," said Captain Acton cheerily. "I love his old father, and I am strongly disposed to like his son; and I am an ill judge of human nature if I am wrong in predicting that the command I have given him will lead to his reformation. I have ever found it true that the way to make a man honest is to let him understand that you have a cordial faith in his good intentions. He must be a black-hearted rogue beyond hope who disappoints the high and reassuring expectations you give him to know you have formed of him."

"Mr Lawrence has a beautiful voice," said Lucy. "How touchingly he sang 'Tom Bowling!'"

"I could love him for his way of singing 'Sally in Our Alley,'" said Miss Acton. "But the song in his mouth has not the moving sweetness papa gave it."

At this moment Captain Acton cried out, halting as he uttered the words with his eyes fixed in the direction of Old Harbour: "Bless my soul! what can have happened? Is the French Flotilla in sight?"

"The French Flotilla!" exclaimed Miss Acton. "In sight, do you say?"

"What can be the meaning of it?" said Captain Acton.

"What do you see? The French Flotilla?" cried Miss Acton in a voice tremulous with agitation. She darted her eyes through her glasses over the sea.

"If the French Flotilla is not in sight," said Captain Acton, "what can be the intention of Mr Tupman rising at this very early hour and getting his brig under weigh? For certainly the *Saucy* is making a start for something or somewhere. Do you see her sheeting home her canvas, Lucy?"

"She is going out for a little cruise, no doubt," said Lucy.

"I quite agree, but it is so unusual for Tupman to be out of bed at this hour that we cannot but think that something very important and dangerous has called him from his moorings. No, sister, the flat-bottomed boats are not in sight yet, and I suspect we shall have to go on staring for many a week, and many a month, if not for ever, before we sight them coming along in a shoal with the little cocked-hatted usurper, his arms folded upon his breast, watching the van from the hindmost, for he is one of those mighty conquerors who are very careful of their own precious carcasses."

It was as Captain Acton said: the *Saucy* brig-of-war was getting under weigh, and it might be safely concluded for no other purpose than to exercise the crew by an off-shore trip. Captain Acton and the two ladies stood watching the little toy figure away down in the river's mouth. Sail was made with man-of-war despatch; all the clews were sheeted home together, the yards at the same time mounting, so that all at once it seemed the little vessel broke into a broad, bright, shapely glare of canvas, slightly leaning from the breeze as she softly crept round and pointed her bowsprit seaward, and whitening the water under her with the power of a floating body of radiance.

"Well done, Tupman!" cried Captain Acton, who watched the manœuvre with a sailor's interest. "Sluggard as you are, you have your little ship and her people well in hand. I wonder if there's a foreigner afloat that could have made sail with the despatch that brig exhibited?"

The little leaning vessel, diminished by the distance from which she was surveyed into a size fit only to be manned by Liliputian sailors, crept like a small white cloud along the placid water of Old Harbour, and rounding the pier hauled the wind for a southwesterly course. They watched her as she streamed onwards with a sparkle as pretty as a rainbow at her fore-foot, and a short scope of trembling lustre astern as though she towed a length of satin. A few minutes before she disappeared from the sight of those who viewed her from the lawn of Old Harbour House, past the bluff or round of cliff on which stood the dropsical old lighthouse, she dipped her flag manifestly in response to a hidden salutation, and scarcely had she vanished when there stole out from the edge of the cliff round which she had gone, the slanting figure of a large three-masted schooner with the English ensign at her peak. She was steering directly for Old Harbour. Though she had evidently come a long journey, she made upon those silver-white rippling waters a far handsomer figure than the brig. She was clothed from truck to waterway with sails which reflected the light of the morning with something of the splendour of polished metal. Her hull was black, but she was inclined sufficiently by the breeze to reveal a narrow breadth of copper sheathing, which sprang pulses of wet dazzling light upon the eye in keen flashes like gun fire.

"The *Aurora!*" cried Captain Acton. "How nobly she sits! How her sharp bows eat into it! Does not she come along handsomely? What a slaver she would make! Nothing flying the British flag could catch her. I did not conceive her due before next Wednesday. She has not been nabbed this voyage, at all events."

"She floats in like a swan," said Miss Acton.

"A most unfortunate image, sister," rejoined the Captain, laughing; "for a swan's white bulk sits low upon the water, whilst yonder beauty is all airy, cloudlike height."

The breakfast bell at this moment summoned them from the lawn. At table Captain Acton said that he had asked Mr Lawrence to meet him at his office down on the quay at half-past ten. This office was in a little house a few minutes' walk from the warehouses. Captain Acton employed a person who looked after his affairs, who, with the assistance of a couple of clerks, saw to the delivery and loading of cargoes, to the needs of the ships in respect of gear, canvas, carpenters' and boatswains' stores, and so forth. But not the less did the gallant Captain take an interest in his own business. He was laudably anxious to promote the prosperity of Old Harbour and Old Harbour Town, but though he was a rich man—a very rich man indeed in those days, having come into a fortune of eighty thousand pounds, together with the finely wooded and beautiful freehold estate known as Old Harbour House—he was by no means disposed to lose money in marine speculation; so he kept a keen eye upon the books, examined narrowly all the demands which were made for the ship's furniture, closely watched the markets in rum, sugar, and coffee, and having a clear perception of the risks of war, justly appraised the value of his tonnage to those who desired consignments through his bottoms.

Shortly after breakfast he left the house and walked by way of the lane to the Harbour.

Lucy was not a young lady to sit idle. She could find something to do in every hour in the day. As Miss Acton did the housekeeping, Lucy was left to her own inventions, and being a girl of several resources, she was very happy in pleasing herself. Miss Acton went to look after the affairs of the home, and to attend to the needs of a little congregation of poor who were ushered into the housekeeper's room one after another every morning, excepting Sunday, where they stated their wants and obtained such relief as Miss Acton's closets, stocked from her own purse, could supply; and if they did not get always exactly what they wished, they were sure of tender and consoling words, of sympathetic enquiry into their troubles, of a promise of some stockings for little James next week, of a roll of flannel for old Martha the day after to-morrow. Pleasant and instructive it might have been to witness this old lady in her hoop and flowered gown asking questions, handing purges, promising little gifts of apparel to the poor people, who ceaselessly sank in curtsies, or plucked at wisps of hair upon their foreheads whilst they scraped the ground behind with their feet.

Lucy first of all spent three-quarters of an hour in drawing. She was a charming picture as she sat in the library bending over her board; her eyes dwelt in their beauty of lids and heavy lashes, sometimes with a little fire of pleasure, sometimes with a little life of impatience, upon the motions of her pencil and its results, and perhaps not always did she think of what she was about, for now and again the pencil would stand idle in her hand, the natural glow of her cheek would slightly deepen as to some visitation of moving thought; her eyes would lift in languor from her work to the open window, upon the bit of landscape which it framed, beautiful with the small darts, and curves, and lights of springtime in the trees, they appeared to brood in contemplation from which she broke sometimes with a faint smile, sometimes with an expression upon her sweet lips which found a deeper loveliness for her naturally pensive look.

When she had done with her drawing, she went to the piano and passed another half-hour at that instrument, then took up some work which she presently neglected for a novel, and shortly after eleven o'clock she mounted to her bedroom to prepare herself for a drive with her aunt.

At half-past eleven a carriage and pair drove through the gates and stopped in front of the house, and there fell from the box a groom in a livery of brass buttons and orange facings, who posted himself opposite the hall door and with crooked knee studied the entrance with trained intentness. He was not kept waiting long. The hall door was opened, and Mr Bates, the butler, appeared with a shawl and rug and the pug. A few minutes later Miss Acton and Lucy entered the carriage, one nursing her pug, the other her terrier. And when some parcels were put in they were driven away.

"I can think of nothing better than sulphur for poor Mr Eagle's feet. Here is a packet of it, enough, I believe, to enable him to walk in sulphur for quite a fortnight," said Miss Acton.

They had arranged to drive as far as the bridge, where they would quit the carriage and walk along the wharves to view the *Aurora* and give the sulphur to Mr Eagle. But there were several places to be visited first of all: Mrs Bigg was to be enquired after; a little basket of comforts in the shape of tea, sugar, and the like was to be left at Mrs Lavender's, whose husband had fallen into a disused pit, and after lying in it all night, during which it rained heavily and continuously, he was discovered by a boy, and later on hauled up with both his legs broken. Several such errands of kindness and compassion must render the drive to the bridge circuitous.

As the carriage went down a lane into the main road, it overtook Sir William Lawrence, who was stoutly trudging along in the direction of Old Harbour, striking the ground as he went with a staff with the regularity of the pounding of a wooden leg whose owner marches steadily.

"Pray, get in! Pray, get in, Sir William!" cried Miss Acton, after telling the coachman to stop, and in a few moments the hearty old gentleman was seated opposite the ladies and the carriage proceeding.

"I am on a visit to Old Harbour," said the Admiral, "to inspect the *Minorca*. Now that my son is in command of her I am doubly interested in the ship. Were you ever on board of her, Miss?"

"Yes, sir," answered Lucy. "I paid her a visit with papa when she returned home before this voyage, but I was never in her cabin."

"We will explore it together. I hope to have the pleasure of handing you over the side, ma'am," said the Admiral to Miss Acton.

"If the ship is perfectly motionless I might venture to step on to the deck," answered Aunt Caroline, "but I could not enter the cabin, sir. I believe the smell would instantly oppress me with nausea. I am a shocking bad sailor; even the sight of a rocking ship at a distance provokes an indescribable and a very disagreeable sensation."

"You, madam, are not to be so easily upset," exclaimed the Admiral, looking with undissembled admiration at the beautiful, glowing girl seated opposite, never more fascinating than in the dress in which she had apparelled herself this morning. Her large hat sat lightly on one side her head, and the fringes of her rich and abundant hair were like little pencilled shadowings upon her fair brow, save that now and again the passage of the carriage made these fairy tresses tremble. "My son passed a delightful evening at your father's."

"Nobody could have been more agreeable, sir," said Miss Acton. "He has a sweet, strong voice, and sings with great feeling."

"Oh yes, he has the makings of a fine fellow in him," exclaimed the Admiral, with his face clouding somewhat. "It is not for me to say so, but there was a time when I was proud of my son. Such was his zeal and gallantry in the Service that I sometimes flattered myself the day would come when, like Lord Nelson, he would have a gazette to himself. His opportunities in the Navy are passed. Even if he could be reinstated I doubt if he would return, so lively, unnaturally lively, is the resentment and aversion which the sentence of the court-martial excited in him. It is a pity—it is a pity!"

The hearty old gentleman sighed, and his eyes reposed in thought upon the face of Lucy.

She may have found an intelligence in his gaze which it did not possess. Her cheeks were a little warmer. She cast her eyes down. The expression of the whole face was peculiarly pensive.

Whatever may have been the thoughts in the Admiral's mind at that time it is certain that among the mortifications and regrets his son's conduct caused him, must be ranked the consideration that Mr Lawrence, had he governed his conduct with prudence, would have stood a very good chance of winning the hand of Lucy Acton. The Admiral knew that his son had proposed to the lady, and his partiality as a father could not blind him to the reasons of his rejection. He had cause to suppose that in his quiet, unostentatious way Captain Acton had taken a favourable view of Lawrence's suit. But the sentence of the court-martial, and his subsequent lazy, sottish life ashore had utterly extinguished the lieutenant's chances so far as Captain Acton was concerned.

Naturally Sir William grieved over this consideration. Here was a beautiful girl and an heiress, belonging to one of the oldest families in the country; her father had exhibited no marked ambition in the direction of her marriage; he was willing to leave her to choose, having confidence in her judgment, and convinced that her choice would be dictated by regard to her own happiness. Like Sir William,

he loved his old calling, and a naval alliance would have been gratifying to him. There was indeed much for the poor old Admiral to
deplore, and no doubt Lucy had some delicate sense of what might
be or should have been as she sat with her cheeks a little deepened
in colour and her eyes pensively bent downwards.

The carriage stopped opposite the steps on the bridge down
which Sir William, holding Miss Acton by the hand, conducted the
old lady with admirable solicitude for her safety, begging her not to
hurry, but to lean upon him and not trust to her cane. The two dogs
were left behind.

The scene of the quay-side was gay and indeed festive. The few
ships had hoisted colours in celebration of the *Aurora*'s arrival and
the large flags of those days streaming from mast-head and gaff-end
and ensign-staff and jack-staff combined with the brilliant blue of
the sky, the light and lovely greenery of spring that clothed the
ravine's slopes, the sober hue of the cliffs, the white shape of the
squab lighthouse past which some gulls were wheeling, the choco-
late tint of the revolving windmill, the sober grey of the houses and
the diamond sparkle of the river with its softened reflection of
bridge and banks streaming into its heart in dreamlike shadow of
what was mirrored: this combination, I say, coupled with the motions
and colours of human life on the quay-side, albeit the beer hour had
struck and the picture owed nothing of animation to the workmen,
fascinated the eye with the calm, the freshness, and the glory of a
little English sea-piece, Sabbath-like in repose, lighted by the sun of
April beaming in a perfectly fair heaven.

Naturally the arrival of the *Aurora,* as of any ship, but particularly a vessel belonging to the port, must be an incident full of active
interest. The wives and children of the crew lived in Old Harbour
Town; the men were related to two-thirds of the people of the place.
The return from a considerable voyage of a ship in those days was
not the commonplace familiar happening of every day which it now
is. Ships sailed in convoys, and arrived in groups at long intervals.
Again a ship was attended with a passion of interest which is no
longer felt. Will she fall in with the enemy? Will she escape him?
There was much to tell after a voyage in those days no matter into
what regions of the globe a vessel sailed: new lands to discover;

amazing and enriching products of the soil to be reported. New races were to be met with. Indeed in 1805 Sydney Cove in New Holland, which had been settled by Phillip in 1787, was scarcely thought of as a new land in this country, it was too recent and remote; it was to supply reports later on, news which was to startle and excite the nation, differing only in kind from the information ships returned with from the East Indies and China and the great continent of South America.

Therefore, when a ship was newly come home even to a little maritime scene such as Old Harbour, there was plenty to hold groups in animated converse on the quay-side.

The *Aurora* had hauled in to her berth; the crew were busy in unbending her sails. The *Minorca* lay close enough to establish a contrast, and everybody would have admitted that if the barque was a smart ship for her time, the three-masted schooner built by the Americans was as shapely a fabric as the gracefullest then afloat. The Admiral and the ladies paused before her on their way to the *Minorca*, which lay further on. They would not go on board; there was too much confusion. The captain, however, stumping the quarterdeck and shouting orders, saw and recognised them. He was a thick-set man, brick-red in complexion, with deep-red greasy hair, ear-rings, brown eyes, and a mouth that through some injury was drawn a little way up into his left cheek. He came to the bulwark-rail with his hat in his hand, and as the Admiral and the ladies stepped to the quayside to speak to him, he exclaimed: "Happy to see you, ma'am. And my hearty respects to you, Miss, and I hope that Admiral Lawrence is none the worse for remaining ashore."

"Glad to see you safely back, Captain Weaver," cried Miss Acton.

"What a very quick voyage you have made this time, Captain Weaver!" called out Lucy.

"Some Frenchman had the scent of ye, Captain, hey, and gave you heels?" exclaimed Sir William. "There's sometimes the virtue of half a gale of wind in a round shot, eh, Captain?"

"Why, sir," answered the Captain, "it is true that we was chased, but that didn't make us the voyage the young lady's obliging enough to praise us for. Off the Scillies a French frigate hove in sight on the weather bow, but what could she do with us? I eased off and got her abeam, soon afterwards on the quarter; I then luffed, sir, making a tight jam of it, and crossed her bows at the distance of about three mile. She threw a few shot at us, but what's a frigate a-going to do with a vessel as can look up as the *Aurora* does, until by thunder the wind seems blowing fore-and-aft?"

He ran his eyes proudly over the spars of his vessel and along the length of her.

"I am glad to know that you return and find your wife and little boy well," said Lucy.

"Oh thank you, mum, thank you, and its deeply beholden I am to you and Miss Acton for calling and enquiring after them, not to mention presents which leaves my Sarah most grateful indeed.That there little Tommy of mine grows like a ship you're arisin'. Because I'm his father I'm not goin' to pretend he don't improve every voyage."

"Put him into the Royal Navy," said the Admiral.The King wants chips of old blocks like you."

"No fear, sir," called the Captain over the bulwark-rail, with a steady shake of the head and a smile that merely ran his mouth higher into his cheek. "I've set my 'eart upon making him a lawyer. He shall end like old Mr Greyquill, as rich and as comfortable; and when he's old he'll hang out a white head of hair like a flag of truce, to let the world understand he don't want any more quarrelling."

"Good!" cried the Admiral with a laugh and an applauding flourish of the hand, and with this laugh, and smiles and bows from the ladies, Sir William and his companions pursued their way to the *Minorca*.

It was apparently a morning half-holiday with Old Harbour Town. Groups stood or walked about the wharves in talk. Most of the people respectfully saluted the ladies and the Admiral, who, one or another, had for every other person a kindly sentence or a pleasant smile. Standing in the gangway of the *Minorca* was Mr Lawrence, who had manifestly seen the party approaching, though himself had been hidden from them by the interposition of the main shrouds. He crossed the planks which connected the ship with the shore, and stood with his hat in his hand as though they were royalty.

"Is Papa on board?" asked Lucy.

"No, madam. I left him at his offices about half an hour ago."

"We have come down to look over your ship, Walter," said the Admiral, sending from the wharf-side a sailor's knowing glance up at the masts and spars of the barque. "You'll not have had time yet, but I trust whilst you're in harbour you will set a good example to others by keeping your gear hauled taut and your yards square to a hair by lift and brace."

"She shall look as smart as she can be made to look, sir," answered Mr Lawrence. "Permit me to conduct you on board, madam."

He had the grace, sense, and tact, to offer his hand to Miss Acton, who said: "Do not let go of me. Those are very narrow planks. If I should be left alone in the middle, I should turn giddy and tumble."

"Trust to me, madam," said Mr Lawrence, and taking the old lady by the hand he marched her on to the planks, and they went in safety over the side into the ship. The Admiral and Lucy followed.

The decks were empty, the men were at dinner. She was a flush deck ship, that is to say, her decks ran fore-and-aft without a break. She was steered by a wheel placed aft, which was unusual. Her deck furniture was simple: she had the necessary companion-way to the cabin, a little caboose or kitchen abaft the foremast, and abaft that again a long boat secured keel up to ring bolts by lashings. She also carried a couple of boats secured under the bulwarks. Her artillery was trifling: four eighteen-pounder carronades, two of a side, the purpose of which it was idle to enquire, because, as she carried but twelve seamen, two boys, a steward, and a cook, she was not likely to make much show of resistance against a pirate with the blood-red flag of "No Quarter" at his mast-head, or any ship of the enemy which, though but a lugger, would certainly be far more heavily armed and manned than the *Minorca*.

"A fine sweep of deck," said the Admiral. "Lord, how the old spirit comes into one with the feel of a ship's plank under foot!"

"Is Mr Eagle on board?" asked Miss Acton.

"No, madam. He is ashore getting his dinner."

"Will you give him this packet of sulphur, and tell him to put a little into his stockings? I hope it may do the rheumatism in the poor man's feet good."

Mr Lawrence pocketed the packet with a bow. Occasionally his eye went to Lucy, but he never suffered it to dwell, nor indeed did he seem to mark his sense of her presence by any particular behaviour. He was perfectly sober, his eyes clear and beaming, his cheeks painted with a little colour, and his apparel showed care. His father glanced at him and seemed well pleased, and Lucy owned to herself that she had never seen him look more handsome, and that somehow or other no stage seemed to fit his peculiar type of beauty more happily, with a subtler blending of all qualities of its furniture with the spirituality of the man, than the deck of a ship with the rigging soaring.

"It is wonderful to think," said Miss Acton, "how far a ship like this will go. I suppose she would go around the world."

"Again and again, madam, whilst her timbers held."

"Around the world!" exclaimed Miss Acton, looking about her with an expression of awe in her face. "It is a long way from Old Harbour Town to London. But around the world! I believe I should be proud had I been around the world. How few who are not sailors can boast of it!"

"Let me conduct you into the cabin, madam," said the Admiral.

"No, sir, I must be content to stop on deck. It is about twenty years ago since I was on the sea. I crossed from Dover to Calais. We were two days terribly tossed about, and almost lost upon some sands. I lay dreadfully ill all the time, and on our arrival at Calais, when I had strength to speak, I said to Papa: 'We must return by the sea, it is true, to get home, but once I am at home, I will never more put my foot into a ship.'"

"But the cabin is motionless, madam," said Mr Lawrence. "It is the tumbling of the sea that makes you ill. Here we are as restful as a painting."

"The very look of that hole," said the old lady, directing her eyes at the companion-way, "makes me feel as though if I descended I should suffer all that nearly killed me in my voyage from Dover to Calais."

"May I have the great honour of showing you the cabin, Miss?" said Mr Lawrence.

"Yes; since I am here I should like to see the ship," answered Lucy.

"I will keep Miss Acton company on deck," said the Admiral.

Mr Lawrence led the way below.

A barque of five hundred tons, though she would be regarded as a considerable ship in those days, will not supply lofty nor extensive cabin accommodation. This little ship's interior consisted of a cabin into which daylight passed through a skylight in the deck above. In the middle of this cabin was a short table capable of seating one at each end and two of a side. The cabin was painted brown and was somewhat gloomy. The furniture merely supplied the ordinary needs of the occupants. There were four sleeping berths, and a little compartment which was used as a pantry.

"I never was in a place like this before," said Lucy, resting her hand upon the table and gazing round her with the curiosity which a new and striking scene of life must always excite in an intelligent mind.

"The bedrooms are very small," said Mr Lawrence, going to the berth that confronted the aftermost end of the cabin table and opening the door. "But at sea any little hole is good enough to stow oneself away in. Amongst other things, a sailor learns how to sleep, and the habit is so strong with me of slumbering anywhere that if there was room for me I believe I could sleep in a hawse-pipe when the ship is pitching bows under."

"What a very little room!" said Lucy, peering in through the door Mr Lawrence held open. "How fearful to be locked up in such a box when the ship is sinking."

"Oh, you must not think of such things, madam. How fearful to be locked up in your bedroom, though it should be half as big as this ship, when the house is on fire! Would not you enjoy a short voyage? The trip to the West Indies is short. It is a tropical journey, and all the romance of the sea is in it."

"In what things, sir?"

"Oh, madam, in magnificent sunsets, in storms of fire which harm not, though they are as sublime as one might figure a vision of Hell viewed through such tremendous doors as Milton described; in birds of exquisite plumage, and flight which is beyond all other forms of grace; in fish of a thousand lustrous dyes, and the dark wet blue of the long shark; in nights magnificent with such stars as do not shine upon these Islands. For as you strike south, madam, the glory of things which are glorious waxes hourly, the moon expands into a nobler shield, and her path upon the water is a torrent of silver that seems to mark the depth of the mystic realm it sounds—"

As he spoke these words the companion ladder was darkened, and a moment or two later Captain Acton entered the cabin.

CHAPTER V

PAUL

CAPTAIN ACTON paused for a few moments at the foot of the companion ladder with a grave smile on his face.

"This is the first time you have been in this cabin, Lucy, I think," he said.

"Yes, sir."

"Well, and what do you think of the accommodation offered by the *Minorca?*"

"I hope Miss Acton thinks well of it," said Mr Lawrence. "I was trying this moment to tempt her to take a voyage to the West Indies by a poor description of some of the wonders which are to be met in the trip."

"Oh, if we should think of a journey to the West Indies we should not choose the *Minorca*," said Captain Acton. "I confess that I have sometimes myself had a fancy for looking into one or two of the old ports which I remember as a midshipman. The *Aurora* would be the ship. She has a speed that would make me indifferent to pursuit. At the same time there is always the risk of capture, and as I can no longer serve my country by taking my chance of a French prison, I believe I am discreetly advised by leaving well alone, that is until peace comes, if ever it comes. Is not this a very fine cabin, Lucy, considering the size of the ship?"

"I daresay it is, Papa, but how should I know? This is the first cabin I ever was in, and the *Minorca* and the *Aurora* are the only two vessels whose decks I have ever stepped upon."

"Then let me tell you there are countless Naval officers afloat who would reckon themselves in Paradise if they had such quarters as these to live in. Look at the *Saucy!* The well of a cod smack is more comfortable than her sleeping places. Take a corvette or gun-brig stationed on the West Coast of Africa, or kept cruising along the West Indian shores; the heat strikes through the plank and a man sleeps in a furnace; cockroaches in numbers thick as ropes blacken the beams, rats ferocious with thirst are found drowned in the hook pot of cold tea you want to drink. Everything simmers, the paint even below, if there is any paint to be found, bubbles, and you are fed on scalding pea soup and beef blue with brine, the very sight of which raises a craziness of thirst which you slake by rum, for the cooling of which you might offer your year's pay for a piece of ice. Now, these are airy quarters. An admiral might well be content with such a living-room."

He looked into one or two of the cabins or sleeping berths, and examined a stand of arms affixed to a bulkhead just before the companion ladder.

"If, sir, you should be tempted whilst I have the honour of holding command in your service into taking a trip in one of your vessels to the West Indies," said Mr Lawrence, "I hope I shall be the one privileged to navigate you and Miss Acton there."

"Oh, we should be in very good hands—very good hands," answered Captain Acton, lightly regarding him; they had met by appointment not long before at Acton's offices, and there the gallant Captain had taken notice that Mr Lawrence was as sober as he himself was, whilst the care with which he had attired himself had promoted all that was excellent in his person to such a degree that Captain Acton had never thought him handsomer and on the whole a finer specimen of the young British Naval officer.

Indeed he had congratulated himself on behalf of his worthy old friend Sir William on having resolved to give his son this appointment, for it surely looked as though with this gift of a berth, with this opportunity for honourably employing himself and so getting a little money and easing his father of the burden of his maintenance, the young fellow's reformation had begun, and naturally Captain Acton, who was an exceedingly kind-hearted man and a sound

Christian in principle and behaviour, could not but be happy in the reflection that he might prove instrumental in rescuing a handsome young man, a gentleman, the son of an old friend, himself a Naval officer, a person whose character was enriched by many meritorious and some rare qualities, from the ruin physical and moral into which he was fast decaying through drink and an idleness which was a consequence of an aversion to his old calling, and the almost insuperable difficulty of obtaining anything to do whilst loitering in Old Harbour Town and passing most of his time at "The Swan" with Lieutenant Tupman.

"Mr Lawrence would represent the voyage to the West Indies as beautiful, wonderful, and indeed magical, as an Arabian Nights dream," said Lucy. "But you did not tell me of cockroaches, sir," she added with a smile, and with one of those looks which in her seemed a brooding or dwelling of the eye, though if judged of its effect by time the look was scarcely more than a glance; yet this was the consequence of the peculiar beauty of her heavy lids rendered yet more languid by the fringes through which the large dark brown orbs of vision directed their gaze. "And you said nothing about the beef blue with salt which creates thirst before it is tasted."

"We will undertake to keep you free from cockroaches, madam," said Mr Lawrence. "And the beef Captain Acton speaks of is shipped for the sailors. I believe, sir, it would not be difficult to send aft every day such a dinner and breakfast as would convince Miss Acton that at sea all that we eat is not breadgrubs and beef hard enough to carve snuff boxes out of."

"For my part," said Captain Acton, "I don't want to sit down to a better banquet than a piece of really good ship's pickled beef finely grained, and cutting delicately and well fatted, and a crisp ship's biscuit, and you may add a drop of real old Jamaica. I have dined more heartily off such a dish than at many a dinner ashore of ten or twelve courses."

"You were young, sir," said Lucy, "and you enjoyed all that you ate. There was a good deal that you ate when you were young that you would not eat now, and even now I doubt whether you would find the old relish in your prime piece of pickled beef."

Captain Acton smiled, and looked fondly at his daughter, and said pleasantly: "And pray, my dear, what are Mr Lawrence's temptations to a voyage to the West Indies?"

"I think you spoke of sunsets," she said.

Captain Acton broke in: "We have finer sunsets in England than any you get in the tropics."

"Birds of exquisite plumage, and beyond all forms of known grace in flight."

"Ay, but they don't sing," said Captain Acton. "Give me the song of the thrush before all the finest feathers in the world."

"Wonderfully dyed fish—" said Lucy.

"Oh, madam," said Mr Lawrence, with a little blush in his face, "I did not intend my poor representation of the fascinations of a voyage to the West Indies for the ear of so experienced a sailor, and so keen an observer as Captain Acton."

"Well, we may go with you some day, sir," said Captain Acton good-humouredly, "but peace must be declared before I embark. We keep Miss Acton waiting," and led the way up the companion ladder.

Amongst those who just then were standing upon the quay-side gazing with more or less of interest at the *Minorca* and the other vessels moored to the walls, was old Mr Greyquill, whose figure was immediately conspicuous by reason of his long white hair and heavily white thatched eyebrows. And this day he wore a round velvet cap such as might have been suggested to him by a portrait by some old Flemish artist, and a velvet coat. He stood on the wharf a few paces behind some people who formed a little group, and peered at the *Minorca* with the sharp of his hand pressed against his brow seeking to determine the faces he saw on board. He was too far off to recognise the Admiral and Captain Acton, who now appeared, but the moment Mr Lawrence's head was visible above the bulwark-rail he knew him, and seemed to try to catch his eye, but Lawrence, who instantly perceived him, averted his gaze or turned his back, and after steadily staring for some moments under the shelter of his hand the old fellow shuffled off.

"Have you secured a berth, Miss?" asked the Admiral, with a hearty, jolly smile.

"Mr Lawrence paints the voyage to the West Indies in very tempting colours," answered Lucy.

"If Lucy and I should take the trip we should go in the *Aurora*," said Captain Acton.

"You! At your time of life, brother, going a voyage to the West Indies with every probability of the French making a prisoner of you and Lucy!" cried Miss Acton in the high key in which she saluted the ear when she was alarmed.

"My dear sister, we are going to do nothing of the sort. Not that a voyage to the West Indies in such a vessel as the *Aurora* would be a fearful adventure or a terrible ordeal. Indeed I never look at that little ship," said he, turning his eyes in the direction of the schooner, "without a longing to be on her deck when she is fully clothed, when the liberal breeze of the sea blows steadily, and when bending under her white heights she springs like the flying fish from one sparkling sea to another, cradled always by the rocking hand of the swell."

"You should add Papa's description to your list of the charms of a West Indian voyage," said Lucy, with a slight glance at Mr Lawrence.

When a girl has been proposed to by a man and has refused him, and when she is perfectly well aware that his passion remains as great for her as ever it was, she will be coy, shy, cautious, something unintelligible perhaps, in his presence.

"Upon my word, Acton," said the Admiral, "you have just put into words the fancies I have had whilst I have been conversing with Miss Acton. The old spirit will speak in a man, the old love will grow eloquent once again at the suggestion that quickens it into bright memory: and whilst I have been talking to you, I have in imagination paced the starboard side of the quarterdeck, which we will call the weather side; this harbour, these wharves, the Old Town have disappeared, and I am surrounded by a wide ocean in the heart of which this little ship is rushing, streaming her wake like a comet's tail, bursting the surge in rainbow-like arches for her progress, filling the air with the music of shroud and back-stay, and lightening the heart with a sense of freedom which the sea alone can give, and which used to visit me like a sense of gratitude or rejoicing as though something had been given to me that was gracious, beautiful, and rare."

Mr Lawrence viewed his father with astonishment, Miss Lucy with a smile whose beauty was radiant with applause, Miss Acton with an expression of awe, whilst Captain Acton burst out: "Upon my word, Admiral, forgive me for saying so, but I never could have believed such thinking so expressed was in your line of mind. I believe St Vincent would be very pleased did he possess your powers of delivery."

"Oh come, come!" cried the Admiral, "don't make me feel more ashamed of myself than I am. But, Miss Lucy, is not the sea a subject about which you cannot think without being inspired with thoughts high above those which visit you from other topics?"

"When such a man as Nelson is in your mind."

"Yes, Nelson is the great sea-poem of the age," said Captain Acton, "and I find more melody in the thunder of his guns than in the prettiest turns of the poetic measure. Are you going home, sister?"

"Yes, we have done all we came out to do. Where is Mr Eagle? Mr Lawrence, you will not forget to give him the sulphur for his poor feet?"

"I will not, madam, and I trust that the application of it may make him a little better humoured."

"One might notice a man's ill-temper," said the Admiral, "if he were over you; but when he is under you—there used to be a saying in my day—it's in the power of an officer to ride down any man under him."

"I believe Mr Eagle is a very respectable man, though illiterate like most of them in the lower walks of the Merchant Service," said Captain Acton. "This sort of people come on board through the hawse pipe, but at a pinch their knowledge which is uncommonly practical, is sometimes vastly useful. They are acquainted with manoeuvres which would often put their betters to their trumps. They know all about rigging, its straining point, have little tricks above the average seamanship for heavy weather, are learned in the pumps and their gear, and indeed know ships not only with the familiarity of a master-rigger, but of a master builder. One of these men I believe is Eagle, and I think, sir, you will find him all that I tell you he is, though like most of his class he is of a somewhat sour and sullen nature, and quick to grumble. I'll go home with you, sister. Admiral, can we give you a lift? "

"No, I thank you, sir. I am to dine today with Mr Perry. I have long promised to eat a cut of cold meat with him. His cider is the best I know. His cider alone makes him worth dining with."

"Give Perry my kind regards," said Captain Acton.

"And thank him," twittered Miss Acton, "for the beautiful sermon he gave us last Sunday, and tell him I am looking forward to such another next Sunday."

This said, they all went over the side, the Admiral taking great care of Miss Acton as she crossed the planks. Mr Lawrence remained in the gangway. When on the wharf his father called to him.

"Where do you dine, Walter?

"At 'The Swan,' sir."

"I have a few words to say to my son," said the Admiral. "I will bid you good-bye here," and with the ceremonious courtesy of that age, he took leave of Captain Acton and the ladies, who proceeded to their carriage, where they were cordially welcomed by the passionate barking of the pug and the terrier.

Mr Lawrence's eye reposed upon Lucy's figure whilst his father was bidding the party farewell, whilst she walked away on Captain Acton's right, Aunt Caroline strutting and leaning with some affectation on her crutch-cane on his left, the three much saluted by the people who lingered on the wharf, as they went. The young fellow's eyes still reposed upon the girl even as the Admiral came stumping across the planks pounding them with his staff as he walked.

"Well," said he, "I suppose you kept your appointment this morning with Captain Acton."

"Oh, certainly, and his reception was all that I could have expected at his hands."

"Are the terms pretty satisfactory?"

"Twelve pounds a month, and ten percent commission on the freight."

"On the freight?"

"On the money earned by the carriage of cargo, sir."

"I understand," said the Admiral. "This should prove a very

good offer—very good terms. What will this ship carry?"

Mr Lawrence reflected as though mentally gauging depth of hold and breadth of beam, and answered, "I think when flush she should hold six hundred tons."

"Six hundred tons out and six hundred home. That is twelve hundred. I don't know what freights are, but they must rule high, and, kindly creature as he is, Acton is the man to know to what market to drive his pigs. I think you have done very well; besides obtaining occupation which may conduct you to something higher or at least better, you stand to clear about a hundred pounds by this voyage—"

"The value of its wages, sir, will depend upon its length," interrupted Mr Lawrence.

"I know that," cried the Admiral. "But whatever the sum, it is good money and honestly earned, made not as you could make it in this place, and better a hundred pounds gained by toil which a man's conscience approves and applauds, than one hundred thousand fetched from the pockets of others by the crime of gambling."

He looked steadily at his son whose eyes were fixed upon the carriage which the Actons were at that moment entering.

"Did you observe Mr Greyquill," continued the Admiral, "on the wharf behind a little crowd of people viewing the ship under his lifted hand? He was there when you came on deck."

"I saw him."

"What brings that old man here peering and mopping and mowing? Has he heard of your appointment? I wish he may not be hatching some scheme, planning some design to end this, your fortunate command, by arresting you unless you pay him up in full."

"I don't know what his intentions are," said Mr Lawrence with some blood colouring his face. "I saw the old rascal plain enough, but avoided his eye as I feared he might have the insolence to step aboard and address me in the presence of Captain Acton and the ladies, and yourself, sir. But if he has heard of my appointment I cannot conceive that he meditates my arrest as an alternative to my paying him in full, which he knows I cannot do. I should tell him that by waiting he will receive payment by instalments. This I can manage now that I have money coming to me. Will he stop his sole chance of receiving back his loan by clapping me into gaol?"

"Why, perhaps not," answered the Admiral.

"He would be a fool as well as a villain for so doing. Take an opportunity of putting the matter to him as you put it to me. I do not want to see your chance obstructed nor Captain Acton's kindness embarrassed by any action on the part of old Greyquill. And I beg, sir," continued the old officer speaking slowly and solemnly, "that during the rest of your time ashore you will behave with that discretion which can alone secure you the continuance of Captain Acton's goodwill. You are going to dine at 'The Swan'? I am sure you will understand what must signify a report that you were not master of yourself, for," continued the old Admiral with emphasis, "it is idle to believe that the best natured man in the world will confide his property and the care of valuable lives to the custody of a man who is not fit to take charge of himself."

"You may trust me," said Mr Lawrence, making Sir William so low a bow that it might have been thought that they were strangers, and had met on an affair of ceremony.

The young man watched his father roll away towards the steps which conducted him on to the bridge. His face was sunk in thought, a peculiar gloom was in the expression of it. His beauty even in repose always had something of sternness in it: now as he watched his father's diminishing figure his mouth gradually put on an air of bitter hardness, and a frown gave severity and even the light of anger to his eyes.

He was lingering on board until the hour when the ordinary at "The Swan" was served, and whilst he stood looking over the rail near the gangway, so profoundly self-abstracted that his eyes, turning idly, seemed without speculation, Mr Eagle came across the planks. He limped a little, and the expression of his face was uncommonly acid with pain and the nature of the man.

"Oh," said Mr Lawrence, waking up, "here is a packet left by Miss Acton for you for your feet." He handed him the sulphur.

"I am much obliged I am sure," said Eagle. He put it to his nose. "I have tried it again and again," he said, "and it ain't of no more use than if you was to rub in snuff. But she's a kindly lady to remember me," said he, putting the packet into his pocket. "And I hope, sir, as when you meet her you'll present her with my humble acknowledgments."

Mr Lawrence gave him a nod and then turned his head away, not desirous of further converse with a man he regarded as inferior to a boatswain's mate or master-at-arms upon a man-of-war.

Eagle was on board to see to the arrival of cargo which came into Old Harbour very leisurely in waggon-loads at a time. The *Minorca* was now receiving commodities for the passage out, but she did not sail till the 3rd of May, and was not yet more than half full up.

Mr Lawrence looked at the clock which was affixed to the house at the end of the wharf in which Captain Acton had his offices, and was about to leave the ship to make his way to "The Swan," when a man who had been standing a few moments on the quay side at the foot of the gangway boards, stepped across and saluted him.

Mr Lawrence exclaimed: "Oh, it's you! What do you want?"

The man was almost a caricature owing to malformation and other deformities. His red hair flamed; he was hunched, his arms were as long as a baboon's and seemed designed for climbing. His legs were arched and at the same time crooked at the knees, so that he appeared to be stooping whether he walked or stood, and to complete the suggestion of his origin he had a trick of scratching himself like a monkey. He was about twenty-five years of age. Whose son he was he could not have told. He preeminently belonged to the parish.

Lawrence had got to know of his existence by one day sauntering into the justice's court. Among the prisoners charged with various misdemeanours was this man, who had no other name than Paul. He was accused of having taken a vegetable, a cabbage or a turnip, from a field which lay invitingly open, and the punishment inflicted was a fine or a term of imprisonment. Mr Lawrence, struck by the extraordinary appearance of the man, or witnessing a very great hardship in a pauper having to pay for so mean a thing as a turnip by a considerable term of incarceration, put his hand in his pocket with a sailor's liberality, and finding the money that was wanted, handed the amount to an official of the court, and the man went free.

The man waited outside for Mr Lawrence. When he appeared he seized his hand, and fell upon his crooked knees and kissed and slobbered his hand, and blubbered, with tears trickling down his face, "that so help him his good God, come what might he would do anything, no matter what, to serve his honour, he would die for his honour; let his honour command him to jump into the river then and there and drown himself, he'd do it if only to please him." His gestures whilst on his knees, his extraordinary grimaces, the strange, wild terms in which he expressed his pathetic gratitude for this con-descension of a gentleman in taking notice of, and rescuing from gaol a poor, pitiful vagabond, a child of the parish, a no man's son, nor woman's either, a creature who lived he could not tell how, sometimes by stealing a raw vegetable, sometimes by running an errand, sometimes by the bounty of a tradesman who might fling him a crust, or of some drunken fisherman who might toss him a shilling to sing him a song and dance as he sang, a performance so hideously uncouth that Hogarth would have immortalised it could he have witnessed it; his gratitude, in short, was so diverting, at the same time moving in its appeal to pity, that Mr Lawrence could scarcely forbear a laugh, and indeed did laugh when he got rid of the fellow and walked away.

"I understand that your honour's got command of this ship," answered Paul.

"Well!" exclaimed Mr Lawrence, eyeing him with that sort of regard with which one views some hairy, human-like importation of the likeness of a man, and perhaps better looking than some men, from an Indian or South American forest.

"If your honour hasn't shipped a steward, sir, I should be mighty glad if you'd take me. I could sail round the world with you, sir. I'd love to be your shadder. Wherever your honour goes, I'd like to be there."

The strange face of the fellow with its red eyebrows and red eyelashes, and red fluff upon his upper lip, and compressed nose, ape-like or sheep-like, so that the nostrils seemed to be squeezed out of position, and to gape from either side, quivered with feeling, with intensity, and passion of desire.

Mr Lawrence, with a ridiculing smile, said "What do you know about waiting on people in the cabins of ships?"

"What I did should be to your honour's satisfaction. I could lay a cloth and set a dish, and I'd learn in as many hours as much as it would take others days."

"But you were never at sea. You'll be sick in your hammock, and I shall be wanting some one to wait upon me."

"Oh yes, your honour, I've been to sea," answered Paul with prodigious earnestness. "I've been in smacks. I've knocked about all my life in boats belonging to this Harbour. Sick! No fear, your honour. I'll sarve you for nothing."

Mr Lawrence looked at the red-headed, monkey-faced, pleading creature, not, in that look designing, it was manifest, to give him the berth; but all on a sudden his face slightly changed, an idea seemed to flash up in him and work in his countenance, just as a light kindled suddenly within a mask made of something transparent might, by the intention of the artist, change its look.

"What's your name again?" he said.

"Paul, your honour," answered the fellow, brightening instinctively with the face Mr Lawrence now viewed him with.

"No other name—no matter; Paul will do very well for the books."

He mused a little with his eyes fastened upon the ship's decks. For a space he was deeply sunk in thought. Presently his eyes rose to the figure before him, and he examined him as curiously as though he had never before seen him.

"Be here," said he, "on Saturday next. It may be that I'll give you the berth. No more words. Off with you!"

The fellow made a dash with his hand at a red forelock, and in his crooked gait went through the gangway and walked away up to the wharf, just as Mr Eagle rose out of the main-hatch.

Mr Lawrence walked to "The Swan." The entrance was under a covered way into which the stagecoach drove for baiting. Mr Lawrence walked into the bar and observed a letter fixed in a frame of red tape stretched across a board covered with green baize. As he was in the habit of receiving letters at this house he looked at this one and saw that it was addressed to him. He pulled it out of its mesh of tape, and addressing a middle-aged, comely woman who sat in the window in the bar where she supplied lookers-in with pots of frothing beer, or directed them to such parts of the house as they desired to visit, he asked when that letter had been left, and was answered that the letter carrier had brought it in about two hours before.

He seemed to know the handwriting on the envelope, and there was a frown upon his face as he broke the big seal. He read it where he stood. It was a letter from a Captain Rousby informing him that he owed him the sum of one hundred guineas, that this money as a debt of honour had been payable immediately on proof of the loss of the wager, but that so far from having received it, Captain Rousby had been waiting for nine months without obtaining further satis-faction than the now wearisome and well-worn excuse that Mr Lawrence could not immediately pay, that he was expecting to obtain employment in the course of the month which would enable him to discharge this debt with interest if Captain Rousby thought proper. The Captain informed Mr Lawrence that last week Mrs Rousby had presented him with twins, a catastrophe which greatly increased his expenses at a time when he was without employment, and when money was never more urgently needed. Captain Rousby then went on to inform Mr Lawrence that if a portion of this debt, say twenty-five guineas, was not sent to him by the first of June, it would be his unpleasant duty to visit Old Harbour Town, call upon Sir William Lawrence and state the facts of the case to him as an officer and a gentleman. If he could obtain no satisfaction from the Admiral, it would be his painful duty—a duty that must be singu-larly distasteful to a man who had been a messmate and shipmate of Mr Lawrence—to take such steps as his lawyer might advise.

When Mr Lawrence had read this letter through, he was in the act of crushing it by one of those spasmodic motions of the hand which accompany a sudden violent gust of wrath, he met the eyes of the female in the bar fixed upon him; in her gloomy beer-flavoured recess, faintly luminous with hanging rows of highly-polished drink-ing pots, and a sideboard well within laden with metal vessels for drinking from and for holding drink, the landlady of "The Swan," for such was this decoration of the bar, had manifestly been studying his face whilst he read. She knew him very well, and she was also well acquainted with his habits. In a breath on meeting her eyes he changed his resolution, and folded up the letter into its original creases, giving her a smile which did not seem in the least degree forced, and saying to her in his pleasantest manner, "Is the ordinary on?" and receiving her answer after she had darted a look at an invisible clock in her room, "In another three minutes, sir," he passed on and went upstairs.

The ordinary was held in a long room next to the room in which the seafaring men congregated. As a meal it was renowned in the district. Coarse it might have been called, coarse and plentiful, but it was of that sort of coarseness which makes very good eating. Mr Short, the landlord, was a liberal caterer, and he excelled in choice of rounds of beef, in joints of venison, in legs of pork and mutton, in fine dishes of veal; and this ordinary was always graced with a precedent dish of fish, which was invariably fresh from the sea, and whether turbot, cod, hake, soles, and many flat fish which the smacks brought with them into Old Harbour, were delicious in freshness and flavour. Short's cheeses, too, were always very fine, dry, crumbly, flakey, nutty, and without being too strong they flavoured the bread or the biscuit with what the palate knew to be real cheese. His cellars held a very fine old port, but it was seldom asked for unless some person of distinction and importance occupied a seat at that teeming and appetising board. Short brewed his own beer, and a delicate amber draught it was; there was no better beer brewed in England.

This ordinary was held every day, for there were always people passing through Old Harbour Town, and then Old Harbour Town itself was liberal with its own supply of guests, pilots, smack-owners and others who found it cheaper and much more convenient to get a cut at "The Swan," than to sit down to an ill-killed and ill-cooked joint, or a fried chop or steak in their own homes. The ordinary was frequently graced by the presence of distinguished people. A lord would occasionally take a chair; several neighbouring squires were regular frequenters when business brought them into those parts. Captain Acton had often made a meal at that table, and so had Sir William.

Mr Short occupied the head of the table, and the oldest frequenter who happened to be present the foot. Mr Short took his seat when Mr Lawrence sat down, and all the people who had come to eat were then assembled. In a picture they would figure as a homely old English lot: men in bottlegreen coats, in red coats, in purple waistcoats, in plain pilot cloth, here and there a dandy built up in the latest style, here and there an old fogey who stuck to the fashion of the last century and figured in a little tye wig, a frill very fit for the harbouring of snuff, a cutaway coat with immense pockets, such as Boswell might have been found drunk in, in Edinburgh, and shoes with buckles.

Mr Short said grace, and prayed for the King and Royal Family, and for the utter ruin and confusion of the French, Spanish, and all our enemies. In two or three places the walls were adorned by maps, with which no navigator of this age would dare to risk his life fifty miles out of sight of land. A spinet stood in a corner; it was sometimes customary when the ordinary was ended and the sentiments had been brought to a conclusion for any one who could perform, to sit down to this spinet and accompany any gentleman who was good enough to oblige. But it was always understood that the song must carry a chorus which everybody present knew so that everybody present might join in it, hence the same old melodies were very often heard in that long room with the low ceiling, and its clock whose voice was audible all over the house at night.

Mr Lawrence was a quality guest, and being a frequenter, had a place of his own, which was on the left hand of the landlord; thus he got the fish of his choice, the cut of meat he liked best, the best draught of ale the house could supply, and this ordinary was too useful to him to allow him to be in debt to it.

Short was a large fat man with a pink face, merry little drunken eyes almost buried out of sight in hairy eyebrows and eyelashes; his pear-shaped nose was so purple at the end that it might have been supposed he had just been fighting his way through a hedge full of nettles. He treated his patrons as guests, and of those he knew, would ask familiarly after their relations, and how their businesses went and the like.

Mr Lawrence sat very silent, yet ate with appetite because what was put before him he relished, but it was observed that he limited himself to one tankard of beer. When the ordinary was ended, pipes were put upon the table, and jars of tobacco, and then Mr Short, without rising, exclaimed:

"Gentlemen! before I give you a sentiment I shall be pleased if you will allow me to propose a toast. It was only known to me this morning that my highly respectable friend on the left, Mr Lawrence, the son of that distinguished officer, Rear-Admiral Sir William Lawrence, has received, through his friend Captain Acton of His Majesty's Navy, the command of that beautiful barque, the *Minorca*. I am sure that there is ne'er a gent here who takes an interest in our Old Harbour, and who has the honour of the acquaintance of Captain Acton and Mr Lawrence, but will feel proud and delighted that that beautiful ship, the *Minorca,* which we all claim now as belonging to our town, will be commanded by as fine an officer as ever walked His Majesty's quarterdeck. Gentlemen all, I give you the health of Captain Acton, Mr Lawrence, and the *Minorca,* and may prosperity attend the beautiful ship, and may she return home to gladden the eyes of all well-wishers of our grand old town by loading our store-houses with more foreign produce."

Mr Lawrence looked startled when this toast was begun; but he composed his face as Short proceeded, and when everybody was extending his glass to him and wishing him all the good-luck that Short desired, he was receiving the general salutation with a composed smile and an air of courteous appreciation.

One sat at the table who peered at him hard when Mr Short began. This was a middle-aged man in a brown wig. He was one of the two clerks kept by Mr Greyquill, and regularly dined at "The Swan's" ordinary, a repast which had never once been decorated by the presence of Mr Greyquill, who, living in rooms over his offices, chose to eat for his breakfast a little fish which he bought from a man with a barrow with whom he haggled, and for his dinner a cutlet or a piece of steak, just enough for one, with vegetables, and for supper whatever might have been left from breakfast or dinner, and if nothing was left, then a piece of "hearty bread and cheese," as he would term it, and a glass of beer.

The man with the brown wig peered with his head on one side at Mr Lawrence, as though Mr Short's toast conveyed a piece of news to him.

When the landlord had made an end, and the healths named had been pledged, Mr Short, filling a pipe and inviting those of his friends who were smokers to follow his example, asked old Mr Sturgeon, a well-known smack owner, for a sentiment, who in a feeble voice, and eyes from which the light of being had almost been extinguished by time, broke out in a sort of hiccough: "As we ascend the hill of life may we never meet a friend."

This was enough for Mr Lawrence, who perfectly understood that all the sentiments which were likely to be delivered at that table he had heard over and over again. He rose, made a bow to the landlord and the company, and walked from the room to the adjacent room, which was made a reading-room of by the pilots, smacksmen, and others, and sitting down at the long table, took a sheet of some paper which was there for the accommodation of the frequenters, and after thinking deeply, undisturbed by the sound of singing which started next door, he began to write in pencil, obviously making a draft of a communication he proposed to copy there, or more probably elsewhere.

Certainly what he wrote about did not refer to the letter he had received on his arrival at "The Swan." This may be assumed, as he never referred to that letter which lay in his pocket. He wrote leisurely and with absorption, never heeding the noise next door, and when he was done he carefully read through what he had written, and with his handsome face stern with the quality of resolution and the temper which enters into great or violent undertakings as their impulse or seminal principle, he pocketed the letter, and left the room by another door.

CHAPTER VI

THE LETTER

MR GREYQUILL'S office was in High Street. He used two rooms for his professional affairs, and the rest of the house, which was a small one, he lived in. He was an attorney, and a flourishing one: so mean that his name had passed into a proverb, but honourable in his dishonourable doings, so that though every man agreed that Greyquill was a scoundrel, all held that he kept well within the lines of his villainy, and that he was unimpeachable outside the prescribed and understood rules of his roguery.

Two mornings following the day on which Mr Short had proposed Mr Lawrence's health, old Mr Greyquill rose from his chair at his office table, and said to his clerk in the brown wig, who sat within eyeshot at another table in the adjacent room, that he was going to collect his rents at Greyquill's Buildings, and that he would not be back before half-past twelve. He never looked so white as he did this morning. His white hair seemed to rest like a cloud upon his head and shoulders. His eyebrows bore so strong a resemblance to white mice that no one could have overlooked the similitude, particularly as each eyebrow flourished over the bridge of the nose a few little dark hairs which resembled tails. His waistcoat was white, not having come from the wash above three days, and his stockings were white.

He left his house and walked down the road which led to the bridge, but instead of crossing the bridge he descended a short flight of steps abreast of the flight that led to the wharves. These steps conducted the passenger to the river-side walk that went up the banks of the stream, and a very sweet walk it was this morning. The bright river trembled in prisms and gems under the pleasant breathing of the wind, which was aromatic with the odours it culled in its flight over the country, the birds sang gaily with here and there a deep flute-like note. It was a morning lovely and delightful with the virginal spirit of spring, when all creation seems new, when no

note in the trees, no sweetness in the air, no bloom or flash of white
on the bough, no timid wayside flower that seems to have sprung
into being since yester eve and glances at you coyly from its little
wayside bower, but delights the senses as a beautiful surprise, as a
something remembered but never so fresh, so appealing.

A bend of the river's path shut out the view of Old Harbour Town
and the Harbour, and just when Mr Greyquill reached this turn, he
saw Mr Lawrence coming along the road, having manifestly gained
it by a little bridge, some distance beyond which was another way,
but rather roundabout, of getting to Old Harbour from Sir William
Lawrence's cottage.

Mr Lawrence looked very well; his colour was fresh, his eyes carried the light which nature intended them to take, but which his
hand was perpetually seeking to extinguish by draughts of strong
liquors. He had been extremely temperate for three days, and his
resolution was producing its fruits in his general appearance. It is
indeed surprising how short is the period asked for by Nature even
from men who live harder and drink harder than Mr Lawrence, to
restore to them as much of their healthy old good looks as in some
cases makes them almost irrecognisable.

"Good morning, Mr Lawrence," said Mr Greyquill, making the gentleman a low bow. "I may take it that you're going to the ship which
I am pleased to hear Captain Acton has given you the command of."

"You are very kind, sir, to take an interest in my affairs," answered
Mr Lawrence with slight sarcasm.

"I think I have some reason, Mr Lawrence," answered Mr Greyquill,
drooping his head to one side, and looking at the other with a con-
fidential and familiar expression which was scarcely a smile, but
which teased the hot blood of Mr Lawrence as though the look
masked an insult. Mr Lawrence viewed him in silence.

"I may trust, at all events," continued the money-lender, "now that
you are in receipt of money—and if the terms have been correctly
named to me they speak very highly in favour of Captain Acton's
generosity—that you will give my debt your immediate attention,
and that if you cannot pay all, you will pay as much as I have a right
to expect from the amount you receive."

"You shall be paid, sir," said Mr Lawrence.

"It would be convenient to me if you would fix a day for the first payment if you cannot pay the whole," said Mr Greyquill.

"I shall not be able to pay you anything this side my first command of the *Minorca*. If I hand you the sum of twenty-five guineas after my return, that is, when I am paid off by Captain Acton, I believe you will not have much reason to complain, sir."

Mr Greyquill shrugged his shoulders.

"Twenty-five guineas is a very small proportion of three hundred pounds," he exclaimed.

"It is not three hundred pounds, sir," answered Mr Lawrence, with the countenance of a man who is resolved in his intention, but desires to speak with prudence and good humour.

"But from my point of view it is three hundred pounds," cried Mr Greyquill. "What is the good of money without interest? I enter in my books the interest on my money as a part of my money, and if you tell me I am not to speak of my interest when I speak of what is due to me, what is my situation? How am I to live? The profit the butcher makes by the sale of his carcasses is the interest upon his outlay; deprive him of that and he will not sell you meat, because he could not afford to do so."

"The butcher does not charge at your rate, Mr Greyquill," said Mr Lawrence with a faint smile.

"I will not declare what the butcher charges!" cried Mr Greyquill, a little warmly for so sleek a man. "But take my word, the British tradesman, whether tinker, tailor, butcher, baker, and we'll throw in grocer as we do not value rhymes, charges at rates which if reduced from profit to interest and called by that aggressive term discount, would represent every shopkeeper in the nation as big a scoundrel as the most voracious of your money-lenders, sir."

He bowed as though to the applause of an audience, and looked the better pleased with Mr Lawrence for having heard him.

"Well, Mr Greyquill, twenty-five guineas when I'm paid off on my return home. I can say no more, and can promise no more."

"You speak like a gentleman to me in this matter, which you do not often do when I refer to it, nor your father neither—"

"Sir William Lawrence has nothing to do with my affairs."

"Still, he might recognise my claim and your debt, and treat me perhaps with the commiseration with which he would pity himself if he lost three hundred pounds."

"You have not lost it, Mr Greyquill."

"No, sir, and from my conversation with you this morning I am satisfied I shall receive every penny. I wish you a truly prosperous voyage and a safe return home, and that the Frenchman won't be the means of dishing more hopes than your own."

He made another of his bows, and Mr Lawrence saluting him with a slight smile and a lifted hat, passed on.

Just at the bend of the road not ten paces from where they had been standing, Mr Lawrence drew forth his pocket-handkerchief to blow his nose, and with it there came out of his pocket and fell upon the road unobserved by him, a large sheet of paper folded into four. Mr Lawrence blew his nose and went round the corner, and the paper would have been out of sight had he looked behind.

Old Greyquill, trudging on busy in thought with Mr Lawrence's debt, was moved by some idea of the man to look behind him. Mr Lawrence had disappeared. Quite discernible from where Greyquill stood was the sheet of paper Lawrence had let fall. Old Greyquill stopped, peered, reflected that it might be a letter that he himself had unconsciously been toying with and had dropped, or that in some other way had let fall from his pocket. He retraced the few steps that lay between and picked it up, and proceeded with it in one hand, whilst with the other he fumbled for his spectacle-case.

He immediately saw that it was a sheet of paper about the size of foolscap, but somewhat squarer, of a bluish tint; it was provided free of cost to the frequenters of the sailors' reading-room at "The Swan." He well knew the paper, for many a letter written upon it had he received. It was of a convenient size for those who used it, as first of all it was ruled on one side, which enabled a man to steer a straight course with his pen. The page was likewise so large as to enable a man to write big, and few who used it could write small. It also supplied plenty of space for erasures, whether of expression or spelling, and this was useful. When folded into four and sealed or wafered, the sheet became a letter which needed but the address to qualify it for the post.

In the case of the sheet Mr Greyquill held, it had been folded to resemble a letter, but it had not been made one; it bore no address, and the communication started at once without the prefatorial "Dear sir," or the like, and it closed without signature or initials. But Mr Greyquill immediately saw that the handwriting in pencil was Mr Lawrence's, and that the document must have fallen from that gentleman's pocket just now when they parted.

We have seen that the frame which bounded Mr Greyquill's portrait of honour was large. Most men recognising the handwriting would have denied themselves the right of reading this letter, because they had found it lying in a public roadway, for two reasons: the handwriting was known to them, and the recent presence of the writer where that letter was found would have identified it as its owner's business in no wise to be intruded on by a man of honour.

But this sort of argument did not fall within the frame of Mr Greyquill's picture of integrity. It was a letter lying ready for anybody's hand in a public way; next, it was not addressed; third, it was not signed; and fourth, though the contents were apparently in Mr Lawrence's handwriting, yet some people did write, as Greyquill knew, so wonderfully alike that there was no reason to conclude without strong internal evidence that the letter Mr Greyquill held was written by Mr Lawrence. Whatever else it was, it was certainly a draft roughly pencilled of a letter that had been copied in ink and no doubt despatched. Here and there was an erasure in ink, which proved that it had been copied in ink and corrected in certain places by the pen that was transcribing it. He had not proceeded far when his eyebrows, which, as we have heard, inimitably expressed the aspect of two white mice, arched their backs to an extraordinary degree as though in imitation of a cat when enraged; his mouth took on the posture of a whistle; with his eyes rooted to the sheet he stopped and scratched his head until he nearly tumbled his hat into the road.

Just then certain large white-bosomed April clouds which had been leisurely sailing up from over the sea began to discharge some rain, and one shower was so smart that Greyquill took refuge in a small wayside barn, where, until the rain ceased he had the opportunity of reading the letter several times.

His astonishment was unaffected and amazing; with the habit of senility he kept on muttering to himself aloud whilst he perused and re-perused the letter.

"Is it possible! Is this the officer and the gentleman! Could an egg so full of criminal matter find any black fowl willing to hatch it in so pleasing a nest! And I am called an old scamp because I part with my honestly earned money for a consideration which is trifling in comparison with the benefit I confer, the help that I am to the man in need. This will require thought. I shall need to think pretty considerably before I decide. Meanwhile, Mr Lawrence, I wish you a prosperous voyage, and I wonder what you will do when you find out that you have mislaid this letter, a copy of which to somebody or other, as pretty a scoundrel as yourself no doubt, you have unquestionably by this time posted?"

Meanwhile, Mr Lawrence walked towards his ship. He should have been on the whole well satisfied with his meeting with Mr Greyquill. Perhaps the profound indifference which in reality possessed him as to the old scrivener's willingness to accept twenty-five guineas, or, in short, anything as an instalment, was because he had long felt that the old man never durst take extreme action. Greyquill knew that Mr Lawrence was very popular in his own particular way in Old Harbour Town and the neighbourhood. He drank and treated, and in a high degree possessed the liberality of the sailor. The townspeople were proud of him, not only because he was a handsome and finely built man, but because he had shone in many deeds of gallantry whilst in the Navy, and everybody was agreed that when Mr Lawrence was court-martialled the Service lost as fine and plucky a seaman as was ever afloat, and one to be recalled to his duties with apologies and without delay.

Admiral Sir William Lawrence was also highly respected, and people spoke with pride of his living in their neighbourhood. It was likewise well known that Mr Lawrence was a friend of the Actons, and in a small town of small gossips the idea if not the circumstance of Mr Lawrence having offered for the hand of the beautiful Miss Acton was not likely to be neglected or overlooked, and to do the gossips justice, they imputed the rejection of the handsome and dashing young Naval officer to his loose habits.

Mr Lawrence well judged that if Greyquill locked him up for debt Old Harbour Town would rise against him. His windows would certainly be broken, his person might go in danger, for there was more than one who had suffered at the hands of Greyquill who would be grateful for any sort of excuse to administer a sound cudgelling to the old man, and take his chance of the law, fortified by the conviction that if it came to a fine the amount would be subscribed several times over.

Mr Lawrence's business on board the *Minorca* did not keep him long. He was primarily there to see to the arrangements of his own cabin, and also of another cabin aft which it was his design to convert into a sickbay. This end was chiefly accomplished in this cabin by the rough construction of a couple of bunks.

Just before he left the ship, the young fellow Paul, whom he had told to come down on Saturday, stepped from the fore part of the ship where he had been watching two or three men caulking, and gave Mr Lawrence his usual salute of a pluck at a forelock and a scrape of a hinder foot.

"Yes," said Mr Lawrence, running his eyes over him, "the articles are opened at Mr Acton's offices. Go and tell the manager——but here—" He pulled out a card upon whose face was some printed address, and with a pencil struck out the address, and wrote to the effect that the bearer called Paul had been engaged by Mr Lawrence as his cabin servant. These lines he initialed, and giving the card to the youth, bade him present it at the offices before one o'clock, or he would find them closed.

"Have you no better clothes than what you wear?" he said.

"No, sir."

"You may give an order for a suit of decent apparel fit to wait at table with, for I want you to understand that your duties may bring you to wait upon ladies and gentlemen, though you know nothing about that. Do you hear?"

"Ay, your honour," answered the fellow with a grin decidedly above a clown's intelligence.

"You can pay for the clothes on your return, or by drawing an advance which Mr Acton's manager will let you have. Do you know Miss Acton?"

"The lady that lives at Old Harbour House along with Capt'n Acton?" answered Paul.

"I mean Captain Acton's daughter."

"I should think I do, sir," answered Paul, grinning.

"You know her well enough, for example," said Mr Lawrence, critically surveying him as though he took counsel within himself whilst he talked, "that if I gave you a letter for her and for none other"—he frowned, and with some passion emphasised *none other*—"you are not likely to mistake, you are not likely to give it to another."

"I couldn't mistake, your honour. I know the lady as I know you, and if so be as I did mistake, then I hope your honour would blow my brains out, for I shouldn't leave your side till your honour did."

Mr Lawrence, with a nod and an expression of face that was scarcely a smile, quitted the ship, and on the wharf found Mr Eagle, who had as a matter of fact for a minute or two been watching him.

"That young fellow came aboard not long ago," said the mate, "and I asked him his business. He replied that he was to be cabin servant by your choosing. I was nigh telling him he was a liar, for I couldn't suppose that the likes of him and his rags would suit a gent as has sarved the King, and been waited upon, as I understand they do in the Sarvice, by Marines."

Lawrence smiled, and answered: "The Marines may not be all you think them, Mr Eagle, though they are a noble fighting corps. I took a pity upon that young fellow. I once helped him out of a difficulty, and his gratitude rose to the height of a dog's, which, as you know, is very superior to man's. His ugliness interests me as the sort of beauty you find in the toad or the snake or other things which make ladies scream. He can bring dishes aft as well as another, and will look a very pretty young man in a new suit of clothes. I may not be down to the ship again till Monday. Good morning, sir."

He walked away, leaving Mr Eagle staring apace, and as he was going over the side, Paul, who was coming down, received a very acid, watchman-like look from the mate.

Mr Lawrence pursued the same road home by which he had gained Old Harbour. In all probability had Mr Greyquill not looked back, the young gentleman would have found his letter where he had unconsciously dropped it. That side of the bridge—the up-river water path—was much unfrequented, save on a Sunday, when lovers walked along it, and now and again a little family dressed in their best. It was many chances to one that the two or three who had passed along that path since Mr Lawrence and Mr Greyquill had stood in conversation upon it, would have picked up the letter or even taken notice of it, so very remote from their ideas of things worth stopping for and examining on the highway was a folded sheet of paper.

Mr Lawrence walked on. He thought of old Greyquill when he passed the place where he had stopped to talk. He crossed the quaint old bridge duplicated in the river, which streamed with becalmed surface up here and mirrored with the precision of a looking-glass the hues and shapes of every bird that swept the glassy surface for an insect, and gaining a rich lane formed by seven or eight hundred years of growth, for a monastery had stood here and a knight had had his manor where now the land was without relic of stone or brick; but the vegetation left by these people flourished, and though not above half a mile in length that lane formed one of the most glorious, soothing, enfolding, impulse-creating walks in all that country-side which abounded in little paradisaical reaches of a like kind; I say Mr Lawrence crossed the bridge, and emerging from the lane struck the high-road, and presently gained his father's cottage.

Even in three days the weather had worked a miracle in the increase of the beauty of the orchards in which the Admiral sat pipe in mouth, tankard at elbow, embowered; a sort of figure who when at his window would have greatly puzzled the Knight of Spenser's *Faerie Queene;* for what should such a shape secretly ambushed in a spot fit only for the dancing tread of the fairy, or the gaping stare of the ogre who tries to see how the land lies by peering through two apple boughs, what should such a shape signify, briefly arresting the clouds of smoke which rose from his lips by vain efforts to extinguish by copious draughts from his tankard the magical fires that blazed in its interior? Whether the Knight would have tilted at the figure or pricked his horse into headlong flight is a conjecture that must be left to those who have read the poem and know the man.

The Admiral just now happened to be at dinner. A shoulder of mutton and onion sauce with potatoes roasted with the shoulder and such other vegetables as the season yielded was a dish fit to set before a king, and the monarch who turned up his nose at such a dainty should be made to banquet on nothing but the fare they give kings upon the stage. Indeed, Sir William would tell his friends he knew for a fact that a shoulder of mutton was the favourite dish of His Royal Highness Prince William. If it was objected that the joint yielded more bone than meat he had his answer:

"Sir, I once said to a sailor who had obtained a berth ashore on sixteen shillings a week, 'How do you manage to rear your family? How many are there of you?' 'Why,' he answered, 'there's me and the old woman and four youngsters and grandfather!' 'You never see meat, of course,' said I. 'Oh yes, we do,' he answered. 'Meat!' I cried, 'on sixteen shillings a week and seven people to support, four of them hungry youngsters!' 'Well,' he answered, 'I doos it in this way. On Saturday I goes to the butcher and buys a shoulder o' mutton; on Sunday we 'as it 'ot; on Monday we 'as it cold; on Toosday we 'ave what's left of the cold; on Wednesday what's left of the cold we 'ave made into ishee-ashee; on Thursday we makes what's left of the ishee-ashee into ashee-ishee; on Friday we does without; and on Saturday I goes to the butcher and I buys another shoulder of mutton.' Now," the Admiral would say with his face warm with triumph, "name me any joint but a shoulder of mutton that will supply what kept this family in meat, or the like of meat, from Sunday to Thursday?"

The Admiral made his son welcome with unusual warmth.

"I never tasted a finer flavoured piece of mutton. This jelly, too, lifts it to the dignity of a haunch. Those spring cabbages are very tender. We do not eat nearly enough vegetables in this country. What purifies the blood like a well-cooked spring cabbage that melts in the mouth? I am in hopes that we shall get a very good show of potatoes. Are you fresh from the ship?"

He asked this question with much importance. Indeed, during the last two days he had manifested great interest in all that concerned the Merchant Service; had found out, for instance, and avowed the fact to Captain Acton, that our Colonial Empire was founded by British Merchant seamen who, in the employ of merchant adventurers, sailed into all parts of the globe and established settlements, and often fought for the preservation if not for the conquest of principalities over which the King's flag now waved. He also pointed to the Honourable East India Company, and asked if our own or any Navy were superior in their capacity and splendour to those ships, and whether our Navy treated their officers with so much consideration, liberality, and prudent foresight for each man's well-being.

"Yes, I have come straight from the *Minorca.*"

"Will you complete your lading by the date announced for your sailing?"

"I think so—I hope so. I am very well disposed towards that scheme I have put into being—the construction of a sick-bay. Every ship should have a sick-bay. You must agree with me, sir."

"Wherever room can be found a sick-bay is most important," answered the Admiral.

"A man falls sick of small-pox. What are you to do with him? You can't cure him, and you can't heave him overboard. But because one falls ill it surely does not follow that the others should go sick. Besides, we carry no surgeon, which was an additional incentive to my suggesting a sick-bay to Captain Acton."

"Oh, you have done well. Acton will value your foresight. A sick-bay is a valuable detail in a ship's catalogue."

They talked of this and of other matters connected with the *Minorca,* and then the Admiral went to the window to fill his pipe, and Mr Lawrence to his bedroom.

Some thought whilst eating with his father had occurred to him, and he felt in his pocket for the copy of the letter which he had drawn out with his pocket-handkerchief and which Mr Greyquill had got possession of. The handkerchief was there, but the letter was not. When he had drawn out his handkerchief and felt and found the lining of his pocket bare, when, in short, he completely understood that the letter was not where it ought to be and where he knew it should be, he turned as pale as the muslin curtain that partly veiled his window, started with an abrupt swagger of motion as though he had been struck violently behind, then with the energy of madness felt in all his pockets, pulling out everything, meanwhile gazing around the room with eyes which seemed on fire with their vigour of scrutiny and passion of fear.

He endeavoured to recollect himself that, by calming his terrors his memory might better serve him. Urgent alarms often induce vain hopes which we should laugh at in the cool mood. He believed he might have put that letter down in his bedroom, and perfectly well knowing that he had not done so, and yet coaxed by a will-o'-the-wisp hope, he ransacked the room as though he knew that in it was to be found a gold piece of value whose discovery demanded a careful search only. What was certain in his mind was that that letter was in his pocket when he walked that morning to visit the *Minorca*. He remembered withdrawing it from his pocket, but in what part of the walk he knew not, and re-perusing a portion of it to refresh his memory. He tried to find comfort in the recollection that the letter bore no address and no signature. But a thundercloud of horror came down on this feeble streak of sunshine when he recalled the damning, incriminating contents of that sheet which he had scrawled in pencil at "The Swan Inn." Whoever found it would know that Mr Lawrence, and Mr Lawrence alone, had written it, and this, too, irrespective of the handwriting.

But here he found another little hope; some squalls of wet, one very heavy, had set the kennels running shortly after he had met Mr Greyquill, and if that letter had lain exposed to those three or four deluges, it not only stood to be changed into a mere rag to the eye which none would dream of even glancing at, but the writing must have been washed out to a degree to render the sense of the letter unintelligible. He considered that it was not above two or three hours when that letter was in his pocket, and that it must have fallen somewhere betwixt his father's house and the *Minorca* in that time, for he had taken the same road to and fro. He reflected that that road was but little used compared with the lane that led to the bridge where the Actons' carriage had stopped. Understanding as a sailor the preciousness of time, and conceiving that if the letter had by some strange mischance fallen during his walk unobserved by him it might still rest in the spot where it had dropped, insomuch that chance—for the fellow was a gambler at heart—might concede him yet an hour, even two hours, in which to find it, he put on his hat and marched out of the house, just saying to his father in the window that he had an appointment and should miss it if he didn't hasten, and then stepped out, casting as he went to right and left of his path eyes as piercingly scrutinising as those which the madman darts when he seeks for the philosopher's stone.

It is needless, of course, to say that this searching walk was in vain. Whatever lay white in his road he rushed at, and in his gizzard he cursed the vast number of pieces of white paper which did somehow, as though distributed by innumerable malicious Greyquills, attract his eye and retard his progress whilst he turned them over.

On his way this side the bridge he met an old man with a stick who stopped in his lame walk to turn about any little heap his eye met. This old man was attended by a dog, who smelt at what the man touched.

"Have you seen a letter," cried Mr Lawrence, "a broad piece of paper folded into four lying in the road?"

"Seen a what, your Anner?"

"Where are you from?"

"From Oozles."

Mr Lawrence repeated his first question.

"I don't know what you mean," said the old man.

Mr Lawrence easily perceived that he didn't, and went on his way always hunting with his eyes. Past the bridge he met another old man, a peasant with silver hair, fit, dressed as he was, to walk upon any stage, and immediately take part in any performance that included a peasant, a foster-child, and a baron. This white hair gave him a reverend look, and his legs were strangely bandaged round about, and his smock was a gown in which he could have preached a sermon without exciting much suspicion as to the propriety of his dress.

"Have you seen a letter folded in four lying in the road?" shouted Mr Lawrence.

"I'm a little 'ard of 'earing," was the answer, and the picturesque old man put his hand to his ear shellwise.

Mr Lawrence went close to him and shouted.

"Gard bless your worship," said the old man in a sweet voice and a face beautiful with the touches of the pencil of time upon a countenance originally open, gracious, and good, "I ha'nt received a letter since her last from my poor old woife, and that 'ull be twenty year ago, as I know by the laying of the foundation stone—" Mr Lawrence broke away, and asked no more questions during the rest of his walk.

He saw no letter—nothing like it. He went on board the *Minorca*, and seeing the mate at the main-hatch, asked in an off-hand way if a copy of a letter had been found in the cabin, or any other part of the ship that morning.

"No, sir."

And there was an end. With wrath in his heart, and cursing himself again and again as a barnyard idiot fit for spread eagling only to carry such a missive as that about with him when its miscarriage might prove his destruction, might even now be working it, he stepped on to the wharf and came across Paul.

"Here!" said he.

The youth approached.

"I have lost a letter this morning," said Mr Lawrence, explaining its form and size, "and it must have fallen from my pocket somewhere between my father's house and this ship by way of Old Friar's Road. If you can bring me that letter, or find out if it has been found, and if so, by whom, before we sail, you shall have five pounds."

"Simply a letter, your honour, folded into four, without address, written in pencil, and not sealed?" said the hunchback.

"That's it!" exclaimed Mr Lawrence.

"I'll do my best, sir, and I'll work from dawn to night to find it, if it's to be found," was the answer.

CHAPTER VII

WHERE IS THE "MINORCA"?

MR LAWRENCE was for a few days very uneasy, but uneasy is a mild term to express the state of a man's mind that starts at a look or an exclamation, who fancies he is whispered about when two go past him talking, who expects that every man who approaches him is going to speak to him about the letter he has found, who imagines that every look that his father fastens upon him is a prelude to a tremendous attack, who is willing to attribute the silence of Captain Acton to the consideration of what steps in the face of such an enormity should be taken by him against the son of his old friend Sir William Lawrence.

But Lucy Acton smiled and curtsied when he passed as usual. Old Miss Acton was nervously polite in her way in her little chirrupy salutations. Captain Acton was sometimes down at the ship, but had nothing to say about the finding of a letter good or bad.

Therefore after a few days of miserable anxiety, during which he was remarkable for sobriety and for conspicuous regard to his personal apparel, Mr Lawrence allowed the subject of the letter to slip from his mind, satisfied that it had been reduced to pulp by the wet that had fallen on the morning he lost it, or that it had been blown by some sportive stroke of breeze into a corner, or a place where it was as much lost as if it had dropped from his pocket into the ocean.

As evidence that Mr Lawrence was improving in general esteem, a brief conversation passed at Old Harbour House on the fourth evening following the day of the loss of the letter. Captain Acton had invited some friends to a rubber of whist. Sir William Lawrence was to be amongst the guests, but as he lived near he was always late, explaining that the fact of his living near excused him for taking plenty of time. Miss Lucy was lovely in black muslin spangled with stars as the hair is dusted with gold.

Whilst they waited for Sir William the conversation turned upon his son.

"How greatly Mr Lawrence has improved, not indeed in manners, for he was always a very fine gentleman, a very pretty gentleman, but in appearance, since you gave him the command of the *Minorca,* Captain Acton."

This was said by Lady Larmont, the widow of an East India Director, who had achieved a reputation for beneficence in the district without spending very much money.

"What I much admire in Mr Lawrence," said Miss Acton, "is his art in making a leg on entering a room. His art in this way rises to a degree that is very unusual in men nowadays, and I should think particularly in sea-faring men. His deportment embraces the whole room. A man has a right to claim some sort of excellence who can make a leg with skill."

"'Tis a very old-fashioned term, madam," said General Groves, "current in my time, but I question if much understood in this."

"It is most happily explained in the play of the *Man of the World,*" said Miss Acton. "I was never more pleased than by Sir Pertinax Macsycophant's reply to his nephew's question how he had made his way in the world. Sir Pertinax replies, 'By booing, sir.' A great deal of money and fine social positions have been obtained by booing."

"Hence the value of being able to make a leg in your opinion, madam," said General Groves.

"If trousers come in legs must go out," said Lucy. "What is the good of being able to make a leg with elegance if fashion compels you to conceal the eloquent member?"

"Well said, Miss, well said!" cried Miss Proudfoot, who was a very good hand at whist and very quarrelsome over the game.

"I don't believe myself," said Miss Acton, "that trousers ever will come in. Men whose calves are of a good shape and who have long been in the habit of admiring and cherishing them, will be very reluctant to conceal them in those ridiculous unmanly garments called trousers."

"As the majority of men strut this petty earth on drum-sticks," said General Groves. "I expect that in a few years hence the universal male wear will be trousers."

He looked at his own legs. Time had somewhat shrunk them.

"Mr Lawrence has wonderfully improved of late," said Miss Proudfoot, with a glance at Lucy. "I should say that when in the Navy he was one of the handsomest men in that glorious Service."

"All praise of him is gratifying to me for his father's sake," said Captain Acton, whilst Lucy sat in silence with the shadow of a smile lurking about her mouth, but invisible in her soft, dreamy half-veiled eyes.

"Would not you like to take a trip to the West Indies in your father's ship, Miss?" said the Reverend James Prettyman, who had been headmaster at a fashionable school for young gentlemen for many years past in a city about twenty miles distant from Old Harbour Town.

"Only the other day," replied Lucy, "I told Mr Eagle, the mate of the vessel, that I could not imagine a pleasanter trip than a voyage to the West Indies in the *Minorca,* but I stipulated that the sea should be always smooth."

"There it is!" said Miss Acton. "Give me a sea as smooth as our lawn, and I will accompany you, my dear."

Here Mr Pierpoint, who held some influential position in connection with Old Harbour and was one of Captain Acton's frequent guests at his whist tables, exclaimed: "The master of the *Aurora* told me, a day or two ago, that Mr Lawrence was attempting a wonderful innovation in Merchant ships by the introduction of a sick-bay, after the custom of men-o'-war."

"It is true, sir," said Captain Acton, "and Mr Lawrence loses nothing in my esteem by his idea and application of it. The Merchants care nothing about their sick. 'A sick man is no man's dog,' I believe, is one of their adages. Every vessel, supposing her to be above a certain tonnage, whether flying a pennant or not, should have quarters properly fitted for the reception and treatment of the sick among her crew."

"I should think so indeed, poor men!" exclaimed Miss Acton.

"Suppose she carries no surgeon?" said Mr Pierpoint.

"Her master should be able to dispense physic with the aid of a book," said Captain Acton. "Besides, the idea is to isolate the sufferers from the rest of the crew in the black, wet, slush-lighted holes in which Merchant sailors are forced to live in dozens, breathing the aroma of their own breath, and creating such an atmosphere that the wicked halo of miasma gleams a corpse-light round the flickering, stinking flame which hovers at the mouth of the spout of the lamp."

"What an awful picture!" cried Miss Proudfoot.

"Who'd be a sailor in the Merchant Service!" exclaimed General Groves.

"It is a noble life," said Lucy. "But it must be nobly lived."

"Oh, madam, I thank you," exclaimed Mr Prettyman. "To live nobly you need pure air to begin with. But it certainly does young Mr Lawrence great credit to be the first, as I apprehend from this conversation, to introduce sick quarters for sick men on board ships. I doubt even if the East India Company's vessels are fitted with such humane receptacles."

"And yet Nelson," said Lady Larmont, "liked the Merchant Service so well that he was reluctant to leave it to enter the Royal Navy. When he came from his West India voyage in a Merchant ship his favourite saying was, 'Aft the more honour. Forward the better man.'"

At this moment the conversation was interrupted by the bustling entrance of Admiral Sir William Lawrence, when of course the conversation was immediately changed from the subject of his son and sick-bays to other matters.

The *Minorca* was announced to sail on Tuesday, 3rd May, at half-past twelve o'clock. All her people without exception lived in or near Old Harbour Town, consequently her crew was quickly assembled. On the day previous they had bent all sails, rove all running rigging, done all that was necessary to render a ship fit for the sea. She lay between two other vessels, but was readily distinguished, not only by her rig but by the height her masts towered above those of the others.

It had been arranged between Captain Acton and Admiral Lawrence that the latter should breakfast at half-past nine with Captain Acton, who would then fill an hour with transaction of certain business which he could deal with in his own house, leaving the Admiral to amuse himself in the grounds with his pipe, and, if

he chose, a telescope; after which they would walk leisurely down
to Old Harbour, go on board the *Minorca*, and take a farewell view
of the vessel with a Godspeed to her new commander.

Lucy over-night had said she would join them, but she did not
appear at the breakfast table. Her father enquired for her, and was
told that she had left the house an hour earlier, or perhaps more,
to take the morning air and a walk with her dog.

Neither Captain Acton nor Miss Acton witnessed anything strange
in the absence of Lucy from the breakfast table. She was in the habit
of taking these early walks, and would often turn into a cottage
whose inmates she well knew and breakfast with the occupants,
enjoying more the egg warm from the nest, the home-cured rasher
of bacon, the pot of home-made jam, the slice of brown bread and
sweet butter, the bowl of new milk, or the cup of tea which on such
grand occasions would be introduced by her humble friends, than
the choicest dainties which her father's cook could send to the
breakfast table at Old Harbour House.

"I expect you will find her down at the wharves waiting for the
ship to sail," said Miss Acton. "I met Mrs Jellybottle yesterday. She told
me that Farmer Jellybottle had received on the previous day a large
parcel of very substantial eatables from his brother, who is head gardener at Lord Lancaster's. Lucy has possibly been tempted by the
display."

"Here is her dog anyhow!" exclaimed the Admiral, as the little animal marched into the room and stood near Lucy's chair with fore-
foot lifted as though she awaited her mistress.

"How sits the wind?" enquired Captain Acton, who being used to
his daughter's occasional absence took no particular interest in her
failure that morning to attend the breakfast table.

"I believe," said the Admiral, casting his eyes at the window, "that
it blows a pretty little off-shore breeze from the north. The sea is
rippled by it into a dark blue, and your ship will sail into it with
almost square yards."

"No ship of mine departs without my heart accompanying her,"
said Captain Acton. "I believe I am bound to go in one of them to
the West Indies some day or other, but not whilst there's an enemy's
cruiser to be met with in the circle of the horizon."

"I suppose, sir," said Miss Acton to the Admiral, "that there is no further news of the descent of the French."

"Plenty of news, madam," answered the Admiral, "but most of the reports are lies born of fear. The French never can get a footing upon this land."

This led to a brief argument between Captain Acton and Sir William, who was making a prodigious breakfast off a large crab, which he affirmed was much more delicate eating than the lobster, as the shrimp is sweeter than the prawn, though people whom the actor Quin loved to deride were of a different opinion. He had begun with crab, and was now ploughing heartily through a dish of eggs and bacon, with a view to letting go his anchor in some savoury sausages. Captain Acton fed capriciously, as a man who thinks of his digestion more than his appetite.

After breakfast the Captain went to his library to transact certain business with a lawyer and one or two others, Miss Acton to the housekeeper's room, there to receive certain poor people, and Sir William Lawrence, filling his pipe, waited in the grounds until Captain Acton should appear, and diverted himself as best he could with conversation with the gardeners and in admiring the springing flowers.

He came from the kitchen garden and was standing in the middle of the lawn, where he obtained a view of the sea betwixt the bluff on which stood the windmill and the other bluff on which stood the lighthouse. He sent his gaze in the direction of Old Harbour. It was a heedless gaze. He took no particular note. Alongside the wharves a number of small vessels were moored. They somewhat crowded the eye with their rigging and spars. The brig-of-war lay in her accustomed place off the pier. Apparently it was not Lieutenant Tupman's intention to put to sea that day.

All of a sudden the Admiral's gaze, that was somewhat heedless— that of a man who takes in a general prospect without regard to particulars—grew intent: his eyes were fixed on Old Harbour. In a minute they grew more than intent: astonishment dilated them, and they were not without the sparkle of alarm. He rubbed his eyes, and removing his pipe from his lips strained his gaze once more at the shipping in the Harbour.

"Good God!" he ejaculated, "where is she?"

Only a little bit of sea lay within his sight; that which he had seen ran in blue ripples between the points of cliff which framed the entrance to Old Harbour. Though the scene was distant, his sight, for a man of advanced age, was fairly good, and even all that distance off, he could without much difficulty distinguish the fine lines of the *Aurora*'s masts bearing their trucks high above the spars and rigging of the vessels abaft and ahead of her.

He walked to a bed of flowers at which an under-gardener was at work, and said to the man: "Have you good eyes?"

"I can see a good bit, your honour."

"Do you know the *Minorca?*"

"Oh yes, sir."

"Could you distinguish her if she's in the Harbour at this distance?"

"Why, sartinly, your honour," answered the man, looking at the Admiral.

"Then tell me if you see her," and the Admiral watched him with such an expression of face as he might have looked with at a falling barometer in seas distinguished for cyclones and typhoons.

The gardener gazed and gazed, and his intent regard crumpled his brow, for he seemed ambitious to be able to say he could see the ship. After a considerable pause, during a portion of which the man sheltered his eyes with his hand, he exclaimed: "If the *Minorca*'s a three-masted vessel, square rigged forward, fore-and-aft rigged on the mizzen-mast, then all that I can say is, your honour, she ain't among that shipping down there."

Without speech the Admiral walked away swiftly on the stout staff he was used to carry, striking the sward with it till you witnessed the energy of his thoughts with each blow, and, entering the hall of Old Harbour House, took down from its brackets a very handsome, and for those times, powerful telescope with which he returned to the place he had left, where he might obtain the best view of the Harbour that was to be got from the grounds of the mansion.

He levelled the tubes at the shipping, but witnessed no signs of the *Minorca*. He was amazed. The glass sank in his hand, and he rubbed his naked eye and fastened it again upon the Harbour. The vessel was to sail at half-past twelve, and it was now about a quarter past ten, and the *Minorca* was gone. The old gentleman took aim with his glass at the little breadth of sea that was in sight, in a hopeless way conceiving that a sail, invisible to his bare vision, might leap into the lenses out of the distant blue recess, and proclaim herself to his nautical eye as the ship that was gone. Nothing was in sight.

He stood musing. It was, as we have seen, about a quarter past ten. Captain Acton would not have completed his business until something after eleven. Should the Admiral invade him with the announcement of this strange disappearance of his ship? He considered the matter a little, and concluded that it must be impossible but that, although Captain Acton had been silent on the subject at the breakfast table, he must know the business of his ship, and that it was understood between him and Mr Lawrence that if the wind served, or anything unforeseen befell, or if Mr Lawrence in his judgment chose to sail before the time announced, he was at liberty to let go his fasts and blow into the open at any hour he pleased. Thus it struck the old man, though secretly he did not regard his own reasoning as sagacious.

Nevertheless he determined to await Captain Acton's arrival from the business which was holding him in his library; so he lighted his pipe afresh with his singular little pistol-shaped pipe-lighter and struck about the grounds with his staff, blowing great clouds out of the depth of his meditation, and often heaving a sailor's blessing at the two points of cliff which interrupted the view of the sea to east and west of the coast.

It was a few minutes past eleven when Captain Acton came out of the house talking to Miss Acton, who was followed by her own and Lucy's dog.

"Sorry to have kept you waiting so long, Admiral!" exclaimed Captain Acton.

"Why, sir," answered the Admiral, "I don't see that we should be late if we did not go at all."

"I don't quite understand," said Captain Acton, gazing with friendly interest at the jolly, round, weather-dyed face of Sir William, whose looks certainly at this moment did not wear the jocund complexion they were used to carry.

"Your telescope is in the hall, sir," said the Admiral. "But your sight is very good. I presume that you are aware that your ship has left her berth, and is not in the Harbour."

"Not in the Harbour!" cried Miss Acton. "Good gracious, has she sunk, do you think?"

Captain Acton sent a swift and searching glance at the shipping in the distance. He then with quick steps fetched his glass. By his movements and countenance the Admiral immediately perceived that he did not know his ship had sailed. He pointed the telescope at the shipping. The *Minorca* was certainly not one of them. The river flowed bare from the sea under its bridges to its inland recesses, and offered no creek nor shelter to the eye for a vessel of any tonnage. If the barque was not in the Harbour, she had put to sea. Both observers on the lawn were sailors, and did not need to be told this.

"If your son has sailed," said Captain Acton, with a face charged with perplexity, doubt, irritation, and astonishment, "he had no authority to do so. What has caused him to take this step? Surely as a sailor who has served the State, he, before all masters in the Merchant Service, ought to understand the meaning of the word of command."

Sir William's countenance resembled the expression that probably decorated Captain Marryat's Port Admiral when he was told in no uncompromising language, "You be damned!"

"And where, pray, is Lucy?" said Miss Acton, in a voice querulous with alarm and other feelings, for Miss Acton was one of those old ladies who are always praising Providence for its blessings, but who are very willing to find calamity in trifles. "She is a long time gone. Who says that she breakfasted with the Jellybottles? And at what time did she leave the house? And if Mamie went with her why is she here?" she added, turning her eyes upon the little terrier.

The hall door was wide open; a footman was crossing the hall. Captain Acton called to him.

"What time this morning did Miss Lucy leave the house?"

"I don't know, sir. I'll ascertain, sir," and the man disappeared.

"The *Minorca* not in the Harbour!" exclaimed Miss Acton, staring at the cluster of rigs, beyond which rose the breadth of narrow sea shining in a blue tremble to its horizon. "No accident could have happened or you would have heard, brother."

"Miss Lucy went out at about half-past seven, sir," said the footman.

"Come, Admiral, we will walk to the Harbour and enquire into this matter," said Captain Acton, who was somewhat pale and looked extremely disconcerted.

"But where is Lucy?" cried Miss Acton.

"Send the people about and make enquiries," answered Captain Acton. "She is making calls. It is the *Minorca* that has disappeared."

"But what a dreadful responsibility to leave upon my shoulders," said Miss Acton. "Suppose those I send about come back and say she is not to be found? It is more than I can bear. The charge is too awful! What am I to do if she is not to be found?"

"But she is to be found," cried Captain Acton, surveying his sister with a quarterdeck severity of look. "What do you think? That Lucy has run away with the ship? She has breakfasted somewhere and is gossiping somewhere else. I leave you to make enquiries, sister. The area to be covered is not wide. She will be telling you where she has been before we return. Come, Sir William, this is the most extraordinary thing that has happened to me in my time!"

The two gentlemen set out at a vigorous pace, leaving the poor old lady overwhelmed, motionless, and gaping with the alarm raised in her by this enormous obligation of discovering whether her niece had breakfasted with the Jellybottles or with other folks, where she was, and why she had not returned since half-past seven that morning.

All the conversation of the two officers consisted of idle speculations as to the cause of the *Minorca* having sailed some hours before the time announced for her departure. It was clearly necessary that Mr Lawrence should have much business to do before he could quit his moorings, and that if the ship had sailed as early as the Captain and the Admiral suspected, her captain had completed all necessary arrangements on the previous day. For first the loading of the vessel was to be fully completed, and all the necessary papers and documents to be on board, the clearance or transire from the Customs duly obtained, and the master furnished with copies of the charter party or memorandum of charter party and of the policies of insurance on both ship and goods.

"I saw Mr Lawrence on several occasions yesterday," exclaimed Captain Acton, "and he did not suggest by a syllable that he was making ready to sail early this morning before the various officials he would have to see were aboard."

The Admiral struck his staff strongly upon the earth and stopped to look through a break in the hedge in the lane or road which they were descending, at Old Harbour: the Captain stopped too; they stared amain.

"But he must have had some object!" cried the old Admiral, whose face was strongly flushed with heat and conflicting passions. "We shall very shortly find out what that object is, and I shall feel very greatly astonished if it does not satisfy you, sir, as well as myself."

They resumed their walk. When they had reached the bridge they found old Mr Greyquill, leaning over the rail, and gazing with intentness, with a sort of lifting leer which could not be defined as a smile, though it was like the shadow of one, in the direction of Old Harbour. This person was not used to address either of the gentlemen on meeting them in the public streets. They were accustomed to nod in silence. But this morning as the Admiral and the Captain passed him, the Admiral so close as to brush his coat-tail, the old scrivener turned with a rapid motion and exclaimed, still preserving his singular leer: "I beg pardon, gentlemen, but as I fail to see the *Minorca* amongst the ships, may I enquire if she has sailed?"

"That, sir, is the errand which is carrying us to the wharves," answered the Admiral, and the two passed on, whilst Mr Greyquill, retaining a hold on the rail of the bridge with his hand, gazed after them with an unchanged face.

It was hard upon twelve o'clock when Captain Acton and his friend reached the wharves. Though there was plenty of shipping about to suggest occupation there was little apparently doing. Here and there a song was monotonously sung by sailors or labourers who were leisurely taking in or discharging cargo. Had the *Minorca* sailed at her appointed hour the little Harbour would no doubt have looked gay with colours flying on the ships and plenty of gossips to see the vessels off on the wharf.

Captain Acton and the Admiral turned into the Custom House, and the first person they met after leaving it was Josiah Weaver, master of the *Aurora,* a thick-set man of a dark-red complexion rendered more glowing still by the sun, greasy deep-red hair, ear-rings, and brown eyes which moved sharply in their sheaths.

"I find," cried Captain Acton, eagerly addressing him, "that the *Minorca* has sailed. How is this? Do you know anything about the matter?"

"She left the Harbour at about a quarter past eight this morning, sir," answered Weaver.

"At about a quarter past eight!" exclaimed Captain Acton. "What was Mr Lawrence's object in quitting his berth before the fixed time?"

Captain Weaver faintly smiled, slightly glancing at Admiral Lawrence.

"When I saw the ship starting," said he, "I walked over to her and asked Mr Lawrence, who was standing right aft watching the crew working, making sail and so forth, what made him in such a hurry, and he answered that he had received news on the previous night of a French cruiser that was hovering over this part of the coast, that when last seen she was standing to the east'ard, and that he had made up his mind to sneak the *Minorca* out at daybreak if possible so as to have the heels of her should she shift her helm, as he had no mind to start his first voyage in Captain Acton's employ by being taken by a French cruiser and locked up for a time no man could determine."

"And that was the reason for sailing which he gave you?" said Captain Acton.

"Yes, sir."

Captain Acton looked at the Admiral, who was staring sternly into Captain Weaver's face.

"Mr Lawrence told you," said Captain Acton, "that he had received the news of this cruiser last night. At what hour, do you think?"

"That, sir, I couldn't say," answered Captain Weaver. "But we might take it as his having heard it after eight o'clock."

"In that case he must have intended during the day," said Captain Acton, addressing the Admiral, "to sail early this morning. For, as I have explained to you, he could have had no time to do his business at so early an hour at which he started this morning, nor would the officials be seen at that time. Therefore he must have made the necessary arrangements yesterday for what he contemplated as a daybreak departure this morning."

"Does the ship call anywhere in England before her final departure for her port?" asked the Admiral in a voice that proclaimed his heart hot with bewilderment, doubt, and anger.

"No, sir," answered Captain Acton.

"A pity!" said the Admiral, striking the ground with his staff. "Otherwise I would have posted it, caught him, and asked him his reason, which to satisfy me would have to prove infinitely more intelligible than the one Captain Weaver has repeated."

"I saw him two or three times yesterday," said Captain Acton. "He had nothing to say about French cruisers in the offing. Nor did he give me a hint that he was taking the necessary steps to quit this Harbour early this morning."

"Is the ship in sight?" exclaimed the Admiral.

"No, sir. A man came down from the cliffs," answered Captain Weaver, "and I asked him that question, and he said she'd rounded the coast to the west'ard."

"The pilot," said Captain Acton, "was John Andrews. Was he on board, do you know?"

"Yes, sir," answered Captain Weaver, "I took notice of him on the fok'sle."

They could obtain no further information from Captain Weaver. They called at "The Swan" and saw the landlord, who told them that he had seen Mr Lawrence on the previous day, that, in fact, he had lunched at the Inn and sat next him, but had said never a word about the change in the sailing of his ship. They called upon Mrs Andrews, the pilot's wife, who informed them that Mr Lawrence had told her husband the day before that the hour of sailing had been changed, and that the *Minorca* would leave Old Harbour shortly after eight o'clock instead of half-past twelve.

"Did Mr Lawrence state the reason of this change?" enquired Captain Acton.

"Not to my husband, sir, who naturally thought the matter all right, and said he would be on board at half-past seven."

They met Lieutenant Tupman of the *Saucy* brig-of-war, a large, fat, purple, smiling man, with the word grog, written in small red veins over his nose and parts of his cheeks: obviously a good -natured, drunken fellow who would fight, no doubt, if a Frenchman opposed him, but who preferred his bed and "The Swan" to frequent sentinel cruisings in his little ship of war. Both gentlemen knew him slightly. They ventured on this occasion to stop and accost him. They asked him if it was true that news of a French cruiser being off the coast had come to hand, and he answered that he had not heard of such a ship being near the coast.

The replies of other questions put to Mr Tupman were equally unsatisfactory, and it now being past one o'clock and the information the Captain and the Admiral had obtained not being worth the questions that had elicited it, they stepped on to the bridge and walked in the direction of Old Harbour House, the Admiral saying that he would accompany the Captain to his home, as he was anxious to hear if Miss Acton had obtained news of Lucy.

CHAPTER VIII

WHERE IS LUCY?

CAPTAIN ACTON and the Admiral walked a few hundred paces in silence, each lost in thought. Very abruptly the Admiral stopped, obliging his companion to halt.

"If I have your permission, sir," he exclaimed, "I will at once send a messenger in a post-chaise to the Commander-in-Chief at Plymouth, and after stating the facts request him to send a ship to overtake or intercept and arrest the *Minorca* and you will then be able to ascertain direct from my son the meaning and causes of his extraordinary conduct."

Captain Acton resumed his walk, and the Admiral rolled by his side beating the ground.

"That idea has occurred to me," he said, "and I have dismissed it, sir, for what reception would the Commander-in-Chief give such a message as you propose? The master of a ship, who is fully empowered to act in the interests of his owners, chooses to leave a certain harbour some hours earlier than the time announced. The reason he gives is that there is a Frenchman in the neighbourhood whom he is anxious to avoid and escape. The Commander-in-Chief's sympathy would be with him in that. It is no case of piracy to ship a pilot, and the mate and crew which the vessel carried last voyage; and besides, sir, would the sloop, corvette, or frigate which the Commander-in-Chief might choose to send, overhaul the *Minorca* if your son determined that his purpose, whatever it may be, should be prosecuted without interruption? She is certainly as swift as the fastest thing that we have in the Navy, and there is no reason to suppose that any vessel as fast would be despatched in chase. Plymouth is a long distance from this spot, and messengers are not always the rapid people we desire them to be. No, sir, we have to accept the position as it is. The ship has sailed; Mr Lawrence's conduct is unaccountable. We must continue to regard him as the honourable, well-meaning man which I have found him during our association in the matter of this command, and I must await with a certain degree of confidence a letter in which he will communicate the full meaning of what is now unintelligible to us."

The Admiral bowed in silence. He was the father of the person they were talking about. Captain Acton's acceptance of an incident which must instantly prove sinister to a suspicious intelligence was noble and gracious, and it was certainly not for the father to endeavour to prove his son a rogue and a scoundrel, and perhaps worse still, in the teeth of the disposition of his employer to continue to place trust in him.

When they were within ten minutes' walk of Old Harbour House, they met Mr Adams, who was an agent for a gentleman who lived

in London, and who owned a great deal of property in the neighbourhood of Old Harbour Town.

"I beg your pardon, squire," said Mr Adams, addressing Captain
Acton, who with the Admiral was passing on with a nod, "but I
understand that enquiries are being made after your daughter."

Both the old retired officers instantly stopped.

"Has she returned home?" asked Captain Acton.

"I cannot tell you that, sir, but this morning at about a quarter
before eight o'clock, I was about ten minutes' walk this side Old
Harbour Bridge. I was going up the road and met your daughter,
who was alone, coming down. A few minutes after I had passed her,
I happened to look round and perceived that she had been stopped
by a young man, humpbacked and otherwise deformed, well known
to me as a fellow who used to hang about Old Town, and called by
the single word Paul. As your daughter was alone I slackened my
pace and continued to look to see what the man wanted with her,
and observed that he gave her a letter which she read, and I heard
her exclaim on reading it: 'Oh dear! I hope it is not serious,' and she
immediately walked swiftly on followed by the fellow called Paul.
She turned the bend of the road, and I pursued my way."

"I beg your pardon," exclaimed Captain Acton, whose agitation
was marked when Mr Adams ceased to speak, "but may I enquire if
you are quite sure that it was my daughter whom you met?"

"Sir, there is but one Lucy Acton in this country, and no man who
has set eyes on her is ever likely to forget her beauty and sweetness."

Captain Acton bowed, but his distress was lively.

"What sort of a fellow was this who stopped Miss Acton?"
enquired the Admiral. "Was he a pauper? Broken clothes, whining
voice, the suppliant's demeanour—that sort of thing?"

"I have known the fellow by sight some years. He got his living
by running errands, and has in his day, I believe, been watched with
some attention by the magistrates. He is a red-haired, hunchbacked,
long-armed man with rounded legs, and I marked a peculiarity in
him whilst he addressed the lady which I have before taken notice
of when passing him as he lounged in the sun, or stood waiting in
a door: I mean that whilst the young lady was reading the missive,

he scratched his left shoulder precisely as a monkey scratches himself."

Captain Acton started, and stared hard at Mr Adams.

"Did you notice how he was dressed?" he asked,

"In a camlet jacket. There was something of the sailor's rig in his costume."

"Then the fellow," said Captain Acton, "is steward of the *Minorca!* This gentleman," said he, addressing the Admiral, "has exactly described the figure of a man who passed me in the cabin two or three days ago when I was talking to Mr Lawrence. Judging that he belonged to the ship, and being struck by his appearance, I asked Mr Lawrence who he was, and he answered that he was a poor devil whom he had shipped as a steward or captain's waiter out of pity, and he said something about having once paid a fine for the man to rescue him from a term of imprisonment to which he would have been sentenced for some trifling offence."

The Admiral's face wore an expression that was almost imbecile with bewilderment.

"From whom was that letter? Who is the person that Miss Lucy has fled to help? It cannot possibly be my son, sir. If he had met with a serious accident, would the ship have sailed? But even if he had met with a serious accident and left the duty of going to sea with the mate, would he have sent to Miss Lucy? I am utterly beaten. I see nothing, and can conjecture nothing!"

Captain Acton with a violent effort had by this time recollected himself.

"I am much obliged to you, sir, for your information," he said to Mr Adams. "We may find her at home, sir," he said, addressing the Admiral. "An explanation will simplify the miraculous. Good day, sir, and many thanks."

He bowed to Mr Adams, and again set off with the Admiral for Old Harbour House.

"To me it is impossible to suppose," said Sir William, "that my son could have written the letter which Mr Adams saw your daughter reading. Captain Weaver told us plainly that my son was aft on the quarterdeck of the *Minorca* at the time that she was hauling out from the wharf. It is perfectly clear therefore that no accident could have befallen him. Nor is it imaginable that, even if he had met with a disaster, he would dream of communicating with your daughter. Why your daughter, sir? If they are on bowing terms we may take it that their intimacy scarcely goes farther. Depend upon it, there is some man in connection with this business, in whom your daughter is interested—of course, sir, you will understand me to mean as a sweet and beautiful Christian sympathiser, as one to whom every sort of misfortune appeals, to whom suffering and misery are quick to make themselves known, being sure of heartfelt, womanly pity. The moment I have had a peck, after hearing whether Miss Lucy has arrived at home, I will devote the rest of the day to enquiries about this person who wrote the letter which Mr Adams saw delivered."

"Speculation is idle," exclaimed Captain Acton, with a slight flavour of impatience in his manner. "I am profoundly puzzled. There can be no question from Mr Adams's statement and from my own observation that the fellow who delivered the missive is cabinboy, or steward, or whatever you please to call him, of the *Minorca,* chosen by your son, as he admits, though it seemed to me as I looked at him that nobody less likely and less inviting for such a post could have been found in the district."

These and a few further words brought them to the gateway of Old Harbour House. They entered and found Miss Acton in the dining-room.

"Well," she cried in a voice of tremulous eagerness, "have you heard of her?"

This was proof conclusive that Miss Acton had not.

"She has not returned, then?" said Captain Acton.

"No, nor can I get to hear of her," answered Miss Acton, whose voice trembled with tears and terror. "Wasn't she down on the wharves?"

"We have heard of her, but not as we could wish, sister," said Captain Acton. "But what have *you* done to find her, or to hear of her?"

"Why," answered the old lady, "I sent George and Joseph on horseback to every house where she is known, and she has visited none, nor been seen by any this morning. Yes, Mrs Moore as she was

passing our gate, caught a sight of her coming out of the house at
half-past seven, or at some such time, and gave her a curtsy and
received a smile. But nobody else that George and Joseph met and
called upon has seen her this day. What have you to tell me about
her?"

Captain Acton repeated Mr Adams's statement. The old lady's face
was slowly moulded into a mask that her friends would scarcely
have recognised by the horror and terror that worked in her.

She cried: "A dirty fellow giving her a letter, and beguiling her and
luring her into some dreadful place, perhaps to her destruction! Oh
dear! oh dear! what is to be done? Can't she be discovered? Can't
the bell-man raise the alarm? Who can the wretch be that wrote to
her? And why should she rush away to his help? Oh dear! oh dear!
what is to be done?"

"I'll do something," said the Admiral. "I'll call upon you this evening
and tell you what I have found out. Farewell for the present. No, I
thank you, I must go home first and I'll get a bite that awaits me,
and then away to Old Harbour Town, and the place shall be dredged,
and the fellow who wrote the letter found, and the lady restored to
her home if wrong has been done her, if there is one ounce of
energy left in this old composition."

He bowed with the vehemence of a man who butts at another,
struck the floor hard with his staff, and rolled out on legs that
showed themselves more expeditious than his years seemed to
promise.

Captain and Miss Acton sat down to dinner. An elegant repast was
rendered insipid in every dish by the absence of Lucy. The Captain's
excellent if fastidious appetite was gone and his eyes often wan-
dered to his daughter's vacant place. Brother and sister had but one
subject in their minds; they talked but little, however, for servants
were present.

When they were alone, Miss Acton exclaimed: "I hope I may be
forgiven if I do him a wrong, and I love his old father, who is the
soul of honour and a fine example of a true gentleman of the sea,
but I cannot help thinking, brother, that Mr Lawrence has had a hand
in our Lucy's disappearance."

And the worthy old lady's eyes grew dim as she pronounced the words "our Lucy."

Captain Acton started from a reverie and looked at her attentively.

"You want to imply," he cried, "that there was an understanding between Mr Lawrence and my daughter?"

"I cannot imagine why the steward of the ship came to be employed, as Mr Adams tells us—an assertion you justify by saying that you saw this man in the cabin of the vessel—unless Mr Lawrence sent the letter."

Captain Acton expanded his chest, and a look of haughtiness entered his face.

"Sister, is your opinion of Lucy such that you imagine she can have anything to do with Mr Lawrence unknown to me?"

But a quality of stubbornness was one of Miss Acton's characteristics.

"He offered her marriage, brother."

"Yes. And she rejected him with the peremptoriness which I should have expected in her."

"A woman," said Miss Acton, "cannot but think with more or less kindness of the man who offers her marriage and who loves her. She may reject him, but she will always feel a tenderness for him."

"But do I understand," said Captain Acton, "that you mean that Lucy was secretly attached to the man whose hand she declined, and that she speeds to him at the first call that is made upon her by such a missive as the fellow Paul delivered?"

"I cannot but think," answered Miss Acton, "that Lucy had a secret hankering after Mr Lawrence. He is exceedingly handsome. In bearing he is superior to any man of quality I ever met, and for fine manners you must look to the aristocracy of this country. He can make a leg with the grace equal to any master of elegant salutations; and though his character is bad, yet there are many points in him which women admire, and I say," she continued, with perseverance and a fixity of meaning truly astonishing in an old lady who in most matters scarcely knew her own mind, who was easily filled with terror, and who seldom acted without consulting her friends, "Lucy has a secret liking for the man, which could scarcely escape the observation of any one who watched them when they are in company."

With an expression of face that was near to amazement Captain Acton said: "Do you want me to believe that Lucy has eloped with Mr Lawrence?"

"Lord forbid! She is too God-fearing, and too nobly and sweetly moulded as a woman to be capable of any such descent."

"Then I do not understand you," said Captain Acton.

"What has become of her?" cried Miss Acton, sinking suddenly into her tremulous voice and into a manner of alarm, bewilderment, and general confusion of mind. "What shall you do to find out?"

"As I am quite convinced," said Captain Acton, "that Mr Lawrence has nothing to do with this business, and as I feel persuaded that the call made upon her is by some man or woman—for how are we to know the sex of the person who wrote that letter?—in whom her charity is interested, and whom she has been helping according to her wont in ways unknown to us, I shall devote the afternoon as Sir William intends, to making enquiries in Old Harbour Town and about the wharves——"

"But she cannot be in Old Town or even in the district," broke in Miss Acton, "or why did she not return to dinner? She has had the whole morning. From a little after seven till now is a very long time, and a hundred acts of charity may be performed in less."

Though Captain Acton was not a man to be influenced by his sister's opinions he knew her to be in many directions a shrewd, observant woman, who could deliver herself of many stupid antiquated notions, whilst at times she would astonish him by the sagacity of her views and the penetration with which she interpreted human motives. We shall not be surprised, therefore, when we learn that shortly after dinner he ordered his mare to be saddled, and rode straight into Old Harbour Town, where he stabled the mare at "The Swan" and walked direct to the wharves, first of all to learn if anybody had seen Lucy down at the shipping early that morning.

He made for the *Aurora,* and found Captain Weaver on board. He immediately related Mr Adams' story, and asked Captain Weaver if he had seen Miss Lucy Acton down by the *Minorca* or near her, or aboard of her shortly before she sailed.

"No, sir," was Captain Weaver's answer. "I came on to the wharf as the *Minorca* was warping out, and talked with Mr Lawrence from the quay-side. I saw nothing of the young lady, who, depend upon it, sir, would have immediately caught my attention had I seen her."

"It is very strange," said Captain Acton, "that that mis-shapen fellow made by Mr Lawrence the steward of the ship, should be employed to convey a letter to my daughter at so early an hour when there was very little likelihood of finding the young lady abroad."

"The whole job of the ship sailing before her time is a mystery to me, sir," said Captain Weaver.

"Walk with me, and we'll endeavour to find out if Miss Lucy Acton was on the wharf after the hour of half-past seven this morning, and before the *Minorca* sailed."

Captain Weaver knew many who were engaged on the several wharves, and so indeed did Captain Acton. They asked two or three score of different persons the question, but the majority had not been down on the wharves at that time, and the few who were at work declared that they had not seen her. It seemed impossible to Captain Weaver as well as to Captain Acton, that so beautiful and well known a lady as Miss Lucy should make her appearance on the wharf at a time of day when scarce more than labourers were about, without being either recognised or seen, and her presence borne witness to by those who did not know who she was.

They went on board the several vessels lying in the harbour, but the answer they received was that of the wharf: Miss Lucy Acton had not been seen, or at all events noticed.

"I will leave you," said Captain Acton, "to make further enquiries, sir, and you will be pleased to immediately communicate with me at my home should you meet with anybody who can positively swear that my daughter was down here between seven and eight this morning."

He seemed convinced by these enquiries at the wharves that at all events Mr Lawrence could have had nothing whatever to do with the communication which Mr Adams had seen Paul place in the hands of Miss Lucy. Who, then, was the sender of the note, and how was it that Paul, who should have been on board his ship since she was on the eve of sailing, should have been engaged to carry the letter? There was really no particular reason why the writer should be a man. Why should not she be a woman? She might even be a relative of the fellow Paul. Lucy was a girl of singular kindness, who was always helping others and going amongst the poor and ministering to the afflicted; and though Captain Acton could not positively say, he might readily believe that she had one or two or three poor sufferers on her list whom she saw to and helped with her purse, and one of these—possibly a woman—might have written the letter in a moment of urgency intending it for delivery at Old Harbour House.

Captain Acton walked slowly towards Old Harbour Town. He was sunk in thought, and was in deep distress and at a loss to know what to do. He had no machinery of police to command. 1805 was a year very primitive as compared with 1905. He reflected that the first step in the disappearance of his daughter as represented in the statement of Mr Adams might indicate nothing in respect of the real cause of her disappearance. Because, suppose his surmise was correct, and that she had hastened to the help of some afflicted or humble person whom she befriended, she might, after having left the place wherever it was, have met with some disaster; she might have fallen over the cliff—she might on some roundabout way home have been robbed and left for dying; in short, when a person mysteriously disappears a hundred reasons for his or her envanishment will occur to the mind, and any one of them may so satisfy, so convince, that those who accept it will go to work as though it were the truth though it possess but the very attenuated merit of being a conjecture.

At six o'clock, greatly wearied, Captain Acton mounted his mare at "The Swan" stables and rode home. He was very pale. Indeed this man loved his daughter, who was his only child. His immediate question, put with bright-eyed passion to the servant who came to the door, was, "Has Miss Lucy returned?"

"No, sir."

"Has news been received of her?"

"I don't think so, sir."

"Has Admiral Lawrence been here?"

"No, sir."

Captain Acton walked into his house and sought his sister, whom he found alone in the dining-room. She was seated on a highbacked chair knitting. Her own and Lucy's dog lay at her feet. She started at the entrance of Captain Acton, dropped her knitting in her lap, and half rose at her brother, clutching the arms of the chair.

"Well!" she cried in a note that was like a suppressed scream with excitement, fear, and expectation. "What have you heard? Is there any news of her? What have you to tell me?"

He sat down, looking very weary.

"I have heard nothing of her, sister. Nobody saw her on the wharf at the time the *Minorca* sailed, and there was plenty about, labourers ashore, and sailors in the ships."

"Then what have you done to find out what has become of her?"

"Believing that she might have met with some accident—God knows of what serious nature—on her return from the person whose letter she received"—Miss Acton looked stunned at such an idea—"I called at Arrowsmith's first of all, and wrote out a placard, offering a reward of fifty guineas to any one who can find Miss Lucy Acton, who can state her whereabouts, or who can give any information as to her disappearance since half-past seven o'clock this morning, which was dated and the day named. This placard will be printed and pasted in Old Harbour Town, and over a wide area of the district before nightfall. I also gave a copy of this placard to the bell-man. What further publicity could I command?"

"But what do you fear, brother? What could have happened to her?"

"Why, suppose on her way home by way of the cliffs, or by any other of the roads by which this house may be gained, she fell upon the rocks, or was met by a band of gipsies, or attacked for her money and left for dead—"

His feelings overcame him, and he looked upon the ground in silence.

"Nothing of the sort, I am sure of it!" exclaimed Miss Acton. "Who hears of such outrages happening here?"

"But to fall over the edge of a cliff is not an outrage," said Captain Acton.

"She is too careful. She may safely be trusted. Besides, are there not blockaders stationed along these cliffs, and would not one see her on the rocks? No, no, no! an accident is not the cause of her disappearance. The more I think, the more persuaded I am that Mr Lawrence has had a hand in this horrid business. Why did he sail so early and long before his time? Why was his steward Paul engaged to carry the letter?"

"You again want to imply, sister," said Captain Acton with a darkling face, "that my daughter has eloped with the man she rejected."

"Rejected, but she has a hankering for him still," said the old lady with one of those smiles of knowingness which make the lineaments ghastly when bitter sorrow and tragic trouble are the topics talked about.

Captain Acton left the room to refresh himself with a change of apparel, and returned after a brief absence. He was a man of considerable but not powerful self-control. He entered the room with a face that indicated a certain resolution of mind, and said to his sister: "I have been thinking, perhaps, that we have been unnecessarily flurried and somewhat hurried in our conjecture and efforts. I believe I have done well in giving all possible publicity to the fact that Lucy left her home this morning and has not returned. But when I come to reflect that even now it is not twelve hours since she started on her early walk, I consider that she has not been long enough absent to cause us the bitter anxiety we have felt and are feeling. Suppose after visiting the person from whom she received the letter, she breakfasted with a friend on the other side of Old Harbour Town. This friend may have induced her to stop to dinner; a drive might follow. There are hundreds of things in this business which when explained would seem perfectly reasonable, so that at any moment she may turn up and tell us the story of her day's outing and wonder that we should be so troubled because of an absence that she makes perfectly comprehensible. I shall hold to this view," he continued firmly, "until the night is advanced. If she does not return to-night then we must take further steps to-morrow."

"What steps?" asked his sister. "What steps have not been taken that remain to be taken?"

He had suddenly sunk in reflection and did not answer her.

"I should be uneasy in my mind in any case," said Miss Acton. "But that odious steward of the *Minorca* being in the business together with the unwarrantable sailing of the vessel hours before her time, fills me with dread and terror, and I cannot, brother, listen to what you say about her breakfasting and dining with a friend and going for a drive, and so forth. She would guess at our suspense and anxiety. Is our Lucy a girl to cause unnecessary pain and unhappiness, not indeed to those who love her as we do, but to the humblest creature in the world?"

Just then the door was opened, and the footman announced "Admiral Sir William Lawrence."

The old gentleman entered, not with his familiar deep-sea rolling gait, but slowly and wearily, and with an air of dejection. Lucy's dog welcomed him by barking and rushing at his shoe and trying to bite through it. Miss Acton rose and sank in a curtsy which is to be seen in these days only on the stage, but her kindly heart quickened her gaze for anything that invited sympathy, and she immediately said: "Sir William, you are quite worn out. You need refreshment. Pray sit, pray sit! What will you take?"

"We will have some brandy and seltzer water," said Captain Acton, pulling the bell, knowing this drink to be as great a favourite with the Admiral as hock and soda water was with Lord Byron.

"I am sorry to say," said the Admiral, sinking into a chair, "that I have brought no news."

"I have scoured Old Harbour Town and can obtain no information," said Captain Acton; "but it is certain that no one seems to have seen her down on the wharf between seven and eight this morning."

"I heard the bell-man recite your notice," said Sir William, speaking leisurely, as one who is tired out; "that, and the bill which they were beginning to paste as I came this way, should help. I've walked my legs off. I have enquired everywhere. I, too, asked if Miss Lucy had been seen down at the harbour at any hour this morning. But my fixed idea was, and still is, that the person who wrote to her through the *Minorca*'s steward was somebody that she helped, somebody in poverty and want, and I called upon everybody likely to know of the existence of such an individual; but to no purpose. The parson, the apothecary, all the tradespeople I looked in upon, could tell me nothing. Once I thought I had run the person we want to earth. Mrs Moore, who keeps the greengrocer's shop, told me that there was an old woman who lived in a cottage just out of Lower Street, out of whose house she had once seen Miss Lucy Acton issue. I got the address, called at the cottage and saw a squalid female who said she was Mrs Mortimer's niece, and that Mrs Mortimer had died that morning at five o'clock. She said it was true that Miss Acton occasionally visited Mrs Mortimer and brought her little comforts and read to her. I got no further. This is the extent and value of my report, and I am as profoundly puzzled," said the Admiral, raising the glass of brandy and seltzer and examining it before he drank, "as I was this morning."

"She may turn up at any moment," said Captain Acton, with more gloom than the hope his words expressed justified. "She has only been twelve hours missing."

"Only!" cried Miss Acton. "Sir William," she went on slowly, nodding at him whilst her face hardened, "I have a conviction which my brother does not share. It seems to me, sir, impossible to think of the unexpected and terrifying departure of the *Minorca* hours before her time, and the conveyance of a letter by the steward of the vessel, without feeling the conviction I speak of."

"And what is that conviction, madam?" asked Sir William, from whose jolly round face fatigue had robbed much of its warm colour.

"I regret to have to say it," said Miss Acton, but I must think—I cannot help it, that Mr Lawrence's hand is in this strange disappearance of my niece."

Captain Acton slightly frowned upon the old dame, and exclaimed: "I think, Caroline, you should have withheld your conviction, for the present at all events, from Admiral Lawrence."

Sir William looked firmly and somewhat sternly at Miss Acton and said:"I am very sorry, madam, that you should hold this opinion, very sorry indeed. I had thought you the friend and well-wisher of my son—in this respect eminently the charitable and warm-hearted sister of Captain Acton. But if you mean to imply that Mr Lawrence wrote the letter to Miss Lucy, then you have to confess (which would be an indignity done to a beautiful character) that your niece was a willing recipient of my son's missive, that she hastened to him on reading the contents of his communication and that in short, the design of the *Minorca*'s premature sailing was that Mr Lawrence and Miss Lucy Acton should elope—a thing not to be dreamt of— at an hour when few were abroad, and when there was little or no chance of the news reaching her home that Captain Acton's daughter had sailed in the *Minorca*."

Scarcely had the old gentleman pronounced these words when a footman, throwing open the door, exclaimed: "Mr Greyquill presents his humble respects to Captain Acton, and desires leave to speak with him."

"Mr Greyquill!" cried Captain Acton.

"Mr Greyquill!" echoed the Admiral, looking with a changed face at the footman.

"Mr Greyquill!" cried Miss Acton. "Why, he may have come with news of Lucy. Bid him step in!"

The footman disappeared.

"What on earth but some news of my daughter can bring Greyquill here at this hour?" said Captain Acton.

The Admiral looked deaf, and continued to stare at the door, which in a few moments was again flung open, and Mr Greyquill entered.

CHAPTER IX

MR GREYQUILL'S VISIT

MR GREYQUILL entered the room by two paces, and placing his hand upon the spot where he supposed his heart to lie, made three separate bows to the company, each of the "Your most humble and obedient servant" school; it was an expression of ceremony which for mingled respect and senility should have pleased, as it no doubt did please, Miss Acton.

He was a figure striking in its way as he made these bows, with his long, snow-white hair, his heavy white eyebrows, his long curling nose, the purely congenital satiric leer that characterised the formation of his thin lips; and his faded dress, which was a very good representation of his mind, aided the impression produced by his face.

Admiral Lawrence gave him a nod which was barely a mark of recognition. Captain Acton bowed to him in silence. Miss Acton cried out:

"Pray step in, Mr Greyquill, and be seated!"

Greyquill sidled rather than walked in and sat down on a chair removed from the others and observing enquiry strong in each face as those who watched him would not condescend to enquire the purpose of his visit, but waited to hear it, he said "I was coming out of Lower Street this afternoon, when I heard the bell-man recite the announcement that Miss Lucy Acton had been missing from her home this morning since between seven and eight o'clock, and a reward of fifty guineas is offered to any one who shall proclaim her whereabouts, or who shall help to restore her to her family."

"That is so," said Captain Acton, viewing him gravely.

"Have you news of her?" cried Miss Acton.

"I wish to state, sir," said Mr Greyquill, addressing Captain Acton, "that if I should prove instrumental, not in the restoration of Miss Lucy Acton to her home, but in your discovering where she is, and how she got there, my candour will be due entirely to the very great respect I entertain for the young lady who has always had a kindly word for me, and whose character is an extremely lovable one, and to the regret, I may say indignation, that one so young, beautiful and rich, should fall into such unworthy hands."

He glanced at the Admiral, who returned the look with a compressed brow, whilst with his right hand he seemed to be keeping time to an inward and secret tune with the play of his fingers upon the knee where the leg of his breeches fell into his stocking.

"Oh, pray continue, sir! Pray continue!" cried Miss Acton in a voice that was almost husky with the hysteric quality of her emotions.

"In other words, sir," continued Mr Greyquill, still addressing

Captain Acton, "I beg to state that if I should be so fortunate as to help you in your trouble I desire no money reward, nor should dream of taking any."

Captain Acton merely bowed.

"I have not met with the usage," old Greyquill went on calmly steadily exasperating Miss Acton by a preface that was disgusting and needless whilst she thirsted for the one essential fact, "that I certainly think I deserve from either Admiral Sir William Lawrence, nor his son, Mr Lawrence." He spoke with so complete a neglect of the Admiral's presence that the old gentleman might have been out of the room. "They have no claim upon my kindness."

"We shall be thankful to receive any news of Miss Lucy Acton," said Captain Acton, with that collectedness of manner which implies the glazing by a vigorous will of passions growing turbulent.

"Two or three days after your appointment of Mr Lawrence as master of the *Minorca,* I chanced to be going by way of Old Friar's Road to visit some houses belonging to me. At the bend of the road, which conceals the bridge and Old Harbour Town I met Mr Lawrence, and we exchanged a few sentences on the subject of the sum of three hundred pounds which he owes me. He informed me that when you, sir, had paid him off on his return he would hand me the sum of twenty-five guineas in part payment of his debt. We each pursued our way. When I had gone a few yards I stopped and turned to look after him. He had disappeared round the bend of the road, but just about the place where he and I had conversed I saw something white. It was a letter. Thinking I had dropped it in unconscious play of my hands during our talk, I returned and picked it up."

The old man put his hand in his pocket and pulled out the letter, which he held on his knee, whilst he continued: "It was not addressed, as you will presently see, but the contents which I took the liberty of reading, the letter being open and manifestly a stray article which was anybody's property, assured me that it had just now fallen from the pocket of Mr Lawrence, who had brought it out possibly with his pocket-handkerchief, but who would not know of his loss by looking behind him as the turn of the road hid it from him. I was greatly astounded by the contents of this letter, which is in Mr Lawrence's handwriting, and somewhat incensed by reading that he termed me an old scamp, I, who had proved his friend at a time when friendship was valuable to him, and who have shown him every consideration since. Will you read the letter, sir?"

Mr Greyquill left his seat and stepped across with the missive to Captain Acton. The Captain glanced at the contents, and without reading extended the letter to the Admiral, saying: "Is this your son's writing, sir?"

The Admiral took the letter, ran his eyes over it, and answered, returning the letter to Captain Acton: "It is."

"It is a draft or copy," said Captain Acton. "It is undated, and it is without the formal beginning of My dear, etc."

He then read slowly and deliberately, the handwriting being good and clear:

"I should have answered your letter sooner but I have been so worried by debts and difficulties, by compulsory idleness and the absolute impossibility of finding anything congenial to do, that I have had no spirit to communicate with you or anybody else. But the wheel of fortune which has depressed me to the very bottom, has by another revolution, raised me. I must tell you that I am very heavily in debt. Even in this antiquated hole I owe an old scamp, named Greyquill, three hundred pounds, of which I have only had two hundred. I am in debt, some of them debts of honour, to several men, a few of whom I have spoken of in my time as brother-officers, and one of them quite recently threatened me with the law. In addition, I owe a lot to various tradespeople in London and elsewhere. So that my personal liberty hangs by a hair, and at any moment I may find myself clapped on the shoulder, arrested for debt, and flung into gaol, there to languish possibly for the remainder of my days, for it is quite certain that my father cannot, even if he would, come to my help. His private means are very small, and his pension inconsiderable, and though he has behaved very well in maintaining me since I quitted the Service, and allowed me to use his cottage as a home, he is a man whose morality is high and severe, and he is the last person to part with a farthing in discharge of debts which he regards as dishonourable.

"I had made up my mind to ship before the mast in a vessel

bound to America, where I should have left her, and sought my fortune in a new country; when through the great kindness that a rich gentleman in this district has for my father, I was offered the command of a barque called the *Minorca,* a handsome little vessel of about five hundred tons, on terms which a Merchant shipmaster would consider liberal, but which to one, in the face of what I owe, are as a penny piece in the value of a guinea. Captain Acton (R.N., retired)—you may have met him—is the owner of the two little ships. He lives in a beautiful old house planted in the midst of a fine prospect of gardens and orchards. He has one child, a daughter, a young creature so beautiful that the instant I saw her I irrecoverably lost my heart to her. I offered her marriage; she rejected me, probably because she had been told that I was a drinker and a gambler. I am, nevertheless, determined to possess her as my wife, and with that view have promptly conceived a stratagem or plot which should either end in enabling me to pay off all my debts and live at peace in this country, or be hanged as a pirate."

The Admiral, who had heretofore discovered no signs of life, started in his chair and clenched his fist.

"It is you, my dear Dick, and old companion, mess-mate and friend, with whom I have enjoyed many a jaunt to which I could never recur without passionately lamenting the days that are no more, who will help me in this desperate undertaking. I propose to navigate the vessel, not to Kingston, Jamaica, to which port she ought to be bound, but to the port in which you live, Rio de Janeiro. By a ruse which must prove successful, I think, I shall inveigle Miss Lucy Acton on board, and everything being ready, shall make sail immediately after she is carefully confined in my cabin. I have had a cabin set apart for my own use, which I represented to Captain Acton was to serve as a sick-bay. This drama has been well rehearsed. When far out at sea the crew will be summoned aft. I shall read some pretended sealed orders from Captain Acton, requiring me to carry the ship to Rio de Janeiro, and to sell her, if possible, after discharging the mate and crew, who will receive from Captain Acton, on application, treble the amount of their wages they would have got for sailing the vessel to Kingston. I shall also take care to destroy the ship's papers. And my story will be that I was overhauled by an

American cruiser, who sent an officer on board. He examined the box of papers and took it away to show to his Captain, as he considered them unsatisfactory. The cruiser then braced her main topsail yard to the wind and sailed away with the box of papers. On my arrival, we will consult together as to the safest course to be adopted for the sale of the ship and cargo, by which time I have no doubt the lady will have agreed to marry me either for love, or because she has been placed in a situation which must render marriage imperative to her in the name of honour. With the money which I shall make, thanks to you, through this business, I will pay off all my debts in England, and Lucy Acton being my wife, or promising me her hand, I may count with absolute certainty upon the forgiveness of her father, who is not likely to abandon his only child for a behaviour that was no fault of hers, and the rest must be left to time.

"I think our man to help us for a liberal commission will be your friend, José Zamovano Y Villa. His scrupulosity in financial matters is not likely to prove a great hindrance, eh, Dick? I shall follow this letter soon after the ship that takes it, so that you will not have long to wait before seeing me after you have read it."

This letter was unsigned. It was manifestly a rough draft of the posted letter which had been amplified before it was sent. Captain Acton's hand dropped with it on to his knee. He exclaimed:

"That is the end—there is no name."

On which Miss Acton screamed out: "What did I say? Are not my words true? To think of our beloved Lucy imprisoned in a ship! Sailed away with, never to be seen more perhaps, in the hands of—of—oh, what is to be done? What is to be done?"

The Admiral started from his chair to his feet. His face was full of blood, his hands were uplifted, and his fingers tightly locked. He cried, in a voice that was like mimic thunder in its power, and breaks, and falls:

"I will hire a vessel and chase him; I will pursue him, though he should lead me to the very gates of Hell. Oh, my precious God! I, who have ever striven to act my part well in the service of my country! I, who have ever struggled to live an honourable and a stainless life as a gentleman and a sailor! Why am I dishonoured and degraded by the possession of such a son?"

He unclasped his hands and buried his purple face, and stood rocking and reeling as though he were about to fall in a fit, and sobbed twice or thrice with that dreadful note of grief in his dry-eyed agony, which makes the tearlessness of manhood in suffering one of the most pitiful, painful and pathetic of spectacles. Captain Acton laid his hand on the Admiral's shoulder.

"Bear up!" he said gently. "Presently we will discuss the matter calmly. God is good, and this blow may not prove nearly so heavy as we now think it."

With kindly pressure he obliged the old seaman to resume his seat, and then turned with something of fierceness upon old Greyquill.

"May I ask," said he, flourishing the letter, "how it is that you, sir, being fully admitted by the perusal of this document into the base plot Mr Lawrence was hatching, should have chosen to keep the intention to yourself, when by the revelation of this letter you could have put it out of Mr Lawrence's power to carry off my child."

Mr Greyquill stood up. His eyes had a peculiar light in them, a faint flush was painted on each check, and seemed to make whiter yet the whiteness of his brows and his hair.

"Sir," he answered, "I am much sneered at in this town and district. I am very well aware that few have a kind word for me. If you, sir, or Admiral Lawrence condescend to bestow a nod upon me as I respectfully pass you in the street, it has the character of the recognition with which you would honour something you disdain, which you are compelled to see, and by that nod acknowledge the existence of. Your beautiful daughter, Miss Lucy, on the other hand, has always been gracious and kind to me. In the light and sweetness of her presence I am sensible of the warmth and glow which make me feel that I am human and a man. There is no office I would not discharge to oblige her. I make money by lending it, but I would give her money—much if she needed it, for the delight I take in her sympathetic, tender and generous nature. When I read the letter you hold, sir, I did not believe that Mr Lawrence would have the power or the art to carry out his scheme of kidnapping your daughter, and I was only assured that his base plot, as you term it, had proved triumphant by the calling of the bell-man, and by the letterpress on the placards which they are pasting about the place. Then I was determined that you should be instantly apprised through the medium of Mr Lawrence's own letter of what had become of your daughter. Otherwise, sir, the loss of your ship by an act of piracy must be nothing to me. Mr Lawrence promises in his letter that he will repay all his creditors, of which I am one to the extent of three hundred pounds. And as I am of opinion that this is his honest intention in order to enable him to dwell in England at liberty, I resolved to keep my own counsel and to await the receipt of my money."

Thus speaking he picked up his hat from the floor, bowed to Captain Acton and to Miss Acton, and left the room without noticing the Admiral.

"What a wicked, dreadful old man!" exclaimed Miss Acton, "to preserve such a hideous secret, and to be willing to wait for payment of his three hundred pounds out of another man's robbery. What is to be done? What will you do, brother? Our Lucy must be rescued. Is it too late? She was here in this house this morning at seven o'clock. The ship cannot be far off. Cannot she be reached?"

Captain Acton, holding the Greyquill letter in his hand, stepped to a bell rope and pulled it. The hue of his face was ashen, the expression cold and severe: such a face as he would carry had he to confront a crowd of armed mutineers.

"What is to be done? What is to be done?" cried Miss Acton.

"What is to be done?" exclaimed the Admiral, starting from a silence in which his form was motionless, though his lips might have been seen moving whilst his eyes were fastened upon the carpet. "This is to be done, madam. I will commute my pension. I will mortgage my household furniture. I will get together every penny that is to be had by realisation of what I possess. I will post to London to-morrow." He pulled out a great gold watch and surveyed it for two or three breathless moments, "and in the river seek and assuredly find a sharp-stemmed vessel which shall convey me to Rio de Janeiro, and I shall be in that spot, if God but grant me wind enough, to greet the arrival of that villain, my son, to secure the person of your daughter, and return her in safety—that I will do!—that I will do!" And the poor old fellow stood up snapping his fingers whilst he flourished his arms at Captain Acton and his sister, and made several mouths in inarticulate phrase.

A footman entered.

"Send George at once" said Captain Acton, "with the gig as fast as the mare can trot to Captain Weaver. He must call at his house first—the Paragon out of Lower Street. If not at home, he must find out where he is, and drive him back here with express orders from me that I must see him without loss of an instant's time."

The footman ran out. Miss Acton looked with eager, tearful expectation at her brother, who addressing the Admiral, exclaimed:

You are a sailor, sir, and so am I, and 'tis natural that we should both light upon the same scheme. But there is not the slightest occasion for you to sacrifice a farthing of your property, nor to post to London tomorrow to find a ship, some little schooner or other swift enough to enable you to be at Rio when the *Minorca* arrives. Such a ship," he said, his face brightening a little with an expression of triumph, "I possess in the *Aurora*. She has discharged her lading. She can be ballasted at once, and if a crew can be assembled by this time tomorrow evening I may be far down Channel in such pursuit as must make the barque's chances of escape hopeless, unless indeed she eludes me in the night, or in thick weather, in which case I shall thrash on and be at Rio a week before she enters the Harbour."

"The *Aurora*," cried the Admiral with a sudden elation, which might have passed as the flare-up of a man in his cups who has sat for a while in maudlin dejection. "By heavens, Acton, you have hit it! where should I find such a vessel for this purpose? Why, aboard of her in a few days you would be alongside the *Minorca*, if you are fair in the scent of the trail of her wake, and wanting that, why, your noble and beautiful little clipper will have been at Rio a fortnight before the barque heaves in sight. May I accompany you?—but you must allow me to do so. You must permit me to be your companion, for, by God, Captain Acton, it is for you to recover your daughter and your property, but it is for me to greet that malefactor, my son."

He smote his thigh hard with the palm of his hand. The noise was like the report of a pistol. He was wont to strike himself thus in the days of his command when angered, or when he expressed a purpose, which he intended to fulfil though it meant life or death.

"Certainly, Sir William," said Captain Acton. "I shall rejoice to have you with me."

"Good, good!" cried the old fellow, and rolling across to his friend, he grasped him by the hand, and held on, looking at his friend with a face a-work with emotion, with an expression indeed that seemed perilously close to further dry sobs.

"But," said Captain Acton, who was perhaps helped to a display of comparative composure of mind by the Admiral's reception of the news, "though if possible we shall sail tomorrow evening or the following day in pursuit, my opinion is, sir, that even if Mr Lawrence were left to his own shifts he would never be able to compass his undertaking. First of all, he has a highly respectable man, who has proved a good servant to me, to deal with in his mate. Will Mr Eagle permit him to carry the *Minorca* to Rio? Will the crew have nothing to say? What will be thought by all hands when it gets about that my daughter is on board, a prisoner in confinement in the cabin? And is my daughter so enamoured of Mr Lawrence that because he has placed her in a highly equivocal situation she will be willing to marry him, or to have anything to say to him on their arrival at Rio?"

"Oh no, oh no!" interposed Miss Acton; "she would not be our Lucy if she did."

"My conviction is," continued the Captain, "that when Eagle and the crew get scent of Mr Lawrence's intentions, and understand the blackguardly act he has been guilty of in trepanning my daughter, they will turn upon him and either do him some serious mischief or lock him up, and under Eagle, proceed direct to Kingston, or if they have not gone far, return to Old Harbour."

"That's what will happen!" cried Miss Acton. "Would our sailors permit a stranger like Mr Lawrence to steal your daughter and your ship and what is in her, and be dismissed from your service by him at Rio Janeiro with promises of your paying them treble wages when they got home, and applied to you? Oh no, no, no!"

"And Mr Lawrence," continued Captain Acton, speaking in a cool voice that was almost sarcastic, "little understands the habits and customs of the Merchant Service when he supposes that owners give their shipmasters sealed orders to be opened and read to the crew in mid-ocean, or when they are well away from their port of departure. This is the practice of our Service, sir, and Mr Lawrence as a Naval man who is ignorant of the habits and discipline of the Merchant ship greatly errs in supposing that the crew will be misled by any such device."

"Suppose," said Miss Acton, "that a French man-o'-war should capture you, and make you prisoners, what is to become of Lucy?"

"We must defy every chance in our determination to recover my child," answered her brother.

"Ay, that must be," exclaimed the Admiral, "even though Heaven should rain French men-of-war."

An hour passed from the time the message was sent before Captain Weaver arrived. Captain Acton desired to see the skipper alone, out of delicacy to Sir William, of whose son it would be impossible to speak without causing the poor old gentleman distress more or less acute. The Admiral found out Captain Acton's well-bred and considerate wish in the one or two hints he dropped, but stuck manfully to his chair nevertheless, and when Captain Weaver was announced, he still remained one of the three occupants of the room.

The skipper entered, red, nervous, with a countenance slightly lifted by astonishment. Of course he knew that Miss Lucy Acton had been missing since the morning, but that was all he did know.

"Walk in, Captain Weaver. Pray, take that chair," said Captain Acton. "I can ask you no questions until I make you acquainted with what has happened."

"Then Miss Lucy hasn't been found, sir," said the Captain.

"She has been kidnapped by Mr Lawrence," answered Captain Acton. "She left this house early this morning to take one of those fresh morning walks which she enjoys, and was seen to receive a letter from the hunchback steward of the *Minorca*. She must have immediately hastened on board the barque, urged by some statement which I am disposed to agree with my sister Miss Acton, was forged or manufactured by Mr Lawrence."

"My son, Captain Weaver, my son!" broke in the Admiral tremulously.

"The best of fathers have known your lot, sir," answered Captain Weaver. "There is no need to go to the Old Testament to learn that."

"The long and short of it is, Captain Weaver," said Captain Acton, "Mr Lawrence having lured my daughter on board the vessel he commands through some ruse which I am unable to explain, made sail at once with the lady on board, not for Kingston, Jamaica, but for Rio Janeiro, where he proposes to discharge the mate and crew after reading to them a forged promise by me that their wages to Kingston shall be trebled on their return and on their application to me. He also proposes to sell the ship and cargo, and he is manifestly acquainted with some scoundrel out at Rio, who, in spite of such vigilance as the officials of Rio may be in the habit of exercising, will undoubtedly discover a market, though not necessarily at Rio."

"Rascally things can be done at sea, sir," said Captain Weaver, whose face, instead of gaining in the look of amazement that had coloured it on his entrance, was slowly settling as Captain Acton proceeded into an expression of hard-a-weather composure. With such a look perhaps a thoroughbred, stout-hearted British sailor would view the calamity or catastrophe that was pressing strong men down upon their knees in devotion, and causing tears of terror to flow from the eyes of others.

"Oh, Captain Weaver, there are many wicked people at sea!" cried Miss Acton. "Think of the pirates! Think of the slavers! My poor, poor niece!"

"Now, sir," continued Captain Acton, "it is not the intention of Sir William Lawrence or myself to suffer my daughter to be kidnapped by an act of treachery which I forbear to say more about in the presence of my honourable and gallant old friend, Admiral Lawrence."

"Oh, Acton," exclaimed the Admiral, "nothing that you can say could approach what I feel, could express what I suffer."

"My intention is," Captain Acton went on, to fit out the *Aurora* at once for a chase. We know where the *Minorca* is bound to. Mr

Lawrence's course must necessarily be yours. Your vessel can sail two feet to his one. If we are unfortunate enough to miss him on the high seas, we shall be at Rio a week or a fortnight before the *Minorca* arrives, to receive him. When can you get your ship ready for sea?"

Captain Weaver reflected. "To-day, sir," he said, "is Toosday. I'll engage to be under way by Saturday."

"Not before?" cried Miss Acton, an exclamation which Captain Weaver received with a faint smile.

"That will be giving the *Minorca* long odds, won't it?" said Captain Acton.

"No, sir. If we took a fortnight to fit the clipper for sea, we should overhaul the *Minorca* or be ahead of her long before she heaves her port into sight."

"What's the distance to Rio, Captain Weaver?" asked the Admiral.

"All five thousand miles, sir."

"What would you call the *Aurora* 's average?" enquired Captain Acton.

"I'll put it low to make sure," responded Captain Weaver, "and call it a hundred and twenty-five miles a day, though a hundred and fifty would be nearer the mark."

The Admiral might have been observed to be calculating by the movement of his lips. "It will be a run, then," said he, "of about forty days."

"At the utmost," said Captain Weaver "and the *Minorca* will want at least sixty."

"What have you to do," said Captain Acton, "that we should wait until Saturday?"

Here the conversation was stayed for minute or two by the entrance of a footman with a tray of sandwiches and cakes, and ale for Captain Weaver, and wine, and the like.

"Why," answered Captain Weaver, who had had time to think, "the *Aurora*'s copper wants cleaning badly. We shall need to take in more ballast. There are the sails to bend and a lot to be seen to aloft; stores to be shipped, and dozens of other matters to be attended to, gentlemen. We're not a Naval dockyard down on the wharves. We can't rig out a dismantled frigate and fill her with men with all her artillery in place and send her to sea in twenty-four hours, and there may be some little difficulty as to a few of the crew. Two or three of them who are married will want a longer spell ashore than this time gives them. If so, and I reckon upon it, I shall need others."

"You think a detention of four days will signify nothing in our certainty of overhauling the *Minorca,* or getting to Rio in advance of her?" said Captain Acton.

"I know the *Aurora,* sir. No highwayman could know his blood-mare which has galloped him again and again clear of the noose of the gibbet better than I know your Baltimore clipper. She'll look up to windward, or hold her course when the *Minorca* is falling points off. She was built to sail, madam, and she do sail. There is nothing in the King's service with her legs. I allow she was born to be a slaver."

"She looks swift even as she lies at rest," said Miss Acton.

"You are not armed, I think," said the Admiral, "whilst the *Minorca* carries some carronades and a stand of small arms in her cabin. Mr Lawrence is a fighting man, and his situation is one of desperation and"—his voice sank as he added—"piracy."

"I do not propose to go armed," said Captain Acton. "Such armament as the *Aurora* of three hundred and ninety tons could carry, and not perhaps without injury to her speed, would prove of little good against an enemy to whom we could only show our heels, whilst as to the *Minorca* if we overhauled her we should hail her to back her topsail, and if she declined we should hold her in sight."

"We might lose her in thick weather," said the Admiral.

"Then, sir, our policy will be to thrash on for Rio."

"You are quite right," said Captain Weaver. "Guns would only be in our way, and sarve to check the beauty, which we don't want."

"Can you explain, Captain Weaver," interrupted Miss Acton, whose irrelevancy was feminine, and whose question was based on her desire to hear something that she could understand, for the talk now as it ran was beyond her—"how it was that Miss Lucy Acton, who is one of the best known ladies who reside in these parts, should pass along the wharves and go on board the *Minorca* to be made a prisoner of and sailed away with, without anybody seeing her— without anybody being able to say that he saw a young female pass along? Even if he could describe her dress without knowing who

she was, we should have been able to conclude that Mr Lawrence
had lured her on board: for we never could have supposed that she
would have gone to him without his being guilty of some base stratagem to inveigle her."

"I can make no other answer than this, ma'am," said Captain
Weaver. "Suppose she was down on the wharves between half-past
seven and eight. Most of the labourers would have been away breakfasting. The few that hung about might not have taken any notice
of her, or if one or two did, then they are people we didn't come
across to question. Most of the men on board the ships in the
Harbour would be in their foc'sles breakfasting and smoking and
the like, and those that were on deck, and few enough at that hour,
might be thinking of other things than people who were passing
by. I don't see how else Miss Lucy Acton's not being seen or noticed
can be accounted for."

"No doubt you are right," said Captain Acton. "I see no other solu-
tion to the puzzle, and a puzzle it is, for," said he, "it is quite certain
that my daughter was down on the wharves and was entrapped this
morning, which explains the reason of Mr Lawrence's hurried sailing."

"I beg your pardon, gentlemen," said Captain Weaver very humbly
and respectfully, "both your honours are sea-faring men who've seen
more of the sea than my larnedest notions could heave into sight
to me, but I should like to say this: if our ship is made out aboard
the *Minorca* supposing we overhaul her, is she likely to back her
topsail to our hail? Mr Lawrence, we may guess, is a detarmined
man, he'll know that you've got the scent of him, and I allow that
he'll keep all on with his ship, even if there should be such a breeze
as would sarve him to run her under water."

"We must hoist foreign colours," said the Admiral quickly and
decisively. "American, I should think; there are many Yankees afloat
like the *Aurora.*"

"Still begging of your honours' pardon," said Captain Weaver,
"suppose the *Minorca* do back her topsail and we launch our
boat; Mr Lawrence makes out his father and Captain Acton in the
starn sheets. Will he stay to receive ye? Won't he fill on his topsail
and be off?"

"You forget," said Captain Acton, "that Mr Eagle and my crew are on board, and they will have something to say in response to Mr Lawrence's orders."

"Your honours," said Captain Weaver, "I am greatly mistaken if Mr Lawrence don't prove one of the hardest and most difficult skippers that ever took command of a ship. He'll get his way, though it should come to his sending balls to do it through the brains of those who try to stop him."

"If the *Minorca* won't heave-to after catching sight of us in the boat," said Captain Acton, "we must return to the *Aurora* and follow her. Then, as I have said, we must head under a full press for Rio."

"But will Mr Lawrence make for Rio," said Captain Weaver, "when he understands by the *Aurora* chasing that you have found out his port of destination?"

"Something at sea must be left to chance," said Captain Acton a little impatiently. "Since you cannot be ready before Saturday Sir William and I will have time to weigh your conjectures and views. I shall be down early to-morrow morning, and hope to find that you have made a fresh and vigorous start in getting the vessel ready for sea."

CHAPTER X

MR LAWRENCE AND MR EAGLE

IT WAS A May morning in the English Channel. Over the soft blue of the sky some large clouds as yellow and tender for the eye to dwell upon as the spume of the sea from the receding breaker, with glories in their brows and glories in their skirts, were sailing slowly and stately on the mild breeze that blew sweet with mingled odours of land and brine from the coast of Old England. There was weight enough in the wind to grace the lines of streaming waters as they ran with feathers of foam, and on this wide plain, with the shores of Britain dwelling in a faint, violet shadow upon the starboard hori-

zon north, but one ship was visible and scarce to be wondered at!
War had swept the narrow seas, and for hours in the day little
more hove into view whether from the cliffs of our country or from
those of the enemy opposite, than sometimes a large convoy glimmering cloud-like as it floated, some compact, some scattered, under
the protection of men-of-war up Channel to London town or to
other ports, or down Channel to their several destinations in various parts of the globe.

Or it might be a cloud of steam-like smoke far off indicating an
action between single ships. An Englishman had hailed a Frenchman
to strike. The Frenchman had answered with a broadside, and before
the sun sets the Englishman with her fore-topmast and mizzen topgallant mast gone is making for Plymouth with a prize in tow.

Or again it will be a smuggling lugger chased by a Revenue cut-
ter with a flash of the sea-snow at her stem and the blaze of a long
gun on the forecastle.

The ship in sight carried in those days a very unfamiliar rig. She
was what is well known now as a barque. She was under all plain
sail and showed many wings, and she lifted sails which Lord St
Vincent when Captain Jervis was the first to introduce into the
Navy, and Merchantmen, always quicker than Navy ships to adopt
improvements or changes for the good, were using them when ships
of the State, at least a good many of them, were still satisfied with
the truck above the topgallant yard.

This vessel was the *Minorca,* which, as we know, had left Old
Harbour shortly after eight o'clock that morning, and now she had
shrunk the Mother Country into a delicate vision, and slightly leaning from the wind was sliding with a steady keel through the water
which beautified the copper that shone ruddily under her weather-
bow with the prisms and crystals and gems of the ocean fountain.
In spite of Admiral Lawrence's admiration of her, she would excite
laughter in this age as an example of the stump-ended fabrics which
the shipwrights of the eighteenth and the nineteenth centuries
were building for sailors. Yet many of these structures made wonderfully long voyages and kept the seas, touching here and there to
careen, for as lengthy a period as the average life of the modern
steel fabric.

The *Minorca's* length did not very greatly exceed her beam. Her bows were round, though they fined down into keenness at her entry under water. She had a large square stern with windows, and her buttocks when her stern fell into the hollow, swept up as much foam as recoiled from the plunge of her bows. Upon the weather-side of the quarterdeck of the ship on this May morning in the English Channel Mr John Eagle, the mate of the vessel, was walking to and fro sometimes directing his gaze to windward, sometimes aloft, sometimes sending it along the ship's decks at the men who were employed on the numberless jobs which attend a sailing ship's departure from port. High aloft, perched on the fore-topgallant yard, was the figure of a look-out man, who was told to report anything that hove into sight and to continue to report how the distant sail was heading. These were Mr Lawrence's instructions.

Mr Eagle looked a very mean sort of man as he walked the deck. Neither by form, face, nor manner did he express individuality or character. The sole feature noticeable in him was a look of sullen-ness, a sour, sneering, quarrelsome air about the mouth, to be found perhaps in the curve of his thin lips.

Whilst he walked Mr Lawrence came up from the cabin through the companion-hatch, and after standing a few moments looking about him, he stepped to the side of Mr Eagle. The contrast between the two men was remarkable. You could scarcely have believed that they belonged to the same nation. Mr Lawrence's tall, elegant, and dignified figure towered above the poor, unshapely conformation of Eagle; his handsome face wore an expression of haughtiness, dis-tance, and reserve. Both Mr Eagle and the boatswain, named Thomas Pledge, who acted as second mate, and the rest of the crew had already discovered that their captain perfectly well understood and remembered that he had been an officer in the Royal Navy, a sailor of His Majesty the King, that comparatively brief as his story was it was brilliant with heroic incident and adventure, and that instead of being greatly obliged to Captain Acton for this command, he con-sidered that he was acting with a very uncommon degree of con-descension in taking charge of a merchant vessel, unless indeed she was a prize to his man-o'-war.

"There is nothing in sight, sir," he exclaimed, as he stood beside

Mr Eagle, who had come to a halt on the approach of the other. "You will please see that a sharp look-out is kept for any sort of sail that may heave into view; and I trust to you to keep a sharp look-out yourself. When fairly clear of the Scillies, I may breathe with some ease."

"So far nothing's hove into sight, sir," said Mr Eagle.

"We have a pretty little breeze blowing," said Mr Lawrence, going to the side and looking over, "and we are under all plain sail. The wind's abeam and her speed is under six. Can she walk in strong weather?"

"She's done nine, sir, in my experience of her," answered Mr Eagle. "But it took half a gale of wind on the quarter to make her do it."

Mr Lawrence came from the ship's side, and said: "Pray continue your walk. I have something of importance to communicate to you," and he looked down into Mr Eagle's face with a curiously mingled expression of contempt, haughtiness and superiority. "It is not customary, I believe," he said, "in the Merchant Service for shipmasters to take their mates into their confidence. It is necessary, however, that I should communicate one or two facts to you in connection with this voyage. I presume you are not aware that Miss Lucy Acton is on board this ship?"

"I saw her come over the side, sir, but didn't know she had stopped," said the mate, with an expression which might have passed for incredulity in the sour, congenital curl of his lips.

"She remained on board, and is in my cabin, and I shall occupy the cabin which was fitted up professedly for a sick-bay."

"Miss Lucy Acton aboard this ship!" cried the mate, giving way to his amazement. "Well, I am truly astonished."

"I don't care a damn about your astonishment, Mr Eagle!" exclaimed Mr Lawrence with haughty severity. "I want you to understand that Miss Lucy Acton is on board this ship, and I desire that you will regulate your behaviour by thoroughly understanding the facts which I am going to do you the honour to impart."

Mr John Eagle made no answer.

"I first of all wish you to understand," continued Mr Lawrence, "that Miss Acton and I are in love with each other. We desire to be married. Captain Acton objects on the grounds of what I am forced to term my poverty; and certainly this quarter-deck would not know my tread if I were not poor. At the same time the greatest esteem and friendship exists between Captain Acton and myself, and his regard for me is sufficiently expressed by his placing me in command here. Do you follow me, sir?"

"I do, sir."

"Miss Acton and I agreed to elope. We found our opportunity in this vessel. This could only be done by contriving what the French call a ruse. It was to be assumed that her father had fallen ill in this ship whilst inspecting her early this morning, and the stratagem was to be carried out by his dictating a letter to me begging his daughter to come at once to the vessel. This she did, and she is now below. Do you understand me, Mr Eagle?"

"Oh yes, sir, I am a-following of you," answered the mate, with a face crippled in meaning by astonishment and by other sensations excited by this extraordinary story.

"Now," continued Mr Lawrence, still preserving his lofty, superior, rather over-bearing manner, as though he would heave Mr John Eagle overboard by scruff and breech if the fellow durst utter a syllable of offence, "it is arranged by Miss Acton and myself that she should feign that I have kidnapped her—sailed away with her, in short, against her will. This attitude we preconcerted, to rescue her from the accusation of having eloped, which might greatly prejudice her in the eyes of her father, and injure her future and fortune. When, therefore, you meet her, which you doubtless will, she will probably with the utmost passion, nay, even with tears in her eyes, declare that she has been torn from her home by a base artifice. And you'll understand, Mr Eagle, that her sighs, her statements, and her tears are merely tricks and parts of a play which has been carefully prearranged between the lady and myself. Do you understand, sir?" he added, looking stormily at his mean little companion from the altitude of his elegant and commanding figure.

"Why, yes, sir, course I do. But I never should ha' thought it. Why of all the young ladies—"

"I'm not asking you for any opinion, nor will any view that you can take concern me. You have the facts, and you will repeat them to the crew, to some of whom she may probably appeal, as indeed

I have advised, that her pretended situation may seem the more real, and Captain Acton by such evidence be more fully convinced. You and the crew will know what to think. It is simply a love affair and my own and the lady's business essentially," and he stopped in his quarterdeck walk, causing his companion to stop, and flamed threats from a pair of eyes as imperious as ever glared command upon another.

Mr Eagle looked as obedient as a quartermaster to instructions sternly delivered by a flogging captain.

"I have another matter to talk to you about," Mr Lawrence proceeded, "and on this head I have to request without the smallest qualification of what you must regard as my orders that you will preserve silence."

"I beg pardon," interrupted Mr Eagle, "but before you go on I should like to say that I am only mate of this ship and take no interest lyin' outside the sphere of my duties that don't consarn me."

"What I have to say," said Mr Lawrence, "will concern you—at least I think so. It will concern you very much indeed. Yesterday, Captain Acton placed in my hands sealed orders with strict instructions to summon all hands and to read the document to you and the men, but on no account to break the seal before the ship had arrived at latitude twenty degrees north, and longitude—about—for we never can be sure of that—thirty degrees west."

Mr Eagle's figure started as he walked. He knew his course to Kingston, Jamaica, as intimately well as you know your home when crossing from over the way to it. He ventured to stare at Mr Lawrence, who went on:

"The nature of these instructions I can only guess at from several conversations which I have had with Captain Acton, who without being in any degree specific, yet seemed to suffer me to read between the sentences of his conversation. And now, sir," said Mr Lawrence with great austerity, "this is the communication you will preserve strict silence upon until the sealed instructions are read. My belief is—understand me: I say that the idea I have arrived at from Captain Acton's conversation—is that I should carry this ship to a port that certainly is not Kingston nor is it in Jamaica, though I am unable to say more, and that he wishes this vessel to be handed over to the representative of a South American merchant who does business in London. What the port may be I am as curious as you undoubtedly now are to learn. I believe also that the whole of us from captain to boy will be paid off at this port and sent to England at Captain Acton's expense, and each man will receive treble the amount of the wages that he would have got for his voyage to Kingston and home. All this I infer from Captain Acton's language, and I may be violating his good faith in me in committing even these conjectures to the strict confidence which I am sure you will observe."

Various sensations were depicted in Mr Eagle's face as he listened. First he looked scared, then fierce by mere force of frown and enlargement of eyes, then sceptical with his sour, sneering mouth, then obstinate, sullen, mulish. He perfectly believed in the statement Mr Lawrence had made. Captain Acton, the owner, was a naval officer, and so was Mr Lawrence. They had agreed to abide in this matter of selling the ship and discharging the crew by a custom of their Service, namely, the sealed instructions.

A very short silence followed Mr Lawrence's delivery. Mr John Eagle then said: "You'll find, sir, that when the crew comes to larn that this voyage aint bein' made to Kingston, Jamaica, but to another place, they'll tarn to and refuse to work the ship, as their agreement was for Kingston and nowhere else."

"That will be mutiny. To refuse an order aboard ship is mutiny. In the Navy we hang men for that sort of conduct."

"Well, sir," said Mr Eagle, who uttered his convictions with the misgiving which fear of the listener excites, "my own opinion is that it wouldn't be reckoned as mutiny. It wouldn't be justice if it was called mutiny, and treated as mutiny. 'Taint the crew that breaks the agreement by refusing to do something which they never shipped to undertake, but the owner who gives 'em a job when at sea which they would have declined to hear of had they been told of it ashore. And I'm surprised," he continued, emboldened by Mr Lawrence's silence, "that Captain Acton, who is a gentleman born, and a man one could sarve all his life with satisfaction to himself and employer, should get rid of his ship and crew in such a fashion. But, perhaps,

set aside for the Captain, though as a matter of fact in Merchant vessels the Captain used to occupy almost invariably the aftermost starboard berth. It was plainly, but comfortably, furnished, the bedstead was like those ashore, and such as in former times Spanish ships chiefly were equipped with. It had a chest of drawers and a washstand in combination, and a table in the middle, at which sat Miss Lucy Acton. Her hands were clasped before her and rested on the table. She shot a swift glance under her beautiful eyelids at the incomer, then looked down upon her hands with a gaze which for motionlessness might have been riveted, though nothing was to be seen of her eyes under their lovely drooping clothing of lids and lashes. She was plainly dressed in a gown whose waist was just under her bosom. In some such a gown, or in some such attire she was wont of an early spring or summer morning to amuse herself in the flower gardens, or to take walks, occasionally remaining to breakfast at some poor neighbour's house. The only conspicuous feature of her apparel was a hat lately introduced from Paris and much affected by the fashionable ladies of London and other parts of this country. I speak of it as a hat: it was in truth a jockey-bonnet made of lilac-coloured silk decorated in front with a bunch of fancy flowers, and on top was a lace veil that hung gracefully down the back.

Mr Lawrence stood viewing her in silence for a few moments, and then approaching the table so that he stood close to her, he said in a voice of tenderness:

"Miss Acton—Lucy—my Lucy: for my Lucy you have ever been in my heart since the day when I asked you to be my wife, and you know—but you must believe—that my adoration of you then has not waned by a single ray of its brilliance—nay, the flame is greater and purer and more glowing than it was in that hour in which you refused my hand, not because you could not love me, nor because you believed the half of what had been told you about me, but because I was in too great a hurry. I had not given you time to find me out and love me as I believe, as I am sure you now do. Oh, my Lucy, this act of seeming treason against you will be forgiven. Your heart will acknowledge that violent as might seem the step I have taken, by no other could we have been brought together, and all the artifices and all the falsehoods I have been guilty of were, you will come to believe, the inspiration of such a love as few men ever felt for the women of their worship."

He knelt on one knee by her side and tried to take her hand. She started from her chair and recoiled some paces. On which he rose and stood towering in his figure and gazing at her, but with a face whose beauty could not have been more perfected than by the expression of the emotion of his heart.

Her native blush, which was one of the delightful features of her loveliness, had vanished: her face was colourless, and this uncommon pallor which one would have thought could only have visited her cheek in the day of dangerous sickness or in death, heightened the wonder, the depth, the power of her dark eyes, whilst those lids of hers which naturally drooped upon the loveliness they eclipsed in slumber, were raised till the vision she might have been said to pour in soft light upon her companion, looked unnatural and wild, the eyes of madness, the incommunicable gaze of any one sooner than the half-veiled, love-lighted sweetness of the orbs of Lucy Acton.

"I asked you when you first came in here to see me what you mean to do with me," she exclaimed in a voice so strained and high, so entirely lacking in its native music that her father, had she been unseen, would not have recognised the tones as his child's.

"And I answered, I will marry you," he replied.

"That is no answer, sir," she cried. "You have basely and cruelly stolen me from my home. I command you to return me to my father! Is this your gratitude for his goodness to you and the affectionate regard he has for Sir William Lawrence, who will be more shocked than even Captain Acton by your unnatural, ignoble, treacherous conduct? Home cannot be far, the ship has not sailed many miles. Return me at once, sir! Ships must be in sight, any one of which will put me ashore. If you detain me, if you carry me I know not where in the hope of my marrying you, you will drive me mad, as I nearly am mad now," and when she spoke these words, she delivered a wild, shrieking laugh, baring her teeth by such strenuous elongation of her lips as left them ashen; and the tragic quality of that ringing dreadful laugh was heightened by the absence of the faintest stroke of merriment in her features.

THE YARN OF OLD HARBOUR TOWN 145

"You are wrong, madam," he said, with an appearance of respect, and even of sympathy colouring the tender voice he employed. "There is no ship in sight. If there were she would probably prove an enemy's cruiser which must end my dream of happiness by our consignment to a French prison. You are in the hands of a man who loves you, who adores you, who is indeed taking his chance of the gibbet to win you. Trust in me. As my wife you shall be faithfully returned to your father, who will not condemn an action which merely anticipates the sanction I was looking forward to when he gave me command of this ship, and brought me by this stroke of goodness closer to you."

"You will return me," she said. "You are not in earnest. This is a bold and awful act of treachery attempted merely to test me. Marry you! Send me back to my father at once whilst my home is at hand, or you will discover that instead of having won a wife, you have driven a girl into a madhouse."

Her wild look, the extraordinary change by dramatisation of the eyes which she held in their soft brilliance fastened upon him, her raised, painful, indescribable voice, her attitude, the hue of her face, might well have suggested to him that her threat was no idle one, that being a young woman of exquisite sensibility she might be so wrought by his inhuman conduct as to lose her mind, her delicate intellect would stagger into madness under the cruel blow he had dealt her in the name of love.

"You are not likely to go mad," he said, smiling at her, and his handsome face with that smile lighting it up might have helped to conquer any woman, though betrayed into the imprisonment of a ship's cabin, and sailed away with into unknown regions, who in her heart of hearts felt towards this man as Lucy Acton did. But not in the way that Mr Lawrence had devised was the victory to be his.

"When am I to leave this ship?" she asked.

"Will you be seated?"

"No, sir. When am I to leave this ship?"

"You know, madam—Miss Acton—Lucy—my Lucy—that I am a man of broken fortunes. I have struggled hard to retrieve the past, but the world is full, and I have been unable to find room in it. You came in my way. I adored your beauty, and worshipped you for your character. You would not accept my hand, but I felt in my secret soul that I was not indifferent to you—nay, that if I could advance higher claims than those of a broken lieutenant and a man with the reputation of being a gambler and a drunkard, you would have listened to me, you would have consented. Nor would your father have objected, for he loves our service, and his partiality for Sir William would have helped me. I determined to win you, no matter the machinery I might set in motion. I was determined to escape the horrible trouble of bankruptcy, and the intolerable menace of a debtor's gaol, by carrying this ship to a port and there selling her and her cargo through the agency of a man who is known to me, and with the money thus got, I mean to pay off all my creditors in England, and return with you as my wife, assured of Captain Acton's forgiveness for your sake, and equally assured of his approval, as it is my intention to hoist the flag of honour as high as my father has mastheaded it, to be a gentleman, to live as a gentleman, and to be deemed by the part I hope to play in the drama of life, worthy of being the husband of Lucy Acton, and the son-in-law of her gallant, generous, noble-hearted father."

She listened to him with the immobility of a ship's figurehead. No astonishment at his extraordinary revelation of intention varied the expression of her face which remained as it was when she shrank from him. Truly a wonderful face, the face of an actress of supreme genius, the face of the inheretrix of the surprising, most excellent art of her mother, the famous Kitty O'Hara. Still did she keep bare her beautiful teeth, still did the tension through the elongation of her sweet lips hold them bloodless, her eyes had lost in their expression their lovely quality of brooding. They stared, and the stare was that of madness. Her colour was gone. Apparently this delicate, fascinating, lovable, gentle girl, possessed powers of will and intellect which dominated Nature herself in her; and even as it is known of some, that they have been capable of arresting the pulsation of their heart and yet live, so obviously in this lady was an influence, a passion, a very wizardry of determination, which suffered her to drive the blood from her cheek, to narrow the eyelid till the eye had lost its familiar seeking and dwelling look, till the mouth took the form that was to convey the intention of the artist.

Her only reply to his speech was (as though she had not attended to his meaning), "Are you going to keep me a prisoner in this cabin?"

"For a day or two only, madam," he answered, with his face flushed with disappointment, for he had hoped his candour would have produced a very different effect. "But I may tell you frankly that Mr Eagle and the crew know that you are on board, and I should have played my part ill had I not provided that nothing you can say, no entreaties that you can make, will persuade them that your elopement is not voluntary."

"Oh, sir, I had never thought you a villain!"

"You shall never find me one!" he cried with impetuosity. "But I am to win you, and will you tell me the poet or the philosopher who has ever spoken of the strategies employed in love as villainy?"

She continued to stare at him. Her figure still seemed to shrink as though in her first recoil when he tried to take her hand. Her face then suddenly underwent a change, her mouth relaxed what in homely features might have been called its wild grin; she frowned; her eyes took an unsettled look. There was something in her countenance that could hardly have failed to arrest the attention of any one who had a tolerable acquaintance with the insane. Mr Lawrence seemed to see nothing but Lucy Acton in her beauty.

"You have stolen me from my home, sir," she exclaimed in a piteous, almost whining voice, "and I am without clothes except the dress that I am wearing, and they will soon be in rags, which will flutter if I begin to dance."

"I am thankful to hear you speak of dancing. If ever your clothes should become rags and flutter to the measures of your feet, your beauty will still make them a finer garment, at least in my sight, than the apparel of royalty in state. But you shall not want for clothes," he said, speaking in his gentlest voice, which, as he held command over fine vocal powers that rendered him at the piano, or at any other instrument, a sweet and engaging and manly singer, would have been found soothing by any ear that had not Lucy Acton's to hear with. "Your dress will last you till our arrival, and then you shall have plenty; whatever your choice selects you may already call your own."

She delivered the same wild, screaming laugh which had before filled the cabin with its insane music, and said, dropping her note into one of plaintiveness, whilst she extended her skirt with both hands as though she was about to make a step or two in a dance: "Think of poor Lucy Acton in rags! Think of the lady who was notable, before a liar and a rogue stole her from her father, for her fine dresses and modish hats and bonnets; oh, think of her"—she paused to sigh deeply—"in rags, a prisoner in a ship owned by her father, who would kill the wretch that tore her from his side!"

And thus speaking she turned to the bulkhead, and putting her arm against it buried her face in her sleeve, and fell to sobbing so piteously that you would have thought her poor little heart was broken.

CHAPTER XI

PRINCESS TATTERS

MR LAWRENCE approached the figure of the young lady sobbing against the bulkhead, and placed his hand lightly upon her shoulder. She shook him off with a passionate convulsion of her whole form, which was full of disgust, aversion, and contemptuous wrath. It was a masterpiece of movement, eloquent in the highest possible degree of what she chose him to believe was in her mind. Her mother, Mrs Kitty O'Hara, had been famous for her artful strokes in this way. No actress surpassed her, and few were the equals of Mrs O'Hara in the remarkable gift of personification of passion by action.

Mr Lawrence drew back a step.

"Loving you as I do," he exclaimed softly, "loving me as I know you do, my dearest girl, my sweet mistress, the sole star of my desire, how must it grieve me to see you weeping, how much more that I am to think those tears flow through me? But I have faith in time, in the unconquerable quality of my love, and in the assurance of my soul, for though I have descended to artifice to enable me to win you, pure gem of your sex as you are, you do not despise me for my struggle. You recognise and approve an effort which has cost me many little pangs; for, dearest madam, my sweetest Lucy, 'tis all for love, and the world would be lost for me if you denied me, if I did not win you."

She stayed her sobbing to exclaim in the high, strained notes she had before spoken in: "Send me home, sir! send me back to my father! There are ships about. You speak falsely if you say there are no ships. We are still near my home. Do as I say before you drive me mad!"

She rounded from the bulkhead as she pronounced these words. Her eyes seemed to be on fire; her checks glowed. Again she bared her teeth in her wild, insane grin. She appeared transformed. He knew that certain violent and heart-changing passions and emotions could so work in a beautiful face as to make it look repulsive and devilish, such as jealousy or criminal insult, but he never could have believed of Lucy Acton that her loveliness could undergo the amazing transformation he witnessed; for he did not think to recall that her mother had been a great actress, and that this girl might have inherited perhaps the finest side of her genius.

"There is no ship, I assure you, madam. They have my instructions on deck to keep clear of any sail that heaves into sight, because I am not the man to allow my dream of happiness to be dissolved by a Frenchman's capture of this vessel. And what must we expect to find in these narrow waters but the ships of the enemy intent upon easy captures, bloodless prizes such as the *Minorca* would make?"

For answer she threw herself down upon the deck. She fell as though in a swoon, and lay motionless with her face buried once more in her arm that now reposed upon the carpeted planks. Her tears or sobs assured him that she had not fainted, and understanding that his wisest policy would be to leave her to her thoughts, he cast an adoring look upon the prostrate figure and quitted the cabin, slamming the door noisily after him that she might know he was gone, but silently turning the key outside, for it was not then his intention that she should go on deck and meet the crew until the statement he had made to Mr Eagle had passed in growling whispers through the men.

It was customary on board the *Minorca* and doubtless in many other ships carrying merchandise, for the mate to dine in the cabin with the captain in his watch below, that is to say, when he had no duty on deck. The second mate kept a look-out, and when the chief mate was done, the second went below to dinner. If the mate had the watch during the dinner-hour, he remained on deck until he was relieved by the captain.

The cabin dinner-hour on board the *Minorca* was one o'clock. When Mr Lawrence first met Mr Eagle, and perceived that he was little superior to a working hand before the mast, he had made up his mind to hold no intercourse with him outside the absolute requirements of the ship's routine. He had told him plainly that he desired to dine alone, and that when the mate's duty kept him on deck he, Mr Lawrence, would relieve him after he had finished his meal. This arrangement perhaps secretly pleased Mr Eagle, even on the spot when it was first named, for he easily witnessed in Mr Lawrence a man so out and away superior to himself that he judged he would feel like taking a great liberty every time he sat down with the master of the ship.

The dinner was served this day at one o'clock. The humpbacked steward brought the dishes aft from the galley or caboose, as the little cooking place used to be called. The ship had only just come out of port, and she had brought with her a stock of fresh provisions, meat, and vegetables, and the like, which would supply the cabin and the forecastle with fresh messes for some days. Mr Lawrence had also caused a couple of hen-coops to be filled with poultry.

In those times sailors lacked the addition of the harness cask and bread barge, to the bitter wooden beef and the coarse worm-eaten ship's biscuit which science and experience have contributed to the scurvy-making fare which seamen are obliged to eat. Yet a sort of provision was made to supplement the brine-hardened meat and the worms of the sailor's bread. The captain of a man-of-war, for instance, at sea, would breakfast on coffee, toast, potted beef and tongue, sliced à la Vauxhall. Whole legs of mutton were tinned.

Mr Lawrence sat down alone in the plain little cabin of the *Minorca* on this the first day of the vessel's sailing, and upon the table were placed by Paul a boiled fowl, a piece of boiled bacon, a round of cold fresh beef boiled, a dish of sausages, and two or three dishes of vegetables. Paul having already received instructions placed a tray furnished for a meal beside his master on the table; and Mr Lawrence cut some fowl and bacon, adding vegetables, and filled a small tumbler with red wine, and then, stepping to the door of the berth in which Lucy Acton was confined, he almost noiselessly inserted the key and softly shot the latch, and resumed his seat, and Paul, bearing the tray of food, knocked on the door, and receiving no reply entered, and the motion of the ship upon a long, steady heave of swell slammed the door to after him.

Mr Lawrence, with his back turned upon this cabin door, heard Lucy's voice, but not what she said. If Paul answered her his voice was so sunk by the awfulness of her presence, by all that she meant being at sea, by all that she had typified to this forlorn vagrant when on shore, that his accents were inaudible in the cabin.

After a few minutes he came out. He approached the cabin table and stood close. His face wore a mingled look of astonishment and fear, and he was very pale. He was as grotesque as something fanciful in a fairy story, with his red hair, hump, long arms, rounded legs, and whilst he stood he scratched himself as a monkey does. His chin was enormous, and out of all proportion to his face.

"Is Miss Acton eating her dinner?"

"No, sir."

"What did she say to you?"

"Why, your honour, when I went in she looked at me and burst into a laugh that turned my blood cold."

"She didn't know you to be the man that gave her the letter that brought her here?"

"She didn't look as if she remembered me, your honour, and she said nothing about it."

"What did she say?"

"Why, your honour, she says whilst I hold the tray, 'What are you?' 'I'm the ship's steward, your ledyship,' says I. 'Ay, but what else?' says she. 'What forest was you caught in?' I didn't understand her, sir, and didn't answer. 'Do you come from Africa?' says she, 'or have you broke loose from a travelling wild beast show?'"

Mr Lawrence arched his eyebrows. Certainly he did not recognise the sweet and sympathetic Lucy Acton in these questions.

"And then she says, frowning as though she'd up with a knife off the tray and run it into me, 'What have you got there?' 'Your dinner, your ledyship,' says I. 'Put it down upon the floor!' says she in a sort of shriek, as if she was trying to sing. 'Don't you see I'm in tatters? They've got me here who am a princess at home, and these are my rags and all I've got,' says she, spreading her dress with her hands as though she was goin' to skip. 'Beggars in rags feed on the floor: they feed so. Anywhere's good enough for them. I've seen 'em sitting on the edge of ditches eating. Put the food on the floor! That's how princesses in tatters dine.' I did as I was ordered, your honour, and came away."

"Go in presently and see if she's done, and ask if she'll have some fruit pie or cake, and report if the tray is still on the deck."

"Yes, sir," answered Paul, who was not sailor enough to say, "Ay, ay, sir," which should have been his speech.

Mr Lawrence was exceedingly thoughtful. What opinion he was arriving at, whether he was beginning to think that the girl was really mad or that she was merely acting with extravagant absurdity in the hope of disgusting him, you could not have told by looking at his face.

In about ten minutes after Paul had made his report, Mr Lawrence told him to knock on Miss Acton's cabin door and enter. This time the door swung to and fro, and Mr Lawrence, who had turned in his seat to follow the steward's movements, saw Miss Acton upon all fours upon the deck with her face close to the tray, as though she was taking up the food with her mouth. A swing of the vessel hove the door to its latch, and hid the extraordinary picture.

A minute or two later Paul came out, shutting the door after him.

"I saw her," said Mr Lawrence. "She is on her hands and knees. What did you say?"

"I asked her if she'd have some fruit pie or cake. She didn't look up nor answer. She's chucked most of what I took in about the cabin."

"She has made no meal, then?

"I couldn't tell, your honour. The piece of chicken is on the bed, and I see the piece of bacon under it. I dunno what she was doin' with her nose a-nuzzling of the tray as though she was a-smelling of the salt."

"Don't enter the cabin for half an hour. Then go in and clear up. And if she speaks, make no answer, and take no notice of her, but clean up the mess."

He left the table, and turned the key softly in Lucy's door, withdrew it, and went on deck. The breeze that had blown the *Minorca* out of Old Harbour still sang in her shrouds, but with a fresh and a stronger song. The sea ran in lines of brine which flashed friskily. The mountainous clouds sailed down the blue heavens with the solemn majesty of line-of-battle ships draped in sun-empearled cloth from truck to waterway. The bluff-bowed barque was darting foam from her to right and left as she thrust through the streaming waters and rolled with dignity, slowly to leeward and yet more slowly to windward as she brought the violet shadowed cavities of her canvas to the wind. The hens were noisy in their coops, and cocks crew. The sound of waters broken and in motion was musical. The shadows of the rigging slided gently to and fro over the wide breadth of white planks. The men in the picturesque garb of the merchant sailor of that day, some of them in striped pantaloons flowing to the shoe, some in short-cut blue jackets, and most of them in round hats, were distributed over several parts of the ship. Mr Eagle walked the weather side of the quarterdeck. In reply to Mr Lawrence's question, he said that nothing had been in sight and nothing was in sight. This Mr Lawrence verified by a searching sweep of his gaze round the horizon, and Mr Eagle went below into the cabin to eat his dinner.

When he was there he bade Paul go forward and tell Mr Pledge that dinner awaited him. This privilege was Pledge's because, though he was the ship's boatswain and also her carpenter, he kept watch and headed the starboard division of the crew as second mate.

He was a tall, lank man, rather knock-kneed, with a long neck, and, which was very unusual in those days, his chin was garnished with a quantity of straggling reddish hair. His face looked as though it had been put together without much judgment. His nose, which was broken, was not in line; his mouth was somewhat on one side, one eyebrow was raised and the other depressed. His eyes were small, of a deep, moist, soft blue. He had served in the American Navy, and had much to tell about Yankee captains and commodores. He was dressed in the garb of the common sailor, and it is not wonderful that Mr Lawrence should decline to meet him at table, which, if it did not make their footing equal, must bring them into relations the fastidious, haughty, handsome naval officer would regard in an uncommon degree objectionable.

He entered the cabin and took his place. Mr Eagle at the foot of the table carved the boiled beef. When they were fairly under way with their dinner Paul went forward, and the two men were alone in the cabin, out of hearing of Mr Lawrence's ears through the open skylight if they suppressed their voices, equally out of hearing of the inmate, under lock and key, of the captain's cabin.

Though Mr Lawrence had communicated the intelligence of the girl being on board and of his holding sealed orders from Captain Acton in confidence to Mr Eagle, the sensations excited in this plain and acid sailor by the extraordinary, astounding, and unexpected revelations had filled him to bursting point with a fever and passion for giving the news. In short, the man's mind was much too small to retain what had been poured into it, and of course it overflowed. To whom other than Tom Pledge could he speak? Pledge and he had sailed in Captain Acton's employ for two or three voyages; they were friends, and visited each other ashore where each had a little cottage and a wife. So after a careful survey of the skylight, which lay open just above the table, and a cautious look round, Mr Eagle said: "Tom, did you observe me and the Capt'n walkin' up and down this morning in conversation.?"

"Ay," answered Pledge, "and I wondered what there was between ye to keep ye so busy in talk."

Mr Eagle again looked up at the skylight, and said as softly as his gruff voice permitted: "What d'ye think, Tom, of our sailin' under sealed orders from Captain Acton which the Captain's to read in latitood twenty north and longitood thirty west? The contents of them sealed orders aren't exactly known to the Capt'n, but he told me from what Capt'n Acton let fall, he believed that the ship was to be carried to another port, and there handed over to a Spanish gent as was a-waitin' to receive her, and that the whole ship's company was to be discharged and sent 'ome at Captain Acton's expense and the wages they had agreed for trebled. What d'ye say to that?"

Pledge, who chewed slowly as a cow the cud, watched his companion steadfastly, his temples throbbing with the action of his jaws, and said: "Do you believe it, John?"

"So help me God, yes, then, as I sit here," answered Mr Eagle.

"Who is to work the ship for him?" asked Pledge. "For you may depend upon it that if the crew are to be carried away to an unbeknown place, they'll all go below to a man, for Jack's as good as his master when it comes to his having to do something which he didn't agree for."

"I put it as you do, though in different words," said Mr Eagle, "and he answered that Captain Acton's orders must be obeyed, that the crew's refusal would be mutiny, and that if they wouldn't work the ship to a port, where he could ship a fresh crew, he'd heave a-back the main-topsail yard and wait for a man-o'-war to come along."

"Well, I'm jiggered!" said Mr Pledge, now looking slightly startled, for he was an old sailor, he well understood the despotic powers of the captain of a ship, and he readily perceived that Mr Lawrence's threats in case of refusal by the crew were to be carried out.

"But that's not all," continued Mr Eagle, with another glance at the skylight. "It ain't 'arf all, and I think you'll agree with me that the rummiest part's got to come."

"Another slice, John!" said Pledge, pushing his plate, and cutting a big chunk from a loaf.

"Who d'ye think's aboard?"

"Who?"

"Why, Captain Acton's daughter, Miss Lucy Acton!"

"What's she a-doing' of *here?*" enquired Pledge, pulling away his plate heavy with meat and fat.

"She's a-running away with Mr Lawrence!"

"Or is Mr Lawrence a-running away with *her?*"

"According to his yarn," said Eagle with sour solemnity, "they've rooned away with each other."

"Where is she?" asked Pledge.

Eagle dumbly pointed to the Captain's cabin. "It's an artfully laid plot," said he, "if the Capt'n's to be believed. She's supposed to he locked up agin her will. By-and-by she's to go among the sailors and swear that she's been carried off by violence. This is to make her father believe that she never consented to run away, as she don't want to lose the fortune as 'ud otherwise come to her."

"Wasn't there some talk a bit of a time past of him a-courting of her?" said Pledge.

"Why, yes, now that you remind me, I recollect."

"Well, John," said Pledge, "it's not for me nor the likes of me to interfere in such a galavantin' job as this. If the young lady's been run away with with her own consent, it's not for me, I says, to pay any attention to what's 'appening. People who fall in love with each other and are objected to by their relatives will sometimes carry on their business in a way as might make pious, respectable old pari-ents feel their hair standing short up on their heads. I've lived long enough in this 'ere world to descover that no good ever comes to a man by messing about in other people's consarns. But when it comes to this ship being navigated to another port than the one agreed for, why, naturally you set me a-thinking, John. I don't know nothing about them sealed orders you refer to, but it seemed strange to me when I heard of it, and it's strange to me still, that Mr Lawrence should have been chosen to command this vessel when the berth was yourn by right of sarvice. Was it because Captain Acton couldn't be sure of your a-executing his wishes? What d'ye think yourself, John? You've got to consider it's two naval officers acting together; they know each other's mind, and I guess that when Captain Acton chose Mr Lawrence to take charge of his ship he knew that he was in the 'ands of a man who'd listen to no talk, who was used to man-o'-war's discipline, and would act if it came to having to shoot men down so as to gain his ends."

Mr Eagle, whose views were undoubtedly in accord with Mr Pledge's, viewed his companion in acid silence.

Just about this time the steward Paul came down the companion steps with the cabin key which he had received from Mr Lawrence. He took no notice of the two men seated at the table, but stepped to Lucy's door, knocked, paused, inserted the key, and passed in. He emerged in less than two minutes holding the tray that was covered literally with broken victuals, and locking the door was about to step up the companion ladder when Mr Pledge said: "Who've you got locked up in that there cabin?"

"You must ask the Captain that, sir, if you want to know," Paul answered.

"You dog! D'ye know I'm second mate? Answer me, or I'll flay ye before sundown," said Pledge, turning scarlet.

"I durs'nt," whined Paul. "I've the Captain's orders to keep my mouth shut," and he hastened up the steps.

He was followed by Mr Eagle, who thought it about time to relieve the Captain.

Mr Pledge had eaten his last morsel of cheese and was leaving the table, when his attention was arrested by a knocking on Lucy's door, accompanied by the cries of a female; but what she said he could not hear. So Mr Pledge, taking some steps, stood close to the door.

The voice of Lucy within cried out: "Is anybody there?"

"I'm here, ma'am," answered Pledge.

"Who are you?"

"I'm Thomas Pledge, acting second mate of this 'ere ship, ma'am."

"Open this door!"

"I can't, ma'am, it's locked," and in proof of his assurance, Pledge turned the handle and shook the door.

"I demand to be set at liberty!" cried Lucy, in the strained, wild voice that had frightened the hunchback steward. "The villain who commands this ship lured me into her by pretending that Captain Acton, who is my father and the owner of the vessel, lay seriously injured through an accident, and wished to see me. I demand to be returned to my home! I have been stolen away by a base artifice. The crew of this ship are the servants of my father, and they would know his wish must be to recover me, and your duty, and Mr Eagle's, and the men's, is to turn the ship for Old Harbour, and surrender me up to my father. If this is not done I shall go mad. I am mad now. The wretch who by a lie has seduced me into this vessel, has driven me crazy."

And with that she fell to singing, from which she broke off after a few moments to burst into a shrieking, lunatic laugh.

Thomas Pledge's mind was of a very common order. He had gathered from Eagle that the girl was to pretend a situation of acute distress, that when she was married her father should not hold her responsible for her elopement. Her words might have carried weight, and even conviction, but for the song and loud unmeaning laugh that closed them, in which Mr Pledge saw nothing but acting, not having experience of insanity in any shape or form. And shouting through the door, "I'll go and report to the Captain, ma'am, that you're locked up and want to get out," he turned, with the intention of making for the companion ladder, when he saw Mr Lawrence standing a few paces abaft the steps, tall, stern, frowning, his face fierce with the strain, and indeed almost fury, of the attention with which he had bent his ears to catch the syllables of Lucy through the bulkhead.

Mr Pledge started like a guilty thing surprised.

"What are you doing at that cabin door, sir?" asked Mr Lawrence. "I do not enquire what you are doing in this cabin, for, according to the custom of this ship, and perhaps of others in your Service, you take your meals here. But what are you doing at that door, conversing through it with the lady inside?"

"The lady thumped and I went to see what was the matter, sir," said Mr Pledge, awed in his old man-o'-war instincts by the overbearing, I may say, the overwhelming demeanour of Mr Lawrence, which was to his words as the thunder of the explosion is to the message of the firearm.

"Has Mr Eagle been talking to you about the subject of our conversation this morning?" said Mr Lawrence.

Now, Tom was too sound a shipmate to betray John. He answered doggedly, as though Mr Lawrence as well as himself must be aware that he was trespassing on ground he had no right to tread: "We yarned of course together. We've sailed together afore, and can always find something to talk about, sir."

Mr Lawrence seemed to read the man's thoughts. Unscrupulous as was this Naval gentleman, he was an extremely clever fellow. Preserving a severe austerity of countenance, a demeanour upon which the word discipline was writ large, he exclaimed: "It is not my intention to ask you if Mr Eagle has broken his faith with me and communicated to you the confidence I imparted to him this morning. You are, sir, by virtue of your rank aboard the ship free of this cabin, and it is therefore desirable that I should trust you. The lady in yonder berth is Miss Lucy Acton, who consented to elope with me, providing it should be understood by all on board that she was being kidnapped or stolen from her home. That this should appear, it was arranged between us that she should be locked up as though she were a prisoner, and then in a day or two I should enlarge her, and she would go amongst the crew and speak of my cunning and stratagem, and her desperate lot in being torn from her father's home. All which would in due course reach her father's ears, and mollify his wrath at her giving me her hand in the existing state of my fortunes, and preserve to her the fortune she must inherit as Captain Acton's only child. Now, sir," continued Mr Lawrence in his frowning, imperious way, "this is submitted to you in confidence, and it is manifestly my wish that some of the crew should credit her story that they may give the evidence we desire when they are called upon to tell what they know!"

"Well, sir," answered Mr Pledge, pleased by the skipper's candour and condescension, "it's not for a plain sailor man like me to put his hand into such a tar-bucket as this. I know my bit, and I'm a-willing for to do it, and if the hands get to hear the story of the lady it'll come from her or from that there humpbacked steward who waits upon her, and not from me, for I'm for minding my own affairs, and sticking like a barnacle to a ship's bottom to the ondertakings I enter into."

He said this with a grave nod of the head, that the significance of the closing passage of his speech might be mastered, for it was then running through his mind that more lay behind the presence of Lucy Acton on board than Mr Lawrence suspected he knew: by which he referred to the sealed orders.

Mr Lawrence made no answer, and Mr Pledge seeing that he was to go, went on deck by the only exit, namely, the companion ladder. Immediately after he had passed through the hatch the steward Paul descended.

"Did you clear away the mess from Miss Acton's berth?" asked Mr Lawrence.

"Yes, sir."

"The lady, I presume, ate nothing?"

"I couldn't see that she had, your honour."

"When you have cleared this table, go forward and tell the cook to cut a plate of the most delicate beef and chicken sandwiches he can contrive. Get a bottle of red wine and a glass, and be ready to carry the refreshments to the lady when I've left her."

He approached Miss Acton's door. Lucy was seated on a locker under a window, three of which embellished the stern of the *Minorca*. The ocean as the ship lightly depressed her stern, was visible through this window, a blue field decked with flowers of foam that rose and sank. The large glazed space filled the cabin with light, which trembled with the pulse of the white wake streaming fanwise, and with the shivering of the sunlight into splinters of diamond brilliance by the fretful motions of the breeze-brushed waters.

Miss Lucy Acton sat with her eyes veiled by downcast lids fixed in a stare as lifeless as the dead upon her hands, which lay clasped in her lap. So motionless was she, you would have said she slept. Much of the lovely bloom that always gave to her lineaments a choice sweetness was absent, but not the less did as much of her face as was visible express its refined and delicate beauty.

When Mr Lawrence entered she did not raise her eyes, nor whilst he stood looking at her did she discover by any sort of movement the least knowledge of his presence.

"Lucy!" he said, speaking the word in the wooing voice of love.

She made no sign. He repeated her name as though startled by her immobility in which an element of tragedy might have been found in the singular, unwinking fixity of her stare upon her hands. He stepped to her side, and peered closely into her face and listened to hear if she breathed. Oh yes: she breathed, she was alive. But though he put his face so close to hers that she might have felt his breath upon her check, her form did not move by so much as might indicate the passage of a thrill, her eyes remained as steadfast in their gaze as though they were painted.

He withdrew a step, and exclaimed: "Lucy, why will you not speak to me? Why will you not look at me? You know that all this is done in the holy name of love, and God who knows me knows that I would not cause you a pang, that your beautiful eyes should not be shadowed by a tear drawn by any action of mine if I could have believed that loving me as I know you do, that loving you as you know I do, you would have come to me at the summons of my passion, and hand in hand with me as my wife, taken your chance of all that might have followed."

The emotion of an impassioned heart, the melody of a rich and manly voice were in his words, and no man, though he should hate the fellow for his wrong-doing, could have doubted his sincerity whilst listening to his speech. Add to this his superb figure, his handsome face glowing with feeling, the hereditary dignity of his demeanour; but these were expressions of his meaning which she would not raise her eyes to witness.

All on a sudden and when the silence that followed had not lasted ten seconds, she sprang to her feet with a shriek; she dashed her hands to her face, she rushed as though pursued to the other end of the cabin, and there crouched with her face, to the bulkhead, hidden in her hands; and thus she stood rocking herself sideways, moaning: "Why am I not sent home? Why am I here a prisoner? What will my father think has become of me? Home, home, home! In the hands of a man that dare rob his employer! At the mercy of one who of all Captain Acton's friends and acquaintances should feel the most deeply obliged to him." She wheeled round and out of her incommunicable attitude and language of distress, and said, looking at him vacantly with a cold, pale smile: "Are you Mr Lawrence, the son of Sir William Lawrence, Captain Acton's friend?"

"You know, madam, that I am," he answered, bowing with graceful suavity, and with a light smile that was like saying, "I understand the import of your tactics, and am willing to wait and watch you."

"I know, sir," she exclaimed with the vehement indignation and contempt conveyed by that perfection of art which conceals art and which is a gift of intuition beyond the reach of those not born with it, "that Sir William Lawrence has a son, and that he was dismissed from the Navy for a brutal, drunken outrage of which he alone, of all the gentlemen and officers in the Service, was capable."

He coloured brightly at this, and his frown was as though a shadow had come between him and the light that revealed his face.

"I know," she continued, still preserving her accent of scorn and viewing him with eyes that did not seem to be hers, so did she contrive to diminish the breadth of the beauty of the lids, so did she manage to look passions and feelings which the memory of her oldest friend could never have recalled as vitalising her brooding, half-hooded gaze: "I know that this man came ashore and lived upon his father who was poor, and drank and gambled until his name provoked nothing but a shrug, and that one day in a fit of pity, for which doubtless he has asked God's pardon, Captain Acton, who loves Admiral Lawrence, gave his poor creature of a son command of a ship. This I know," she said, letting her eyes fall suddenly from his face down upon her fingers which she seemed to count as she proceeded. "But I had always supposed that there was some spirit of goodness left in Mr Walter Lawrence. I believed that though he might gamble and drink and live in idleness upon the bounty of his father, he with all his imperfections was a man incapable of outraging the feelings of a young girl, incapable of betraying the generous confidence of one who stood to him as a warm-hearted friend. Can you be that Mr Lawrence?" she said, peering at him in such a peculiar fashion, with such archness of contempt that a spectator, short-sighted and at a little distance, would have supposed she was looking at the handsome fellow through an eye-glass. "Oh, I am going mad to suppose it—mad to think it possible!"

She flashed her hands to her forehead, sobs seemed to shake her, she turned on her heel and went to the big stern window, and looked out upon the sea.

He seemed to have been struck dumb by the fury of her candour. His teeth were fastened upon his under lip, his cheek had grown pale.

"Will you leave this cabin," she said without turning, "and acquaint the first ship you meet with that you have a young gentlewoman on board who desires to be set ashore in England? I do not ask you," she continued, with the cutting sneer that was on her lip as plain in her voice as though her face was visible to him, "to return this ship and her contents to their lawful owner. But if you suppose that you are going to gain me by keeping me a prisoner in this den, if you imagine that all the horror which my soul can feel for a wicked, unscrupulous man is not likely to be with me in all thoughts of you that come to me with your presence, or fill me with madness when I am alone, then better for you if you should go to the stack of muskets which is in the cabin, load one and shoot yourself."

And clapping her hands as though she was in the box of a theatre ravished by some transcendently fine performance, she once more delivered herself of the maniac laugh which had curdled Paul's blood and which though ringing from lips, though proceeding from a face hidden from him, seemed to strike Mr Lawrence as nothing which she had spoken had, and save but for the swaying of the ship he stood as motionless as a statue facing another statue whose back was turned to him.

CHAPTER XII

MR LAWRENCE REFLECTS

WHEN MR LAWRENCE found that nothing he could say, nothing he could implore, nothing he could entreat his companion to forgive provoked Lucy into looking round from the window through which she gazed at the sea, nor caused her to alter her posture, which curiously suggested with dramatic art that she was alone, that the man was gone, that she was engrossed by thoughts of her own, he withdrew. After closing the door he seemed to hesitate over turning the key, but turned it nevertheless and pocketed it as before.

The cabin was empty. Mr Pledge was again superintending work forward. Mr Eagle kept the look-out. This was the ship's first day from home. The watches had not been set, and it would be "all hands" with the ship's company until the second dogwatch came round. The vessel swayed on the heave of the swell with the ponderosity you would have looked for in one of her mould. She creaked in every timber. She pitched rapidly, albeit the blue afternoon hollow was very shallow, but the sullenness of the sturdy round bows was in her longwise motion. If Lucy meant to be sea-sick she was neglecting her chance, for here was movement more fitted to discompose the land-going stomach than the lofty billow that is swung by the storm. But so far this sweet and amazing young lady had proved herself as good a sailor as Mr Lawrence himself.

Whilst he stood in reflection at the cabin table, the steward Paul came down the steps bearing a tray of refreshments so prettily decorated as to prove that the ship's cook had been chosen with judgment. The pyramid of sandwiches might have kindled a light in the dulled eye of one lying oppressed with nausea. In addition were a plate of cold tongue, a small plate of brawn, with two or three other delicacies. On the tray stood a bottle of red wine and a tumbler. Mr Lawrence told Paul, handing him the key as he gave him the directions, to take the tray to Miss Acton, place it on the table in perfect silence, and quit the cabin, making no answer if she spoke to him. When this was done and the key received by Mr Lawrence, he took a tumbler from a rack out of the skylight and entered the berth which under the name of "sick-bay" had been fitted up for his own use. Here he contrived to find a bottle of brandy, a small caulker of which without water he swallowed.

This interior presented a very inhospitable look; its rough-hewn bunks might have been intended for the accommodation of prisoners. The deck was without carpet. Indeed the only colour or warmth which this melancholy hole presented to the eye or the mind was to be found in such wearing apparel as swung from hooks, in Mr Lawrence's sea-chest, in the nautical instruments, in the shelves with their little burden of tin box, a few books, and so forth.

He sat down upon his chest, folded his arms and sank into thought. Had he needed a motto for his reflections he might have found one in the Duke of Gloster's speech:

"Was ever woman in this humour woo'd?
Was ever woman in this humour won?"

He had been so transported by his scheme for winning the beautiful young girl whom he worshipped that his survey of the vast canvas of his intentions was in reality restricted to but one corner of it, so that he saw only a little of the whole truth. First, and certainly foremost, he had counted upon her love for him, which, however carefully the secret might have been kept by her, was witnessed by him every time they had met, and flourished as a conviction in him. He had looked for her forgiveness for the rashness, and, it may be added, the cruelty of his conspiracy of love, and he never could have believed that in the sweet image of the girl dwelt such a character as she had exhibited since, after inveigling her on board into his cabin, he confessed that the story which had brought her to him was a lie, and with a face filled with the light of worship for her avowed his intentions.

In some strokes of this character he might have indeed believed that she was merely acting, but other features had impressed him to such a degree that, though he was determined—not yet, perhaps—to accept the suspicion, or the persuasion of his own opinion, he, behind the darkest curtains of his heart, felt a fear that his stratagem would force her reason from her brain, that she would go mad when she clearly understood that the ship was bound to Rio to be feloniously sold there, when she realised that she had been ruthlessly torn from her father, from her home, and all that she loved, and that her name must ever bear the stain, happen what might, of Mr Lawrence's ignoble feat of abduction.

But as a rule men who act with excessive imprudence are endowed with a quality of self-complacency which enables them to persuade themselves that "it's all right," and to this belief they cling until time and experiment prove that it's all wrong; whereupon their moral being falls to pieces, they become mean, cheap, and weak, and bewail their folly under the name of misfortune.

Mr Lawrence having meditated awhile, rose from his chest, unclasped his arms, and whistling softly the familiar air of "Wapping Old Stairs," quitted his naked, forlorn, inhospitable berth.

As he advanced towards the companion steps the hatch was darkened by the figure of Mr Eagle, who, on catching sight of the Captain, cried: "A sail broad on the larboard bow, sir!"

Mr Lawrence rushed back to his cabin, whence he took from a shelf a telescope of uncommon power for those times, the gift of no less a man than Captain Acton after intelligence had been brought to him of a particular heroic piece of behaviour on the part of Mr

Lawrence. With this telescope he sprang on to the deck, and levelling it at the sea over the lee bow, viewed in the lenses the picture of a large man-of-war with two white bands broken by gun-ports. She was far away, yet not so distant but that a hand's breadth of her black side could be seen shivering in mirage betwixt the lower white band and the wool-white tremble of water running aft. All the men of the *Minorca* were on deck at work here and there. They looked at Mr Lawrence as with levelled telescope he stood on the quarterdeck viewing the distant battleship. They all belonged to Old Harbour Town; all had heard of him, and a few knew him by sight. They were members of a group of inhabitants who felt that the presence amongst them of a man whose sea story though brief was brilliant did them and Old Harbour Town honour, and they regarded him as he stood with the glass at his eye, as though they should say, "Yon's a man-o'-war, and she may be a Johnny; but there's the Jack who will know what to do with her." And, may be, some of those who thus reflected cast their eyes upon the figure of Mr Eagle, who stood near enough to the Captain to enable the sight to master the details of a very striking contrast.

"Hoist the ensign!" exclaimed Mr Lawrence.

Mr Eagle, breaking into a run, sent aloft at the peak of the barque the meteor flag of Old England.

"British!" said Mr Lawrence in a moment, as though speaking to himself, "as I thought," holding the man-o'-war in view in his telescope, and marking the slow soaring of the British flag to the gaff-end of the two-decker.

The Captain's exclamation had been overheard, and the gaze of the Merchant seamen of the *Minorca* was fixed upon the figure of one of those fabrics which could never light up with their cloud of sail the confines of the sea or the nearer fields of water, without exciting a thrill of interest or causing the heart to leap up in momentary transport of patriotic pride. She was under fore and mizzen jury topmasts. With the main all was well, and the spars lifted their canvas to the moon-like royal without hint of wreck or suggestion of wound. Either she had been in action and had come away crippled, or had been in trouble on a lee-shore or amongst rocks. And still she painted a stately and a swelling picture upon the blue sky past her, The sun was westering; his yellow light flung upon the distant canvas the delicate sheen of fine silk. From the hand's breadth of black side under the lower white band, the stately roll to leeward flashed lightning-sparks from the wet, and, as she slightly pitched, the upheaval of her bows exhibited at the fore-foot the snow-like crumbling of foam. She passed in grandeur and in tranquillity.

All the hearts aboard the *Minorca*, British as they were, must wish that that gallant show might not fall in with something superior to herself in weight of broadside and perfect in equipment aloft. Though every man felt that the sequel of such a rencountre must be the inevitable one: that is the sailing of the jury-rigged two-decker in company with a powerful prize both bound, let us suppose, for the sweet and lovely waters of Plymouth Haven.

Mr Eagle approached Mr Lawrence, who turned upon him suddenly.

"The sails of that ship," cried the Captain, "must have been in sight some time before you reported her. When I came on deck she was hull up. Is this your idea of keeping a look-out?"

"I reported her as soon as I saw her, sir."

"Wasn't she reported from the masthead?"

"Yes, sir, and then I saw her and reported her to you."

"And this is the way that a look-out is to be kept aboard this ship," said Mr Lawrence with a biting insolence of scorn, and that sort of pity which enrages more than kicks or execrations. "If you don't hold to the instructions you receive from me, sir, you'll soon find yourself eating black bread in a French dungeon with straw from a sty for a bed."

He made a step to the ship's side, and the mate without answer slunk away to leeward.

About this time the breeze began to freshen. The horizon slightly thickened with some windy change in the atmosphere and with the shadow of the evening. The *Minorca* under all plain sail heeled into the white smother of spume alongside, and as she sprang crushed the surge with her round weather-bow till the bright brine sometimes leapt like a fountain athwart the forecastle. Mr Lawrence watched her behaviour with attention, and often sent a look at the creaming road of wake which was so brilliant and long that, as the shadow deepened, the tail of it was lost to view.

In the second dog-watch the crew were mustered aft and divided into watches. It was tolerably certain that down to this moment no hint had found its way amongst them that their course would presently be for any other port in the world than Kingston.

Mr Lawrence supped alone as he had dined alone, and, as he intended, to breakfast alone. At sea the last meal which in the old forecastle days consisted of black tea and ship's biscuit was invariably called supper. At six o'clock Mr Lawrence sat down to the last meal of the day. A tray for the inmate of the Captain's cabin was prepared. It was furnished with tea and milk (for the ship was but one day out, and though she wanted a cow she could not need at least a day's supply of milk), bread and butter, slices of ham and biscuits. When the steward came from the cabin Mr Lawrence said: "Did the young lady speak?"

"No, sir."

"What is she doing?"

"She is pulling feathers and other stuff out of her bed which she has drawed from its place on to the deck, and she is sitting alongside of it a-fluffing of the feathers over the cabin floor."

"Did she look at you when you entered?"

"She didn't seem as if she even saw me, your honour."

"Has she eaten anything, can you tell me?"

"When I fetched her tray last time, sir, I noticed that some sandwiches and tongue was gone, and there was a little red wine in the bottom of the tumbler, as though she had drunk some and left a drop."

"She has ripped up her mattress and is throwing the inside of it round about her!" Mr Lawrence frowned, pursed his lip, and stared upon the deck with a strange admixture of gloom and anger.

In truth there had come into his mind the remembrance of a person who had fallen mad, and amongst the earliest indications of his insanity was his tendency to tear up everything that would yield to the power of his fingers, including his clothes.

"By-and-by," said he, "go in and clear the mess up. Take no notice of her, nor heed her if she speaks. Then fetch the mattress from the upper bunk in my cabin and place it on her bedstead."

He finished his supper in a very gloomy mood. His character has been imperfectly drawn if it leaves upon the reader the impression that he was no more than a gallant, handsome, hectoring scoundrel, a drunkard, a liar, and a gambler. He was more than this, and better than this. In him was a very great deal of honest, sturdy, British human nature, and amongst those who saw the white skin of his character peeping through the rags and tatters of his morals was the young lady whom he had locked up in his cabin. Was he driving, had he driven her mad? This was an awful thought to him, a figure, a presentment on the canvas of his scheme which his utmost imagination never could have painted. He was passionately fond of her. In truth he was risking his neck to win her. His inmost sensibility as a man and as a gentleman was in perpetual posture of recoil over the reflection that his hand it was that had made this gently nurtured, beautiful, adorable girl a prisoner in a little ship that was rolling to a port in which she was to be fraudulently sold. He thought of her in the lovely drawing-room of Old Harbour House: the soft illumination of wax lights; the sweet incense of flowers; the piano whose keys were accompanied by her own melodious warblings; her little dog; all the comforts and luxuries which wealth could provide her with; all that a tender-hearted and loving father could endow his only child whom he loved with. And then he thought of her torn from all this pleasantness and sweetness and elegance, so robed that in a short period she must become beggarly to the eye; after her father's hospitable and plentiful table, fed with the poor fare of a common little ship.

For some time after he had closed his knife and fork he sat at table shading and supporting his forehead with his hand, his elbow resting, and deep thought was in his attitude. To one who knew his story he submitted a picture for memory to cherish. Night was near, though not yet come, but its shadow was upon the ship, and three or four stars like little balls of quicksilver ran to and fro athwart the gleaming black panes of the skylight glass. The hum of a steady breeze in the stout shrouds, in the cat-harpings, in the drumming hollow of many sails sounded like the strains of an organ muffled to the ear by the walls of the church that holds it. The low thunder of the surge washing past the ship was as constant as its

accompaniment of the concert of creakings, jarrings, shocks in bulkhead, rudder-post and strong fastenings.

Mr Lawrence started suddenly, stood up, looked round him, and
viewed steadfastly for a space Lucy's cabin door. Then muttering to
himself, "To-morrow—to-morrow!" he made his way towards the
deck.

He had half mounted the cabin ladder when he was brought to
a stand by a sound of voices, of men speaking hard by the companion-way.

"What beats all my goin' a-fishing," said Mr Thomas Pledge in a
voice which, in spite of its being subdued, and in spite of the noises
of the wind aloft, and of waters washing along the bends yearning
and seething, was distinctly audible to Mr Lawrence as he stood in
the shelter of the companion-way, "is this: this 'ere ship belongs to
Captain Acton. His purchase of her was square and above-board. Why
should he go behind his own back, in a manner of speaking, and
put a man that was an officer in the Royal Navy in charge to carry
her to a port, and sell her by stealth, as though she was a piece of
plunder, and the officer in charge ordered to 'and her over to a
fence, which, John, as of course you know, is the vulgar name for a
man as receives stolen goods? Why is the crew kept in ignorance
of Captain Acton's intention? There's no 'arm in a man a-selling of
his own property. But I says there is a good deal of 'arm in a man
deceiving of sailors for making them an offer to do something which
he don't rightfully explain, and which they'd decline to undertake
if they'd been told the nature of it."

"In all what you say I agree with you, Tom," answered Mr Eagle,
"and I should have thought that Captain Acton was the last man on
this earth to have behaved himself in such a way. For my part I have
always found him so straightforward that the needle ain't truer to
the Pole than he is to his rightful and honourable meaning."

"Ay," said Pledge, "but don't you forget that the needle swings, and
leaves the Polar mark points off."

"But he swings back again," said Mr Eagle, "and is true as God's
law allows him to be in every atom of steel that goes to the making of him. Have you talked at all forrards about this here matter?"

"Not yet," was the reply.

"Well," said Mr Eagle, "I'm for leaving these 'ere coils on the pin until the time comes for chucking the fakes down and lettin' go, by which I mean I'm for waitin' until the Capt'n calls the 'ands aft and reads to 'em the sealed orders he told me about. It'll be time enough to speak up when we know what Captain Acton's instructions to him are."

"You may be right," said Pledge, "but I should oncommonly like to larn what old Jim is a-going to say to this 'ere traverse." Meaning by old Jim the oldest hand forward, and one who had served Captain Acton ever since that retired Naval officer had commenced shipowning.

At this point Mr Lawrence, who judged that as much had been said as was likely to interest him, put his foot over the coaming and passed on to the deck, walking, without heeding the presence of the two men, to the binnacle stand. He inspected the compass, and then looked along the deck. Only one figure was now visible, and he had started to stump the planks in the true deep-sea look-out fashion.

It was, of course, as Mr Lawrence had foreseen. Eagle had betrayed Mr Lawrence's confidence, and Pledge manifestly was thirsty to carry the report into the forecastle. As this was a part of Mr Lawrence's programme his mind made no other comment upon it than that he was pleased to discover that honest John Eagle, as Captain Acton held him, was a rogue who could not keep a secret although imparted by so exalted a personage as the commander of a ship, and that in breaking his promise the sour, shallow-minded mate was doing exactly what Mr Lawrence wished.

The night came down in a heavy shadow that was not lightened by its burden of stars. The foam of the sea looked as spectral as the faint astral splashes in the velvet deeps on high through which sailed many visionary shapes of cloud. A little time before it fell dark, and when the soft, moist crimson of the sun that was set yet lurked in the west, the steward Paul went aft with lanterns for the cabins occupied by the Captain, the mate, and Miss Lucy Acton. The great cabin, or living-room, was already lighted by two lanterns which swung from hooks on either side the skylight fore-and-aft. The lanterns Paul bore were small, of iron frames fitted with glass, and in them was consumed a mesh which was fed with oil.

Mr Lawrence was in the act of passing from the cabin steps to his berth when Paul, who had received the key from him, came out of the interior tenanted by Lucy. He looked pale in the lantern light, ugly, and grotesque, and his face wore an expression as though he had been terrified.

"Have you hung up the light in Miss Acton's cabin?" said Mr Lawrence.

"Yes, sir."

"What is she doing?"

"She was lying on the mattress I took in."

"Did she speak?"

"No, sir. At least not at once."

"Has she ripped up the mattress?"

"I didn't see she 'ad, your honour."

"What next?"

"As I turned after 'anging the lantern up I found her stannin' behind me with a knife in her hand; one of the knives I took in the tray, and didn't miss when I cleared away. She says to me, speakin' through her teeth like as though she was tryin' to talk whilst holding on to something with her mouth, and in the strangest, thinnest voice I ever heard in all my life, like when you're trying to file down the head of a nail, 'What do you want here, you loathsome creature? You come fresh from your forest. Go back before I kill you!' And she flourished the knife which glittered in her 'and as though it was a-fire, on which I ran out, sir."

It would have been difficult to tell what was in Mr Lawrence's mind as he stood viewing Paul for some moments in silence, after that arched-legged hunchback had ceased. He said in a voice without a tremor, in tones as steady and collected as those in which he would ask a man how he was or bid him good-morning: "Have you ever met with mad people?"

"Yes, sir."

"What proof have they given you that they were mad?"

"A-tearin' up of their clothes and a-goin' about without shame. He was a man called Micky Cruppin, sir. Another 'ud stop at every pool to wash his feet. I knowed a man who wouldn't attend sarvice 'cos he said that the devil always came in, and took a seat beside him. There was old Mother Compton, who'd spit at a dog if he barked at her, who used to do her washin' on the Sabbath, sayin' that she was too good to go to church, and that the parson ought to be 'anged for having committed a forgery where he last lived. And this she'd say of a new parson just as she would of t'other who had gone afore him."

"Do you think Miss Acton mad?" said Mr Lawrence, speaking with an effort, but determined to have an independent opinion and willing to believe that the wretch who stood humped, pallid, and terrified before him might be able to distinguish clearly what was obscured by his own prejudices, wishes, and dread.

"Yes, sir, I do," was the answer, swiftly delivered, as is the characteristic of conviction.

Without further speech Mr Lawrence passed into his cabin.

'Till midnight he was frequently up and down. The mate in charge rounding upon his heel would see the figure of the Captain, who might not have long before gone below, rising and falling against the stars as he stood grasping a back-stay, watching the darkling ship as she crushed the phantom lights of the deep out of the black coil of surge with its trembling lading of stars of the sea-glow, and ever and anon sending the eye of a man, who has been used to looking out for ships of the enemy, around the gloom of the horizon. But the mate of the watch did not know that Mr Lawrence varied this routine of vigilance by often standing in his own cabin with his ear pressed to the bulkhead that separated Lucy's berth from his, with the idea of catching any noises that might be made within.

Shortly after midnight he softly turned the key in Lucy's door and looked in, and deeming that she lay asleep he passed in, closing the door behind him, that the roll of the ship might not slam the door and awaken the sleeper. The light was dim, but sufficiently clear for eyes that had come out of the gloom or darkness. A mattress lay upon the deck close against the bedstead, which was emptied of its furniture, and upon this mattress was stretched the figure of Lucy Acton. She was fully dressed as in the day, save that she had removed her jockey-shaped hat. The bolster from the bedstead supported her head. Some of her dark hair had become disengaged and lay loosely about her cheek, giving the purity of marble to her brow in that light, and her sleep was so deep that she lay as though dead. On the deck close beside her grasp was a common table knife.

Mr Lawrence made a step and quickly picked up the knife and drew back again, conscious that the fixed gaze will often awake a slumberer even from deep repose. He stood close to the door viewing this picture of a sleeping girl in a ship's little cabin irradiated by a dim light, whose motions with the rolling and the pitching of the ship, filled the darkling interior with a hundred dancing spectres. His marine ear would take no heed of the voices of the ship in that cabin, the groans and murmurs, the low whistlings and rusty strainings. This was a concert which his seasoned sense of hearing must miss or overlook in his perception of the picture he viewed.

He gazed at the sleeping figure for two or three minutes and then left, again locking the door. He entered his own cabin and stretched his form along the lower bunk; but used as he was to sleep well in an hour betwixt one scene of slaughter, of belching broadsides, of fierce and murderous boarding and another scene scarred by the cannon flame, terrible with its thunder of guns whose muzzles yawned close to the muzzles of the foe, slumber was not to be his.

Was it possible that Lucy's situation had driven her out of her mind? Her behaviour throughout the day had been extraordinary. Features of character had appeared in her in the extravagance of her moods and humours which he never could have conceived would, though latent and demanding the summons of insanity to become visible, have formed a part of her nature. She, the gentle, the sweet, the refined, the tender, the sympathetic had exhibited even coarseness. Could she be mad, and yet slumber so soundly? How do the insane sleep?

He contrasted her wretched bed on that cabin floor with her home bedchamber which he figured—he had never entered it; a room sweet-scented with the flowers of the creepers at the windows, white and fair in the apparel of a girl's bower of rest, elegant in its equipment as were all the rooms of the home of the Actons.

He loved her passionately, even to madness, and must win her. But he never would have sought to win her at the price of her reason, had he foreseen the blow his stratagem must deal her. He must turn robber to rescue himself from a life-term of imprisonment as a debtor, and he could not steal his friend's ship without stealing his daughter too, because he knew that his act of piracy would as effectually end all chance of his possessing her as a wife as though she lay as dead as Juliet in her tomb.

He was on deck early in the morning. Daybreak had turned ashen the surface of the sea. The wind was a steady breeze, and the *Minorca* crowded with every cloth she carried saving her stun-sails, plunged and pitched, and frothed, and foamed in prodigious fine style as she was swept onwards by the wind that was a point abaft the beam. The sun rose in wet pink splendour on the larboard quarter, and by his light, which threw out the sea-line like the crystal rim of a tumbler against the heavens which were full of travelling clouds, Mr Lawrence swept with his glass the whole brimming circle. There was nothing in sight.

Mr Pledge walked the deck in charge of the watch. When Mr Lawrence appeared Pledge saluted him in man-o'-war style, but Mr Lawrence's policy towards Pledge was the same as his policy towards Eagle. He would not sit at meals with him, or have anything to say to him outside the necessities of strict discipline and the ship's routine. Pledge saw pride, haughtiness, and contempt in the handsome face that was turned to him when Mr Lawrence condescended to ask a few questions about the ship's rate of going, and the like. But this much the Captain added: "Did you ever serve in a man-o'-war, sir?"

"Yes, sir," answered Pledge.

"British?"

"American, your honour."

"Well, the Yankee's discipline is taut, though not so taut as ours by the length of a log-line to a lead-line. You therefore understand the necessity of obeying orders?"

With some astonishment Thomas Pledge answered: "I do, sir."

"I told Mr Eagle to keep a bright look-out for ships, and he reported one to me when she was hull up. She might have been a Frenchman, and if so, we should now be occupying her hold. You will please keep a bright look-out for ships, sir!" he added, with which he stepped to the weather-side of the quarterdeck, and Pledge crossed to leeward thinking to himself: "If he talks to old Jim like this and with that there face and manner, he'll find out that the discipline of the British Merchant Service ain't all his Navy ideas would like to see it. Damn me, on top of his talking to me like this, if I don't 'ave a yarn with old Jim after breakfast, and blast the consequences," and he sent a scowl at Mr Lawrence, who was looking to windward.

CHAPTER XIII

LUCY'S MADNESS

THE MONOTONOUS and commonplace demands of everyday life on board ship as well as on shore will enter into the most exalted and uncommon forms of romance at sea. Whether Lucy Acton was mad, or whether she was merely acting a part, it was as certain she must be fed as though she was a vulgar, homely, steerage passenger with nothing more poetic and soul-lifting in her life than the faded portrait of the milkman who wooed and then jilted her.

The cabin breakfast was served at half past eight. A tray for Lucy was placed at the side of Mr Lawrence, who with his own hand furnished it. He then directed Paul, whilst giving him the key, to leave the door unlocked on quitting the berth, and, turning in his chair, he watched the hunchback enter. But the door, as before, was closed by the swing of the ship, and he caught but a glimpse of the interior, which did not frame its inmate.

This time Paul was for some minutes in the berth. He came out, leaving the door unlocked as ordered, though shut, and stood beside Mr Lawrence to make his report.

"How does the lady seem?" said Mr. Lawrence.

"She made me put the tray on the deck, sir," answered Paul, "and I see her running her eyes over it, and she says, 'Where's the knife, you man of the forest?' I says, 'I don't know, mum.'"

He paused.

"Nothing but a slice or two of tongue was sent to her," said Mr Lawrence, "that requires a knife to cut it with. Go on! Tell me what followed."

"After she told me to put the tray on the deck, and looked at it and asked about the knife, she stares at me just as I was about to go, and then your honour, her face changes as if she'd pulled off a mask. She smiled with so cunning a look, such a trembling of the eyelids, that I reckoned she'd got something hidden and was going to stab me with it, and she lifts her shoulders all the while, a-looking at me with a cunning smile and trembling eyes, till I supposed she was a-imitating of my figure; and then she whispers so soft that I could just hear what she said, whilst she beckons to me, smiling: 'If I show it, swear you'll keep it a secret.' ' I don't know what you mean, ma'am' I says. 'Here,' she says, with her cunning smile, and still abeckoning. 'But if you don't keep the secret I'll kill you as sartin as that you was born in a forest.'"

Here again the fellow paused, apparently striving to find words to produce his picture.

"Go on!" said Mr Lawrence fiercely. "What did she show you?"

Paul started, and answered: "She took me to the locker that's under the window, and, lifting the lid, pointed down into the inside, and began to laugh with a strange, crying noise, like a cat quarrelling, and then says she, 'Do you see it?' There was nothing in the locker, saving that in one end of it she'd made a sort of bird's nest out of the bed feathers which I 'adn't swept away, and in it was her rings, a piece of soap, a salt-cellar which I hadn't missed from the tray, and what I took for a ball, but which, I allow, was her gloves rolled up tight. 'Do you see it?' she said, looking so cunning and a-whispering so mysterious, it was more like dreaming than living to see and watch her. 'That's my secret!' and then she slams the lid of the locker to, with a noise which I thought your honour would believe was a pistol-shot, and says, frownin' and starin' at me with eyes that seemed to be in a blaze, 'If you says a word about what you've seen I'll kill you.'"

The fellow ceased. He had told all he had to relate, and he was by no means such a fool as not to see in his listener's face that he had related much more than enough. He scratched his thigh as a monkey would, and fell to waiting upon his master.

When Mr Lawrence had finished breakfast he went on deck consistently with the innovation he had made in the ship's routine aft to relieve Mr Eagle, who had come on watch at eight o'clock, and who now with Mr Pledge went to breakfast in the cabin.

It was a very fine, clear, sparkling May morning far down in the English Channel, and still the sea stretched desolate to its dim blue recesses: which, had all been right with Mr Lawrence, would have pleased him very much indeed, but he had something else to think of. The waters frolicked in little sliding runs; it was a chasing dance of waters with the billows pointing their white satin shoes under their brilliant skirts of liquid blue. Mr Lawrence walked the deck, and seemed to be keeping a bright look-out as he swept the horizon with the glass he had brought with him, and often his stern, haughty, and handsome face was directed towards the men, who seemed to know that a vigilant eye had hove into view through the companion, and they clapped a fresh colour of activity into those motions of limbs which accompanied their labours.

But in truth Mr Lawrence was all the while thinking of what he had heard from Paul, and every time he took a turn his gaze went to the companion hatch, whence, now that her cabin door was unlocked, he expected at any moment to see the figure of Lucy Acton emerge.

What would she do if she came on deck? And what was he to do if his treatment of her had driven her mad? It seemed like all the world to a very little, for here was this one man in conflict with really stupendous circumstances brought about by himself. Upon his hands was the girl of his heart, the most adorable of women in his opinion, as mad—if he was to trust the evidence of his own senses and the report of his steward—as any howling, grimacing, jibbering inmate of a lunatic asylum. Upon his hands, too, was the ship with a crowd of sailors, the ship to be feloniously sold, the sailors to be fraudulently got rid of: and much must depend upon the reception accorded him and his friend Dick, if it ever should come to the *Minorca*'s safe arrival at Rio de Janeiro, by the intelligent scoundrel whom he had named in his letter as Don José Zamovano y Villa.

Mr Eagle did not keep him long waiting, and when that surly, awkward seaman arrived Mr Lawrence went below and found Mr Thomas Pledge in the act of leaving the table and the cabin, with his jaw still working in mastication. It was clear that Mr Pledge had no intention of keeping his seat, even though he had not entirely swallowed his last mouthful, when Mr Lawrence hove in sight.

As the second mate climbed the companion steps Mr Lawrence stood with his hand upon the table and his eyes fastened upon Lucy's door, thinking. It was clear he was hanging in the wind, as sailors say. He could head a boarding party, he could look a loaded cannon full in the muzzle, he could risk seizing the siderope which was connected with a fuse for exploding the powder-room of a pirate that was to be boarded and taken; but he seemed to lack heart for such an enterprise as his opening of that door, and his entrance into that berth signified.

He formed his resolution, and stepping to the door, knocked. He received no answer, whereupon he entered.

He started as though he was confronted by something totally different from the lady he expected to see. In truth Mr Lawrence had never seen Lucy Acton with her hair down. Always when they met her hair had been dressed in the prevailing mode, with a little fringing or shadowing of wisps on her fair brow and curls on the beautiful outlines of her shoulders. Whether her hair had become disengaged from its fastenings in the night, or whether the deck mattress had done half and she with her fingers had let fall the rest, matters not; she was before him clothed all about her back and breast with her abundance of soft dark hair.

She was kneeling or crouching at the breakfast tray which was upon the deck, and when Mr Lawrence entered, she held in one hand a piece of cold tongue, a bite or two out of which she was eating, and in the other hand a white biscuit. The cup was half-full of tea. She did not lift her eyes when he entered, nor seem to be aware that another occupied the cabin besides herself. She looked at the piece of tongue with a smile which was a miracle of idiotism in its perfect conveyance of no meaning, then bit what was in her mouth, then smiled again; and again as suddenly frowned with a marvellous swiftness of transformation of facial expression. So that whilst she looked, she appeared idiotic in one instant, in the next she wore a strange and alarming look of angry madness, dreadful to witness, working in her lineaments so sweetly feminine, so purely gentle.

Her natural colour had not wholly faded from her check, but the bloom was very faint indeed, once removed only perhaps from pallor, so that her eyes, which in the full glow of her beauty were as a sorceress's for liquid softness and the lambent lights of passions and emotions, making one think of a dark midnight sea illuminated by the moon, gathered a keenness of outline, a vitality of colour and play which of themselves would have suffered her to pass as the mad girl she was or figured to be.

"I wish, madam," he said, "I could see you seated more comfortably. But I wish more that you could see into my heart, what I feel there, and how my pain is infinitely keener than yours, because my love for you, my inexorable passion for you, my determination to win you and make you my own for life, paralysing the efforts of those who would keep us asunder, make the very soul within me shrink to behold you so uneasy, so unhappy, so reluctant to cast upon me one look—even one look—to persuade me that my stratagem was based upon my conviction that I am not indifferent to you, nay, that deep in your spirit your love for me dwells as a jewel in a casket that yourself dare not open, though willing that I should."

She continued at one moment smiling her idiot smile, at another moment frowning her madwoman's frown, whilst he spoke. Then looking up she seemed to perceive him for the first time, sprang erect with a wonderful convulsion of terror in her whole form, and a sharp, short, piercing shriek of distress.

"Who are you, sir?" she cried, brushing her hair by a fling of both hands from her brow and cheeks. "How durst you intrude upon me? Do you know I am a woman—a lady—a lady—a princess—the

Princess Tatters, sir, the daughter of a great and powerful lord who would condemn you to be hanged if he caught you here!"

It was sure that neither the spirit nor the inspiration of the genius of the famous Kitty O'Hara was far distant from her child when this sweet and astonishing young creature executed the above feat of dramatic gymnastics and delivered the words just recorded.

The bewildered man stared at her as though he was himself bereft of reason. Amazement, confusion, love, pity, horror, doubt were amongst the expressions which ran through his countenance like shadow chasing shadow.

"My dearest madam!" he cried. "My sweetest Lucy!" and here he clasped his hands and swayed with passion in his posture of piteous and painful appeal, which rendered him as a figure a really noble piece of flesh and blood, exalted as it was by its peculiar manly beauty of face. "Is it possible that you do not know me? How can I act to undo the dreadful distress my love has brought upon you? Oh, thou fair and everlasting darling of my heart, have those secret sweet feelings with which you regard me no power to influence your moods, to control these strange manifestations, to——"

He drew his breath in a gasp and stopped, arrested by her suddenly turning her back upon him and bowing with the exquisite grace of the finished curtsy of those days to what Mr Lawrence guessed was an apparition.

"It is good of your Royal Highness," she exclaimed in softly modulated, respectful tones, uttered in a measure that gave them a courtierlike dignity, "to visit me in my loneliness and distress. The great Duke of Clarence, sir"—again she curtsied—"will ever be remembered with love and pride by a kingdom whose glory lies in the deeds of her sailors, for his devotion to the sea, to those who sail it, and who bleed for their country upon it."

She seemed to listen in a profoundly respectful attitude to the reply of the vision, and then said as though in answer to it: "Your Royal Highness, I am imprisoned in this ship by a man who is the son of a sailor and was himself a sailor until he was expelled from the Service of which your Royal Highness is one of the most brilliant lights, by a shameful and a barbarous act unworthy of an officer and a gentleman. He hopes to marry me, sir, by stealing me from my father, who was a captain in the Royal Navy, and who trusted him. I entreat your Royal Highness's influence to procure my immediate liberation from this wicked man that I may return to my father who will be breaking his heart over my disappearance and loss."

She pronounced the words "who will be breaking his heart" in a plaintive Irish accent. But it did not occur to the listener that the apparition she apostrophised was not H.R.H. the Duke of Clarence but Mrs Kitty O'Hara, her mother, who was as famous in her day as Peg Woffington and equal to Mrs Jordan in some scenes of romping and roguishness.

Like most sailors of his time Mr Lawrence possessed the instinct of superstition, a quality or element which has contributed the most brilliant of the rays to the glory of the romance of the sea. He was sensible of an emotion of awe as he watched Lucy bowing to and addressing a royal apparition so well known to him as the Sailor Prince whose viewless eye might be taking in his story whilst the wild-haired girl bowed apparently to the bulkhead or addressed the thin air.

She appeared to be listening: then with a profound curtsy, said: "I thank your Royal Highness for your gracious condescension. It is not my wish that this unhappy man should be severely punished. If, sir, it should be your pleasure to order him to be executed, I would travel twenty miles upon my knees to beg him off. I am reduced to this one gown, and am now the Princess Tatters. My cruel gaoler will not suffer me to use a knife to cut the food he sends me. Look at that tray, sir! I feed upon the floor because I have been made a beggar of, and as though I were a savage, I am obliged to use my fingers to eat with."

Here she paused and looked round at the tray as though she would have Mr Lawrence catch a sight of her face, whose composite expression of indignation, distress, and eager yearning for help and sympathy was heightened and scored by the mad look her eyes wore, and the unmeaning smile which deformed her mouth. She again addressed the apparition.

"Can I trust your Royal Highness with a secret? . . . How good you are, sir! Your Royal Highness shall see my treasure, but you are too great as a Prince, and too virtuous as a man, to betray me."

With that, and looking round about her with insane cunning glittering in her eyes as diamonds tremble in the dancer's ear, as though she feared she might be watched by another in that berth, albeit her manner persuaded Mr Lawrence that she did not know he was looking on, she went to the locker, lifted the lid and disclosed her treasure-hidings of rings, soap, and the rest of it, looking up meanwhile as though into the face of a person who was bending a little to catch a sight of that nest of feathers, but looking up with such marvellous vitality in the composition of her lineaments, and in the penetrating glare of those eyes of hers which in hours of repose and content seemed to brood upon what they viewed, that Mr Lawrence could almost swear that he beheld the spectral shadow of the Royal apparition into whose face she gazed, stooping and peering into the nest at the end of the locker.

She spoke again to the phantom, but this time in such a mere muttering of words that the listener caught nothing of her meaning, and then sank her figure in a profoundly respectful curtsy whilst she seemed to kiss a hand extended to her.

She stood a few moments with her hands clasped before her at arm's length, and her head bowed as though deep in thought, then went to the tray again, knelt beside it and continued her meal, taking the biscuit and the tongue in her hands without seeming to be in the least conscious of the presence of Mr Lawrence.

"Madam," said he softly, "after so lively a conversation with your Royal but unrevealed visitor, have you no word for me—no look——"

"I have no piano in this cabin, sir," she answered, without raising her eyes. "And I have no heart to sing without music."

"I do not ask you to sing," he said. "Give me but a word, give me but a look. You tear my heart by this behaviour."

She looked up at him suddenly with her eyes trembling cunningly again as when she asked the phantom to view her treasure, and with a look impossible to portray but which convinced him that she did not know him, and in a voice that was almost tender with its note of seeking after sympathy and help, she exclaimed: "Are you come here to liberate me, to restore me to my father, who weeps because he thinks I am lost, to rescue me from the wicked arts of a treacherous man —oh, tell me so, tell me so!" she cried, springing to her feet, and extending her arms.

What could the unfortunate, infatuated, handsome rascal say? Her appeal was poignant by virtue of her deep distress, the misery of her condition, the insane disposition of her beautiful face, wild and almost white in its shadowing of hair. What could he say to her? His countenance was filled with the confusion of his mind. His heart beat tumultuously with love that raged with its sense of helplessness. These phrases do not exaggerate a state that nothing but the highest form of genius could delineate in its astounding complexity of adoration, despair, horror at the consequences of his own lightly undertaken act, honour that could be no stranger to a valiant nature, and a resolution to persevere and conquer as a consequence of the character that could lay upon its owner's soul this enormous obligation of the betrayal of the girl he worshipped and the man who had stood his friend when the world was sterile, and he must either flee the country or rot in gaol.

"Madam," he said in a broken voice, "it is plain that I have brought upon me something that I had not foreseen, and if you are the sufferer, I am the loser, and of the two the keener sufferer by my loss. This door, madam, will remain unlocked, and you are at liberty to come and go as you please."

He made her one of those elegant and stately bows which was his greatest charm in the eyes of old Miss Acton, and left the berth, closing the door.

Did he believe her mad, or did he conceive that she was merely feigning a part?

It may be at once said that he had very little doubt that her ruthless abduction based upon the fear that her father had met with a serious injury, coupled with her imprisonment and the terrors excited in her by the knowledge that she was being carried away into a remote part of the world and that she was entirely at the mercy of a man who had proved himself a scoundrel, had disordered her intellect, had played havoc with her nerves and brain, so that though she might recover her reason should she be rescued or returned to her home, she must continue mad whilst in his ship or associated with him.

If he doubted her insanity at all his suspicion had no stiffer ground than the shallow sand on which reposed his hope that she was acting. Throughout this passage he did not think to consider her as the child of a great actress. To him she had always been a gentle, sweet, undemonstrative girl ingenuous in speech, kind, charitable, beloved by the poor, one whose pursuits were amiable and pure. She was nimble and poetical with her pencil. She sang pretty songs prettily. Her beauty informed with a colour of its own the melodies her fingers evoked from the keys or strings of the instruments she touched. He could not think of her as having the talents of an actress, or even the tastes of one. He had never heard of her taking a part in a performance above a charade. Nothing, therefore, but madness or an extraordinary dramatic genius which it was impossible for him to think of her as possessing, could create those parts which she had enacted before him in a manner so immoderately life-like, so absolutely in unison with what he himself could conceive of the behaviour of madness, that deep in his soul might be found the conviction that she had lost her reason, and that his passionate, unprincipled love was the cause of it.

Shortly before twelve the people of the *Minorca* beheld on the starboard bow one of those bland and beautiful pictures of the sea which have vanished from the face of the waters to be seen no more. The Lizard was painted in a soft, blue looming mass against the sky, and to the right of it upon the sea-line, there sprang like stars in their rising, the white cloths of ships—a numerous convoy from Torbay; they rose fast with a pleasant breeze on the quarter, and one hundred and sixty sail could have been counted with three line-of-battle ships and some frigates to look after them. They were of all rigs known in those days, from the commanding Indiaman armed like a man-o'-war, hoisting her huge main and fore-yards by jeers, loosing her vast topsails out of the tops, clothed as no ship now goes clothed with sprit-sail and sprit-topsail, water sails and other devices in canvas to catch even the faintest cat's paw that should tarnish the burnished calm, down to the little snow bound to Lisbon; a gallant, an imposing, a splendid sight, when every hull was shaped upon the sea which seemed to be transformed into a mighty plain, brilliant for leagues with the shining white cones of tents.

Mr Lawrence, who was on deck at noon, wisely concluding that the then peculiar rig of the *Minorca* would challenge the attention and excite the suspicion of one or another of the convoying men-of-war, hoisted British colours, and as no observation of the sun was deemed necessary when there hung plain in sight the famous promontory of the Lizard from which a departure was to be made, he overhung the rail gazing apparently with absorbed interest at the grand spectacle of ships which were making a more southerly course than he. Indeed he was so absorbed either by that "vision splendid" or by thinking of the mad pictures he had witnessed in the little berth from which he had lately emerged, that he failed to notice that some of the hands forward for whom the dinner-hour had arrived and who were hanging about the caboose, were staring at him with a degree of obstinacy which perhaps had he regarded it he would have deemed something more than strange, as they had a fine show to arrest and detain their gaze on the bow. One of the most steadfast of these starers was the man Mr Pledge familiarly styled Old Jim.

At noon Mr Eagle, who had been in charge of the watch since eight o'clock, was relieved by Mr Pledge, and went below. On enter- ing the cabin on his way to his berth, he started and stopped dead on beholding Miss Lucy Acton standing at the table and looking up through the skylight. She had gathered up her hair, but in such wise that had it not been for the jockey-shaped hat which she had resumed she would have looked as wild as though her tresses hung about her shoulders and down her back as in her berth.

If she was sensible of the entrance of Mr Eagle she did not for some moments running into a minute or two appear to notice him, but continued to gaze fixedly through the skylight as though she beheld something that riveted her vision through the open glazed cover.

Mr Eagle did not speak. Indeed, having started, he came to a stand and scarcely moved, staring. Of course he knew that the young lady was on board, but realisation had not been completed in his narrow, shallow understanding, because down to this moment he had not been able to use his eyes to see her. But now she stood before him, Miss Lucy Acton indeed, but Lord defend him! how changed! "Why," he reflected with the velocity of thought, "it was only a few days ago, in a manner of speaking, that she comes aboard this vessel when we was lying at the wharf and asks after my rheumatism, and says she'd like to make a voyage to the West Indies if the weather could be kept fine and the sea smooth. And I couldn't help thinking to myself that I never could imagine a smarter and a more modish young party than she looked, whilst now—well, if this rooning away to sea with a man is to be called love, bust me if it ain't only another name for madness. For what young lady in such sarcumstances as that there with a beautiful 'ome, carriages, sarvants to wait upon her, and a loving father to give her everything that she wants, and more than she wants, would dream of rooning away to sea with a man with no other clothes than those on her back, onless she was as mad as that there Miss Lucy Acton looks."

She turned her eyes upon him when the surly shell-back had come to this part of his thoughts, and frowned without recognition in her face as he read it. She stared at him, not with the heavy lidded, beautiful eyes of Lucy Acton, but with orbs of sight whose glances seemed keen as rays of light as they shot from under her knitted brows. Though her fair forehead was deformed by a scowl, her lips were curved into a meaningless smile—the very expression of the idiot's highest facial effort, and all meaning or no meaning that was in her countenance was accentuated by the unusual, uncommon, very faint tinge which had taken the place of the habitual bloom of her checks and paled her into an aspect of distraction, wildness, and insanity.

"Do you belong to this ship?" she asked.

"Of course I do, ma'am," answered Mr Eagle, with profound aston-

ishment moving in his face as though it were some vitalising sub-
cutaneous influence that stirred in one part of his visage at a time.
"Don't you recollect me, ma'am?"

"Who is in command of this ship?" she enquired in a low, harsh
voice, almost a whisper. "Whoever he is," she rattled on, "I am his
prisoner. I am being carried away into captivity, I who am a princess,
though soon to be clothed in tatters. If you are a man with a heart
have mercy upon me, and turn this ship and steer me home!"

Eagle stood dumbfounded. He was prepared to hear her represent her state in such fiction as had been preconcerted between
her and Mr Lawrence. But he never could have supposed that sim-
ulation of madness was the posture of mind she had pre-arranged
to feign, and she looked so mad and spoke so madly that it was
impossible for such a stubborn, sour old fool to see the truth or
know what she meant.

He gazed at her with the vacancy of a confounded mind, per-
plexed not infinitely, for few understandings were more limited, and
then said: "I've got no power here, ma'am. It isn't for me to steer
the ship, if you was to condescend to go on your bended knees,
which the Lord forbid. Indeed, ma'am, I don't know what to say, and
only know what I've been told, and can but judge by what I see.
It's not for me as mate of this vessel to mess about with something
that may be all right or all wrong. There's one in this ship as could
break me and would break me if so be I gave him the chance, and
a chance he'd find"—here he lowered his voice and looked up at
the skylight—"though no other captain would think of taking advantage of it. If you've been wronged, I'm 'eartily sorry for it. And if it's
all right, why then, ma'am, I wish you joy, though it's a very bold
henterprise—a very bold henterprise," he added, and he gloomily
shook his head and sourly viewed her.

Whilst this singular conversation was being conducted in the
cabin, a scene in the tragicomedy of which this book is the relation
was being prepared on deck. The convoy on the starboard bow had
considerably risen and was scattering, and flags from the armed fabrics which watched the vessels streamed at gaff end and mizzen
royal mast-head in signal to the slow sailers and to other ships
whose blockheads of masters, indifferent to the safety of the

bottoms they commanded, acted without reference to the possibility of the enemy heaving into view, and some of them with the contemptible determination to prove their independence by giving the commodore and the naval officers in the other ships as much trouble and annoyance as skilless seamanship could provide.

Mr Lawrence kept the *Minorca* away a point or two that he might hold the convoy in view and hang upon their quarter without drawing close as though he was one of the convoyed ships, for it must be intelligible even to the most inexperienced in sea-going affairs that Mr Lawrence had no wish to invite the attention of one of those British men-o'-war.

He leaned over the rail, and then walked the deck, whilst Mr Pledge paced to leeward. On a sudden Mr Lawrence became aware that the whole ship's company were on deck forward in the neighbourhood of the caboose, and that a few talked together with frequent glances aft, whilst others stared in the direction in which he moved, deliberately and obstinately.

He stood a moment before he made a turn for another quarter-deck excursion and viewed them, and then walked right aft with his back turned to the bows of the ship, and in such an attitude that should the man at the wheel look over his shoulder he would not be able to see what he was doing. What he did was to pull from the pocket of his coat a pistol whose priming he quickly examined; he replaced the weapon, which was of a lighter pattern than the cumbrous engine which in those days men stuffed into their belts, and none by observation of his coat would conceive that he went about armed with a loaded pistol. This done he wheeled round and walked the usual distance forward.

As he advanced, one of the sailors came away from a little crowd of men manifestly with the object of addressing him. This man was Pledge's friend "Old Jim." He was about forty-five, with a neck as long as a piece of broken pillar, and lantern jaws deformed by a growth of mustard-coloured hair sprouting in single fibres. He had but three or four teeth in his gums, two of which shot outwards and lifted his upper lip. He was generally reckoned the ugliest man in Old Harbour Town, and esteemed by his brethren of the jacket as one of the best sailors that ever stepped a ship's deck.

"May I have a word with you, sir?" he exclaimed in a coarse, hoarse, broken voice.

"What do you want?" said Mr Lawrence, halting and viewing the fellow with a frowning face and lips which grew tight-set the instant he closed them.

"I beg your pardon, sir——" began the man.

"To the point! Out with it and bear a hand!" exclaimed Mr Lawrence with a stern, contemptuous glance at the huddle of faces forward, and then slightly turning his head to see in the tail of his eye what Mr Pledge was doing.

"Well, sir, it's like this," said the man, pronouncing his words forcibly in his determination to show a bold front. "Us sailors who agreed to sail this 'ere ship to Kingston in Jamaica have got to hear that we are bound to another port, though where it is ain't know'd."

"What's this matter got to do with you?" said Mr Lawrence fiercely.

"It's got to do with us all, sir, not alone with me," was the answer.

"If it's the owner's wish that this vessel shall be carried to another port, there she shall go; and so you have it. Now, go forward!" said Mr Lawrence, and he moved as though about to turn on his heel.

A murmur broke from the men.

"We are not willing to carry this ship to any other port than the port we agreed to, sir," said Old Jim, speaking with great firmness, the murmur that had risen behind him having stimulated his fortitude.

"I think you are a mutinous dog," said Mr Lawrence in a snarling, sarcastic voice, but preserving a frown that was portentous of an intellectual thunderstorm through the darkness of which the eyes would flash lightning. "Do you see those men-of-war out yonder? I need but make a signal to bring an armed crew aboard, and then you shall be carried into the first port that's convenient and discharged to make way for a crew of willing men—men willing to obey their commander, who must be willing to obey his owner."

"There's no good in threatening us with your armed crew. We agreed for Kingston," said a voice.

"Who said that?" shouted Mr Lawrence, with the blood red in his face.

"Me—Thomas Hanlin," was the answer, and a sailor made two or three steps and stood close to Old Jim.

"Mr Pledge," cried Mr Lawrence, "clap that man in irons! go and fetch them, sir!" and rounding again upon the man, and approaching him by several paces, he pulled the pistol from his pocket and levelling it direct at the man's head, cried in a tone that left not an instant's doubt of his resolution in the mind of every man who saw and heard: "If you utter another syllable I'll send this ball through your brains!"

As he flung himself into this posture of taking aim, with some of the crew about the caboose cowering as do men who seek to dodge a missile, whilst Old Jim and the other stood in the foreground steadily staring at the enraged officer with the blood in his cheeks, Lucy Acton came on deck, and, standing with her hand upon the companion-way, wild-eyed, and pale and dishevelled, with a mien of distraction which was a marvellously true copy of madness in momentary halt, watched the proceedings.

CHAPTER XIV

THE "LOUISA ANN"

IT WAS ON the 4th of June 1805 that a large, handsome three-masted schooner was softly, with a keen cut-water, rending a way for herself over a smooth breast of sea. The sound under the bows was that of a knife shearing through satin, and the note fell softly with a silken noise upon the ear, without tinkle of bell-bubble, or serpent-like hiss of expiring foam. Upon the stern of this schooner was painted in long white letters the word *Aurora*.

The breeze was so light that it was scarcely to be felt on deck. The gaff topsails faintly swelled with a summer-like softness and tenderness of gleaming curve and delicately-fingered shadow; but the heavier canvas hung with an occasional sway of boom only, as though the little ship was at rest in a harbour into whose water breathed the slow, low swell of the outer sea.

It was half-past seven in the morning; the sky was blue from line to line, but the monotony of the morning's brilliance of azure was relieved by a few little steam-white clouds which floated small violet island shadows under them. The horizon was a clear line, a sweep of crystal against the blue crystalline heaven it brimmed to.

The decks had been washed down, the ropes coiled away, and everything was neat, sparkling with the swabbed brine from pump or bucket, and the whole a pleasant picture to the eye with its lofty fabric of wide white canvas, its glossy black sides descending into a ruddy coat of copper sheathing which charged the water immediately under with a yellow light as of fire, the canvas forward lifting and drooping in wings of triangular cloth like the pinions of a sea bird that gently flutters its plumes as it slowly breasts the water to the impulse of its webbed feet. Smoke from the chimney of the little galley rose for a space in a straight line, then curved like the liquid column of a fountain. The cook was preparing breakfast for the cabin, and the savoury smell of eggs and bacon in the process of cooking made the scarcely breeze-disturbed atmosphere in, the neighbourhood of the schooner's kitchen shore-like and home-like, and in every sense delicious to hungry sailors whose breakfast was black tea, ship's biscuit, and such remains of yesterday's beef as they might have preserved.

The *Minorca* had started early on the morning of 3rd May. The *Aurora* followed her in pursuit on the 8th May, sailing on the afternoon of that day. Her nimble keel had been delayed by contrary winds, and down to this date—namely, 4th June—she had failed to even approach the average daily speed which Captain Weaver had predicted of her in her chase of the barque. She had met with one adventure only so far: it was sufficiently filled, however, with excitement and danger to suffice for twenty.

When in the Chops of the Channel the weather thickened all round: a dingy drizzle of rain curtained the horizon into the distance of a cannon shot, and out of this sullen dimness which was not to be shifted nor broken into spaces showing recesses, the surge came in a steel-dark curve upon whose polished back the foam that fell from the head of the billow cast a deeper gloom filled with raven gleams like water at night. A bright lookout was kept. The *Aurora* under all plain sail sprang through these glooming waters, and the brine swept from her weather-bow in sharp shootings of brilliant hail.

Suddenly a little before eleven o'clock in the forenoon the deck was hailed from aloft, and a sail reported three points on the weather-bow. She came out of the thickness like one of the heads of seas, in a shining light of canvas; she was sailing large; she showed herself as an iceberg leaps from the snowstorm of the Antarctic Ocean. A brig-of-war with foam to the hawse pipes, and the white band along her side broken by guns!

She was within a couple of miles when she shaped herself out of the rain-thickened murkiness. The *Aurora* was making a free wind, and every stitch of canvas was doing its work. Was yonder stranger French or English? The Admiral and Captain Acton, who were both on deck, left Captain Weaver to his own devices, sensible that they were in the hands of a shrewd, well-seasoned, practical sailor, who knew his ship better than they did. "We'll test her," said he, and the tricolour was run aloft. No flag aboard the brig was to be seen in response. The schooner was crossing the stranger's bows when the brig suddenly let fly a shotted gun at her. Whatever her nationality it was plain she was not satisfied with the show of bunting flying aboard a vessel that any practised eye could at once see was not of French paternity.

"Keep her away three points!" cried Captain Weaver, which shift of helm would leave the schooner in fuller possession of her powers of flight. And immediately afterwards he shouted: "Haul down that lie, and hoist the British Ensign! She shall have the truth, and it'll make the truth known to us."

Scarcely was the ensign blowing from its halliards when the brig fired a second shot, and as the passage of the *Aurora* and the shifting of her helm had brought the brig's trysail-gaff into view the schooner's crew saw the French flag streaming from the end of it. Immediately the *Aurora*'s change of course was perceived the brig trimmed her canvas for a chase; she set stun-sails from lower boom to both topgallant yard-arms; these additional wings threw her out against the weeping gloom in a large, looming, menacing mass irradiated by an occasional flash of bow gun which dyed her canvas with a sudden yellow glare as of lightning. But these explosions were soon stopped, and the pursuit was continued in silence.

It was idle, however, to call it a pursuit. It was a procession with the leader walking fast ahead and the follower lagging. On board the *Aurora* they saw the brig's round bows bursting the surge into sheets of brilliant whiteness which raced under her row of iron teeth like the foaming cascade of a weir; whilst alongside the keen fore-foot and the clean copper and beautifully moulded run of the *Aurora* the brine swept past with no more noise than a shower of rain upon the sea, in a narrow band on either hand which, uniting at the rudder, rushed off in a ribbon of wake that shone like pearl.

It was not long before the brig that was chasing on the schooner's weather-quarter swelled and paled in distortion with the encompassing thickness, and presently she was a pallid square, and then she became a smudge after which the rain curtain dropped upon her, and she vanished. Then it was that Captain Weaver luffed the schooner to windward of her course, and she went ahead with flattened-in sheets, leaning to it and severing the flint-coloured billow with her sharp tooth of forefoot: and so she held on, until, had the weather cleared, the brig, even had she taken in her stun-sails and hauled the wind with yards sweated fore and aft, would have been found dead to leeward and far away beyond all dream of prize money amongst the French crew.

"I can't conceive of anything," said Captain Weaver, smiling with something of pride at the Admiral and Captain Acton, "born—I don't care in what shipwright's yard, whether British or French or Roosian or Spaniard—as is going to have more than a look at the *Aurora* when it's her pleasure to show nothing but her heels."

Nevertheless it was an adventure fraught with danger to the schooner, and neither the Admiral nor Captain Acton needed to be informed that had the weather been a little thicker and the brig a knot or two faster so that she could have brought the schooner within range of her broad-side, it was odds if the fall of a mast or the ruin of a sail had not resulted in the *Aurora*'s company finding a lodging in the brig or under hatches in their own little ship and sailing for the nearest French port, with the pursuit of the *Minorca* immediately ended.

But the essential object of Captain Weaver and the very first desire of Captain Acton and the Admiral was the overtaking of the *Minorca,* her capture, and the rescue of Lucy.

To this end it was extremely necessary that they should speak to ships to ascertain if the barque whose rig would make her remarkable had been sighted or spoken, and if so when and where? They had fallen in with two or three vessels which after very careful inspection they had considered safe to speak. But they could obtain no information. Nothing answering to a ship rigged as the *Minorca* was had been sighted. So Captain Weaver stuck as best he could to his course for Rio, though much hindered by opposing winds. It was to be hoped if the *Aurora* lay fair in the wake of the *Minorca* that the winds which had delayed the schooner had also baffled the barque.

Now, as we have seen, the 4th day of June had come, and the *Aurora,* with a light air aloft which put a gentle breathing into her gaff top-sails and lighter canvas, was slowly scoring her way through the heart of a wide circle of Atlantic ocean, along which the swell ran gently, whilst the surface at a distance resembled a motionless sheet of ice under a blue sky.

Admiral Lawrence was walking the deck alone. Captain Weaver stood on the weather side of the wheel viewing the vessel as she leisurely floated forward. They had kept a look-out aloft with the perseverance of a whaler. The signalman was furnished with a glass with which he continuously swept the sea-line from beam to beam. The Admiral, great as his trouble was, looked uncommonly well and hearty. His cheeks wore a deeper dye of colour. He rolled along the deck with enjoyment of the sensation of the plank, whose motions were timed by the sea.

As he rounded in one of his fore-breakfast strolls, Captain Acton stepped out of the deckhouse, for this schooner was furnished with a deck structure a little sunk so that you entered it by a short flight of steps, and in front of it stood the wheel. The house contained six berths each lighted with a window; the foremost larboard berth was the pantry, and next door to it, abutting upon the sleeping place which the Admiral occupied, was the spare room for Lucy.

Captain Acton's face as he emerged was grave and pale. His restlessness and anxiety had increased with the voyage and the obstruction of the wind. Realisation of the loss of his daughter was a pain in him that was a a wound deeply planted, and there was no remedy but the recovery of the girl. He joined the Admiral after looking aloft and around him, and exclaimed: "Very slow work, sir. If it's to be this sort of thing the *Minorca* will not find us at Rio; and if she fetches Rio before we do, my child is lost to me."

"I cannot see that, sir," answered the Admiral. "What can my son do? She will not have him, and he must therefore leave her at Rio, because I have never imagined that he will be able to sell the barque and her cargo without exciting enquiries which he dare not challenge. If therefore he puts into Rio, it will be with the hope of inducing Miss Lucy to marry him there and promptly—an issue which he will have satisfied himself upon before his arrival. And if, as 'tis certain, she will have nothing to do with him, he will leave her at Rio and make haste to sail to where he can dispose of your property without risk. But," he continued cheerily, observing that his companion held his peace, manifestly unconvinced by the Admiral's arguments, "we have no right to assume that the weather is always to consist of baffling breezes or light airs like this; and, sir, consider that what is bad for the schooner may—indeed should—be bad for the barque. There is but one course for Rio from the port we hail from. I have watched Weaver's navigation with anxiety, and have full confidence in his judgment. I have again and again considered his chart and prickings and in all that he said and says I have agreed, and still agree."

"But," said Captain Acton in a tone that marked the depression of his spirits, "you must remember that this visible girdle of sea has, even in brilliant weather and from the mast-head, but a narrow width, and we might even now be abreast of the *Minorca* which is sailing yonder, or yonder, hull and spars down to a fathom below the sensible edge."

"We've allowed for that, sir," said the Admiral. "'Tis a contingency which has had a very full share of contemplation. If we miss her and pass her in the way you suggest, there is still Rio to receive us, where we will await the *Minorca*'s arrival. And in that you will get your way, and crown this struggle with success. So that let us miss her by failing to sight her as you say, it can but mean that we shall be first and ready for Mr Lawrence."

"True," answered Captain Acton.

At that moment the man at the masthead with the telescope still at his eye, shouted the magic words: "Sail ho!"

"Where away?" yelled Captain Weaver from the side of the wheel.

"Right ahead, sir."

"How standing?" bawled Weaver.

After a brief pause: "Coming for us, sir. We are rising her."

But the schooner might be rising her through overtaking her, and nearly a quarter of an hour must elapse before the sailor aloft could shout with emphasis down to the deck that the sail was standing right for them and that she was square rigged.

The circumstance of a sail heaving into sight was necessarily brimful of excitement and interest to Captain Acton and the Admiral. She might prove a peaceful trader or a man-of-war, a friend or an enemy, a privateer, or as likely as not the *Minorca* rolling home in charge of Eagle and her crew, who, conscious of the presence of Lucy on board, and having learnt that the ship's destination was any port but Kingston, had mutinied, and locked up the Captain in his cabin, and turned tail for Old Harbour Town.

But the breakfast bell had been rung, and leaving Captain Weaver and his mate to keep an eye upon the stranger and to act with the prudence which was to be expected of a man of Weaver's sagacity and experience, Captain Acton and his companion entered the deckhouse. Here was a cheerful little interior, gay with sunshine, which sparkled in the furniture of the breakfast-table, on which smoked as relishable and hearty a meal as was to be obtained at sea in those days. The two gentlemen found much to talk about, and perhaps because of an argument they had fallen into, their sitting, was somewhat lengthened: until just when they were about to rise, Captain

Weaver came to the cabin door, and after with the old-fashioned courtesy of his period, begging their pardon, he exclaimed: "The sail's now clear in the glass from the deck."

"What is she, do you think?" said Captain Acton.

"She looks to me, sir, a worn-out bit of a brig about a hundred tons. Most sartinly there's nothing to be afraid of in her."

"She's not the *Minorca?*" cried the Admiral.

"No, sir, she carries no royals."

On this Captain Acton and his friend went on deck. The schooner was travelling three or four knots one way, and the stranger was heading directly for her at some small pace, so that the speed of the two vessels being combined, the sail might be expected to show a clear hull; which she did, and with the aid of their telescopes, Captain Acton and Sir William confirmed the conjecture of Captain Weaver. She was either a little brig or a brigantine—her after-sails were concealed; her burden was very small. The dusty and rusty complexion of her canvas neutralised the brilliance which most ships' sails shine with when the silver glory of the morning sun pours strong upon them. By half-past nine, three bells by the schooner's clock, the stranger was on the larboard-bow with her main topsail to the mast, and so close that it seemed almost possible to distinguish the faces of her people.

She was a little brig, and an immense but ragged British ensign fluttered at her trysail gaff-end. She had been painted black, but the fret of an ocean long kept, the hurl and whirl of prodigious seas which were like to founder her, the blistering heat of tropic suns,the viewless fangs of the wind had so worn her sides that she was mottled with patches of different colour as though she was suffering from some distemper which ravaged vessels of her sort when the voyage was of great length. She rolled wearily, as though her old bones were worn out, and every time she hove her bilge to the eye she disclosed a very landed estate of weed, long, serpentine, trailing, like the huge eel-like growths which sway from black rocks in the white wash of breakers.

"Ho, the schooner ahoy!" shouted a man, standing close to the larboard main-shrouds.

"Hallo!" was the answer from Captain Weaver.

"We are the brig *Louisa Ann* of Whitby from Callao, one hundred and seventy days out, bound to the port we belongs to. We are short of provisions, and should feel grateful if you could let us have a cask of beef."

This was clearly delivered, and every syllable caught on board the *Aurora.* Captain Weaver looked at Captain Acton, who immediately assented.

"Send a boat and we'll give you what you want!" shouted Weaver.

A few men were to be seen racing aft, and in a minute or two a squab boat descended from a pair of davits as stout as catheads with four men in her, two to row, one to bale, and one to steer.

Whilst they were coming Captain Weaver said to Captain Acton: "The master of that brig, sir, seems to have his wife aboard."

But though Captain Acton and Admiral Lawrence heard him, their eyes were busy with the boat as she approached, and neither raised a glass to determine the appearance of the female.

The man who steered the boat was the captain; he climbed over the side of the *Aurora,* and presented the aspect of a man not unlike Mr John Eagle; he looked sour with succession of bad weather, with little ships that made nothing but leeway on a wind, with immensely long voyages, with shortness of rations and fresh water, and with the aridity of the ocean which he had been forced to keep for nearly the whole of his life.

"I should be much obliged for a cask of beef, sir," he said, after touching the narrow penthouse of a queerly constructed fur cap. "It's still a long way home for that there *Louisa Ann,* whose bin a hundred and seventy days in bringing us so fur."

"Have you spoke any ships lately?" asked Captain Weaver.

"The last we spoke," answered the man, "was the day before yesterday. And we took out of her by request of her master, a young female who was said to have gone mad, but for my part I never met with anybody saner. She's an additional mouth, and a cask of beef would be grateful."

"A young female!" said Captain Acton. "What was the name of the vessel you took her from?"

At this point the Admiral levelled his glass at the brig. The master of the *Louisa Ann* went to the side and shouted down, received an answer, returned and said: "Her name was the *Minorca.*"

"The *Minorca!*" shouted Captain Acton. "The day before yesterday! And you received a young lady from her?"

"By God!" cried Admiral Lawrence in a voice of thunder, letting fly the profanity with the bellows of a boatswain, "why, Acton, there's Lucy aboard that brig! I can make her out plain in this glass."

"She's a beautiful young lady—highly eddicated," said the master of *Louisa Ann.*

Captain Acton levelled his telescope. He did not need to long survey the figure of the woman who was standing near the tiller that was grasped by a man. The lenses brought her face close to him.

"It is Lucy!" he said, in a voice in which awe and amazement were so mingled that one should say the apparition of a ghost, of something spiritual and fearful to the observer, could not have filled the hollow of his mouth with that tone.

He was now seized with a passion of delight.

"Lower a boat, Captain Weaver! Lower a boat!" he shouted, losing his habitual gentleman-like coolness and calm in the overwhelming sensations of that moment. "Bear a hand now! Be quick! It is the lady for whom we have been chasing the *Minorca.* Quick, I say!" He stamped his foot.

"She is waving her handkerchief!" cried the Admiral, with his eye at the telescope. "God bless her! God bless us all! What a miracle of discovery!"

"A relation, sir?" said the master of the *Louisa Ann,* addressing Captain Weaver, whom he had immediately perceived was not of the standing of the two Naval gentlemen.

"My daughter, sir!" cried Captain Acton.

"Then I'm proud and 'appy to have been the instrument of a-bringing her to you. I'm a father myself and can understand your feelings, sir," said the captain of the brig.

But congratulations were not in place in such a moment as this. A fine boat of the *Aurora* was alongside manned by five sailors, who being clad in much the same sort of apparel, carried a sort of war-like aspect as though the boat was proceeding from something heavily armed and much to be feared. Captain Acton and the Admiral sprang into her with the agility of boys, thanks to the energy infused by the apparition of Lucy waving her pocket-handkerchief, and whilst they were being swept to the brig Captain Weaver asked her master one or two questions.

This was the story his interrogatories elicited. On the day before yesterday the brig that was very short of provisions and water sighted a vessel, which on her approach proved to be so rigged that the master declared he had never seen the like.

"She carried nothing but fore-and-aft sails on her mizzen-mast," said he.

On which Captain Weaver exclaimed: "The *Minorca,* of course. She was French, and what's called barque-rigged."

Well, the *Louisa Ann* backed her topsail, and the strangely rigged ship backed hers, and the master of the brig, not choosing to ask too many favours at once, hailed to know if she could spare some fresh water, as they had run to an allowance that was close upon famine.

He was received on board by a tall, commanding, handsome man, who, on the arrival of the master of the *Louisa Ann,* said he was welcome to a supply of fresh water, and that in return he would ask him to receive a young lady who had gone mad during the voyage from England, and convey her to that country. Her name was Miss Acton. She was a daughter of Captain Acton of Old Harbour Town, and the captain of the *Louisa Ann* might make sure of a handsome reward for his services from the father. The lady, the tall, handsome man said, had consented to elope with him, and they were to be married at Rio de Janeiro; but she had gone out of her mind. The fine, handsome man felt he could do nothing better than to restore her as soon as possible to her friends. The captain of the brig said that he had but a poor accommodation for a lady of her quality, but wanting the fresh water very badly and likewise reflecting that he might receive a handsome reward, and learning from the fine, handsome man that Miss Acton was by no means violent, but on the contrary gentle and melancholy, he consented.

"And how did she seem," said Captain Weaver, "when she got into the boat?"

"She never spoke nor smiled," answered the captain of the brig, "but got quietly in and sat quietly down, and kept her eyes fixed upon the thwart that was next hers whilst the water was being lowered; but afterwards when I got her over the side and put her into the best cabin we could accommodate her with, she began to talk, said she thanked God for her deliverance, and was grateful indeed to Him for now being on her way home. And she spoke as clear and collected as I do, and is no more mad than I am. But she did not let me into the job whatever it was. She hasn't given me an idea as to her elopement and the reason of her being sent aboard me, and I'm always a-wondering what the trick is."

The *Aurora*'s boat was swept alongside the brig, and Captain Acton and the Admiral clambered over the side up a short flight of steps, and in an instant Lucy was clasped in the devouring embrace of her father. Such an old-world scene taxes the highest gifts of the pen or the brush. This *Louisa Ann* was about fifty years old; she was nearly as broad as she was long. Her fore-mast was stepped far in the bows; her decks were stained and grimy; the paint had faded out of the inside of her bulwarks. Her sails were patched and so dingy that they might have been coloured as a smack's. Her rusty sides were lined with yawning seams amid which three little circular windows were merged with no accentuation from the dirt-shrouded glass which prevented the sea from entering the blistered, worn, mani-coloured hull. Her sailors looked as though they were shipwrecked: long-haired, bearded, sallow, in clothes considerably tattered, in aspect melancholy and dejected with lack of nourishment, dullness of sailing and ceaseless motion: for here was the tub wallowing like a buoy in a popple upon a smooth sea, and the frightful weather she would make off Cape Horn or in a gale of wind the imagination of a sailor could readily picture by witnessing her motions now.

On the stage of this little marine theatre the father clasped his daughter, whilst the Admiral, with emotion damp in his eyes, looked on. Captain Acton released his child and surveyed her, whilst the Admiral seizing both her hands, raised them to his lips, one after the other, mumbling in broken tones: "May God bless you! I thank God we have found thee!"

She was dressed, of course, in the costume in which she had been kidnapped, and like the sailors she looked very much the worse for wear and tear. Her jockey-shaped hat, so modish and even rakish when purchased, had fallen into a confusion of headgear, a something that might have wanted a name had it been found on the highway. Her hair looked wild in the inartistic dressing it suffered from. Her rich and characteristic bloom had faded, and what lingered was but as a delicate faint flush of expiring sunset. But even as she stood, not the most cynical and aspish of her own sex would have challenged her beauty, the charms of her figure, the melting sweetness of her eyes on whose dark-brown iris the white lids, rich in eyelash, reposed. Those eyes were wet now, and tears were upon her cheeks.

But what was to be said aboard that loutish old brig, with a crew of half-starved, weedy mariners looking on agape? In a very few minutes Lucy was handed into the *Aurora*'s boat, and the party were making for the schooner as swiftly as the dip and sweep of oars could impel the keen-bowed little fabric.

"What a wonderful meeting!" cried Captain Acton, blessing his daughter with a smile sweet and good with the pulse of the heart of a father who adores his only child. "You will have much to tell us, my darling."

"Much," said the Admiral.

"Oh yes. It is a story that will make you wonder," said Lucy. "I fear Aunt Caroline was terribly upset when she found me missing."

"Oh, we'll soon stand her up again," said Captain Acton. "Did you recognise the *Aurora?*"

"Oh yes, sir; how could she be mistaken?" answered Lucy. "How beautiful she looked as she came towards us!"

"You have been half-starved in that brig," said Captain Acton, searching his daughter's face, and running his eyes over her dress.

"We'll soon have her back again to her old moorings," cried the Admiral. "She cannot gain in beauty, but the schooner will give her the colour she lacks."

There was very little to be said in that boat where there were five oarsmen to listen. The few of the crew who remained on board the schooner greeted Miss Lucy's recovery and arrival alongside by springing into the rigging and delivering cheer after cheer with much demonstration of arm and cap. She was carefully handed over the side, Captain Weaver receiving her, hat in hand and a succession of congratulatory bows, and without more ado she was conducted into the cabin that had been assigned her by her father, who embraced her again and again when he had her alone, saying that she looked tired, that she must take some repose before she began to tell him and the Admiral what had happened to her. He held her by the hands. He looked at her face; his affection, his gratitude, his delight overwhelmed him.

"Oh my dear, dear Lucy," he cried, "little can you conceive how the man who carried you off has made your aunt and me, and his father, suffer!"

"He acted wickedly in luring me on board only to steal me," said Lucy, "and he is wicked to rob you of your property. But oh, father, villain as he seems, his behaviour to me was that of a gentleman— and—and I am sorry for him."

Captain Acton's face changed with the astonishment wrought in him by his daughter's words and manner of speaking, and instantly to his memory recurred the remark of his sister that, if Mr Lawrence was in love with Lucy, she was equally in love with him, though she made no sign save to the scrutinising eye of an old maid.

"We'll talk of that later, my dear one," he said. "You'll find several changes of apparel in those boxes. I left it to your aunt to pack them. She would know what you needed, though we had no hope of falling in with you in this way. Some breakfast shall be got for you in the cabin when you are ready, and then you will tell the Admiral and me your story."

After further endearments between this devoted father and his daughter, Captain Acton closed her cabin door and went on deck.

He found Captain Weaver, the master of the brig, and the captain of the brig in conversation. The skipper of the brig had made no entry touching his falling in with the *Minorca*. He could depend upon nothing but his memory and to the best of his recollection he had given to Captain Weaver the latitude and longitude in which he had spoken the *Minorca* on the morning before the previous day. It was at least certain that the barque was within easy sailing reach of the schooner; it was equally sure that the schooner was almost directly in the tail of the wake of the *Minorca* and that if Captain Weaver continued the course he had been steering he was bound to overhaul her, providing the schooner was the swifter vessel.

Leaving Captain Weaver to converse with the skipper and to supply his wants, Captain Acton passed his arm through the Admiral's and led him aft.

"Now," said he in a soft voice full of the emotion which his daughter's preservation and restoration had filled him with "now that my dear child, by the mercy and goodness of Almighty God, has been returned to me I am for heading straight for Old Harbour Town, for she has had enough of the sea—more than enough, and I am for having her at home, safe again, She has gone through much, she looks ill, she needs the rest and nursing she can only get at home."

The Admiral was violently agitated. He exclaimed in broken tones: "If this is your decision I implore you to reconsider it. You, sir, who are the soul of benevolence would not act with heartless cruelty towards an old friend, but heartlessly cruel you must prove to me if, with the opportunity which this schooner provides and with the *Minorca* within a few hours' reach, you suffer my worthless, ungrateful son to make away with your property, and render me hopeless and helpless as a man who has no means to repay you the loss you must sustain."

Captain Acton was silent for a few moments. He then said: "My dear friend, have you reflected upon all that your son's return to England must signify to him?"

"Your property must be recovered. My son must take the consequences of his acts. I know what it means, sir—the gibbet and chains—for thus they serve the pirate," exclaimed the poor old Admiral, grim and desperate.

"God forbid!" exclaimed Captain Acton, whose spirits, it could be seen, were suddenly and violently disordered by the Admiral's speech. "They hang no pirate without a prosecution. Who is to prosecute? Admiral Lawrence's old friend, Captain Acton? No, sir, by the holy name of that good God who has restored my child to me, not I!"

"Oh, Acton, Acton, you overwhelm me!" murmured the Admiral, turning his head away to sea, and speaking with a voice that trembled with the tears of a man's heart.

"What I meant was," said Captain Acton, tenderly pressing his friend's arm, "if your son returns to England he may be arrested for debt, in which case his actions of abduction and piracy may be brought to light, and if I was not compelled to prosecute, I should be held guilty of conniving at a crime. All this must be avoided, and can be avoided."

"It can be avoided, and still your property may be preserved to you," exclaimed the Admiral. "My unhappy son will throw himself upon your mercy——"

"It shall be extended sir, it shall be extended," broke in Captain Acton.

"And we can land him privately," continued the Admiral, "at an English port, where habited in the clothes of a common sailor he will seek a berth before the mast, and sail away—to be heard of no more."

Here this fine old seaman fairly broke down, and stepping to the bulwarks, hid his face in his hands, whilst convulsion after convulsion seemed to rend his sturdy figure.

Captain Acton waited until this unconquerable fit of grief should have abated. He then went to his friend's side, and, passing his arm round his neck, said: "My dear old friend, keep up your heart! We will pursue the *Minorca* and regain her if possible, and depend upon it, your son shall be made to suffer as little as can be helped. Meanwhile, let us wait until we hear Lucy's story."

CHAPTER XV

NELSON

BY THE TIME that Lucy was seated at the cabin table of the *Aurora* at the meal which had been prepared for her, with her father on one side and Sir William Lawrence on the other watching her with riveted eyes, listening to her with impassioned attention, putting such questions as must naturally arise from this most extraordinary adventure, the brig *Louisa Ann* was about three miles astern rolling and flapping onwards for Whitby, her larder enriched by two casks of beef and a cask of fresh water, whilst in her master's pocket was Captain Acton's address; for it had been agreed that in consideration of the brig's skipper having taken Miss Lucy Acton aboard his ship, he was to receive the fifty guineas reward which had been offered for her recovery, and which Captain Acton would forward when on his return he should know where to address the skipper.

And meanwhile Captain Weaver had received instructions from Captain Acton to continue his chase of the *Minorca,* and the schooner under full and large breasts of canvas was gently leaning from a pleasant little breeze which had sprung up whilst the *Aurora* was sending meat and water to the brig, and was sliding with some show of nimbleness through a blue surface that was summer-like in peaceful rippling, in beautiful dyes, and in splendid distances.

The cabin that Lucy was now to occupy had been fitted up and furnished with all possible reference to her needs, for it had been hoped that if she was not overtaken at sea she would be found at Rio, and Acton's and his sister's expectations were not so forlorn but that they believed the *Aurora* would return with the girl, and the possibility was to be provided for with as much foresight as could be bestowed on the circumstance of her return as a fact. The boxes contained such wearing apparel as she herself might have chosen from her wardrobe. The toilet table was comfortably supplied: indeed nothing that she was accustomed to use in dressing herself was absent.

So, then, as she sat at table she almost looked the same beautiful Lucy Acton who had left her house early one morning for a walk in which she had met the hunchback Paul and read a letter he gave her. The old rich colour was indeed lacking; no charm of hat, no grace of coiffure, no elegance of costume could immediately qualify or dispel the languor of fatigue in the eyes, the delicate shadow pencilled by worry and an enormous mental strain under the eyes, and a general expression in movements of silence or repose, of anxiety, pain, and another quality which you might have seen was present without being able to give it a name.

One or two questions of no moment had been asked and answered when the Admiral exclaimed: "I beg, dearest madam, and you, Captain Acton, will forgive me for perhaps unseasonably thrusting in, by asking if you can tell me that atrocious, and to me heartbreaking as has been the conduct of my son, he acted nevertheless during his relations with you on board the *Minorca* as a gentleman?"

"He did. I can assure you on my word of honour, Sir William," answered the girl, with a glow and fervour that caused her father to again attentively examine her face with an expression which changed the look it was wearing. "In my feigned madness I reproached him in language which I knew was not ladylike. I called him a scoundrel, and a rogue, and many injurious and aggravating words which came into my head I flung at him, acting all the while the part of a madwoman. Yet, sir," she said, turning to her father, "never once did my violent attacks upon his temper and character cause him to forget himself. He bowed to me, he madamed me, he was throughout as gentlemanlike and respectful as I had ever found him when we met at Old Harbour House or in Old Harbour Town."

The Admiral put his hand upon hers.

"I thank you for this gracious assurance," he said, in a voice deep with feeling, with eyes which looked humid as they reposed upon her, and with a faint smile like the first illumination of the face by a dawning happiness.

"Did you act the part of a madwoman?" said Captain Acton.

"Yes, Papa. When I found myself his prisoner and at his mercy I quickly thought over what I should do to rescue myself. I understood, first of all, that I must disgust him if possible." Captain Acton and Sir William exchanged a look at this stroke of *naïveté* and lightly smiled. "How was I to disgust him?" continued the beautiful young creature. "I made up my mind to pretend to be mad."

"And you are so fine an actress as to have been able to persuade so intelligent a man that you were actually mad?" enquired Captain Acton with some astonishment.

"I was determined to try. I could see no other way of frightening and disgusting him."

"The spirit of her mother came to her aid," said the Admiral, who had heard much of the genius of Kitty O'Hara.

"Ha!" exclaimed Captain Acton, looking fondly at his child, "I don't doubt it is in you. But you have suffered it to rest as an unsuspected quality."

"And you made Mr Lawrence afraid of you?" said Sir William.

She answered by relating the story of some of those freaks with which the reader has been made acquainted; she described other acts of madness which had taxed her imagination to devise. She was mad to all who spoke to her because, as she justly said, "it would have been ridiculous for me to have been mad to the Captain and sane to everybody else in the ship."

Captain Acton listened to her with profound interest. He was greatly impressed and moved by his daughter's exhibition of traditionary genius. She recalled his wife, of whom he was passionately proud and fond. He had never imagined that Lucy had the talent of an actress, but the dramatic character of her narrative and every point in her extraordinary relation convinced him that she was a born artist, and that accident had compelled her to reveal to herself gifts of power, perception, and imagination of whose existence she had been as ignorant as her father.

"My love," said Captain Acton, "will you tell me how it happened that you should have allowed yourself to be lured on board the *Minorca?*"

"I will tell you exactly," said Lucy, and the Admiral bent his ear. "It was a very fine morning and I was awake early, and I thought I would walk as far as the pier and back, intending to be home before you read prayers. I left Mamie behind, as she has a trick of running into the water, and she swims so badly that I am afraid she will one day be drowned. On the way I met the red-haired hunchback whom I had seen about Old Harbour Town at times. There was something in his manner that made me think he was making for Old Harbour House. He saluted me very respectfully, and gave me a letter written in pencil. In my excitement and alarm I did not know what I did with it. If I put it in my pocket it was not there when I felt. It was signed by Walter Lawrence, who wrote that Captain Acton had come on board the *Minorca* had stumbled over something the name of which I forget, and fallen a few feet into the hold, which lay open. Mr Lawrence believed that Captain Acton was not dangerously hurt, but he was in a very bad way and in great pain, and he had asked Mr Lawrence to write to his daughter Lucy and acquaint her with the accident and beg her immediate presence, but she must on no account make the disaster known to her aunt or to any other member of the household.

"I was completely deceived by this letter," continued Lucy, "and hurried to the ship followed by the hunchback, who conducted me downstairs and opened a cabin door. I entered, thinking to find you there, sir. The door was instantly shut, and I found myself alone with Mr Lawrence."

"The villain!" muttered the Admiral.

"But could you suppose, my love, that I should be down at that ship at so early an hour?" said the Captain.

"I was too much agitated to reflect, Papa," Lucy answered. "It seemed so natural—so reasonable—and I hastened to the ship, in the belief that you were lying in her seriously hurt."

"But suppose that fellow Paul had not met you?" said Captain Acton.

"Mr Lawrence is very daring," answered Lucy. "I can easily believe that the hunchback Paul, as he is called, had orders if he did not meet me to go to the house and deliver the letter to me in person."

"But wouldn't Mr Lawrence guess that I should be at home at that hour, and that you would know I was at home?" said Captain Acton.

"The Devil," said the Admiral, "is very bountiful to his servants in his gifts of opportunity."

"True!" answered Captain Acton. "Fortune certainly favoured Mr Lawrence. And now, Lucy, I want you to explain how it was that neither I, nor the Admiral, nor Captain Weaver, could find a single living creature to tell us that you had been seen passing along the wharves to the *Minorca?*"

"I am sure I cannot answer that question, sir. I was not disguised, nor was my face concealed. I wore my jockey hat. My spirits were in too great a hurry to allow me to take any notice, but I am quite sure that there were very few people about; none of these might have known or observed me, and it is not surprising, therefore, that you should not have guessed what had become of me."

"What excuse did Mr Lawrence make to the men for sending you into another ship?"

"I cannot believe that he made any excuses at all. He is not a man," Lucy answered, with a faint smile which was certainly not unsuggestive of that sort of expression which the human face puts on when its wearer speaks with secret pride of another, "to make excuses for his conduct to the common sailors under him. Indeed, Papa, I don't know which side would be more surprised: he, in excusing his actions to the sailors, or they, that he should condescend to explain. When I first went on deck after being kept in the cabin the scene I witnessed might have been on the stage of a theatre: the crew stood in a body in the fore-part of the ship; two men were a little in advance of them, and at one of these men Mr Lawrence had levelled a pistol. There he stood, pistol in hand, and the sailor, stubborn and defiant, never budged. I felt faint. I feared he would shoot and kill the man."

"He didn't shoot, then!" cried the Admiral.

"No, Sir William; something like a scuffle followed, and Mr Pledge, who, I believe, was the boatswain, acting as an officer on board, holding some irons in his hand, seized one of the men, but I thought in a very gentle, friendly way, and carried him below."

"Did no mutiny amongst the crew follow?" enquired Captain Acton.

"I think not. I am sure not. Mr Lawrence awed them all. I could never have believed in such a commanding, overwhelming manner as he put on."

The Admiral drummed with his fingers upon the table, looking down.

"But pray, Lucy," exclaimed Captain Acton, "what was Mr Eagle about? Did not he know that you were Mr Lawrence's prisoner, though he might not have been able to guess that it was Mr Lawrence's intention to navigate the ship to Rio to sell her there? Did not he make any effort to rescue you by appeals to the Captain, or by so working up the crew as to determine them to sail the ship back to Old Harbour Town?"

"I can assure you, Papa," answered Lucy, "that Mr Eagle is a very silly, sour man, in whose rheumatism I shall no longer take any interest. He thought I was mad, and was as much afraid of me as he was of Mr Lawrence, and was careful to avoid me. As I just now said, if I was to be mad to Mr Lawrence, I must be mad to the others, and fully believing that I was mad, the crew would naturally think that the most humane course Mr Lawrence could adopt was to send me home by any ship that would receive me."

"You must have acted your part well, my child," said Captain Acton, viewing the girl with admiration and fondness.

"I was forced to act many parts. Every day the strain grew more and more unsupportable, and I prayed for the end to come in the way I was working for. I was obliged to act many parts, some so base, sordid, even disgusting, that my heart sickened at my imposition, and the internal struggle with my feelings was as hard as my external efforts. I had to invent my parts and rehearse them."

"What were the characters which could convince so shrewd and intelligent a man as Mr Lawrence that you were mad?" enquired Captain Acton, the habitual gravity of whose face was replaced by a constant expression of astonishment.

"I pretended to hear voices, and answered, of course, when Mr Lawrence was present," said Lucy. "I would bow to visionary persons and address them. One was the Duke of Clarence, whose hand I kissed while Mr Lawrence looked on."

Captain Acton's eyes opened wide; the Admiral gurgled a nervous laugh.

"I secreted my rings and some rubbish, and made signs with a mad face to Mr Lawrence to come and look at the treasure I had hidden. I took my meals on the deck crouching like an animal. I would shriek with laughter which had nothing to do with what was said. A later and most difficult effort was to believe that I was Mrs Siddons."

"What on earth have you been reading in your day about madness to give you such extraordinary ideas?" said Captain Acton.

"I can't tell how the fancies came to me," said Lucy. "I know that mad people see apparitions and reply to imaginary voices. I also remembered old Sarah Hutchinson who was thought mad because she was always trying to tear up things: her sheets, her gowns, anything that might be given to her. It was the remembrance of this disease in her that made me rip up my mattress and scatter the feathers about the cabin."

"Some of these days, madam," said the Admiral, "I trust you will favour me with a sample of the genius that terrified Mr Lawrence and led to your recovery, for which God be praised."

She looked at Sir William, and with that look her face underwent a change—the change that had amazed Mr Lawrence, that transformation of beauty into alternate idiocy and bright-eyed madness, that marvellous facial motion which had done more to convince her kidnapper that his act had driven her mad than all the rest of her impersonations put together. Her rich and beautiful eyelids seemed to shrink up into the sockets in which her eyes were lodged; the eyes themselves seemed to sparkle with the uninterpretable passions of the afflicted brain; the faint bloom which her cheek wore when she stepped on board faded as the picture of a red rose overhanging its reflection in water disappears at the blurring by the wind of its liquid mirror. Her lips were elongated and parted, and grey with tension, and her teeth, white as sea foam, were set. The whole expression of madness was incomparably life-like.

Sir William started back in his chair, crying faintly: "My God! Look at her, Acton!"

The father caught that surprising face of dramatic genius a moment before she composed her features to their natural calm beauty of drooping lid and brooding eye and sweet expression of lip, and the tenderness, the gentleness, the goodness that was her heart's and her soul's, and the foundations of her moral nature.

"Well, Lucy," said Captain Acton, after fetching a deep breath of astonishment, "should I die insolvent, you will know your fortune. You have it in your face: I don't question the rest of your performance. 'Tis the very spirit of her mother, sir. Small wonder that Mr Lawrence was convinced."

"The British stage misses a splendid figure, a shining light, in your neglect of it, madam," said the Admiral.

"Oh, I have no taste for acting. I have no ambition to be an actress. This effort was forced upon me. How was I to disgust him, sir?"

Again at this ingenuous remark the Admiral and the Captain exchanged a smile.

"Do you think, my dear," said Captain Acton, "that the crew know they are being carried to Rio de Janeiro? I believe, sir," he continued, addressing the Admiral, "that in Mr Lawrence's letter that Mr Greyquill brought to us reference was made to certain sealed orders given by me to the captain of the ship to be opened and read to the crew in a position that was or was not named—I forget."

"I have no doubt that the crew know that the ship is not being steered to the West Indies," answered Lucy. "In silent weather in my cabin I could hear any conversation that passed in the room where Mr Lawrence or his officers sat at table, and more than once I overheard Mr Pledge and Mr Eagle talking about the ship's navigation, wondering to what port Captain Acton had in his sealed orders directed Mr Lawrence to carry the ship, to sell her and dismiss the crew. I therefore supposed that the rest of the men would know that the ship was not bound to Kingston."

"I judge by this," said Captain Acton, addressing the Admiral, "that my sealed orders"—he smiled sarcastically, and the Admiral listened with a frown—"have not yet been read to the crew by Mr Lawrence."

"Where is the *Aurora* going?" enquired Lucy.

"We are pursuing the *Minorca,*" answered Captain Acton.

She looked down upon the table with a grave face. "She is not far distant," she said, speaking as though in soliloquy. "It is only three days ago that I was on board of her. This swift vessel is certain to overtake her. And what then will happen?"

And as she said this she suddenly lifted her eyes half-veiled, dark, and beaming to her father's face.

"The Admiral and I," answered Captain Acton, talking as though slightly embarrassed, though moved by other feelings, "consider that we cannot do better than remove Mr Lawrence into this ship, and carry him to England."

"And what after?" enquired Lucy, observing that her father paused with an expressive look at Sir William, "I mean what after as regards Mr Lawrence?"

"You do not wish him to be hanged for piracy, even if abduction be not a hanging matter," said Captain Acton with a smile in his eyes as he met the Admiral's.

The girl shuddered. "I know they hang for piracy!" she exclaimed. "It is what must happen if you convey him to England."

"He must be prosecuted before they can hang him," said Captain Acton, whilst the Admiral's regard was fastened upon Lucy's face with such tokens of affectionate gratitude and surprise which rose to a passion of delight as made the worthy, poor old man's jolly, weather-scored, truly British countenance moving to behold. "And who is to prosecute him? I alone am the sufferer. I alone can prosecute. Am I likely to do so? Am I the man to bring my friend's son to the gallows?"

"No, sir, no!" cried the Admiral in a deep, trembling voice.

"But though you do not prosecute him, sir," said Lucy, "might not his story become known so that he might be arrested for piracy, and charged and convicted on the evidence of his crew?"

"You are a Portia," said Captain Acton.

"She reasons exquisitely well!" exclaimed the Admiral, slowly and dolefully wagging his head.

"We propose to provide against all that your fears picture, my dear," said Captain Acton, who could no longer doubt that Aunt Caroline was right, and that there had been, and that there still lived, a deep secret liking or love for Mr Lawrence in Lucy, which had not suffered but rather gained by his rascality, "by landing Mr Lawrence

at an English port where he is unknown, where habited in the garb
of a common merchant sailor he will seek, and of course obtain,
employment before the mast, and sail away clear of all dangerous
consequences of his conduct."

"Sail away, madam, into the remotest part of the earth to be seen
no more—to be heard of no more," said the Admiral, trying to master his face as he spoke. But he failed and turned his head from his
companions, and would have buried his face in his hands but that
he would not have them know that his love for his son was deeper
than his horror at his conduct.

The silence that followed was eloquent with recognition of the
poor old gentleman's trouble. Lucy left her chair, and going close to
the Admiral said, yet not so low but that Captain Acton overheard
her: "It will not be as you say, Sir William. Indeed it must not be. So
fine a character besmirched by acts into which a very bitter necessity has forced him, ought not to be found in the common garb of
a humble working merchant sailor, nor buried in some distant parts
where he can never shine as a man of fine and heroic spirit fit to
fill the highest position in the service he has left; and above all, and
which is best, sir, capable of bitter regret, of deep feeling, of exert-
ing the power by which the humbled man is alone able to struggle—I mean the power of self-regeneration."

She spoke like a young wild-eyed prophetess; her tones had a vigorous, dramatic clearness which made her voice new to her father's
ears. Her language, which seemed exalted beyond her age, beyond
anything one would look for in the lips of so calm, modest, and
undemonstrative a girl, she appeared to make peculiarly appropri-
ate to her years and sex, by her delivery, her melodies of accentuation, the easy grasp with which, it was clear, she held a subject that
was deep in human nature.

The Admiral rose, and addressing her as though she were the con-
sort of a king, said: "Madam, as the father of the person you speak
of, I ask Almighty God, who is merciful and knows the human heart,
to bless you for your words."

Captain Acton was silent. He was astonished. He had never
observed his daughter as Aunt Caroline did. He was wanting in feminine sagacity where the heart is concerned. He saw that if his

daughter was not in love with Mr Lawrence, she was dangerously near that passion; she seemed to him to have been transformed into a sweetheart by usage which would have made the heart of most young women fierce with hate and horror. She was under a spell which she thought to break by the practice of an inherited art, as miraculous in effect as it had been unsuspected in being, and she had left her kidnapper seemingly as enamoured of him as though his behaviour from the beginning had been strictly honourable and chivalrous, an additament to the passion which his gallant record, his lofty bearing, and his handsome looks had inspired in her.

Her rising from the table had caused the gentlemen to rise. They went on deck. Lucy said she was tired and would be glad to take some rest; her accommodation on board the *Louisa Ann* was very wretched, and she had scarcely been able to sleep on account of the gruff voices, the alarming creaking and groaning noises, and a strange hideous smell which probably came from the cargo, all which she must always associate in memory with the *Louisa Ann.* She wished however to see the *Aurora,* and for some minutes she stood on the deck with her father and the Admiral beside her, gazing round the picture as though entranced. Once again her lovely eyes seemed to brood even in their glances; they appeared to dwell with a dreamy delight on what they beheld. Through her parted lips the sweet breeze rushed, and the hair upon her brow flickered like shadows cast by the wavering of a silver flame.

The bright, mild wind came gushing steadily over the bulwark rail; the decks were slightly sloped, and their seams ran black, as defined as the ebony lines ruled by standing rigging in moonshine, and the planks between shone like ivory. On high the heeling structure was a vast surface of canvas, with three square yards at the fore for the fore topsail and topgallant sail, and over the swan-like stem of this American clipper—for a clipper she was—the immensely long bowsprit and jibboom spread the foot of huge triangular wings which gave the hull a grand and noble look forward, as though she was about to spring from the water in the brilliant flash of foam which darted from the wet and metalled fore-foot, to form one of the squadron of cream-coloured clouds royal in their progress with trailing robes of glory.

"What a contrast," exclaimed Lucy, "to the *Louisa Ann!*"

She turned her eyes into that remote part of the sea on the quarter where the *Louisa Ann* hung transformed by distance and sunshine into a star of day. So marvellous is the magic wrought by the wand of the deep in its passage over even such shapeless enormities as the Whitby brig.

When she had drunk her full of the wide scene of sea and sky and milk-bright schooner in the midst, with never a break the clear horizon round save the *Louisa Ann* that was fast fading, Lucy went below, followed by her father, who kissed her again in a transport of delight at having recovered her, and in being able once more to hold his adored child to his heart, and before she entered her berth to lie down and rest, he said to her: "I am so overjoyed, my darling, in having recovered you that I take no interest in the *Minorca.* Mr Lawrence may do with her what he pleases—I have you."

She smiled and kissed him, and then said: "But oh, sir, his poor old father! You have regained me, your only child, but Sir William, an old, a good man, an upright, a beautiful character, must lose his son, an only child too."

"He shall not lose him through me," said Captain Acton, speaking with the solemnity with which he might utter a sentence in a sacred building. "Sir William shall never be made to suffer at my hands. I will not lift a finger to prosecute Mr Lawrence, who, if he ever returns to Old Harbour Town, will be safe from all but his creditors."

She slightly coloured as though surprised into an emotion of happiness, and again kissing her father went into her berth, and Captain Acton returned to the Admiral slowly and thoughtfully.

It was early next morning, about six bells—seven o'clock—when an event of the deepest historic interest to those who took part in it, broke the routine of the chase of the *Minorca* by the *Aurora.* The wind was a little to the north of west, and blew a gentle breeze which rippled the waters upon the long-drawn swell that came heaving from horizon to horizon, from north-west to south-east, as though a gale of wind had been lately blowing or was to come. Though freckled with high fine-weather clouds the dome of heaven sank in purity to its girdle of sea line, and from the deck at daybreak nothing was in sight.

But soon as the east changed from darkness into a pale luminous grey, with the stars fading above the soaring haze of light as through they fled in scatterings, a sailor trotted up the forerigging of the *Aurora,* and shinned as high as the topgallant yard over which he flung a leg with his back against the mast, and taking the telescope that was slung upon his back in his hands, he slowly and steadily directed the lenses round the girdle of brine which was now faintly stealing into a visible horizon in the west, and his silence betokened to Captain Weaver, who stood on the quarterdeck with eyes fixed upon the fellow up aloft, that nothing was in sight.

Captain Weaver was carrying out the instructions he had received at Old Harbour Town. He was chasing the *Minorca.* The recovery of Lucy had led to no change in those instructions. Though Captain Acton in his gratitude for the restoration of his child was willing to relinquish the pursuit and to leave the *Minorca* and the handsome piratical scoundrel who had sailed away with her and Lucy to their fate, he had not revealed his thoughts to Captain Weaver, nor to the Admiral, and the *Aurora* at this hour of daybreak on a day in June 1805, was steadily stemming in chase of the barque which she was to capture, Captain Weaver did not exactly know how. For the *Aurora* was unarmed, whilst the *Minorca* mounted four pieces of artillery, and was in command of a naturally desperate fighting and fearless spirit, one whose neck would certainly be broken by the hangman if he was taken: unless indeed his crew turned upon him, and backed their yards and stopped the ship, that her owner might come by his own, despite Mr Lawrence's levelled pistol or any threats he might make use of in reference to the powder magazine. "But," Captain Weaver had thought to himself on several occasions, "time enough to know what's a-going to happen when we heave the *Minorca* into view or draw abreast of her, for who's to tell but that we are bound to miss her, in which case we shall receive her at Rio, providing her skipper hasn't got scent of us and shifted his hellum for another port, and then there can be no blazing away of carronades on one side and a trimming of sail to keep clear of shot on the other."

Just as the sun rose the Admiral came on deck, and as the old gentleman stepped over the coaming of the sunk door of the deck-house and mounted the two or three steps that carried him on deck, the man on the topgallant yard, with his telescope shooting straight from his eye into the south-west quarter of the sea, bawled: "On deck there! Two sail, a point and a half on the starboard bow."

Scarcely had the words been received by the ears on deck when he shouted: "Two more sail, just astern of the two first."

"What's this going to be?" exclaimed the Admiral to Captain Weaver.

Another call from the mast-head, and yet another and another and another in brief intervals of scarce half a minute's duration each; and at last fourteen sail were reported in sight on the starboard bow, sailing large, heading north-east or thereabouts so that the course of the *Aurora* would bring her into the thick of them.

At this moment Captain Acton came on deck. He saw the cloud of sail in an instant and the Admiral having taken the ship's glass from Captain Weaver's hands, Acton rushed into the deck-house to get his own fine telescope.

"A small convoy, sir, I think," said Captain Weaver.

"No, sir," responded Captain Acton, with his eye at his glass. "Line of battle-ships, and three smaller vessels," for by this time the distant fleet by combination of its own and the passage of the *Aurora* through the water had lifted above the horizon to the topsails of the hindmost, the courses of the van swelling and falling plain in the lenses as the structures bowed upon the large, wide, steel-coloured swell tinctured by the day-spring.

"I agree with you, Acton: a fleet of men-of-war," said the Admiral.

"British or French?" enquired Captain Acton, letting his glass sink whilst he looked at his companions. "Before we sailed the news had got about that Villeneuve meant to go for the West Indies. It may be his ships returning." He pointed his glass again, and counted: "Eleven sail of the line and three frigates."

"Villeneuve's force was greater, sir," said the Admiral. "It was reckoned at eighteen or twenty line-of-battle ships."

"All the same we must mind our eye," said Captain Acton. "Shorten sail, Captain Weaver! But furl nothing! And stand by to get away close hauled on the larboard tack before we're within gunshot."

Lucy came out of the deck-house. A long night's rest had restored much of the bloom to her beauty. She wanted something of the freshness, but she lacked nothing of the sweetness and the loveliness with which she fascinated the gaze at home. She ran to her father and kissed him, shook hands with the Admiral, and bowed to Captain Weaver most cordially.

"What a lot of ships!" she cried.

The crew were busy with letting go halliards and brailing in and clewing up, and the *Aurora* floated forward, slowly swaying her mast-heads with languor and dignity as the heave of the sea took her and rocked her. The ships rose until every hull was visible.

Eleven line-of-battle ships, as Captain Acton said, and three frigates. They flew no colours: nothing in that way could be seen save the little patch against the flecked sky that denoted the flag-ship.

"If they are not British, sir," said the Admiral, after a prolonged squint through the glass, "I'll swallow my cocked hat when I get ashore."

"I could swear to one of them as the *Superb,*" said Captain Acton, who had also taken a prolonged view of the ships through his glass. "She is a slow sailer. I know that she is rotten to the core for want of a dockyard. If I am not greatly mistaken, her stun-sail booms are lashed to the yards, and she is the only one with stun-sails set, which means that her rotting keel marks the pace for the rest. Hoist our colours! We'll chance it."

Captain Weaver sped aft, and in a few moments the English Ensign soared to the mizzen-gaff end and streamed out fair to the sight of the approaching fleet.

"British, as I guessed," cried the Admiral.

"And here comes a frigate to speak us," exclaimed Captain Acton, as one of the smaller vessels which had hoisted English colours came out from the crowd with yards braced for the shift of helm and, leaning under her silk-white towers of cloths, and rolling as she came, made directly for the *Aurora.*

The schooner was washing slowly along under her three lower gaff sails only, and the frigate that carried everything but studding sails was speedily within ranging and hailing distance. She was the

Amphion, without much beauty to detain the eye, unless the gaze climbed aloft where every sail was cut and set with the perfection that was the characteristic of the British man-of-war, and where the running and standing rigging was ruled as delicately against the sky as though exquisitely pencilled on paper, and on high, just under the gleaming button of the truck, shimmered the long pennant in fluctuating dyes like a thread of a girl's golden hair floating on the breeze. But her sheathing was rusty and ungainly with marine growths, and her sides wanted the paint-pot, but the run of the hammock cloths was as white as snow, and her row of cannon and the sparkle of uniform buttons and the colour got from the marine sentry posted here or there, heightened the war-like spectacle to the degree of a marine piece charged with the loveliness of finish and precision and imposing and stirring with the spirit of war.

She put her helm over, and sailing broadside to broadside with the *Aurora,* hailed her from the throat of a lieutenant who had hoisted his figure by standing on a carronade.

"Ho, the schooner ahoy! where are you from?"

"Old Harbour Town, England," responded Captain Weaver.

"Have you seen anything of the French Fleet?"

"No, sir, we have sighted nothing of that sort."

This was manifestly all that the frigate had left the other ships to ascertain, and the lieutenant was in the act of springing on to the deck, when Captain Acton shouted: "Pray, sir, can you tell us what those ships are? "

"They are the fleet under Lord Nelson," was the answer, "which have been chasing Monsieur de Villeneuve across the Atlantic to the West Indies, and are now bound to Europe, having missed the Frenchmen."

"I am Admiral Sir William Lawrence," was next bawled. "Will you be so good as to inform me if Lord Nelson is on board one of those ships, and which ship?"

"Yes, sir, he is on board the *Victory.* She is the one that is ahead of and to windward of the ship that has stun-sails set."

So saying, and evidently not much impressed by meeting an Admiral of whom he had never heard in a schooner that looked uncommonly like a slaver or a pirate, the lieutenant disappeared, and a moment or two after, the frigate trimmed sail to rejoin the fleet.

"Nelson!" cried Captain Acton, in a voice subdued by reverence for the name it pronounced, addressing his daughter. "We must run down and have a look at him. The deviation need not be above two or three miles, which will not cause us to lose sight of the *Minorca* by diverting us from her track. Make all sail again, Captain Weaver, and head for that flag-ship. You can see her: she is to windward of the ship with the stun-sails."

All sail was immediately made on the schooner. And with a fine dancing motion thrown into her by the swell, her coppered sides slipped nimbly through the water, graced by the frolic of foam sheared out of the feathering ripples by the sharp stem.

It was not very long before the eleven sail of the line with their attendant frigates were swelling large, bristling, and close to the *Aurora,* at whose signal halliards stood two sailors who dipped to such battle-ships as the schooner passed receiving the acknowl-edgment of small ensigns gaff-ended, and then hauled down to be hoisted no more. The picture was full of a grandeur that borrowed majesty from the sense of the power and the empire the ships sym-bolised. They were lordly in slow motion; they bowed to the swell as though in lofty homage to their mistress the sea; they were ter-rible in triple rows of cannon and by virtue of the traditional mag-nificent spirit, silent and concealed behind their lofty and invincible defences. It was the breakfast hour, but the people aboard the *Aurora* were very willing to wait to break their fast. Not a man but was fascinated by the sight and presence of that tall, majestic ship out there, with the little flag at the fore. For Nelson—the Nelson of the North, of Aboukir Bay, of Teneriffe, of St Vincent, the Nelson of a hundred wounds, the first of all sea chieftains in the history of the world, Nelson, the truest sailor, the kindest shipmate, the man of the purest and loftiest spirit of chivalry and patriotism that ever stepped the planks of a ship's decks—this great, this sublime hero, to be even greater and sublimer in his victorious and immortal death a few months later—*Nelson was in her!*

As the schooner, swifter by two to one than the battle-ships, passed onwards on her road to the *Victory,* the Admiral and Captain

Acton recognised some of the three-deckers in which they had served as midshipmen.

"There's the old *Canopus!*" cried the Admiral. "Lord, what a shivering recollection I have of her main topmast crosstrees!"

"And there's the *Bellisle,*" said Captain Acton. "I was in her"—and he named the period to his daughter, whom he addressed, but who seemed to have no eyes for any ship but the *Victory.* Other ships, the two retired naval officers knew, were the *Superb, Spencer, Swiftsure,* and *Leviathan.*

The position of the *Victory* gave plenty of scope for the maneuverings of the *Aurora.* Captain Weaver, finding that he would rapidly outsail the liner and be ahead and out of hail before half a dozen sentences could be exchanged, luffed the *Aurora* to windward of the *Victory,* wisely declining to be becalmed by the big ship's sails if he stationed his little craft to leeward of her. A lieutenant stood at the forward end of the raised deck, or poop as it really was. One or two midshipmen were visible. The sentry on the forecastle was in sight; otherwise scarce a man was to be seen. The lieutenant hailed as the officer in the *Amphion* had: "Schooner ahoy! Are you fresh from England?"

"Direct, sir," answered Captain Weaver.

Scarcely had the *Aurora's* skipper made this answer when there appeared at the side of the lieutenant a figure whose apparition was so sudden that, like Hamlet's ghost in the theatre, he might be thought to have risen from below through an opening in the deck. He wore a cocked hat athwartships. His frock uniform coat seemed somewhat threadbare; amidst the folds of the left breast of his coat were four weather-tarnished and lustreless stars. The right sleeve was empty and was secured to the breast. One eye was protected by a green shade. He looked a little man alongside the lieutenant who himself was not above the average. Collingwood described him as small enough to be drawn through an alderman's thumb ring.

At the sight of this immortal figure the Admiral and Captain Acton instantly bared their heads, and the whole of the crew of the *Aurora,* springing into the fore and main shrouds, roared hurrahs in such voices as perhaps only British sailors' throats are capable of delivering. Amidst those shouts of rapturous recognition and impassioned pride, could be heard such exclamations as, "God bless you, Lord Nelson!" "Down with the French, and glory to our Hero!" "Hurrah for the grandest sailor in the world!"

Nelson, standing beside his lieutenant, who might have been Pasco (the officer who, on the 21st day of the following October, made the Nelson signal that is as dear as his heart's blood to every Englishman), acknowledged the salutations of the schooner's quarterdeck and the mobs in her rigging by bows and a smile, and a lifting of his hand and certain flapping motions of the stump of his right arm, an action into which he was frequently moved when irritated or pleased.

"I should like to know," he exclaimed, and every ear on board the schooner was bent to catch his accents, with the greed with which a crowd of men might be supposed to extend their hands to catch a shower of gold flung amongst them from a height, "if you have seen anything of the French Fleet under Admiral Villenueve?"

"No, my lord," shouted the Admiral, "I am very sorry to say we have not."

Nelson's stump wagged with annoyance.

"I have followed them to the West Indies," he exclaimed, "with eleven sail of the line, and Villeneuve has eighteen or twenty; but you may tell them at home, if you are returning shortly, that had I fallen in with the French Fleet I should have brought them to action."

"We are honoured by your lordship's command," cried the Admiral. "May I venture to introduce myself as Admiral Sir William Lawrence? And I beg the honour of introducing my friend Captain Acton, late of His Majesty's Royal Navy, and his daughter, Miss Lucy Acton."

Nelson flourished a salutation. Lucy sank in a curtsy that was almost the same as kneeling. Most girls have a favourite hero, and Nelson was hers, and had been hers ever since he came into renown on the glorious St Valentine's Day. Had her father not been fascinated by the figure on the *Victory,* he might have witnessed the almost magical art with which his daughter had alarmed Mr Lawrence into releasing her, by a brief study of her face as she gazed at the little figure on the deck of the *Victory,* with his untenanted sleeve secured to his breast, and a smile of acknowledgment on his pale and worn face, seamed about the mouth with wrinkles such as are sometimes seen in persons deformed in the back, or suffering from spinal complaint.

The *Aurora* and the line-of-battle ship sailed so close that it needed a special vigilance on the part of Captain Weaver to preserve his schooner's spars from the yard-arms of the towering vessel within a biscuit toss. Much exertion of voice was therefore not necessary for conversation, and though Nelson occupied a platform high above the low deck of his schooner, his features were perfectly visible, and his voice fell as clear as though he stood beside those he addressed.

"Any relation, sir, of Lawrence of the *Peterel* and *Curieux* affair?" he cried.

"I am his father, my lord," replied Sir William with a low bow, of which the gravity that coloured it was very intelligible to Captain Acton and Lucy.

"A brilliant piece of work, sir," cried Nelson.

Again the poor old Admiral bowed, this time with a glow of pride, because a sentence of praise from the mighty Nelson excited in the heart of this old sailor a transport that the highest honour conferred by the King himself could not have induced.

"I have had the honour, my lord," exclaimed the Admiral, "to serve under Howe, Duncan, and Sir Hyde Parker, but alas! I came into the world too soon to reflect even a little of the glory with which those who have had the unspeakable happiness to serve under your lordship have covered themselves."

"Ah, three illustrious names, sir," said Nelson. "Howe was the greatest of sea officers. Are you gentlemen making a voyage of discovery or of pleasure?"

"We are in chase of a ship, my lord," cried Captain Acton, "which we hope to capture."

"How? Unarmed!" exclaimed Nelson.

"We hope to effect our end without bloodshed, my lord," said Captain Acton.

"You will be very clever. I wish I could learn how to effect ends

in the same way," were Nelson's closing words, as, saluting the people on the deck of the *Aurora* once more, he stepped back and disappeared, followed by a storm of cheers from the men of the
Aurora, in which the Admiral and Captain Acton heartily joined,
whilst Lucy flourished her pocket-handkerchief, though her hero
was out of sight.

CHAPTER XVI

THE CAPTURE

AT BREAKFAST, which was necessarily delayed on board the *Aurora,*
the conversation, as may be supposed, was almost entirely concerned with undoubtedly the most memorable incident—the meeting with Nelson—in the lives of Captain Acton and Sir William. The
Aurora had hauled out of the Fleet with a dipping flag, and with
wings eagerly straining to the breath of the strengthening blue
breeze that gushed with a tropic warmth over the little seas which
creamed and purred in heads that would easily grow spiteful and
change their fountain-like music into a harsh hissing as of serpents,
was heading as true a course as Captain Weaver could imagine for
the barque that Captain Acton wanted.

Nelson's reference to Mr Lawrence's brilliant action was going to
prove an overwhelming memory to the Admiral.

"When I think, sir," he exclaimed, as they breakfasted, "what a few
syllables of applause signify in the mouth of such a man as the hero
of the Nile, I feel as if I could spring overboard and drown myself
when I reflect that my unhappy son quitted the glorious Service
under ignoble circumstances, and that by remaining he might have
come under the command of Nelson, and gained the splendid
renown which scarce a sea officer who has served under that great
man but has won."

"I for one should not need to meet Lord Nelson and hear him speak of your son to fully agree in what you say, Sir William," said Lucy.

Her father looked at her with a questioning gaze, but made no remark. Nearly all the talk at that breakfast table was about Nelson and his ships and his pursuit of Villeneuve, but shortly before the three arose the conversation had been deflected by a remark of Lucy, on which the Admiral said: "If this breeze holds we shall be heaving the *Minorca* into sight the day after to-morrow, or at latest the following day. There can be no doubt that the schooner is fair in her wake. The Whitby brig seems to have steered a straight course from her to us; and now, sir, Lord Nelson's remark comes home: we are unarmed. The barque carries four guns with which she can pelt us without our being able to make a reply. If she wings us she will escape, and since she will very well know who we are that are in pursuit of her, is my son likely to proceed to Rio? Will he not take advantage of our being crippled to shift his course, and go away to some place, unconjecturable by us, where he will be able to communicate with his scoundrel friend at Rio and the Don with the long name who is to have the management of the nefarious business?"

"You will know, sir," replied Captain Acton, "one of Nelson's favourite sayings: at sea something must be left to chance. I count upon the crew of the *Minorca,* when they sight the *Aurora* and understand her mission, which they will guess without explanation, backing her main-topsail in defiance of your son's firearms and calling upon us to take possession. If this does not happen, I shall not be at a loss, and meanwhile, Sir William, let us get a view of the barque."

After breakfast Captain Acton and Lucy walked the deck, whilst the Admiral, with his big pipe, seated himself right aft all alone, for this little ship was steered by a wheel in front of the deck-house; he sat puffing out clouds of tobacco with his eyes fixed upon the glimmering phantoms of the British Fleet, which hovered in the north-east quarter in a few dim, waning gleams; and the moods of his mind were faithfully reproduced in his jolly, honest, well-bred, kindly face.

The breeze blew bright and warm, and sang sweetly aloft. The brilliant horizon ahead slided up and down past the prismatic edges of the clear and shapely sails which yearned in steady breasts from mast-head to jibboom and bowsprit ends; the parted water rolled past in wool-white lines of yeast; the heavens were alive with the clouds of the air. Nothing was in sight but Nelson's Fleet, fading.

Lucy had related much, but she had much more to tell, and she narrated to her father fresh stories of her madness, and drew several graphic pictures of Mr Lawrence whilst he laboured under the various sensations her genius as an untutored artist excited. She spoke with contempt of Mr Eagle, whilst she had little or nothing to say about Mr Pledge. Her narratives were marked by a strong leaning in favour of Mr Lawrence. Her father could not mistake. Her prejudice, indeed her fondness, was expressed not so much in her admirable recitals and her references to the dignified and gentlemanly manner with which Mr Lawrence had treated her, with which he had received her aggravating, indeed her venomous, references to his past and present conduct, as in the pause, the soft, thoughtful smile, the brief exclamation, the sigh, and now and again the little but significant remark.

"But it is impossible, Lucy," said Captain Acton, "to make a hero out of such a fellow as this: a man who forges sealed orders supposed to be written by me! A rogue who not only steals my property, but kidnaps my daughter by a lie!"

"He must have done well, sir, for Nelson to have remembered him," said Lucy. "And, oh, Papa, will not you make some allowance for the misconduct of a man who is tempted by—by—"

"By what, my dear?"

"By love," said Lucy, hanging her head, whilst the blush that came into her cheeks was like the revelation of the glory of the red rose to the first delicate light of sunrise. Then with a sudden impulse of confidence she added fluently: "He was wasting his time at Old Harbour Town. He fell into vicious habits and modes of getting money which he detested, but the opportunities offered, and strong as he is as a sailor, he proved himself weak as a man."

"As a gentleman!" said Captain Acton, who followed his daughter's words with mingled impatience and wonder.

"I feel that I am greatly to blame in this dreadful trouble," said Lucy. "I am sure that it was his love for me, his desire to gain me as his wife, his horror at the prospect of being an outcast through debt, his resolution to lead an honest life and perhaps a noble life, should I become his wife and should he obtain your forgiveness; these things I am convinced drove him into a sort of madness in which he invented this desperate plot which could never be forgiven in any man who was not as brave and well-bred as Mr Lawrence, nor as—as——"

"D'ye mean handsome, Lucy?" said Captain Acton. "For the dog is that."

"But what is to happen to him," said Lucy, "if you carry him back to England? I would rather hear," she cried, with an emphasis which may have borrowed note and complexion from the impulse of her late impersonations of madness, "of the *Minorca* having sunk and carried him down to the bottom of the sea with her, than live to witness his degradation and perhaps his death and the misery and the broken-heartedness that must come to his dear old father, if you do not prove his friend, and help to reclaim a nature that in its essence is beautiful, and a fulfilment of the purest woman's ideal."

Captain Acton walked half the length of the extent of deck they were pacing, before he spoke. "Your dear mother," said he calmly, "whose genius as an actress I cannot help thinking has descended to you, though never once in all your life have you given me reason for suspecting the existence of a gift, not wonderful by mere power of mimicry, but astonishing by its art of persuading and convincing the beholder that what he sees is the living thing itself: your sweet and blessed mother, though a staunch upholder of her sex, was fond of a saying which she had found in Pope:

'Nothing so true as what you once let fall,
Most women have no character at all.'

She meant by this, as Pope, or rather Horace, held, that a woman may have a very great genius, and yet be so weak in the significant and quint-essential actions of her life as to prove herself characterless. You have behaved with amazing heroism. You found yourself in the hands of one of the most unscrupulous of men——"

"No, sir," she said.

"You are placed in the most helpless situation a woman could find herself in: at sea, locked up in a cabin, and all the crew, who might otherwise have helped you, believing that you were running away with Mr Lawrence, and that your imprisonment and your representations and your madness were part of a programme preconcerted between you and your lover. You realise the horrors and peril of your position, and by virtue of the mother's genius that came to your help, you decided upon a behaviour which you magnificently conducted. So much for the better part of you: but what remains? To be wooed—shall I say won?—it is necessary for your sweetheart to act the part of a scoundrel. He must steal my ship and kidnap my only child, and heap lie upon lie, and then, to be sure, he is a very pretty gentleman, a noble, gallant rogue, at root a man of a lordly soul, of a most chivalrous and fighting spirit to be made much of—in short, to fall desperately in love with."

Lucy bit her under-lip, but certainly the general expression of her face was not one of displeasure.

"So, my dear, you see that your mother was right in putting faith in her quotation, 'Most women have no characters at all.'"

Whether Lucy would have replied to this cannot be known, for just then the hand stationed aloft sung out: "Sail ho!"

"Where away?"

"Right ahead, sir."

But the stranger remained so long invisible from the deck whilst she could be easily distinguished from the height of the fore-top-gallant and then from the fore-topsail yard, and then from midway the altitude of the fore-shrouds, that it was not before the afternoon had passed into a golden brightness of westering sunlight that the ship right ahead revealed her canvas to the quarterdeck of the *Aurora*.

From the moment the ship in sight was reported, expectation aboard the *Aurora* sprang and grew. Was she the *Minorca?* She was undoubtedly square-rigged, but the lenses of the comparatively feeble telescopes of those days could not determine before it fell dusk, whether she was rigged aft with square yards or merely with the mizzen and gaff topsail which made the *Minorca* a barque.

The Admiral was restless; he paced the deck with unwearied legs, and when the sail ahead had hove her canvas into view, he sent endless searchings of her through his telescope, but never could arrive at an opinion. Captain Acton was self-possessed, and his manner was marked by contemplation as though the possibilities the ship in sight suggested filled him with earnest and bewildering considerations.

Lucy was of opinion that the ship must prove the *Minorca.* She well understood that the two vessels could not be far asunder, and quite rationally concluded that the sail ahead was the barque. It would have needed, however, a keener gaze than either Captain Acton or the Admiral was capable of bringing to bear, to penetrate to the girl's thoughts. Whilst the distant vessel leaned like a small orange flame gently blown sideways by the wind upon the early evening purple of the horizon, Lucy would overhang the rail with her brooding, beautiful eyes dwelling upon that far-off vision, and the expression of her face was in these intervals of motionless posture and steadfast regard, as though she was asleep and dreamt, and that her dream was partly sweet and partly vexing and bitter, so that her whole look was that of one who slumbers, through whose sealed lids a vision of sleep slides to the heart to trouble its pulse.

Captain Weaver believed that the vessel was the *Minorca:* because, first, she carried royals; next, because she happened to be where she was; third, the leisureliness with which the *Aurora* rose her seemed to prove that her pace was that of the barque. But the dusk drew round; the gloom of night came along in that thickness of shadow which under such heights as the *Aurora* was then sailing, seemed swift to persons accustomed to the northern twilights. And at the hour in which the shades of the coming night had with their viewless fingers effaced the stranger from the sight of the *Aurora,* and shaken some stars into their places, the sail had been risen by the *Aurora,* till on the heave of the swell her hull to the height of her bulwarks from the edge of the sea was visible. And then she was steeped in darkness.

The moon was without power until shortly after midnight; her light silvered the sails of the ship ahead, and she grew out of the gloom into a fairy-like fantasy that might have been some symmetrical form of moon-touched mist fleeting down the wind, or some snow-robed height whose base lay behind the horizon.

The Admiral was on deck, and so was Captain Acton, and Captain Weaver had also stepped out of the deck-house to take a look round. The stranger was now sufficiently near to be determinable by the glass even in moonshine; and so soon as she sprang into being under the magical flourish of the wand of the moon, it was known for a surety that she was not the *Minorca*. She was square-rigged aft, and made a big, broad cloud as she rolled along under topgallant, topmast, and lower stun-sails. The breeze that had blown throughout the day still blew, and the circumstance of the stranger having kept ahead of the *Aurora* for many hours was proof of her nimble keel.

"She sails faster than the *Minorca,* gentlemen," said Captain Weaver.

"She has the appearance of a frigate," said Captain Acton, working away at her with his glass.

"Is that *your* opinion, sir?" Captain Weaver asked the Admiral.

After a pause, during which he carefully scrutinised the vessel, "She has every appearance of being a frigate," the Admiral answered.

Of what nation, if an armed ship? A wide berth was to be given to the Tricolour or the Spanish Flag. After much debate the order was given for sail to be reduced that the *Aurora*'s pace might not outmeasure that of the stranger, until break of day should yield a better idea of her character. Meanwhile she must be closely watched, and at the first shift of the stranger's helm the *Aurora* must out with all wings and slide away from gun range with the despatch the wind could give her.

The dark moonlit hours thus passed, and the *Aurora* followed the stranger, but at a distance that was out of cannon reach.

At daylight the vessel proved to be a frigate; she was painted black, with red gunports and red tompions. But this was no evidence of her nationality, for it was only comparatively recently that Nelson had caused ships under his command to carry white bands which the portholes for the guns chequered with black squares. And many ships of the State in 1805 were black in hull and some of them yellow.

"We must take our chance," said Captain Acton to Weaver, "and end our doubts in the only possible way. See that our ensign blows clear for the eyes aboard of her."

As the ship ahead was almost stern on, they ran the British ensign to the *Aurora*'s mizzen-mast head whence it streamed, a "meteor flag," in the silver-white glory of the sun. In a few moments the English colours were hoisted aboard the stranger, on which the Admiral delivered a British cheer, which was caught up and re-echoed by a few of the crew forward.

Immediately every stitch of canvas that the schooner carried was set, and bending to the pressure of the fine breeze that was now flashing from right abeam, gracing the multitudinous run of the surge with the various splendours of the morning's light; the three-masted American-built clipper *Aurora* thrashed through it in her pursuit of the black British frigate at a rate of sailing that within three hours brought her within speaking distance of the man-of-war.

Before this happened, however, Captain Acton had called a council of his daughter and the Admiral, and a resolution had been arrived at of which the nature will appear in a few moments.

The frigate seemed unquestionably of foreign build; but the name *Phœbe* written in large characters upon her stern over which from the peak of the mizzen-gaff streamed the flag of our country, was a warranty that whatever nationality her builders had boasted, she was now a British ship. She was somewhat old in years, as was manifested by her fore-mast that was stepped too far forward to please a critical eye, whilst her main-mast stood too far aft, its nearness to the mizzen-mast offending the gaze by an appearance of crowding. But she was very spick and span: as fresh as though just launched; her glossy, black sides trembled with the lustre of the sea; her canvas was spacious and superb in cut and set. The white line of hammock cloths delightfully contrasted with the gilt rope of beading which ran the length of her below the wash streak, and which terminated on the stern in a flourish of gilt scroll amid which the windows gleamed darkly like those of Old Harbour House duskily shining amidst the foliage of creepers.

The regular enquiry was made from the frigate's quarterdeck by an officer, and the regular information was supplied by Captain Weaver.

"I will send a boat aboard of you!" was the shout which immediately followed Weaver's response. "Shorten sail, or shake the way out of her as you please!"

"Just what could have been wished!" exclaimed Captain Acton to the Admiral. "She suspects us. 'Twill save a world of bawling."

Sail was at once shortened aboard the schooner and the helm put down, which held the canvas shuddering in smart ripplings of shadow, whilst on board the frigate the lower stun-sail was taken in, the other stun-sails boom-ended, the main topsail yard backed to the wind and the ship's way arrested, all with the alacrity and quietude which are to be found only in a British man-of-war in perfection.

Down sank a boat from the davits with a lieutenant in the stern sheets, and six sailors to pull her, and in a dozen strokes of the blades feathering in fire to the sunlight and dropping jewels of brilliant dyes ere they were buried for the next foaming impulse, the boat was alongside the schooner. The lieutenant mounted the short length of steps which had been flung over through the open gangway and saluted the little ship as all sea-gentlemen do, or should, when they step aboard a vessel, even though she should be as mean as an Irish hooker.

The Admiral, Captain Acton, and Captain Weaver stood in the gangway to receive the officer, a man whose portrait should be painted by the caricaturing brush of a Michael Scott. He was this side of forty, and a great Roman nose stood out like a flying jib between two gaunt cheeks whose hollows when he was silent made you think he was sucking in his breath. He wore a pigtail under a very old, tarnished cocked hat. His uniform coat was scarcely held together by the tailor's thread, and appeared to have travelled a score of times round the world in an age when a voyage round the world was regarded as something more prodigious than we should now consider a voyage to the moon, if such a journey were practicable. His shoes were rusty; his hose had gone into mourning over an absence of soap that was all the same as the death of his laundress. Yet despite a garb that made a travesty of the human figure there was something distinguished and even noble in the man's bearing. It was to be seen at once (and no masterful capacity of penetration was needed) that in this officer was the gentleman of old blood, poor and proud, a loyal subject whose heart's life was at the service of his King and country.

It might be thought that the first person in the group this gentleman's eyes fastened upon was Lucy. She would be held to appeal in her sweetness, colour, freshness, and youth to a sailor as a nosegay of lovely flowers to a lover of flowers who for months has lived forlorn in a desert of sand. But instead of looking at Lucy, the lieutenant stared at the Admiral with a very great deal of visible speculation in the screwed-up cock of his eye, till his face relaxed with these words: "Pray, sir, did you ever hear of Billy Lawrence?"

"Who commanded His Britannic Majesty's sloop *Merlin?*" cried Sir William. "My dear Fellowes, this is indeed an unexpected meeting. And you knew me before I should have known you!"

They grasped hands.

"Acton, let me introduce an old shipmate—Lieutenant Fellowes. Captain Acton—Miss Lucy Acton."

"Of the Norfolk Fellowes?" enquired Captain Acton, after bows and smiles had been exchanged.

"Ay, sir," exclaimed the Admiral and as a man of Norfolk myself I am proud of the family whose records do honour to the dear old county."

"Pray, what is your ship, sir?" asked Captain Acton.

"The *Phœbe.*"

"Who's her captain?"

"Lord Garlies."

"Ha!" said Captain Acton. "He was at St Vincent."

"As a spectator only, I think, sir," answered Mr Fellowes.

"His lordship evidently suspects us," said Captain Acton, laughing.

"Why, to be sure," said the lieutenant, laughing also, "you have a very slaving, piratical look. Who would expect to find a British Admiral aboard so rakish a craft?"

"But unarmed, Fellowes, unarmed!" exclaimed the Admiral. "You won't want to see our papers, will ye?"

And the worthy old sailor chuckled heartily from his throat to the bottom of his waistcoat.

"Will you step into the deck-house, sir," said Captain Acton, "and learn our strange story, which shall not detain you long."

Mr Fellowes bowed with a smile which charmed Lucy by its good-nature, and by the light it kindled in the man's face, where she witnessed that sort of breeding which her heart, as the hearts of most women who are ladies at heart, delight in. The party of four entered the structure, and the cabin servant was ordered to put refreshments on the table.

"This is the yarn, Fellowes," said the Admiral, who, it had been pre-arranged, was to tell the story. "My friend Acton is the owner of this schooner; he is also the owner of another ship, called the *Minorca*. Now, this ship, of which my friend was good enough to give the command to my son—"

"A fine fellow," interrupted Mr Fellowes. "How is he?"

"Pretty well—pretty middling, I thank ye," answered the Admiral. "But just now in a bit of a fix. It has come to our knowledge that there has been a mutiny on board the *Minorca*, and that the crew are navigating the vessel to Rio de Janeiro—"

"The *Phœbe* is bound to that port," again interrupted Mr Fellowes.

"Good!" cried the Admiral, with an expressive look at Captain Acton—"instead," continued Sir William, "of Kingston, Jamaica, to which place her cargo is consigned. We are following her in this clipper, which outsails her by two to one, and we have reason to know that she is now about two days in advance of us. The *Minorca* is armed: we are not. And your captain will be conferring a very great favour upon us if, seeing that the *Phœbe* is almost as swift as this schooner, he will allow us to keep him company, so that if we jointly fall in with the *Minorca*, her crew may be overawed by the guns of the frigate."

"Lord Garlies, I am sure, will be happy to oblige you, Sir William, and your friend, in any way he can," said the lieutenant. "Pray, how did you happen to hear of the seizure of the ship and her shift of course to Rio?"

"The news was communicated to us," said the Admiral, "in a

letter which had been written before the ship sailed by a conspicuous member of the crew. A copy of this letter fell into Captain
Acton's hands on the very day the *Minorca* left Old Harbour Town,
and my friend immediately arranged to pursue his ship in this smart
schooner when she could be got ready."

The Admiral spoke with a steady face and with a steady voice.
He was giving a version of the story which to all intents and pur-
poses was true, and there was nothing in the relation, as previously
devised, to alarm his conscience as a gentleman and a man of honour by inaccuracy.

"I see," exclaimed Mr Fellowes. "But are you sure of the situation
of the chase?"

"Why, sir, yes, as sure as we can be of anything at sea," said Captain
Acton, who thought it judicious and proper to join in. "Yesterday we
spoke the brig *Louisa Ann* of Whitby, who reported that three days
before, she had asked for some provisions from a ship named the
Minorca whose rig was that of my barque. There is no doubt that
my ship is just ahead of us, and that our superior sailing will enable
us to overhaul her within a week. The effect of the frigate's presence will be to rescue the capture from the trouble of bloodshed.
When your guns are seen, sir, and the character of your ship distinguished, the mutineers will back their topsail yard and leave us
to quietly take possession."

The lieutenant politely nodded his agreement with this view, and
finished his glass of brandy and soda-water. At long intervals, to com-
pare the lapses with the short time he spent on board, he directed
a look at Lucy; but the glance was that of a man who knows that
women do not admire him, and do not want him, a poor, plain and
elderly man: and whose policy, resolved long ago, was to give the
marriageable part of the sex a very wide berth.

The conversation at the Admiral's instance, and to his own and
the relief of Captain Acton and his daughter, was now changed into
a few questions and answers which have nothing whatever to do
with this narrative; and after a visit that had lasted about twenty
minutes, Mr Fellowes took his leave, cordially and with a hearty
handshake bidding his old captain God-speed and farewell, and bowing with dignity and much respect and a pleasant kindness of

expression of face to Captain Acton, and the sweet girl whose story, had the Admiral or Captain Acton thought fit to relate it, would no doubt have exchanged his light, superficial, uncritical regard into a gaze of admiration and astonishment.

"I suppose that is Lord Garlies whom he is addressing," exclaimed Captain Acton, on the arrival of the lieutenant at his ship.

The question was answered by the person thus referred to coming to the ship's side after receiving Mr Fellowes' report. The preliminary hail having been bawled—the two vessels lay close together, and those aboard one might hear the wash of the waters alongside the other, in the falls of silence—the person referred to by Captain Acton shouted: "I shall have much pleasure in complying with your request."

"We beg to thank you most cordially," replied the Admiral, who, in response to Captain Acton's desire, was acting as spokesman in this passage. "May I venture to ask if I have the honour of addressing my Lord Garlies?"

His lordship bowed: upon which the Admiral and Captain Acton paid him the homage of their hats in a well-accentuated flourish of courtesy, for not only was Lord Garlies a brave man and a fine seaman: he was the son of an earl and heir to a title which made a claim that in its way was not less irresistible in 1805 than it may be found a hundred years later.

"The best course we can adopt," cried Lord Garlies, "is to keep the width of the horizons between us. I will take the western and you the eastern seaboard. This from aloft will enable us to command a large surface of sea. The rig of the vessel you are chasing will determine her for us. If I sight such a vessel on the starboard bow, I will hoist a large red flag at the mizzen-royal-masthead; if on the larboard bow, a white flag at the same place. You will hoist your answering signal and manoeuvre to close us; but that shall be as the wind may prove. If you sight your ship, it will suffice if you hoist your ensign at your mizzen topmast head, and an answering signal will tell you that we intend to close with you in chase."

This was deliberately delivered and clearly heard, and, with a flourish of his hand, Lord Garlies stepped back.

In a few minutes sail had been trimmed on both vessels, and

when each had measured a distance that gave the other no more than a sight of her bulwarks upon the sea line, the helm was put amidships and the frigate and the schooner were steered along that course in which they hoped in a few days to overhaul the *Minorca*.

They were sailing in bright latitudes where the weather is warm, where often the sea rolls in a languid silken swell like the gentle heavings of a carpet of the sheen of satin under-blown, where the stars shine with brilliance and the moon at her full has an almost sun-like power. And very fortunately the two ships were favoured with fine and sparkling days vital with favourable winds. Throughout the daylight hours the two ships held each other steadily in view, the schooner under slightly reduced canvas, and the frigate under a press, and at night each signalled her place by rockets discharged at intervals, so that always when day broke the brace of pursuing structures were found to be either abreast, or almost so, each sunk from the sight of the other to the line of her bulwarks.

Came a fine, glittering morning towards the middle of June. It was about half an hour after daybreak: the sun had risen, and the flood of brilliance lay broad upon the sea in the east. Captain Acton was dressing in his cabin, when his door was rapped upon, and Captain Weaver, whose manner was full of excitement, reported a sail in sight, right in the centre of the horizon betwixt the two ships.

"The frigate has hoisted her signal, sir," he said, "and we have made ours."

"I'll be with you in a minute. She is too far off, I suppose, for the glass to resolve her."

"I guess she is the barque, sir, if the frigate's signal is right. They command a greater height aboard of her than we can, and I fancy they have twigged something fore-and-aft on the mizzen-mast."

It was two bells in the afternoon watch—one o'clock—at which hour the frigate and the schooner had closed each other. By this time the ship ahead had been raised to a full sight of her hull. But long before this she had been made out as the *Minorca,* by that unmistakable signal of her character—the fore-and-aft canvas on her mizzen—and top-masts.

The breeze was steady. All three ships heeled to it. The frigate foamed bending under studding sails, the schooner under all the canvas she could set, and the barque leaned under the heavy strain of every cloth she carried.

It would be impossible to describe the feelings, sensations, passions of three of the principal actors in this story. Who can analyse human emotion when its state is one of almost chaotic conflict? Sir William Lawrence being satisfied that the sail ahead was Captain Acton's barque, fixed his face in a mask ironhard with resolution to endure, come what would. His answers were short, and to the point. He had little to say. His tendency to the garrulity of old age had temporarily withered; he was as grim and reserved as though he commanded a line-of-battle ship, whose stern-walk was exclusively his promenade. He was an old sailor and a gentleman: he prided himself upon his descent; he greatly loved honour and loyalty, which is the spirit of honour, and above all, he loved truth. Yonder was his son in charge of a ship he was endeavouring to steal from his benefactor; he had by a base stratagem kidnapped the sweet and beautiful daughter of his friend; he had proved himself a liar, a thief, a scoundrel in the most voluminous sense of the word. The people of the frigate commanded by Lord Garlies might, doubtless must, come to hear all about his wrongdoing, and through them the story would leak with plenty of colour and plenty of exaggeration, into every ward-room and gun-room and cockpit in His Majesty's Service. These were thoughts and considerations to hold the Admiral austerely silent, and keep him to himself whilst the chase continued.

Captain Acton and Lucy often walked the deck deep in talk. The Captain had decided in his own mind to place Eagle in charge of the *Minorca,* with orders to proceed to Kingston, providing there was no disaffection amongst the crew, and Mr Lawrence would be transferred to the *Aurora* and conveyed to England. What excuses would he plead? What apologies would he offer? What sort of a figure would he make in the sight of his father? in the thoughts of the girl whom in the sacred name of love he had used with such reckless cruelty, as to deprive her of her reason, as he supposed? in the opinion of the kindly gentleman whose confidence he had grossly abused? Would he, when landed in England, consent to ship as a sailor before the mast, and conceal himself for the remainder of his life in a distant land? If not, what would he do? What must be his fate?

But though father and daughter talked these matters over whilst they stepped the white planks and whilst the ship ahead slowly enlarged, the topics which engaged them did not contain all, indeed they did not contain even a very little, of the thoughts which crowded Lucy's mind and gave a dozen varying expressions to her beauty in as many minutes.

At about three o'clock in the afternoon the frigate fired one of her bow guns apparently at the *Minorca*, a stern, laconic message to her to heave to; for hours ago it was perceived that the chase was the vessel Captain Acton and the Admiral were hunting; and for hours it must have been known aboard the barque that one of the pursuing ships was a frigate heavily armed, and the other a fabric perfectly familiar to every man in the *Minorca*, as the three-masted schooner *Aurora*, the property of the owner of the barque.

Indeed the chase was now so near that with the unaided vision her men might be seen moving upon her decks, and the Admiral's telescope was levelled at a tall figure that stood solitary and apart upon the barque's quarter, surveying with folded arms and erect carriage the ships which were following him with foam to their hawse-pipes.

When the *Phœbe*'s cannon suddenly thundered, the Admiral dropped his telescope to look at the frigate, and when he again directed the glass at the *Minorca*, the tall figure, that he well knew to be his son, had vanished.

Scarcely had the ball of satin-white smoke, belched from the cannon's mouth, been shredded by the wind and carried low over the heads of the breaking seas in rags and lengths like pieces of a torn silk veil, when the helm of the barque was put down, stun-sail halliards were let go, all in such a hurry that the sails fouled the booms and yard-arms, and painted a scene of confusion aloft, that might have stood as a perfect picture of panic at sea; the yards on the main were laboriously hauled around and the main topsail backed and the barque was at rest, rolling and tumbling very uncomfortably with a great deal of flying and flapping aloft, one man at the wheel, two men standing close beside him in a posture of waiting, and the fore-part of the bulwarks from the gangway to the fore-rigging lined with the heads of the crew.

The barque was swiftly neared by the pursuing ships, and when they were within easy oars' range or hailing distance their way was arrested, and immediately down sank a boat from the frigate's side with Mr Fellowes steering her and six sailors, as before, rowing her. The boat made directly for the schooner.

"Before we board the *Minorca*," said Captain Acton to the Admiral, "we must hear what Fellowes proposes, or what instructions he comes with from Lord Garlies."

But as he said these words one of the two figures on the *Minorca* who stood close to the wheel, bawled, with his hand protecting his mouth from the sidelong sweep of the wind: "The ship's at your sarvice, your honours; and right glad we are that you've overhauled us, as it is about time we was under lawful government."

"That's Eagle!" said Captain Acton. "'Tis clear that the crew have not mutinied against my interests."

He flourished his hand in token that Mr Eagle's words had been heard, and that the rest was to come. The man-of-war's boat swept alongside, and Mr Fellowes, received by Captain Acton and the Admiral, stepped through the gangway.

"Can I put you on board your ship, gentlemen?" he said. "My crew are armed, and their presence alongside may calm the passions of the turbulent among that lot," he added, with a nod at the barque.

The invitation was accepted with many thanks.

Sir William Lawrence was very grave, his looks were stern, almost fierce, as he entered the boat. Captain Acton was cool and thoughtful. His brow was knitted; his lips were set. His demeanour was that of a self-possessed man confronted by a condition of things rendered complex by features extraneous to the main trouble or difficulty, yet confounding it by their existence. Lucy watched the scene from the after-part of the *Aurora*'s quarterdeck. She stood alone in that part of the ship leaning upon the rail, and once or twice her gaze followed the boat that was bearing her father and the Admiral to the *Minorca;* but it was chiefly directed at the barque whose length she explored for a sight of the tall figure whom she had

immediately recognised as Mr Lawrence, whilst Sir William was surveying his son through his glass. She mused upon the amazing passage of her life that had filled the interval between the time of her
going on board yonder ship, believing her father to be lying dangerously injured in her, down to the hour of her transference to the
Whitby brig. Never was her pensive beauty more fascinating than
now, whilst her soft dark eyes brooded upon the ship that had been
her floating prison. What would Mr Lawrence say or think when he
came to understand that her madness was feigned, a dramatic stratagem to obtain liberty and restoration? How would he—but how
could he—face his father whom he had degraded, and her father
whom he had robbed and wronged?

She sighed; the distress of her heart saddened her face with a
meaning as of tears.

Mr Eagle stood at the head of the side ladder when Captain Acton
and the others stepped on board. At his elbow was Mr Pledge. Some
of the crew were grinning, and all seemed to be hugely delighted
by what was happening.

"We have followed and found you, sir," were Captain Acton's first
words to Mr Eagle.

"S'elp me, your honour, it's no fault of any man aboard saving the
party you gave the command of this ship to," answered Mr Eagle in
a profoundly respectful, obsequious, yet sour and protesting manner
and voice as though he had been wounded in a very delicate part
of his honour.

"I'm here to witness to that, sir, and so's the men," said Mr Pledge.

"Reserve what you have to say for my private ear!" exclaimed
Captain Acton, with a severe look and in a stern voice. "Where is
your Captain?"

"He left the deck when the frigate fired a gun," replied Mr Eagle,
"and I haven't seen him since."

"I believe he's done for himself," said Mr Pledge, addressing
nobody in particular; "I fancied I heer'd a shot fired in the cabin."

"You didn't run down to see?" cried Captain Acton. "Come, Sir
William! Will you kindly follow, Mr Fellowes?" And attended by the
two he had named, he hastened to the companion-hatch and all
three ran below.

The cabin—the "great cabbin," as it would have been called by our ancestors—was empty of everything but its furniture. Captain Acton knew his ship. He walked straight to the door of the Captain's berth or cabin—that compartment in which Mr Walter Lawrence had locked up Miss Lucy Acton—and threw it open. The sight that met their eyes caused an instant arrest in the movements of the three gentlemen from one of whom, the Admiral, an exclamation in the note of a groan escaped.

On his face stretched along the cabin floor, his arms extended, his right hand grasping the butt-end of a pistol, was the body of Mr Lawrence. That the pistol had quite recently been exploded might be known by the smell of the gunpowder that lurked in the atmosphere. By the side of this motionless figure lying prone, knelt the distorted shape of Paul, the steward, who, on the door being flung open, and on catching sight of Captain Acton and the Admiral, sprang to his feet and recoiled into a corner of the cabin, with his face blanched by terror which had immediately visited him on top of the wild, uncalculating passion of grief which commonly besieges vulgar persons of this man's mental calibre who are likewise freaks of nature.

After a moment or two of hesitation due to the consternation excited by the unexpected spectacle upon the cabin deck, Captain Acton and Mr Fellowes ran to the prostrate man, and Acton cried: "He has shot himself!"

"Help me to turn him over, sir," said Mr Fellowes. "I don't think he is dead."

They gently rolled the dead, or dying, man on to his back, and the nature of his injury appeared. He was clothed in white trousers, a light blue coat, and a shirt the front of which was ornamented by some light tracing like flowers. He was without a cravat, and his head was uncovered. The left side of his shirt was soaked in blood, and the singed hole through which the bullet had passed from the weapon whose muzzle he had pressed to his breast, was visible in the thick of the dark crimson dye. His face was marble-white. It wore an expression of torture. His lips were parted and grey. The eyelids were half-closed, and the whites of the eye only were visible.

The Admiral stood looking as though petrified. All the wrath that was in him, all the fierce and terrible thoughts which had raged in his heart and prepared his tongue for a delivery desperate and fearful in the mouth of a father, melted, vanished, faded as smoke in the air, as a shred of mist torn from a cloud in the sky, and his face wore an expression of unutterable grief, of horror beyond expression in words, every passion and emotion it displayed being irradiated by the light of a father's love which had seemed to be waning and expiring in its socket, but which found life and power in that mute, irresistible prayer addressed to him as a father by an only son whose valour he had honoured, whose beauty he was proud of, whose life appealed to him more deeply in that his career had been halted by an act of folly when his reputation stood high for heroic daring. He went to the side of the body; he looked down upon the face with tearless eyes, and with that same dry sob in his throat which Captain Acton had heard when the poor old gentleman spoke after Mr Greyquill's visit, then sank upon his knees beside his son, muttering: "Walter, oh, Walter, that it should have come to this! I loved you, my son—may God pity me, and have mercy upon you!"

Captain Acton, deeply affected by his friend's distress, concealed his face by turning his head. Mr Fellowes, who had grasped Mr Lawrence's wrist, cried out: "I feel a thread of pulse. He is not dead. I'll away for our medico, and shall be back with him in a jiffey."

He ran out of the cabin. The Admiral pillowed his son's head with his arm, and gazed at the marble-still features. Never could any man appear more stricken, though 'tis hard to tell by posture or by expression of face the depth of human sorrow, the pang of the wound that death alone can heal. His only son—whom he had cursed for his wickedness—whose professional life, extinguished by an act of drunken madness, had swelled the eyes of the father with the unshed tears of the spirit of a man—lying dead or dying on his arm—self-slain!

"Were you here when Mr Lawrence shot himself?" exclaimed Captain Acton to the hunchback Paul, who cowered in his corner with white cheeks and terrified looks.

"No, your honour," howled the wretch; "I heard the shot and ran in. I'd have asked him to shoot me instead—I loved him, your honour —I worshipped him, kind gentlemen—he was good to me, he was the only friend I ever had in the world. I'd have died over and over again for him."

The hunchback broke down, and roared in tears.

"He lives, Acton," said the Admiral in a low voice. "Some brandy and water might bring him to."

Captain Acton told Paul to fetch some, and the wild, deformed creature of the forest, as Lucy had called him, sped from the cabin on the errand.

It proved as the Admiral had said. After a little brandy and water had been poured between the ashen lips, Mr Lawrence opened his eyes. They opened full upon his father, whose face was stooped close to him. Consciousness was tardy in her awakening, but on a sudden the prostrate, bleeding man recognised his father, and with that look of recognition there must have come to him some vision of memory presenting scenes of his past. He frowned, sighed, turned his eyes upon Captain Acton, and closed them, but not as though he had fainted, for the lids were firm set.

Whilst they waited for the arrival of the frigate's surgeon, Captain Acton asked Paul some questions which the hunchback answered as though when the examination was over the Captain would send him to be hanged forthwith at the yard-arm. In an agony of impatience the Admiral awaited the arrival of the medical man, who, considering that there was a space of blown and running sea for the boat to cross and re-cross, returned with Mr Fellowes in a space of time that was the expression of the habitual and disciplined promptitude of everything in which time finds a place, that is carried on aboard a British man-of-war.

He had been told what had happened, and presented himself equipped with wool, lint, and bandages. He speedily discovered that the pistol had been discharged at the place where Mr Lawrence supposed his heart to beat. The unfortunate man imagined that the heart is on the left side of the body, whereas it is nearly in the middle, and is well protected by the breast-bone and ribs, so well indeed that only a small portion is unprotected. The bullet had passed clean through the chest and left lung, and come out just below the left bladebone of the shoulder. The surgeon, on removing Mr Lawrence's shirt and vest, found the bullet, which had not pierced the vest. The wounds of entrance and of exit were easily seen, and the former was bleeding freely.

When the wound had been dressed, during which Mr Lawrence kept his eyes shut and his teeth set—he was in mortal pain—the Admiral asked him gently if he suffered much. Mr Lawrence opened his eyes and looked at his father, and smiled slightly. Faint as the smile was, mingled as it was with the distortion of anguish, it had in it the charm of a manly beauty which only the decay of the grave could destroy, and in it also were remorse and gratitude. His lips parted in the words, "No, sir," and again his eyes closed.

Captain Acton, the surgeon, and Mr Fellowes went into the cabin, leaving the Admiral and his son to themselves.

"Will he live?" asked Captain Acton.

"I don't see why he shouldn't, sir; the wound is not mortal. But he will require to be very carefully nursed," answered the surgeon, with the coolness and manner of indifference which are a characteristic of the official medical man who is unburdened with stimulating considerations of practice and fees.

"There'll not be much nursing to be got out of this shipful of rough sailors," said Mr Fellowes. "What a fine, manly, gallant young officer was lost to the Service in Walter Lawrence! What made him shoot himself?"

"Do you think, sir, that he could with safety be transferred to the *Aurora?*" asked Captain Acton, with an appearance of anxiety that seemed to render his evasion of Mr Fellowes' question undesigned "We could nurse him there. We are a comfortable little ship, better found—certainly in the way of the cabin—than this vessel."

The three on this hint fell into a brief and earnest conversation, and in a few minutes Sir William was called to participate in the discussion and deliver his views, whilst the surgeon re-entered the berth to consider afresh the condition of the patient.

Meanwhile Lucy Acton watched and waited on the quarterdeck of the *Aurora.* The hour was about half-past four. The breeze was sinking with the sun; it still blew with weight enough to keep the sails of the three ships steady. But the dance of the sea was growing languid, the rolling foam of the breaking head was wanting in brilliance of flash and friskiness of somersault; the blue of the deep was darkening, and spread in violet shot with light blue and purple gleams to the margin of the reflected glory of the sun where the lines of light steeped into the richer colour.

Lucy had watched the sailors of the barque gather in the confusion of studding-sails until the vessel looked as trim and fit aloft as need be; she had also watched the passage of the *Phœbe*'s boat to the frigate, and its return to the barque with one man more, whose position on board she could not imagine, neither that nor the reason for his being fetched. The man-of-war lay near, rolling languidly, lifting her copper sheathing on fire with wet sunshine, pointing her guns at the sea as the bright buttons of her trucks described arcs upon the blue sky like the flight of meteors in the velvet deeps of night. But now at half-past four the girl seemed to witness a commotion on board the barque. A man went aloft to the main-yard arm, and another to the foreyard arm, and some one standing upon the quarterdeck of the *Minorca,* in a voice by which she guessed him to be Mr Fellowes, hailed the schooner, and requested Captain Weaver to send whips aloft to hoist a sick man in a litter aboard.

Lucy, having sought in vain for any signs of Mr Lawrence or her father or the Admiral on board the *Minorca,* ran to Captain Acton's cabin and tried to see the barque through his glass. Unfortunately she could not use both hands; she needed one to keep her eye shut; therefore, when she balanced the glass upon the rail, the rolling of the schooner caused the object she tried to see to slide up and down in the lens like a toy monkey on a stick in the hands of a child. However, with her unhelped vision, she presently saw a something resembling the short stage which is slung over a ship's side for men to stand upon to paint, or do carpentry work, float from the deck of the barque to a certain elevation between the fore and main-yard-arms, where tackles or whips had been rigged; she then perceived this something slowly descend into the man-of-war's boat alongside, into which, immediately afterwards, some figures tumbled from the flight of steps at the gangway, and the boat made for the schooner.

As the little craft rapidly approached, swept onwards by six powerful oarsmen, Lucy quickly began to distinguish the inmates who, in the stern sheets or aft, consisted of the Admiral, Mr Fellowes, and a stranger. She could also see what resembled a stretcher lying with its head upon the aftermost thwart and the heel upon an unoccupied space in the stern sheets. The girl trembled, and wondered, and stared. Where was her father? Who was the sick man? Where was Mr Lawrence?

The boat drew alongside, but not until the arrangement of plank and mattress upon which lay Mr Lawrence had been swayed over the rail of the schooner, and softly and tenderly lowered on to the deck, did she know that the sick man in the ship's litter was the lover whose passion for her had defied the gibbet in its unscrupulous, reckless, daring, headlong determination to achieve.

She ran to the side of what may be called the litter, and looked down upon the face that rested upon a bolster. She clasped her hands. She compressed her lips. No exclamation escaped her, but one saw in her beautiful face the expression of that deep pity which is ever the attendant of love where sorrow is or suffering.

Mr Lawrence's eyes were open. They looked straight up at her; tormented as he was, his pain had no influence over the composition of his feelings. It was a stare rather than a gaze: and in that stare was profound astonishment at the sight of her, likewise amazement at the sanity of a face, which, when he had last seen it, was deformed, as he had believed, by the madness his behaviour had wrought in her; but before all, and stealing into and illuminating the complicated emotions conveyed by his eyes, was the love which had ever beamed in them when he turned them upon her, a light not to be lessened or obscured by any conflict of passion.

The Admiral, Mr Fellowes, and the surgeon had come on board when the litter was being lowered, and stood in momentary pause beside it, whilst men were summoned to convey the wounded man to his father's cabin. Lucy swept round to the Admiral, and with her hands still clasped, cried to him softly: "Oh, Sir William, it is your son—I could not imagine—is he dying—will he die?"

The surgeon who stood close, and who had been gazing at the young lady with admiration of her face and charms of figure and wonder at finding so beautiful a girl in a little schooner at sea, exclaimed: "I am surgeon of yonder frigate, madam. This gentleman will not die, provided he is carefully and judiciously nursed."

"I will nurse him," cried Lucy.

A faint smile lighted up the features of Mr Lawrence, who slightly moved his head to cast his eyes upon her.

"Oh, madam, my dearest madam," exclaimed the Admiral in a voice broken with feeling, "how am I to thank you? What words do your angelic goodness leave me for the conveyance of my gratitude?"

"You will tell me, sir," said Lucy, addressing the surgeon, "what I am to do, and I will do it. Where is he wounded?"

"Near the heart. He shot himself!" said the Admiral.

Some men were now arrived. They picked up the litter with careful hands, and in a sort of procession Mr Lawrence was conveyed into the deck-house, Lucy walking beside him, whilst behind stepped the Admiral, Mr Fellowes, and the *Phœbe*'s surgeon. Once only did Lucy speak in that solemn march from the quarterdeck into the little interior. She looked back and asked: "Where is my father?"

"He is remaining on board the *Minorca* to see after affairs there, madam," answered the Admiral. "I believe Captain Weaver is to take charge of the barque, and Captain Acton will himself sail the schooner home."

The litter was carried into the Admiral's cabin, and Lucy and the surgeon followed.

꙳

Lucy Acton's ardently uttered exclamation, "I will nurse him," cannot fail to an intelligent and imaginative reader to immediately reveal the end of this plain yarn of Old Harbour Town. But many may desire that a specific character should be given to the conclusion of this narrative, and they shall have it.

It would exceed the bounds of possibility to suppose that any charming girl of great sensibility whose heart was disengaged, whose feelings were fresh and sweet, could nurse for the space of five weeks so fine, manly, and handsome a gentleman as Mr Lawrence without falling in love with him. This may be true of ninety young ladies in every hundred. But what was Lucy Acton's case? She was secretly but deeply in love with Mr Lawrence when his own overmastering passion for her impelled him into the perpetration of an outrage upon her person, and a criminal offence against her father. She had loved him with a passion deep and concealed in her spirit long before her abduction, and Aunt Caroline had guessed the truth. She had loved him with an increasing fervency, even after she had been cruelly abstracted from her home, when she knew that her kidnapper's intention was to rob her father of his ship, and the freighters of their goods, and the crew of their wages. And never had she loved him so well as when she was feigning madness with the aim of being transhipped and sent home by him, and when at every interview his eyes reposed upon her with adoration in their expression and his bearing towards her was as gentle, appealing, respectful, and dignified as though he was courting her in hours of health and content, with her father's sanction, and under her father's roof.

But the contradictions of the female heart! What mental physiologist shall attempt more, without certain failure, than to describe with out addling his brains by trying to explain? You might call Lucy an impossible character whose presentment may find a fit frame in a novel, but for the like of whom the ranks of women, warm, living with clear minds and perceptions, must be searched in vain. If this is what shall be thought, let the objection stand: it shall not be reasoned in this place. Enough, if actual facts are recorded.

The schooner occupied five weeks in reaching England from the hour of her parting company with the frigate and shortly after with the *Minorca*. All that time Mr Lawrence lay upon his back; but the wounds slowly healed, and he gradually recovered his strength. And when the schooner brought up off Falmouth Mr Lawrence was nearly well.

He had been nursed by Lucy from the time of his being slung over the side. The wounds were dressed by her hands. Day after day, hour after hour, she sat beside him in his cabin. She carried his tray of food into his little sea-bedroom, and fed him, or helped him to feed himself. And though at night he was watched by his father, the instructions given were that if the patient expressed a wish for her presence, Lucy was to be summoned, no matter the hour of the night in which the call was made.

What could such an association as this end in, but in such a love between the two as must prove irresistible sooner or later as an appeal?

Another element of admiration supplied increase of vitality to his passion when he gathered, from her own confession, that she simulated madness to rescue herself from a voyage whose issue threatened lifelong misery to her, and death by the hangman to the other.

Captain Acton easily perceived what was happening, and might as easily have guessed what was to come. The Admiral was as perceptive as his friend, and as reserved.

Captain Weaver had been sent on board the *Minorca* to take charge of her; Mr Eagle remained as the barque's first mate, and Captain Acton himself navigated the *Aurora* to the English Channel. He had overhauled Mr Lawrence's cabin in the *Minorca* and found the "Secret Instructions" he was supposed to have written, and this paper he would have shown to Sir William Lawrence but for the circumstance of the envelope being sealed with the Acton crest, which signified that Mr Lawrence had taken an opportunity of borrowing a large silver seal which stood upon the library table in Old Harbour House, and replacing it, after using it for a nefarious purpose: Captain Acton had himself used that seal the day before he followed in pursuit in the *Aurora*.

The schooner having touched at Falmouth, proceeded to Old Harbour, where her unexpected arrival aroused great excitement, and provoked much wonderment, and started every tongue into a passion of gossip and conjecture. The crew gave the populace the news that the Admiral and his son, Mr Lawrence, had gone ashore at Falmouth, but whether to stop there or whether to make sail from that port to foreign parts, the jacks were unable to affirm.

Captain Acton and Lucy were strictly reserved—in some directions rigidly silent. Even Aunt Caroline, who had looked carefully after the home, and particularly Lucy's little terrier Mamie, and who swooned away in a bundle of flowered gown and hoop at the sight of her niece, was kept in ignorance of many essential features of this story—where it begins when she steps off the stage—for fear that her tongue should betray more truth to outside ears than it was expedient or desirable they should be made acquainted with.

In the course of a few weeks the Admiral arrived at his little cottage. He was without his son, of whom no news could be obtained. Gossip had ceased to flow when the *Minorca* returned, and the tongues of her crew once again opened the flood-gate of talk. But what could they declare that should convict Mr Lawrence of piracy? They said that the *Minorca* had sailed under secret instructions from Captain Acton which, Mr Lawrence had gathered, imported the sale of the barque at a place named. These instructions were never read to the crew, because she was overhauled by the frigate and the *Aurora* before the defined parallels of latitude and longitude had been reached. Captain Acton never denied that he had given secret instructions to Mr Lawrence. There was therefore no case against the Admiral's son. And from the statements made by the crew, confirmed by Mr Eagle and Mr Pledge, it was generally held by the honest gossips of Old Harbour Town that between you and them and the bedpost, Miss Lucy Acton had eloped with Mr Lawrence, had so acted as to persuade the crew that she had been abducted, and had been recaptured by her father, whose sole motive in pursuing the barque was to regain his child.

Six weeks after the arrival of the *Aurora,* the worthy, the excellent, the benevolent Caroline Acton, sister of the Captain, departed this life. About a month later news filtered into Old Harbour Town that Mr Lawrence, who had perfectly recovered his health, had obtained, through influence, which was subsequently traced to Captain Acton, the command of a small Indiaman. Some weeks later old Mr Greyquill was considerably astonished and gratified by the receipt of a draft for three hundred pounds from Rear-Admiral Sir William Lawrence, with a request that he would credit Mr Walter Lawrence with the sum, and rule his name off his ledgers. It was understood that much about this time other troublesome, but not very formidable, debts incurred by Mr Lawrence were discharged by the Admiral; but as it was generally known that he was a poor man, it was confidently assumed, and not perhaps without good reason, that Captain Acton influenced by Lucy, had supplied the money.

It is certain, anyway, that about nine months after the return of the *Aurora,* Captain Acton, Sir William Lawrence, and Miss Lucy Acton, left Old Harbour Town, for the neighbourhood of London, where after an interval, the exact period of which being uncertain, is not of historic value enough to demand research, Old Harbour Town received the news, this time in print, in the *Annual Register or La Belle Assemblée,* or some such publication of the period, that Mr Walter Lawrence, late of His Majesty's Royal Navy, only son of Rear-Admiral Sir William Lawrence, K.C.B., was on such a day united in the bonds of Holy Matrimony to Lucy, only daughter and co-heiress of Captain Acton, R. N. (retired).

And thus ended the yarn of Old Harbour Town.